Wimbledon Village thrives on the edge of a hill, the utmost southern tip of a large high plateau in South West London. Its northern border is dominated by a wasteland known as the Common, mysterious grounds teeming with wilderness. To the west, the Common spreads further like a plague, where Nature lives unruly, until it grinds against the bustling roads, the public buildings, the suburban houses of the village, where men and women live their dreams and nightmares. All along the southern ridge of the hill the Epsom Downs stretch south into Surrey and at the foot of the hill lies modern Wimbledon Town, constantly moving, growing, as it fades into the desolate urban landscape of Merton. The eastern front meets the signs of modern transportation and modern urbanisation until they all step aside to show the green triangle of Wimbledon Park, as it embraces the hill in a cuddle, as it has done since the earliest of times.

Our story starts in Wimbledon Village. But as the pages unfold, as the fog clears, and our characters come into play, it will become clear this is an alternate Wimbledon. It is a Wimbledon where you and I do not exist…

Titles available in the Wynnman series:

Book 1 – The Wynnman and the Black Azalea

Book 2 – The Wynnman and the Crimson Paths

Book 3 – The Wynnman and the Silver Spectre

Titles available from the same author:

Il Canto Della Chimera Vergine

Beyond Boundaries

Memento Postridie

Arya

The Misadventures of Mister Fast

Beyond Oblivion

THE WYNNMAN
AND
THE SILVER SPECTRE

by
Trevor P. Kwain

The story so far...

Enrico LoTrova opened a bakery in Wimbledon Village in the hope of starting a successful business. Due to a lack of funds, he decides to join the Wimbledon Association of Independent Shops (WAIS) which is organising a fundraiser event at Cannizaro Park. This is where he meets Viviane, the local florist, and Dr Watkins, the curator of the Wimbledon Museum. The three of them embark on an adventure that will lead them to learn about Wimbledon's secret history and the legend of a sorcerer called the Wynnman. First, it was the search for a mythical flower in the beautiful Cannizaro Park. Then, they stumbled across an ancient ritual in the Pool of Elixir, hidden under the Old Rectory, the last surviving manor of Wimbledon. However, they are not alone. A mysterious man keeps crossing their path, on his quest to prove the existence of the Wynnman. Something strange is happening around Wimbledon...

To learn more about Wimbledon and the world of the Wynnman, scan the QR code below or go to: *https://trevorpkwain.page.link/wynnmanuniverse*

The chilly breeze of the mid-winter evening crept through the wild trees and savage undergrowth of Wimbledon Common. A soft, dense mist had taken hold of what was the largest heathland in London. Tonight, the mist floated mid-air against the pitch dark as if it were a ghostly figure dancing across deserted footpaths or around the thick vegetation in a hypnotising embrace. There were no lights at all. The Common was kept as a patch of thick woods and unruly vegetation. Historically, it was owned and used by the Lord of the Manor to raise livestock or collect firewood. Today, it was collectively owned by Wimbledonians who looked after its flora and fauna to keep nature's spirit free from enclosure and construction. The Common had become a place for day walks amid nature, away from the bustling traffic of Wimbledon Village nearby. Hardly anybody ventured through it at night though. That is why, the two feeble round lights came as a surprise to the wildlife of the Common as they pierced the mist with their beams, followed by the rattling of wheels on rough ground.

John and Fran were in a rush to leave the Common and reach the first lamp posts on the border with Rushmere Green, on the northern outskirts of Wimbledon Village, where cars and civilisation became the normality once more. The air felt colder as they rode their bikes fast on the uneven dirt track that led almost the whole length of the Common, north to south, from the Wimbledon Windmill to the Fox and Grapes pub. Despite its imposing width, enough for passers-by and horse riders travelling in both directions, the track was in the same wild state as any dirt track on the Common, full of bumps, holes and mud puddles of all sizes no matter what time of year. The dark evening made things worse, as it was harder to see what was on the road ahead. Both John and Fran had to brake constantly not to topple over or drive into the thick berry bushes along the side of the dirt road.

Sometimes the mist and the beam of their dynamo lights played tricks on them. Dead logs looked like deer about to leap across their path. The creaking tree branches, caressed by the breeze, sounded like eerie voices of something feral hidden in the woods. John and Fran picked up speed where they could. They wanted to get home soon for a nice cup of tea.

'Why did you have to stay late to close up?' moaned Fran glancing at the shadows coming and going past them.

'The boss pays well.' panted John. 'Tomorrow is a big day so I had to check everything down to the last calculation. Now, can you push on those pedals, Fran, so we can get home?'.

'You are the only one doing all the heavy lifting. Where are the others?'

'At the other site.'

Fran shook her head in disapproval.

'If I hadn't come, you would be coming back on your own at God knows what time. Look around you. It's only six in the evening and the place is as scary as hell!'

The two kept riding straight ahead. Fran spotted an uneven shape in the ground coming into view of her dynamo light.

'Look out!' she cried.

John heard and they both steered on impulse to the right, just about in time to by-pass a large, deep puddle.

'Did you see that?' Fran shouted with her heart in her throat. 'You could have fallen into it and got soaked. Can't you see how dangerous it can be?'

'Chill out, Fran!' replied John impassively. 'Almost there. It is worth what Alberyx Enterprises pays me for!'

'We should have taken Parkside.'

'This way is quicker. We'll be at the compound in 20 minutes.'

Fran shook her head again in disbelief as she picked up the pace again. It was the first time she had come to see John at work so late in the day. She was surprised to see how he commuted back home each night. She was also surprised to see what Alberyx Enterprises had been doing to the Wimbledon

Windmill ever since they had taken up the repair work. Earlier, John had been kind enough to let her peer behind the protective scaffolding, covering the whole windmill and hiding their work from public view before its completion. It was a complete restoration project to bring the windmill back to life and up to speed with modern times. It had been a mammoth task, John had explained, which had lasted for months, working long hours non-stop till today. Tomorrow was the big day and Fran was relieved to know John's services would no longer be needed. They could finally spend more time together. Thunder struck in the distance and Fran woke up from her thoughts of renewed domestic life.

'It was not meant to rain.' wondered John slowing down.

'I don't see clouds.' said Fran.

The two continued along the dirt track. It now curved slightly to the right and still no lamp posts could be seen in the distance. John felt something was not right.

'Is this the right direction?' he quizzed, now slowing down almost at walking speed. 'I don't recognise this part of the main path. Did we take the wrong turning somewhere by mistake?'

'I don't know!' shrugged Fran. 'You ride through here every day, don't you? You should know!'

'Well, usually I am on my own without someone moaning in my ear. If you hadn't nagged so much, we would have noticed we were turning in the wrong direction. There are so many crossroads across the Common.'

Fran preferred to ignore his comment. John could not hide how annoyed he was. He was a meticulous man, eager to make sure his work was free of mistakes. It came as part of his profession. Being the chief engineer for the New Wimbledon Windmill project required precision with numbers and careful planning. For this reason, he had been chosen for the job and no-one else. He could never admit to anyone he had got lost in the Common while being perfectly able to navigate through the complex calculations of engineering physics he had been asked to implement.

Thunder struck. Its echo was now very close, even though the night sky still looked clear. The mist thickened in random patches. Both John and Fran felt the chilly breeze on their necks as it rose a little without dissolving the ghostly sea of mist hovering above the dirt track. It engulfed them bit by bit and the dynamo lights of their bikes struggled to cut through it. Then a new sound reached their ears. It was faint but they could tell it was a different one. John and Fran thought it was another rumble of thunder, further away from the Common. The rumble turned into a rushing, repetitive roar, more paced and calculated as if following a pattern or a specific beat. The roaring sound grew louder and louder, not once did it diminish. The silence of the Common was suddenly drowned, overcome by this louder noise, which now seemed to be coming from every unexplored corner of the wild Common. John and Fran looked around frightened. Then the sound moved to a single point in the misty darkness on the dirt track ahead of them. John and Fran came to a halt with their bikes. They took deep breaths trying to come to grasps with what seemed to be the roar of an engine.

'What is that sound?' asked John.

'Is that the sound of an engine? A car perhaps?' guessed Fran.

'In the middle of the Common? No, it's not a car. It sounds more like…a train!?'

John could not believe his own words as he spoke them.

'Oh really, a train in the middle of the Common is more plausible?'

John put his finger over his mouth, asking her to hold her tongue and listen. Fran did not like that. They focused harder on the sound. The rushing roar was becoming clearer. The echo of chuffing steam and striding steel wheels ensued, becoming distinct enough to a point its beat and rhythm could not be mistaken.

'That's a train!' blurted out John with a mixed feeling of fear and surprise.

He was a man who believed in certainty beyond any reasonable doubt, so he was sure it was a train nearby.

'Don't be silly! We are miles away from the closest rail track. Where would it run here anyway? On these muddy roads perhaps? You've been working too hard, John!'

Fran's words did not convince him, but it simply was not the right time to have another argument with his girlfriend at this stage. Both of them agreed they could hear the same sound. The huffing and puffing became more frantic and the roaring more deafening. Something, whatever it was, was getting closer.

'A train?' John asked himself in self-doubt.

'I don't like this.' pleaded Fran, her voice trembling like a leaf. 'Can we please go?'

John could not ignore the hint of fear in her voice. He too felt a shiver down his spine as he stared through the mist into the darkness.

'Let's make a U-turn and get away from here!' he decided aloud.

Before they pushed down on their pedals once again, the wind picked up in strength and blew the mist around. Yet, rather than clearing it away, the mist became a denser, impenetrable cloud climbing up as high as the trees nearby. Fran felt goose bumps on her skin. Thinking it was the sudden cold, she wrapped her arms around her coat and sensed a pricking sensation on the skin of her hands. The fabric had become fuzzy to the touch. John felt the same happening to his coat and he could feel his hair being pulled up by a tickling force. The eerie sound of the train picked up again as the wind died down. Fran and John felt lost and confused; they suddenly panicked when they could no longer see the trees or the shrubs or the starry night over the Common. The mist turned into thick fog all around them. They were terrified but felt stuck to the ground, staring ahead, not knowing where to turn or whether to wait and see what the rushing roar really was.

Then, up ahead, where the sound was coming from, an intense glow grew from a tiny dot to a strong beam of light, much bigger than their dynamo lights. The rushing roar surged to a deafening high-pitched sound, followed by a white wash of bright light piercing the fog and blinding both John and

Fran. It all happened in a blink of an eye before the sound of thunder rumbled once more for the last time. The path was now clear and it was dark again in the Wimbledon Common. The fog had gone, and so had Fran and John.

Dr Watkins pushed the last few boxes to the side. He had been clearing the way for tomorrow's visit, making sure the path covered with metal planks led undisturbed throughout the archaeological site. The curator took a deep breath. He felt hot. The bright LED lights installed on the low hanging walls emanated a strong heat, sometimes unbearable when doing this heavy work. Dr Watkins wiped his forehead and neck with a handkerchief and loosened the top buttons of his shirt. He could not understand how Simon Deeley and his team of archaeologists could spend the day down here in this heat. He glanced at his watch. It was almost six. He then inspected the basement in front of him.

The bright lights had dried up all shadows ever since Alberyx Enterprises had helped set up the site below the Old Rectory. The old shelves had been pushed to the side and all the junk of no historical value had been cleared, reclaiming a lot of space for Simon's team to work in. The metal planks covered the whole of the old stone flooring, making the surface even and easier to walk on. The plank pathway carried on into the small chamber containing the Pool of Elixir. Dr Watkins peeked through an opening into the wall to give it another check before leaving. The chamber had required more work to make it secure after the underground tremors that hit Wimbledon the year before. The whole ceiling and walls were held up with a solid metal panel to prevent them from collapsing. The pool in the middle had stayed quiet and inert ever since the accident.

Dr Watkins walked inside and stood by the pool, stroking the white glove on one of his hands. It was a constant reminder of the burns he had suffered from the fire. The scars had healed but his hand still hurt, and he had been advised to keep his glove on for a few more months. The pool seemed harmless now. It had been emptied, cleaned and scrubbed by the archaeologists and any useful samples had been collected. The carvings on the eagle-like statue perched on the edge of the pool were more visible than ever. Dr Watkins could easily recognise from a distance the mix of runic characters and Anglo-Saxon symbols inscribed on every inch of the statue. Even now, under the glare of the LED lights, the curves and grooves of the symbols cast eerie, imaginary shadows. The statue stood quiet, dark and dull, absorbing all the reflections. It had been a few long months since the archaeological site under the Old Rectory site had opened, and both he and Simon had been slowly deciphering the symbols on the statue from week one. Meanwhile the team from the British Museum analysed the samples taken from the natural rock and from the bottom of the pool. The final evidence gathered over weeks and months had stirred strong emotions among Simon and his colleagues, and a week ago they had told Dr Watkins they strongly believed what they had discovered was probably the best Anglo-Saxon discovery since the dig at Sutton Hoo. Dr Watkins himself could not hide his excitement at hearing that, even if Simon had preferred to share only a few details. The week ahead was an important one: tomorrow, on Monday, Simon would be driving down to Wimbledon to produce the final report to Dr Watkins; and then in the evening they would both present the findings at a special event organised by Alberyx Enterprises at Eagle House in Wimbledon Village.

Dr Watkins smiled to himself, filled with pride. The long hard work was about to pay off. He caught himself staring at the empty bottom of the pool. The dregs of the burnt chemicals had been scrubbed off right away, but somehow the Pool of Elixir still smelled of blood and death. The curator thought it best to make a move and get home in time for dinner. Outside, the biting cold winter made him yearn for the heat from the LED lights. Plus, staying too long under the Old Rectory was causing him to have trouble sleeping. He needed to rest to be in his best shape for tomorrow morning at eight. He went to turn off the lights, and before he hit the switch, the LED lights dimmed and lit up, on and off for a few seconds. Dr Watkins then heard the light bulbs emitting a buzzing sound and thought it must be a power surge. He spun around to look at the rest of the chamber where the shadows danced at the rhythm of the flickering lights, as if following a silent, macabre melody. For a moment, he thought the runes and the symbols on the eagle-like statue flickered too, coming to life with silvery sparkles glinting against the darkened stone. Dr Watkins squinted, unable to tell if it was his imagination. Then the flickering stopped, and the lights returned to normal. Dr Watkins waited in silence. He could hear no more buzzing. The statue stood silent and motionless as it had always been. The curator waited a little longer and then, with a shrug, switched the lights of the Pool of Elixir off. He then moved into the old basement, grabbed his jacket and wrote his name on the register as the last person signing out. The way out was through a tiny elevator built in the middle of the basement, which took Dr Watkins up into the entrance hall of the Old Rectory. It was the easiest way to access without having to use the narrow, spiral staircase. The large mansion was empty and silent.

Outside, in the winter cold, Dr Watkins found himself under the giant scaffolding covering the Old Rectory and hiding it completely from prying eyes and onlookers. Dr Watkins walked the few steps down onto the gravel driveway. The sky above was nowhere to be seen as the scaffolding joined up with slanted panels making a protective roof. Alberyx Enterprises had upped their game with the level of security all around the perimeter of the Old Rectory. Julian Alberon was serious about not letting anyone in or out without permission, and Dr Watkins was reminded of it once again by the guarded turnstile set up in the middle of the driveway.

'Good evening!' said the curator scanning his pass.

'Good evening, Dr Watkins!' exclaimed the guard as he waited for the curator's details to show up on the screen. 'Working late on a Sunday again?'

'Big week coming up. Preparations always happen at the eleventh hour. Did you see the lights up here flicker?'

'Yes, we did. Probably a power surge from the generator. It's a problem due to all these lights installed everywhere to guard this place, especially at night. I don't know which is worse: being down there in that creepy underground site or here in the freezing cold. By the way, it is another cold night. Better wrap up.'

'I will. See you tomorrow morning when Simon gets here.'

The guard nodded and Dr Watkins pushed through the turnstile. The rest of the driveway opened up and the curator walked the stretch of road leading to the entry gates to the Old Rectory. There was another guarded checkpoint here for incoming vehicles. The younger guard in the sentry box kept his eyes glued on the security monitors, nervous about missing something; he checked Dr Watkins's details before letting him through but hardly exchanged any words. New recruit, Dr Watkins thought.

The moment he passed the last checkpoint, the curator was away from the scaffolding and into the cloudless winter night above Wimbledon hill. He was now in the grip of the cold winter air, alone with his thoughts as he walked the private road leading out into Church Road. He relished the idea of getting home as quickly as possible, to put his feet up and have a nice cup of tea with digestive biscuits. He knew though he may have to give one more glance at his papers before the next day. The research was a mixed bag of history and folklore, which he and the team from the British Museum had put together as more information from the Old Rectory was dug out giving more insights into what they already knew about the distant Anglo-Saxon civilisation. There was a section about the migratory route to Britain and how the Anglo-Saxons came to pass through Wimbledon; then one about the way they lived, and more specifically any links to the scarce early medieval remains found around Wimbledon hill over the decades. He had also written a section about ancient customs and how these had slowly faded with the arrival of Christianity. They were mainly stories about ritual symbolism, and old legends about dragons, warriors and sorcerers. Among the fragments of such collective imagination, Dr Watkins could not ignore the fact that there was probably some truth in the myth of the sorcerer who had lived in Wimbledon in the seventh century or earlier. It went by the name of the Wynnman if someone held these fairy tales to be true. Maybe what they had found in the Pool of Elixir could lead them to the true origins of the Wynnman.

Nathan moved the digital knob of his radio transmitter back and forward to keep the audio free from incoming interference. He did not want to lose signal from the frequency range he had been able to listen to comfortably for the last couple of weeks. He now sat hunched over his desk, notepad on the side, moving the knob so gently as if he were a thief cracking a safe combination. Indeed, if anyone knew what he was up to they would treat him like a criminal. After all, listening to the encrypted radio communications of a private company was not legitimate playbook material for a typical journalist, let alone a local journalist for the Wimbledon Gazette. Nathan Glenn though had made it his mission to investigate the affairs of Alberyx Enterprises and had tried in many ways to spy on the secrets he thought the local company was hiding. He knew the risks associated with it, but he did not believe a word of the company's intentions.

He sipped his tea and glanced furtively out of the window. The streets were empty and dark, only lit by the streetlamps every few yards or so. Nathan had the nagging feeling he was being watched. He dismissed the idea and focused on what he was hearing. Lately, he had been able to tap into the channel used by the security personnel at the Alberyx Enterprises headquarters in Warren Farms. He had stumbled on it by chance fumbling with the controls of the digital radio transmitter. His first two attempts had only allowed him to hear conversations in the mailroom and in the food supply warehouse, which did not turn out to be anything exciting. He was listening now to two security guards talking about the upcoming security schedule. The conversation had been dragging on for an hour or so.

'...Main gates locked?' asked one guard completing their routine check.

'Yes. Locked.' confirmed the other guard. 'Routine check complete. Nothing to report.'

'Ok. Done. Now, let's look at the schedule for the week. For the opening of the windmill, we need to ensure transport is ready once the event is finished.'

'Is that for tomorrow? Monday?'

'Yes, I told you that before. Pay attention! Tomorrow, Monday, we have the opening of the windmill. Has transport been arranged to take Julian Alberon to the press conference?'

'Yes.'

'Good. Have we reviewed the security details for the special soirée at Eagle House on Monday evening?'

'Is that the museum event?'

'Yes...can you please get on with the programme?'

One of the guards sighed. He was tired of repeating things to his colleague at such a late hour on a Sunday. Nathan laughed to himself.

Nathan knew about what was coming up. It was no secret. Everyone in Wimbledon was getting ready for a busy week ahead, as a swarm of journalists from all over London had started pouring in as early as Saturday to attend the two social events heavily promoted by Alberyx Enterprises. Local businesses were expecting at least half the turnout of the Wimbledon Tennis Championship so it was a chance nobody could miss. The Wimbledon Gazette saw all these journalists and big TV anchor-men as competition and had asked Nathan to get some interviews and write a good article. But Nathan had bigger fish to fry and little or no interest in reporting on the façade Alberyx Enterprises wished to show. He was hoping to find out more about Alberyx Enterprises's heavy investments in Wimbledon over the last few months. Since the accident at the Old Rectory, Julian Alberon and his company had been able to get so many planning permissions approved one after the other, starting from a full takeover of the Old Rectory, and had even contributed to helping the Council with their public services, such as local roads and gas networks. Yet, when Nathan had enquired if the Council had discussed such big changes with the current holder of the title of Lord of the Manor of Wimbledon, he had not received any response. Nobody knew who had bought the title, and whoever had, was meant to have a say when the conservation area of Wimbledon Village and its surroundings were directly impacted. Nathan's suspicions had been growing for months and he wanted to enquire, despite being asked by the head of staff at the Wimbledon Gazette not to waste his time on gossip. And now, here he was, playing with a tampered digital radio transmitter and hacking into the encrypted radio channels of Alberyx Enterprises. Nathan checked his watch. It was getting late into the evening. The conversation was still going on, but no juicy details had emerged yet.

'… and then I have arranged for the traffic on Wimbledon High Street to be rerouted for Monday evening, at least until all guests arrive. I am sure it will be crowded outside with all the journalists already here in Wimbledon for the opening of the windmill.'

'That reminds me: we need to keep an eye tomorrow for…you know who…'

'Who?'

Nathan cocked his ear all of a sudden.

'You know who… The dangerous man who has been giving a hard time to Alberyx Enterprises…'

There was a silence from the radio. The other guard was probably at a loss.

'You know about the protesters? Do I really need to spell it out?'

'Oh yes! Yes! Them, and their leader. How could I forget? I will check tomorrow morning if our own men are keeping an eye on him.'

'Perfect. Do we have any feedback from the Royal Wimbledon Golf Club for our security requirements?'

'I think they replied…'

There was a sudden interference on the radio. A loud static noise drowned the guards' voices. Nathan cursed under his breath. He could not miss out on a vital clue right now. He put a hand on his ear to bear with the noise while fiddling with the knob. The loud static coming from the digital radio transmitter did not relent. Nathan looked out of the window, worried Alberyx Enterprises may have intercepted his signal and were ready to storm into his house. Outside, the streets were still empty and dark. The streetlamps were flickering, going on and off out of control, and in the distance a couple of car alarms kept wailing non-stop. The whole scene lasted for maybe one minute before it quietened all of a sudden. The sound from the transmitter went back to normal and the voices of the two security guards came clear through the speakers. Nathan blinked. He then looked at the radio and then out of the window again. The street was silent, and the streetlamps were no longer flickering. Everything appeared to be back to normal.

'What was that interference?' said one of the guards.

'I don't know. I thought it was you. Could you hear me?'

'No. I could not hear a bloody thing. Is this set up on the right channel?'

'I believe so. Let me check if this radio frequency is still secure…'

There was a beeping sound and Nathan was quick to switch the radio transmitter off. The speakers went silent. Nathan was now alone with his thoughts. That was a close shave, he thought. He sat back on the chair and let out a deep groan. He was not sure if the security guards could detect his intrusion; yet, he had to tread carefully no matter what. He picked up his mug and took another sip of his tea, replaying the dialogue of the two guards. The security team from Alberyx Enterprises was keeping an eye on a high person of interest. Nathan Glenn had an idea of whom that person may be. There was no journalist or Wimbledonian who had not heard of the man causing so much trouble to Julian Alberon's company: Mr Basil Elders. What surprised Nathan the most was that Alberyx Enterprises deemed Mr Elders dangerous. He could already smell a newspaper scoop for him and the Wimbledon Gazette.

The view from Julian Alberon's house was more appreciated from the second floor and above. To one side, the long stretch of garden at the back kept the neighbours at a distance, giving Sir Alberon his deserved privacy. It was the same for the two side passages, leaving a good five yards or more between the house and the garden walls. Yet, the better view was on the opposite side, from his home office on the third floor. The three-panel window looked over Wimbledon Common, just above the tip of the trees bordering Parkside. Julian loved to admire its beauty undisturbed. He had been at the window for a while, lying on the lounge chair he had purposedly put by the window to enjoy the twilight. The winter evening was on the brink of taking over and swallowing what remained of the day. Julian glanced at the clock. It was not yet six.

The last hour had been fully dedicated to resting his mind and body. He always reserved some time for meditation the day before a great opening event like the one scheduled for tomorrow. This time though it was more important than ever. It was a big one he and his team had been working on non-stop. If Wimbledonians had asked him months ago whether he would be capable of such a feat, he would have said otherwise. He might have just jotted down an idea on a restaurant napkin as he used to do when he started doing business in Wimbledon. Julian knew he always wanted to do better, and his time had come. It was all uphill from here.

There was a sudden twinge of pain in his hand. Julian looked away from the view and looked at his hand, squeezing it gently with the other. He was still wearing his glove; he had not dared take it off after the last team meeting at the company headquarters. The scars he had suffered together with Dr Watkins still reminded him of the terrible fire at the Old Rectory, and he could feel a twinge of pain from time to time, even if doctors had reassured him the skin had healed. Julian grumbled to himself. The idea of healed skin apparently was a matter of opinion. What Julian had been left with was a ramification of scars all over his hand up to the wrist. Since his return to the public eye, he had not had the courage to show it. The glove had stayed on. He had to show confidence and entrepreneurship to Wimbledon.

The business tycoon brushed his worries to one side, darning the pain in his hand for reminding him about the past. It was time to calm his nerves and focus on the future. Tomorrow was all that counted now. He would not be terrorised into backing down now that he was close to launch day. Julian looked back out of the window. The trees had darkened, and the expanse of Wimbledon Common was now an indistinct mass. He stood up from his lounge chair and leaned forward a little, to see if he could spot the Wimbledon windmill. He had been doing that almost every evening over the last few weeks, even though he knew perfectly well he could not see it from his house. He just could not contain himself about the work he had accomplished. He contemplated about what could go wrong and the thought of Mr Basil Elders came into focus. Julian cursed under his breath. His hour of meditation was already a distant memory, and tension was again taking hold of him. He quickly rang the bell and asked a member of staff to fix him a drink. A tipple before dinner and then early bedtime would do him good.

He stood up taking in the pitch dark now before him. Night had finally fallen. The lampshade to one corner flickered momentarily. It was not long before the same happened to the lamps behind him. Something flashed outside the window across the evening sky. Then the hi-fi music system turned itself on and loud classical music blared from the speakers with its tragic crescendo.

'What on earth…?' blurted out Julian.

He spun around and strode to the hi-fi system trying to turn it off. His computer had turned on as well by itself and the blue tint of the screen clashed against the soothing orange tint of the lampshades. Julian lowered the volume of the music. One of his house staff had rushed upstairs with his drink. He too looked alarmed as Julian.

'What happened?' Julian asked.

'We don't know, sir. We had the same thing downstairs in the main lounge. I think I even heard the washing machine turning itself on in the utility room.'

Before Julian could advise on what to do next, the flickering stopped and both hi-fi system and computer turned themselves off automatically. The whole house went back to quiet.

'This is very strange.' commented Julian glancing all around the room.

'Power surge perhaps, sir?'

'Unlikely. Let me check with headquarters at Warren Farms. I'll deal with it.'

The house staff member nodded and left the drink before going back downstairs. Julian quickly picked up his smartphone. He worried something may have gone wrong with tomorrow's show. Maybe he was overreacting, but he had to be sure. Someone at Warren Farms would be checking.

'Hello? Sir Alberon? What's the problem?' answered a man on the line, already worried that the boss had called on a Sunday evening.

'Just checking in.' said Julian. 'Did you witness a power surge over there just now? Did the monitors show any spike in the readings? Are the machines ok?'

'They are both ok, sir. All ready and set for tomorrow and for next weekend.'

'I did see a flash outside my window. Are we sure there was no short circuit, or something else that went awry?'

'Sir, I can see everything from here. Everything is stable. And for the power surge, we did not experience anything of the sort here. Perhaps it was something local to your area. Nothing related to the machines or our infrastructure.'

Julian took a deep breath of relief. He was happy to learn his work was not damaged.

'Rest assured, Sir Alberon. We have it covered.' replied the man on the line in hearing the boss taking a burden off his chest. 'We will run a check on the power grid before tomorrow to be on the safe side.'

Julian thanked the man multiple times and ended the call. He tapped his phone on the chin and laughed to himself. He was worrying too much. There was nothing to fear. Tomorrow would be a success.

In the meantime, miles away from Julian's house, the man he had just spoken to on the phone was caressing his beard, staring at the monitor and glancing at the mess of electronic equipment scattered on the table near him. He chuckled to himself in the darkness of the room and with only the blue tint of the screen to give him company. The clock showed it was way past six o'clock. The world had not ended. He was still there. The room was still there. Wimbledon was still there. Whatever the computer programme was meant to do, it had done something. Something darker.

Monday morning saw the rise of a lazy winter sun, rising unannounced through the hazy morning mist just as every Wimbledonian woke up to start another working week. Simon Deeley was driving down Wimbledon Park, and as he sped across the border between Wandsworth and Merton, he spotted the spire of Saint Mary's Church as he had done almost every morning for the past few months. It was a reminder he was close to his destination. No matter the weather, the spire always peeped in the distance with its golden rooster at the top.

Simon checked the time. Eight o'clock in the morning. He was on time as usual. He hoped Dr Watkins would already be at the Old Rectory. The curator always seemed to take his time and more than once he had arrived late whenever Simon was scheduled to come to the archaeological site at the Old Rectory. Simon Deeley was a precise man, meticulous with detail. He had been working at the British Museum for many years now, starting as an assistant, and now, in his mid-thirties, leading new expeditions and discoveries on behalf of the renowned British institution. He was the one who had received the call from Julian Alberon himself. Simon could not believe his ears back then: Alberyx Enterprises was willing to fully fund the excavation and research at the newly found chamber under the Old Rectory in Wimbledon Village. Thanks to that, Simon and his team probably experienced the fastest turnaround in any of their archaeological exploration. A few months down the line, and he had cracked the code of the Pool of Elixir.

The car drove up the hill, past Rectory Orchards, and finally turned left into the private road leading to the Old Rectory site. Simon slowed down the car until it came to a stop by the sentry box.

'Morning, Mr Deeley!' said the young guard with a yawn.

'Morning. Almost end of shift?' commented Simon with his strong Scottish accent.

'Yes. Almost.'

'Everything ok?'

'As always.'

'Is Dr W here? I suppose not…'

'Dr Watkins, you mean? Actually, he has just arrived. It was if he had never left.'

'Was he working late yesterday?'

The guard nodded and then proceeded to open the barrier to let Simon drive through. He waved to the guard and parked the car in his usual spot on one side of the driveway. The driveway was still quiet. His team and some of the workers hired for maintenance would not be there for another hour or so. Simon quickly checked himself in the rear-view mirror. His African buzz hair cut still looked fresh from the barber, especially after his clean shave earlier that morning. Simon thought it would draw more attention to his eyebrows and eyes. It would be the perfect way to captivate the audience when he would present at Eagle House. He then picked up the box of reports from the back of the car and got out.

The sky had disappeared as he was now under the protective scaffolding they had built over the large century-old mansion that was the Old Rectory. Dr Watkins was waiting just inside, past the second checkpoint through the turnstile. He was in the entrance hall, wearing one of his light blue navy jackets. His blue eyes quickly met Simon's and waved at him with the folder the curator had in his hand.

'Good morning, Simon!' he exclaimed with chirpy enthusiasm.

'Morning, Dr W.'

The curator had become used to the shortened nickname. Simon Deeley was the only one calling him Dr W, and Simon's Scottish accent almost made it sound cool and edgy.

'I am surprised tae see ye here early.' continued Simon. 'It is a first, I must say.'

'I know, Simon.' replied the curator shyly. 'I have to be honest, though. I could not miss today for anything in the world. We may have finally unlocked the puzzle. Is that fair to say?'

'Unlocked is a big word.' smirked Simon. 'I would go as far as saying Wimbledon has a new chapter in history tae explore. You shuid be proud. In the end we worked together oan this.'

'I am, Simon. And thanks to you and your team as well.'

'Good. Now, shall I dae th' honours?'

Simon hinted at the box in his hands and Dr Watkins quickly went to call the small lift so they could descend into the basement. Once there, Simon's first step was always to turn the lights on, log in his arrival and check the status of the environment such as temperature and air composition. He had to make sure a stable average was kept at all times to avoid any damage to wall carvings, old statues and any worn-out remains. Then he would take off his coat and finally relax as he checked the work to be done and enjoy some warm coffee from his thermos. He was wearing his usual faded salmon coloured t-shirt, tight across his slim upper torso, and a pair of mud green khakis. He did not have the tool belt he usually kept around his waist during work. The first time Dr Watkins met Simon, he had mistaken him for a new member of security, misled by his toned muscles and trained physique. His attentive gaze was framed in an oval-shaped faced, with small nose and cheeks, embellished by a pair of green eyes. He never stared; he always gave the impression he listened and cared about what someone had to say.

'Where tae start?' said Simon.

'I have brought some of the books and photographs we had at the Wimbledon Museum.' replied Dr Watkins pointing at the folder he had put on the large table in the basement. 'I am not entirely sure why you would be suddenly interested in Wimbledon Common. I thought all your answers were here.'

'Some are.' grinned Simon, toying with the idea of mystery. 'OK, let me unpack the stuff I brought here with me, and A'll show ye.'

He put this thermos down and proceeded to empty the box on the table. He took out a few old bound reports, each with a worn-out red cover and a handwritten label. There were also photographs and scanned copies of older papers.

'These are from some of our archives. Not everything can leave the British Museum. Hence, copies of copies. However, I hev what I need to illustrate what we may be dealing with.'

'Dealing with?' commented Dr Watkins. 'You make it sound more perilous than it is. Wimbledon is a peaceful town.'

'Not what I've heard in the last twelve months.'

Dr Watkins was not surprised at how news had spread around so fast across London about the accident at the Old Rectory. It had not just made local news.

'So, we hev established the content of the chamber dates back to around seventh Century, or maybe the end of the sixth.' carried on Simon, sipping his coffee. 'We cannot deny the pool is Anglo-Saxon because of the runes and the symbol. However, we could not date the stone well. It is as if half of the material is from the Anglo-Saxon era and the other is much older. Never seen that before in my life.'

Dr Watkins frowned. This last bit of information was news.

'This led us tae look at the natural rock in the chamber. We found out it is older than Anglo-Saxon. The puzzling matter is also th' excavation date. It is clearly man-made, but it goes back to a time as ancient as Stonehenge.'

'Hold on a minute!' interrupted Dr Watkins. 'We've been researching and digging for months and we have concluded this is an Anglo-Saxon site. Now it isn't anymore?'

'It is! But there is more!'

Dr Watkins saw a glint of excitement in Simon's deep green eyes. He was sure Simon felt the same excitement as him. Wimbledon was probably sitting on a past that had been left unexplored for centuries. He could feel the ground under his feet trembling, as if calling out to both of them from the depths of the hill.

'Is this part of your presentation tomorrow night at Eagle House, Simon? I am sure it will cause some stir.'

Simon placed his thumb under his chin and index finger on his nose, tapping gently. He had something on his mind.

'Not really, Dr W. Hence, I asked for this meeting today. Tomorrow night I will mainly be presenting our Anglo-Saxon findings and in particular explaining the legend inscribed on the eagle-like statue on the pool's edge.'

'About the seven relics?'

'Correct.'

Dr Watkins eyed Simon suspiciously.

'Will you talk about legend or fact?'

'We are archaeologists and historians, Dr W. My presentation will keep the human imagination at bay. A person named as "The Wynnman" has existed for sure. Whether he or she is the sorcerer we read aboot, is something to be seen. This is where the last part of the text intrigued me and led to a little side research. Follow me.'

Dr Watkins frowned and quickly followed Simon into the small chamber. The archaeologist strode around the pool and stopped close by the eagle-like statue.

'Do you remember this last section?' Simon asked bending over to point at where the runes and symbols clustered together towards the base of the statue.

'Yes. We had not finished interpreting it. It was tough to understand. Something about mounds?'

'Exactly. Mounds.'

Dr Watkins gave Simon a doubtful look and kneeled by the statue to be at eye-level with the bit of text Simon was pointing at. He knew what mounds were. Britain was full of them, but he was not sure what Simon was getting at.

'All this time we only looked at Anglo-Saxon remains for reference, which were very helpful in linking with the cultural practices beknown to us, but it also meant we looked at the site from that angle alone.'

'Why would you look at it in any other way?'

'The last section talks about the rush to the mounds by the villagers in order to defend themselves from the Wynnman, and how the village learnt from local customs how to find protection. Mounds have been a form of defence, a fort so to speak, since...'

'Prehistoric times?' finished Dr Watkins incredulous.

'Exactly. The legend talks about Anglo-Saxons learning from ancient knowledge. My guess is that it dates to thousands of years. Maybe even older than Stonehenge!'

'Ah Simon!' sighed Dr Watkins. 'You said it. The word 'guess' throws everything out of the window in our industry unless you have solid proof.'

Simon did not look amused. He stood up, looking down on the curator.

'This is why I called you, Dr W. There is a mound in Wimbledon, and glimpsing at your photographs from the Wimbledon Museum, I think I am right.'

'Where?' questioned Dr Watkins standing up.

'Caesar's Camp in Wimbledon Common.'

The curator's eyes widened. He knew perfectly where Caesar's Camp was and also what it had been in ancient times.

'Simon, we hardly have proof of Caesar's Camp being a prehistoric burial mound. We have only ever found arrowheads, broken spears or knives, and fragments of pottery that date back to the Iron Age, I believe. Not much to go on.'

'That was only at the surface, wasn't it? I am talking about going underground. Deep underneath it.'

Dr Watkins's eyes widened further, as if Simon had just uttered a serious religious blasphemy.

'You can't be serious, Simon! You cannot dig there. The Wimbledon Common is a protected asset. You will never get permission to do so without asking the relevant bodies, like the Wimbledon and Putney Commons Conservators or WPCC, the Royal Wimbledon Golf Club, and the Council. To name a few.'

'But you can, Dr W. Work with me to put a case forward. If Anglo-Saxons went there to protect themselves from the Wynnman, be him a local tyrant or some kind of magic man casting spells, then the continuation to our story must be lying underneath with all the answers you are looking for. Think of what it would mean for British archaeology. Think of what it would mean fo' Wimbledon.'

'What if there is nothing down there, Simon? Will you leave me to face the wrath of Wimbledonians as we leave a big hole in their favourite green place on the hill?'

'Nobody said anything about a big wide hole. We have the technology and the resources to make this new archaeological site as less invasive as possible, especially if backed by Alberyx Enterprises. We just need approval to work on that piece of land, and you have all the contacts.'

Dr Watkins sighed in response to the big request Simon had put forward. He walked around the pool, tracing lines with his finger on the millennia-old stonework. He thought about Simon's proposal. Enticing, daring, and surely risky with everything happening of lately.

'It is not the easiest of times, Simon.' replied Dr Watkins, facing Simon across the empty pool. 'Not sure if you heard, but today, in a couple of hours, Alberyx Enterprises announces their new installation on the Common. You've seen the protesters, haven't you? It is clear some people are not happy about touching the Common, as you can imagine. Now this?'

'All I am saying is, have a think about it.' pleaded Simon shortening the distance between them. 'I know Caesar's Camp is on the land owned by the RWGC, the Royal Wimbledon Golf Club. Ye know the owner, don't ye? Lord Cotton, I believe. Good friend o' yours and member of the WAIS.'

'And?'

'Then arrange a meeting and let him hear our proposition.'

'Ours? Since when I am part of it?'

'Ye know better than me how important 'is could be. The Old Rectory was just the tip o' the iceberg.'

Dr Watkins pursed his lips, thinking about what Simon had just said. Indeed, his new lead to Caesar's Camp could open new doors. If he had to find the Wynnman, he had to follow the clues wherever they may lead.

'Let me have a chat with Lord Cotton.' said the curator. 'I am seeing him today at the press conference and I could propose lunch or something. Can we please not talk about this at your presentation on Monday evening?'

'Not tae worry. A'll hint at my latest findings, Dr W, and see the audience's reaction. That should be a good indicator of Wimbledon's support about a new archaeological site… What's that?'

Dr Watkins nodded vaguely and then shook his head realising Simon was now staring at a random point on the natural rock wall of the chamber.

'What?' said the curator at a loss.

'Over thir. That LED light is off.'

'Oh, that. I think there was a power surge last night. The lights flickered for a few seconds. That one must have fused.'

'And ye tell me now?' commented Simon annoyed. 'How many times do I hev to say it? Any abrupt changes in lighting and temperature are critical.'

The archaeologist rushed back to the basement to check his readings again. Dr Watkins followed him without being worried too much. It was not the first time a lightbulb fused. Cabling this whole underground site had been a challenge in the first place.

They both returned to the basement. Dr Watkins glanced at his watch. He had plenty of time before the press conference. He joined Simon at his side. He was busy checking the readings of the whole environment again. He skipped to the evening before and zoomed in.

'What time did ye say?'

'Must have been just before or after six in the evening.'

The archaeologist was quick at sliding the timeline on the tablet, scrolling across the multiple wavy lines going up and down the chart. Dr Watkins did not understand what the problem could be.

'I don't understand...' commented Simon as he finished scrolling sideways.

'What is it?'

'I cannot find the six p.m. slot anywhere.'

'In what sense?'

'I'd better ask one of my team members to run a quick diagnostic on the server. Looks very odd.'

'What does?'

'Look here.' said Simon pointing at multiple charts simultaneously. 'Th' lines are no longer continuous around six p.m. In each chart, there is a ten-minute gap between five to and five past six.'

'Probably the monitor stopped for a while.'

'It's not the monitoring 'at troubles me. If that had bin the case, I wuid see th' time units and then no data for 'at point in time. Here, though, it looks as if th' actual time units have disappeared from all the charts, as if the ten minutes had been cut out or erased.'

'Erased?'

'As if they had never existed.'

The New Wimbledon Windmill, as it was going to be called from that day onwards, was not actually new. It had been around for centuries and it was the key landmark of Wimbledon Common. Everyone knew that if anyone ever got lost in the vast wilderness of the Common, they always looked for the windmill rising above the trees. However, the Wimbledon Windmill had suffered the biggest damage in its history a couple of years before, after a terrible storm. The storm had broken its sails and damaged the central pillar supporting the whole mechanism. Since then, the windmill had been laying in ruins for quite some time, unable to find supporters who would fund a quick restoration to its former glory. Things did not change until recently when the local businessman Julian Alberon put forward plans to renovate it and make the windmill turn once again for the good of the community. Then one day he announced his restoration work was complete.

It was Monday morning. Julian Alberon was standing on a small, temporary balcony high up on the solid blocky scaffolding that had been concealing the windmill for a few long months. The whole restoration plan had progressed with the utmost secrecy and Wimbledonians had been gossiping at what may lie behind the scaffolding. Julian's well-groomed hair and clean-shaven face stared defiantly at the huge crowd below, eager to hear his anticipated announcement. Among the general public, there was the Mayor and members of the Council, plus other business partners that had supported Alberyx Enterprises over the last few months. Julian had waited a long time for this moment, and he felt confident enough despite the restless night before. He peeked at his cards for a quick refresh of his memory. One of his assistants was hidden backstage, perched on a foldable stool, giving him the last instructions and starting to count down before his introduction speech could commence. Julian smiled at the crowd and waved a friendly 'hello' to which the large Wimbledon crowd responded with a cheer.

'Everybody loves him!' said Viviane, her eyes full of admiration.

'Yeah, sure!' replied Enrico with sarcasm shifting one of his trays of sweets on their serving table. From where they stood below, they had the best view of Julian Alberon and the front of the windmill. It was a position reserved especially for the WAIS, the Wimbledon Association of Independent Shops, which Mr Alberon had kindly contacted to organise a promotional feast. Viviane had helped with the floral decorations on and around the windmill. Enrico instead had delivered what he was good at and had prepared another of his sweet specialties. His table was covered with *cantucci* and some almond biscuits with or without candied fruit. He felt it was the best choice for accompaniment to the gallons of hot tea and watered-down coffee sold at the main stand. They were all ready to celebrate the big surprise everyone had been waiting for.

'I wonder what could be behind the scaffolding' whispered Enrico, eyeing Julian and the crowds, as they were both getting ready for the speech.

'I don't know but I am sure it will be mind-blowing.' replied Viviane, never afraid of showing her confidence in Julian's work. 'Have you seen what else he's done around Wimbledon? He even fixed the roofs on the high street and installed solar panels on behalf of the Council and at his own expense! Can you believe that?'

'Dr Watkins said Julian has been very reserved about the whole thing.' added Enrico. 'Nobody knows exactly what he did to the windmill, and the Council only learnt the bare minimum to approve restoration plans. Everything complied with local regulations, apparently. Maybe it is just the same old windmill!'

Enrico looked at the crowds. Whatever Alberyx Enterprises had been up to, Wimbledon had struggled to keep quiet about it for months from the moment Julian's own company, Alberyx Enterprises, had started covering the windmill in order to begin the project. It had only fired up more gossip, more chatter. The result was one of the biggest turnouts in years on the Common since Queen Victoria's visit, and Julian Alberon could not hide his pride.

Enrico looked at Julian, high up on the scaffolding. The two had not seen each other since the horrible accident at the Old Rectory. Despite having spent a short time recovering and still working from home, Julian had been busier than usual from the looks of what Alberyx Enterprises had been doing across Wimbledon. The investment in the archaeological site at the Old Rectory had led to a complete regeneration project for Wimbledon Village, and the New Windmill was one of the first promises Julian had managed to deliver in such a short time. Enrico was impressed. Julian would have been tired from all his work, worn out by fatigue to meet such tight deadlines. Instead, here he was, smiling at the crowds with a self-confidence Enrico could only admire with a little envy. The Italian baker knew he could never have coped with so much work if he were in his shoes.

Plus, he could not ignore seeing Julian's hand in a leather glove. It was the hand he burnt in the accident at the Old Rectory. Staring at it created an odd asymmetry next to the naked pink flesh of his other hand, as if there were some kind of unbalance. Seeing Dr Watkins's glove had also produced the same effect. It was a stark reminder to Enrico who somehow blamed himself for what had happened. He had told Viviane many times he could have prevented it; he had been close enough to warn Julian and Dr Watkins not to get burned. Enrico thought the scars would have healed by now and he wondered how much longer they would take; how long before he was allowed to forget that horrible event.

'He's about to speak!' shouted Viviane excited, giving a nudge to Enrico.

'Yes, yes! *Ossignore…*' sighed Enrico, still unable to grasp Viviane's groupie attitude towards Julian Alberon.

The crowd's soft murmur quietened down as Julian Alberon gently tapped his microphone to check it worked. It was his time. He shifted into his business-like, welcoming stance. His shoulders relaxed, his arms wide open, holding tight onto the railing of the balcony. He then cleared his throat and spoke with attitude and determination, aimed at inspiring his listeners.

'Wimbledonians, councillors, friends, welcome to the inauguration of the New Wimbledon Windmill. Today is another important milestone to add to the long history of our village and of our windmill, which has served our community for centuries. It was in 1816 when it was first erected, and it is today we salvage it from disrepair once more to start a new chapter. I say once more, but this time for good. We all know how the sad story goes. The windmill became abandoned in the late nineteenth century and only in 1974 was it rebuilt as a historical monument thanks to the charitable work of my predecessors. Yet, history repeats itself, and when storms and gales hit the Common more than once in recent decades, the windmill was not strong enough to resist, having been rebuilt in wood and brickwork over and over since Victorian times. I actually became interested in the windmill almost a year ago. For those who know me, I have two things at heart when it comes to Wimbledon: its business potential and its remarkable history, both ignored on most occasions. When the modernisation of Wimbledon became a core part of our agenda at Alberyx Enterprises, the windmill was one of the many things to tackle in my business plan and by coincidence its desperate need for repair came at the right time. It was time to rebuild it as an enduring symbol of our Common that would outlive generations to come. A few months ago, we kickstarted the project we had in mind. Today, Wimbledon enters the future. Without further ado, let me present you the New Wimbledon Windmill!'

Julian Alberon made a theatrical gesture, with a gentle bow and sleight of hand as if he were a magician. The hidden cue to the assistant behind him was her signal. She turned around to peer inside the cavernous windmill and gave the green light to the engineers sitting one floor below around a fully equipped control room. The push of a button was enough to bring the whole cylindrical scaffolding down. It collapsed on itself like a house of cards and a shower of confetti followed with a pompous fanfare. Everyone was in awe, not just for the spectacular display Julian Alberon's team organised, but also for what laid behind the scaffolding. The windmill stood there at its usual location and its shape was unchanged. The sails, the central cone-shaped structure, the wider hexagonal base to hold it all together; it looked the same, except the wood and brickwork had become strands of decoration across the new light but solid metallic building with its silver-like glistening reflection. The sails too were made of a light white metallic grid similar to the one of radar stations. Some of the faces in awe turned to admiration while others, being more conservative, twitched their noses to the odd new structure.

Where Julian Alberon was now standing, which everyone thought was a balcony, was in fact an open man cage at the top of a small crane, stuck in mid-air at the same height as the windmill's pinnacle. He stood with his arms wide open to show his creation. He appeared like a flying wizard and the windmill behind rose upwards like a phoenix rising from the ashes. A clapping of hands ensued from the audience, enough to show the majority present welcomed the new windmill. Julian enjoyed the brief accolade before taking the word once more.

'The New Wimbledon Windmill, ladies and gentlemen. Yet, no ordinary windmill. This is a feat of technological advancement embracing the history of our village and the technical advances we make at Alberyx Enterprises. Most people feel windmills are obsolete. That they are no longer needed. That they are purposeless buildings just for show, for nostalgia. Well, let me tell you, we at Alberyx Enterprises wanted to re-purpose this windmill for good. You are now witnessing the first ever wireless electricity generator, the first of many to be built around Wimbledon. It will allow us to be energy self-sufficient, but it will also provide greener electricity for a more sustainable environment. Just look at the Wimbledon Common around us! Look at that wonderful green area!'

Julian paused to catch his breath and then resumed.

'Join me this coming weekend when the first wave of clean electricity will be officially distributed to the community from our own New Wimbledon Windmill. I will be holding a press conference at the Royal Golf Course after lunch today to answer any questions and provide a more formal statement for the press. For now, feel free to come and see inside and take a peek. Thank you!'

The crowd cheered to Julian Alberon's last words and an encore of applauses followed once again. He stood up there to enjoy the moment waving his gloveless hand as if he were a preacher.

'Isn't he inspiring?' commented Viviane clapping her hands.

Enrico tut-tutted and devoured a *cantuccio* just to keep his mouth busy and away from inappropriate comments. He knew everyone admired Julian Alberon for his successful career and for being Wimbledon's number one benefactor.

'Stop being jealous!' Viviane teased. 'You are always moody when news from Julian breaks out!'

'I am not!' babbled Enrico, mouth full and hands high up to show his innocence.

'Ok, ok. Shall we go and have a look inside?'

She hinted at the crowd starting to queue to marvel at the inner workings of this new machine which looked like a windmill but was something else entirely. Enrico nodded, unable to hide his own curiosity. The last thing he wanted was to argue. Viviane knew he was a little jealous of Julian's success and Enrico only blamed himself for not being clever at hiding it.

The entrance to the windmill was on the opposite side, through a low wooden gate leading to a small opening covered with gravel. Straight ahead a small arched door led inside the hexagonal base of the windmill. Despite the complete overhaul in new metal and synthetic materials, Enrico could see Julian's team had been careful enough to keep traces of its past. The small entrance was still in wood and brickwork, with a nice plaque above commemorating its founder.

CHARLES MARSH, 1816

Enrico and Viviane had to queue for almost half an hour before it was their turn to get inside. The whole visit had been organised as a tour in a clockwise direction. Inside, the windmill was a very tiny and cramped space. Even with most of the old equipment gone, the engineers really had to be creative in how to install a very advanced computer lab filled with cables, shelves and control panels. All the different modular components making up the new technology infrastructure of the windmill were on display for everyone to see, explaining what their function was. Self-standing signposts marking key points of the tour at regular intervals kept playing animated videos to show the benefits of wireless electricity.

When it was almost their turn to step inside, Enrico suddenly felt anxious in front of the heap of machinery popping up from every corner inside the windmill.

'Is this tour going to be long?' he moaned to Viviane in a low whisper.

'What has got into you, Enrico? It is not that big, is it?' she replied as she read one of the signs.

'I don't see how this windmill can generate wireless electricity. What's wrong with milling flour like in the old days?'

'Take it easy, grumpy man.' teased Viviane, ready to enter. 'You will upset the star of the show. I should know better, though, coming from you. Aren't you the self-proclaimed technophobe? If I remember well, you are one who still owns an old Nokia 3310, right?'

The Italian baker grinned. He pulled out his Nokia 3310 and wiggled it in front of her, teasing in return.

'It does its job!' Enrico added.

'What a museum piece!' Viviane replied with a coy smile.

By the time they stepped inside the New Windmill, Enrico felt a lot better. The whole world inside the ground floor of the windmill appeared to be more magical than ever, from the jingles accompanying the explanatory videos to the animated characters showing how wireless electricity would remove the need for electricity cables and supply the most remote places.

'Look who's there! The man of the hour!'

Viviane pointed at one end of the hexagonal room where a small spiral staircase led to the upper floor. Julian Alberon had just come down and was discussing with his assistant and other members of his team. He spoke with grandeur and confidence, never crossing his arms and always keeping his hands active to show his interest and his support. A hand on a colleague's shoulder, a hand holding the drawings or the schedule he was being shown. Enrico and Viviane could see his passion transpiring as he spoke and listened in equal measure, but the Italian baker could not ignore the glove he wore on one hand. It somehow broke the perfect image, as if tarnished or stained. Enrico wondered again if he should blame himself for that, or if Julian Alberon had thought of that in the first place. His technophobia was probably playing tricks on his mind and conscience. Enrico ran his hand through his wavy black hair to find some self-composure, in the hope his gesture would swipe away negative thoughts.

'Hello Viviane! Hello Enrico!' exclaimed Julian Alberon on seeing them.

He dismissed his team and walked up to them with a broad smile.

'Thank you!' he said, giving a hug to both. 'Thank you for coming. It means a lot to me!'

'Don't mention it!' replied Viviane. 'It is a pleasure!'

She nudged Enrico subtly.

'Oh…nice work, Mr Alberon!' Enrico said shaking quickly the businessman's hand. 'Not sure what it does but…nice work!'

'Enrico! Come on! Call me Julian!'

'Julian! Sure. I hope all is well with you. We can see you are back at work with loads of energy after…you know…the accident…'

Viviane elbowed him this time. Enrico could not help himself.

'Kind of you to ask.' answered Julian mildly, not taking notice. 'I fully recovered after a few months. The doctor said it was nothing serious. Unusual but no contamination or bacteria was found after all the tests they put me through. That crimson liquid was an awkward experience. A chemistry experiment gone wrong!'

'How come you keep the glove on?' asked Enrico.

'Safety, I supposed.' said Julian. 'Skin feels sensitive still. I'd rather be cautious.'

'Well, at least it gives you that eccentric look you always strive for!' noted Viviane to show the positive side.

Julian grinned while fidgeting with his glove as he spoke. Enrico could tell Julian Alberon was powering through with his smile and joviality to suppress bad memories from their shared adventure at the Old Rectory. He could see it in the scars from the burns around his right temple and some thin ones on the edges of his face. Faint enough not to see them, if not up close. Enrico thought Julian must have a good make-up team. The curious baker was about to ask more about Julian's health but thought it best to leave it for another day.

'Well, we are glad to be here!' continued Viviane to ease off any uncomfortable silences. 'Any chance for a special private tour of the top floors?'

'Why not?' answered Julian. 'I can do that for special friends. Let me ask one of the engineers.'

As he left momentarily, Enrico groaned. The buzzing of the equipment was becoming annoying.

'Are you ok?' checked in Viviane.

'Yeah, yeah… Just sceptical about all these computers and cables!' replied Enrico.

Viviane rolled her eyes. She was about to add something when Julian beckoned at them from the spiral staircase to come over.

'Green light!' he shouted hanging from the rail and ready to pull himself up to take the first step. 'Come on up!'

'Can you manage?' mocked Viviane turning to Enrico in confidence.

'Sure!' said Enrico playing along. 'And while I'm at it, I can keep my tongue in check, if that troubles you.'

Viviane chuckled. Their banter was no longer unusual. She had become used to Enrico's quirkiness and Enrico on the other hand knew what pleased Viviane and what did not.

The second floor appeared to be narrower as the slanted walls of the windmill rose to join up at its highest point. To Enrico's liking, more computers popped up around the place like mushrooms. The cables branched out around the old brick pillars like artificial ivy from the future taking over the past. One area of the second floor though was clear of all clutter and machinery. It was by one of the two only windows on the floor, wide enough to make the space look bright and fresh. Through the window, looking outside, they could see the stalls and what remained of the crowd who had attended Julian's speech. Behind them the sea of green and wild trees that was the Common extended south towards Wimbledon.

A large easel lay in the middle of the second floor. It had a mix of post-its and charts, but the main feature was a large sheet in the middle of it, showing a technical drawing of the windmill. The printed details explained the design and a few scribbled notes pointed out key components in the structure.

'Let me show you the plans!' introduced Julian with another theatrical gesture of his hand. 'I always think the plans help to get a better understanding of the vision and grasp the whole concept instead of asking my chief engineer to demonstrate how the machine thinks and functions. I am actually going through this at my press conference today after lunch so consider it a special preview.'

He grinned and stood next to the easel waiting for Enrico and Viviane to come forward and see the plans in full for themselves.

'The New Wimbledon Windmill has become a special one.' he started explaining. 'While its sails will still use wind power and turn around with the historic charm that goes with them, what we did was also turn the sails into special photo-magnetic panels that will capture the effects of geo-storms in the Earth's outer atmosphere. The waves received will be channelled here and turned into a small source of electromagnetic energy, enough to feed Wimbledon Village and Wimbledon Town with clean energy.'

'Where does the wireless bit come into play?' asked Enrico.

'Good point! We always hated transmission lines and telegraph poles ruining the countryside. My plan is to build a local network of antenna repeaters, camouflaged like we did for the windmill. It would be our own local power grid, enabling us to extend the signal and carry the electricity wherever it may be needed. The windmill will transform the energy into packs of photons which the antenna repeaters will be able to transform into common alternate current.'

'Wow, Julian!' congratulated Viviane. 'Futuristic stuff! And the council did not say anything?'

'All planning permissions were submitted as required and all my requests were clear from the beginning. It is safe and efficient. The change to the windmill does not diminish or alter its historical value. The best of both worlds!'

'It does look a bit metallic…' noted Viviane.

'I completely understand.' carried on Julian unphased by the comment. 'It is not the first time I've heard this comment. There is a reason behind the light metal structure. We tried our best to avoid a grey block of concrete. While looking more robust, it would have looked horrible. Plus, it would have been a nightmare to manage. As it is now, we ensured the windmill would survive future storms and keep its beauty intact at the same time. Wimbledon will come around to accept it.'

'And what is on the third top floor, under the pinnacle?' asked Enrico curious.

'That area is where the sails are attached and connected to the "brain" of the whole system. We call it the Oscillator, since it helps capture the oscillating wavelengths from geomagnetic energy at the right frequency. Due to its fragility, we do not allow non-authorised, non-technical personnel up there. And that includes me!'

He pointed at a small pulldown ladder leading to a closed hatch in the ceiling where a red sign made it clear who could and could not enter.

'The "brain" connects the receptors to the generators on the ground floor. It then transforms the photons into wireless energy, sends it back up to the "brain" and it is transmitted to the closest household antenna. I repeat, the energy is safe and clean, and only mishandling it on purpose can cause unstable currents. That is why only our chief engineer is allowed up on the third floor. He must be present whenever access is required.'

'Can it blow up?' asked Enrico concerned under the playful eyes of Viviane.

'Nothing of that sort.' laughed Julian. 'It could give you an electroshock or spark a fire when unstable, so we sealed off the whole top floor with the latest safety precautions to contain any possible damage.'

'You are right.' commented Enrico. 'We don't need anything else to happen to this old windmill. There have been too many incidents. How many times did it collapse?'

'Two times, I think. Maybe three. Trust me, Enrico. It won't happen again!'

Julian's answers were well-polished and rehearsed probably under the direction of his public relations team. Yet his self-confidence was so strong and evident that he convinced everyone into seeing and believing in his vision. Even Enrico had to admit that Julian was a self-made man. He had it all. Coming to think of it, Enrico grinned at the fact that Julian had just called him by his first name. Perhaps having a friend as famous as Julian was a good thing after all.

'Will you be joining me at the press conference later?' asked Julian.

'We have an invitation, thanks to Dr Watkins.' said Viviane. 'We will probably make our way soon.'

'I have to say Dr Watkins has been doing a good job. His work with the British Museum at the Old Rectory is outstanding.'

'So we heard from Dr Watkins.' added Enrico. 'We have not seen him as much since he has been helping with the site. We are actually invited to the presentation on their findings tonight. Eagle House, isn't it?'

'Yes. I am excited.' commented Julian without hiding how he felt.

'Will you be presenting too?' asked Viviane.

'I will leave that to my experts. I just had to ensure they had everything to make it happen. Tonight, I will be a guest like you two, and hear what Dr Watkins and Mr Deeley have to say.'

'We heard a lot about Mr Deeley.' noted Enrico. 'Viviane and I have not yet had the pleasure of meeting him, but Dr Watkins keeps talking about how quick and efficient he is. I must admit I am a bit curious to hear what they are going to present.'

'*Ragazzo curioso!*' joked Viviane ruffling Enrico's hair when he least expected it.

'What did you say?' asked Julian.

'Oh, you know Enrico,' clarified Viviane. 'he is always curious about things.'

'True.' nodded Julian, amused. 'If it hadn't been for you, Enrico, everything we found under the Old Rectory would have been lost forever.'

'I'm just a baker…' joked Enrico.

'That is true. And a bloody good one, if you ask me!' added Viviane.

'I agree. That is what I keep hearing!' said Julian. 'I'll have to come personally to the Wynnman bakery one of these days and get the bread myself one day. It has not been easy the last few months.'

'Anytime, Julian.' replied Enrico.

Julian replied with a smile of delight. The Italian baker felt a little uneasy with the business tycoon's stare. He was not made for being at the centre of attention but he realised he was gradually making a name for himself in Wimbledon so he would have to get used to this kind of thing. Befriending Julian was probably an opportunity that should not go amiss to make his baking business thrive even more.

The full crowd had dispersed by late morning. Some had made the choice to reach Wimbledon by car via the long stretch of road called Parkside. The more eco-friendly Wimbledonians had preferred to walk along the wide foot path leading straight across the wilderness to the southern edge of the Common. Its wild shrubbery and thick forest were welcoming and enchanting under the bright winter sky. Back at the windmill, the organisers from the WAIS had stayed behind to clear the stalls and the picnic tables. While stacking empty cake tins, and putting away used mugs and trays, the odd chatter about the new windmill kept creeping up. The new light, metallic structure rising above them was so different and to some it even looked alien. There were differing opinions as is always the case. Everyone though agreed that the debate among Wimbledonians on whether to accept the New Wimbledon Windmill was just about to start.

Enrico and Viviane had not made up their mind yet. They were both in the car park next to the windmill, busy loading Viviane's tiny yellow Fiat 500 with her flowerpots and Enrico's stack of trays from the bakery. The back and forth kept them warm in the fresh winter air.

'I can't believe you wear a chef's jacket even in winter!' said Viviane exasperatedly.

'I like it. And don't worry, I have a pullover underneath to keep warm. You can call it my trademark!'

'I am sure it is. Let's wrap this up quickly and get a move on so we can get to the Royal Wimbledon Golf Club in time for the press conference.'

'What do you think of this then?' wondered Enrico pointing at the silent windmill towering above them.

'It is a breath of fresh air. Change is good!'

'Do you think so?' Enrico looked at her doubtfully. 'I am just surprised Julian went for this "look" while insisting we should preserve Wimbledon's history alive. Shame Dr Watkins was not here! I would have loved to hear his opinion.'

'He has been so busy with the Old Rectory site. To answer your question, I think he would not disapprove. This is better than leaving it in ruins like one of your Roman temples!'

Enrico heard Viviane's chuckle but let the sarcastic comment slide. He glanced at the windmill once more. His technophobia had long gone the moment he stepped outside of the windmill and made their way to the car park next door. Yet, he felt another tingling sensation brewing. This time in his hands, and it was a sensation he knew well. Each time his curiosity went berserk, he felt the urge to bake some bread just to get over what he had been thinking. Something nagged him and it was not the windmill.

'What did you think of Julian and his health?' asked Enrico helping Viviane in tidying up a few flowers in the corner of the boot.

'He looked in great shape to me! So positive!'

'I am not sure about that glove of his. Like Dr Watkins's glove, I find it disturbing.'

'Stop it, Enrico!' sighed Viviane, knowing perfectly what Enrico may be getting at. 'Stop getting worried about his hand and the scars. It is not your fault!'

'You didn't see what I saw in the Pool of Elixir.' reminded Enrico with a sudden shudder. 'The fire. The apparition. It scared the hell out of me and still haunts me in my dreams. Sometimes I think it is accusing me for not doing anything to prevent it...'

'Don't be so harsh on yourself, Enrico!' reassured Viviane. 'It was all an accident. Neither you nor Julian or Dr Watkins should hold a grudge. I know Dr Watkins and Julian do not hold you responsible. Maybe Inspector Baynard does.'

The Italian baker laughed at the way Viviane always tried to lift his spirit. He had missed the inspector at Julian's event. Enrico had even looked out for him, but they both knew it was better the two men did not cross paths that often.

'You're probably, right!' Enrico agreed. 'It's just that we have not seen Julian in a while, and I felt I never made amends. He almost disappeared from public view after what happened at the Old Rectory, working non-stop, and then he came back with all this, riding on the wave of his success. It's incredible!'

'Well, he has done so much for Wimbledon. Funded new schools, saved historical buildings from speculative construction, built new green spaces, and even supported the WAIS in its early years. The list goes on. Next time you see him congratulate him instead of asking what's wrong! He is a good friend!'

Enrico nodded with a sigh of acceptance at Viviane's playful advice and carried the last bulk of the trays to the car. He knew he should be more supportive of Julian. He had helped him and Viviane with their respective shops. He could be a helpful friend indeed.

'I need to catch up with Mr Wyczenski for our next WAIS meeting on Wednesday.' said Viviane. 'Do you mind waiting five minutes by the car?'

'*Nessun problema*! No problem!' confirmed Enrico.

The Italian baker closed the boot and leaned on the car in the middle of the car park, now emptier than before. He took in the view of the windmill against the clear blue winter sky. The cold air was still freezing from the early morning. He wrapped up his chef jacket, the one he wore on almost every occasion, and kept his gaze on the windmill. He was starting to like this new modern windmill. The radar-like sails slightly curved, the silver shine from the light robust metallic structure, the contrast from the brickwork dating back to centuries ago. The best of both worlds.

'You can't do this!' complained a loud man's voice to his right.

Enrico turned his head in the direction of the voice. Next to the windmill, a one-storey detached building stretched alongside the length of the car park. He hadn't noticed it before, hidden as it was by the nicely cropped trees and a well-trimmed hedge recreating a natural fence around the windmill and the low building. Two burly men, with shaved heads, earpieces and bulldog faces, probably security, had come through a double glass door entrance pushing forward a man with greying hair, around the same age or maybe younger than Dr Watkins. He was very tall, taller than the two security guards, but his hunched shoulders and back diminished his height and revealed genuine fear and shock at the threat of the two men.

'I'm still responsible for it.' he shouted. 'It's a breach of contract. Let me back in!'

The tall man tried to free himself from the two men, wanting desperately to get back inside the building, but only found a tough resistance. The two security guards pushed him back harder and harder but were still careful enough not to throw him onto the ground and harm him.

'Please leave the premises, now!' warned one of the two security men. 'You received all the final paperwork confirming the termination of your contract and your services here are no longer required. Please leave before we call the police.'

The tall man was then pushed into the car park at what was deemed a safe distance. Enrico noticed the two security guards had stopped a few yards in front of the double glass door, waiting for the tall man to leave for good.

'Ok, I will leave!' shouted the tall man in surrender. 'This is outrageous. I will bring you two to court, and Alberyx Enterprises as well. This is no right way to treat a long-serving member of the community, and a senior citizen for a matter of fact.'

The guards did not respond to the threat to avoid a battle of words. They just waved their hands at him, telling the tall man to calm down. The tall man grunted with dissatisfaction and turned around to leave. In the haste of it, he stumbled and fell forward hitting his face on the car park tarmac. Enrico stood up from the Fiat 500 and rushed across to help the tall man out. The two guards did not budge or flinch at the scene. They waited a while and walked back inside when it was deemed safe to do so.

'Are you alright?' asked Enrico kneeling to check the tall man was not hurt.

'Fine. Just a bruise.' muttered the tall man wiping dirt from his hands as he sat up on the tarmac.

Enrico stretched his hand out. The tall man looked back at him with suspicion. He had dark green eyes and two pink cheeks blushing against the aging skin. His grey hair was thick and messy. Enrico thought it was because of the fall until he realised it was the tall man's style to leave his hair ruffled. The tall man stood up and brushed off any dirt on his trousers. Enrico took a better look at him. He was indeed very tall, towering over Enrico's medium height like a giant. He wore a pair of baggy chestnut trousers with a sleeveless, brown and white striped sweater over a faded mud green shirt. Enrico thought he could spot some tea or sauce stains on his sleeves.

'Thank you, sir!' finally replied the tall man.

'Don't mention it! Everything ok? I was waiting nearby and realised your situation was somehow… distressful.'

'I'm fine. It's just that these people have no heart or mercy. I have been working here for more than thirty years. And this is how they thank me!'

'More than thirty years?' exclaimed Enrico.

The Italian baker was impressed. He was only a few months away from celebrating his first anniversary since opening his bakery, The Wynnman, in Wimbledon Village.

'Yes!' confirmed the tall man. 'I am… oh, well… I was the guardian to the old windmill until two days ago.'

'Oh, you mean…' stammered Enrico pointing his thumb at the windmill.

'Yes!' confirmed again the tall man with anger. 'Alberyx Enterprises thought they no longer needed me after building this thing. Apparently, it looks after itself. Damn machine!'

Enrico was quick to realise the tall man was not a fan of the new, modern Wimbledon Windmill.

'I am sure the WAIS can help you find something that works for you in Wimbledon.' he tried to reassure him.

'It's not the job, young lad. These people are playing around with things and doing stuff they don't even know about. And worse they don't even realise it!'

'What do you mean?' asked Enrico intrigued.

The tall man looked back at the low building as if worried he could be heard. There was no sign of the two security guards. He then looked again at the windmill.

'Walk with me.' said the tall man.

The two walked the short distance back to the Fiat 500 and in the little time he had, the tall man did not waste a minute to share his thoughts. Enrico understood the tall man wanted to talk after what had happened; perhaps the tall man simply did not talk to many people if he had spent most of his life alone in the windmill as he claimed. The Italian baker looked out for Viviane but she had not returned yet.

'You see, my friend,' started the tall man. 'when you work with things you can't see, like this wireless electricity malarkey, you can only be sure of the results one can see or touch. The rest is faith. Faith that there will be no unexpected consequences or ill side effects. Am I right?'

Enrico nodded vaguely. He was not sure what the tall man really meant.

'I have been around the windmill 24/7 ever since it was closed for this restoration project a few months ago. I was asked to keep an eye on the place day and night so nothing would disrupt the work organised by Alberyx Enterprises. From time to time, especially at night, I have seen electric charges flickering out from the top like the lava spurts of a volcano. Some of them even reached high into the sky on certain occasions and temperatures in the immediate area dropped almost below zero at a speed unheard of. Let me tell you, this wireless electricity will cause weird things to happen.'

'Well, I am sure Alberyx Enterprises has been testing how to harness electric charges in a safe manner if they wish to support Wimbledon.' reasoned Enrico on friendly terms. 'And as for the cold temperature, it is winter after all!'

He was no specialist on the subject of wireless electricity, but he did think the tall man was not either. The old windmill had been used to mill flour a century or more ago, before being turned into a museum. Perhaps there were people who complained back in the day when the windmill was closed and turned into a museum. Today, the new windmill changed again and it was just a sign of progress coming to Wimbledon; it was normal to be scared or sceptical of the unknown. Yet, Enrico could not dismiss the tall man completely when it came to side effects. The thought of an invisible and unpredictable force like wireless electricity made him feel uneasy. Enrico shuddered and focused on the tall man's words, listening to his every word so as not to get distracted.

'Well, my young friend, what if I told you I saw something weirder than just electric charges?'

'Like what?'

'A ghost, perhaps.'

Enrico stopped in his track. The tall man eyed him with anticipation.

'A ghost?' blurted out the Italian baker, incredulous.

'Yes, right there!'

The tall main pointed at a spacious green plain free of trees or shrubs, east of the windmill. It was neatly framed between the street leading out of the car park and out of the Common, and the wide dirt footpath leading south to the village. Enrico could see one or two people walking across it, enjoying the winter sun before its warmth died out.

'Right there in the middle, I saw a ghost!'

'Really?' led on Enrico with a hint of sarcasm.

Enrico thought he may be walking with a lunatic, and he was not interested in hearing more about the tall man's nonsense. Viviane though was not back at the car yet, and so the Italian baker had no choice but hang around and listen until she returned to free him from this scary tall man who believed in ghosts.

'Yes! I saw the ghosts of James Brudenell, Earl of Cardigan and Captain Harvey Tuckett, getting ready for duel as if it was 1840. It was a brief apparition before the mist lifted and made them disappear like sugar dissolved in water.'

The Italian baker had his doubts. He thought he should check the facts with Dr Watkins next time he saw him, to be sure nobody died in a duel here and there was no ghost story among the pages of local Wimbledon folklore.

'And you say the New Wimbledon Windmill did it?'

'Exactly! I would not be surprised if Alberyx Enterprises knows about such events with all their technological contraptions being built and tested down at the Warren Farms compound.'

'Warren Farms?'

'Yes. The headquarters of Alberyx Enterprises, deep in the heart of Wimbledon Common. God knows what goes on in there...'

Enrico thought the tall man spoke about the compound as if it were a secret government base like Area 51. He forced himself not to laugh. The conversation was only going to spiral down to the unimaginable. Enrico glanced sideways looking for an excuse to say farewell to the tall man. Then Viviane's jolly voice returned to Enrico's ear, promising a safe way out of the discussion.

'Quentin!' she exclaimed. 'Quentin Plainstraw. How have you been?'

The tall man turned around, distracted from his conspiracies and thoughts about ghosts. His suspicious scowl eased a little in seeing Viviane.

'Oh, Viviane. So nice to see you.' replied Quentin glumly.

'I see you already made acquaintance with Enrico LoTrova.' she continued, not noticing Quentin's mood.

Quentin eyed Enrico again with renewed interest and with a thorough inspection from head to toe. To Enrico, he looked odd, with his stained shirt and his messy hair laying unruly even when ruffled by the gentle winter breeze. Yet, he could not help feeling sorry for him.

'Are you excited about the new windmill?' carried on Viviane innocently.

Enrico hid behind Quentin's shoulder and made a gesture to warn Viviane not to touch the subject and cut it short, but to no avail.

'It is hideous!' grumbled Quentin.

His face was angry again; his mouth ready to spit venom once again.

Viviane blinked her eyes, bewildered.

'Sorry, Viviane, Enrico.' apologised Quentin. 'Not a good day for me. I already bothered Enrico enough with my misfortunes!'

'What happened? Are you ok?'

'Yes. Well, no. I mean yes. Healthy and all. Unfortunately, my days here at the windmill are over. Alberyx Enterprises no longer requires a guardian.'

'Oh no! I am so sorry!' exclaimed Viviane genuinely. 'When did this happen?'

'Just now.' added Enrico.

'Why don't you go and talk to Dr Watkins?' suggested Viviane. 'He may be able to help.'

'For what?'

'Maybe there is somewhere else in Wimbledon where you can get help.'

'I worked here for thirty years. I am not going to let this infernal machine take it away!'

Quentin showed renewed determination. He was still angry. Viviane and Enrico felt helpless. The tall man realised what he was saying.

'Sorry for my outburst.' apologised Quentin with a sad, resigned look on his face. 'This is not your problem. Thanks for the advice though. I would love to stay and chat, but I need to go. If you excuse me.'

'Of course!' concurred Viviane with a smile full of good intentions. 'If there is anything you need…'

The tall man, Quentin Plainstraw, turned on his heels after giving a polite but reluctant nod and started heading west where at the end of the car park the wilderness of the Common resumed with its tall, thick trees. Their branches reached high and arched over like claws, and for a minute Quentin did not look as tall.

Inspector Baynard had given exact instructions. Nobody except the Wimbledon police or an official employee of Alberyx Enterprises was allowed through the wooden gate leading onto the footpath cutting across holes number six and seven of the golf course belonging to the Royal Wimbledon Golf Club. Access to the area was off limits until further notice and he ensured the other end of the footpath, half a mile down the hill near Beverley Meads, was also blocked off. Baynard hoped such measures would be short-lived, until this whole show was over.

Sergeant Jeremy, though, did not expect to see such a large crowd hanging around in front of the wooden gate. It was right at the end of Camp Road where the narrow road took a sharp bend north into a narrower country lane leading to Warren Farms compound, deeper into Wimbledon Common. The space was so narrow that, on more than one occasion, he had to ask the other policemen to push the crowd of protesters to one side so the odd car could pass through safely while he kept guard at the wooden gate.

The crowd was a restless one, pacific but belligerent-looking, chanting protests and joining in to find strength in their numbers. Some had been there since seven in the morning when the call came through to the Wimbledon police station from local residents at first and then from the custodians at the Royal Wimbledon Golf Club during their early morning check of the grounds. The crowd of protesters had threatened to invade the golf course and push deep into the hill towards one of Alberyx Enterprises's working sites, built right between holes six and eleven, on an unused rough patch of land. Jeremy and the rest of the Wimbledon police had grown accustomed to such demonstrations in the last couple of months. There had been several marches on Wimbledon High Street and many sit-ins in front of the Town Hall. The target was always the same: Alberyx Enterprises.

Jeremy had not expected the civil uproar to reach such proportions and reach this corner of Wimbledon Hill with the threat of invading what was rightfully private property. The events of the morning built up so fast that Inspector Baynard was once again under pressure by the Chief Superintendent to bring back order, especially when it concerned a prominent business like Alberyx Enterprises. The company was very concerned the protest could put their staff of the nearby working site at risk. Any damage to the machine nicknamed "Repeater" would put Sir Julian Alberon's launch plans for the week ahead in jeopardy especially if anything happened on the same day as his long-awaited announcement at the windmill. Both Baynard and Jeremy knew they had a long week ahead of them.

'Stand back!' Jeremy repeated a few times to stress his authority.

The crowd huddled around the wooden gate. There must have been fifty or sixty protesters in total. They stood silent, then chanted again or cried out words of dissent. Always pacific but still belligerent to the worried eyes of Sergeant Jeremy. He dried the sweat off his brow. He then spotted a police car coming on Camp Road, from the direction of Wimbledon Village. The plain colours with a blue siren confirmed it could only be Inspector Baynard coming to oversee the situation. The inspector waved his hand out of the window, as a sign of hope to Sergeant Jeremy, and hit the horn hard to scare the mass of people building up against the wooden gate.

'Move!' he shouted menacingly from the car window. 'Police coming through!'

His light grey eyes met the eyes of the protesters. He gave them an icy stare, something that would restore order again without having to shoot a gun up to the sky or cause unnecessary violence in what was usually a tranquil and respectable place. Jeremy helped push the crowd back and Baynard swiftly parked his car in front of the wooden gate as an extra barrier. The other policemen present joined in and formed a human chain in front of the car. Baynard stepped out and checked it was fine to do so for the two passengers with him.

'What's the status?' asked Baynard.

'Under control so far, inspector.' confirmed Jeremy. 'But I will be honest with you. The situation is a bit delicate.'

'You don't say? Perhaps you should let the Chief Superintendent know that.'

Baynard let the sarcasm sink in and turned to introduce his guests.

'I have here with me Mr Sanders, Sir Julian Alberon's lawyer, and a representative from the Council to verify some of the complaints the protesters have been putting through for months. We go through, we check the work site, verify all is in order and come back. Hopefully, there is nothing wrong with this thing called "Repeater". Am I right, Mr Sanders?'

'Please rest assured, inspector!' said Mr Sanders, his tone formal and bordering the pedantic. 'Sir Julian Alberon, my client, wants to be transparent to the community and show there is no harm behind his plans. The council has reviewed both work sites already, the one here and the one at the windmill. I am optimistic no foul play will be found.'

'There are no journalists here, Mr Sanders, so let's cut to the chase. I hope it is as you say it is. Let's go. Sergeant Jeremy, we should be back in less than an hour. If all is positive, I will call reinforcements to disperse this unlawful crowd.'

Jeremy nodded and let Baynard lead the way with his two followers through the wooden gate and down the tiny public footpath which cut across the golf course. The Royal Wimbledon Golf Club was about a hundred years old. Together with Cannizaro Park and Westside House, the eighteen-hole golf course occupied a portion of what used to be the Lord Manor's Old Park before it was sold to private owners in the seventeenth Century. The footpath Baynard took went on through to the west side of the hill, across the Warrens and down to the Beverly Brook river where Wimbledon territory came to an end.

However, the inspector did not intend to walk the full length of the footpath. The three stopped a hundred metres into it and took a left through another gate to enter the grounds onto hole number six. The smooth green of the fairway stretched unevenly, following the rolling Wimbledon hill on the horizon. About half-way, onto the right, the worksite of the Repeater could not go unnoticed. It was a tall scaffolding in the shape of a thin turret with a couple of temporary pop-up offices at its feet. The Alberyx Enterprises worksite covered a triangular patch of coarse grass, which had always been a disused space, squeezed in between three golf holes. Inspector Baynard was fully aware that this section of land had been lawfully leased for construction by the Royal Wimbledon Golf Club to Alberyx Enterprises. He could not understand what all the fuss was about. It was not as if it ruined the beautiful view. The closest residence was in Camp Road and Camp View, more than five hundred yards away. He played with his thoughts while they walked down the fairway and through the wild shrubbery, the remaining traces of the Old Park's rough vegetation. The conversation with the Chief Superintendent earlier was fresh in his mind. He had to bring back order. Enough of scandals hitting Wimbledon almost every month. From the explosion at Cannizaro Hotel and earthquakes under St Mary's Church to the marching protests in recent months. It had to stop and Baynard had been asked to get to the bottom of it immediately. The inspector stroked his silver goatee thinking about the best thing to do.

Three workers waited for them at the site. The tall scaffolding looked bigger when right under it. The blue cover did not give away much and Baynard struggled to figure out what it was for. The only clue in plain view was the big sign hung across each of the four sides.

THE REPEATER

The future brought to you by Alberyx Enterprises

'Good morning, gentlemen! Inspector Baynard.' welcomed one of the three workers.

His name tag said Richard. He let the other two introduce themselves.

'Please take us through what we have here!' said the representative from the Council.

'Yes…erm…' Richard hesitated.

'Is there a problem?' asked the representative from the Council.

'Our chief engineer is not here yet.' Richard added, apologetically.

'Is he needed?' interjected Baynard.

'Well…erm…he was meant to take you through the site as requested…'

'Is he going to be late?' insisted Baynard, frustrated by Richard's sheepish attitude.

If he carried on extracting information at this rate, they would not be done until tomorrow morning.

'We can't actually get hold of him.' Richard explained. 'Phone goes to voicemail. We tried his girlfriend's number but nothing.'

'Well, it is still mid-morning. We can't call it a case of missing person yet, can we?' teased the inspector. 'He probably overslept. Can anyone here at least run us through the basics while you try to get hold of him?'

'S-sure…' said Richard hardly shining with confidence. 'J-Julian…I mean…S-Sir Julian Alberon…said it should be fine if we went ahead. We know the technical specifications anyway.'

'Good. Then I will let the Council take it from here.'

Baynard moved out of the way to let the council representative step forward with his clipboard thick with forms and checklists. Before they started the tour, a heavy round of questions was fired like a machine gun with the coldness and rigidity of administrative bureaucracy. And for every answer, a box was ticked off. Is the turret a structure built for energetic purposes? Yes. Is it compliant with regulation 33B? Brief hesitation. Yes. Is it radioactive? No. Does it cause hazardous by-products which can harm the environment? No. Does it cause noise which can be detrimental for the surrounding community including both business and residential areas? No…

The questions came one after the other. Baynard did not pay attention to half of it. He probably stopped listening after the first one. He fidgeted with a chewing gum in his mouth, thinking of the day ahead. What a start of the week it was; and it was just the beginning. A text from one of his men at the windmill confirmed Julian Alberon had just unveiled a new machine inside the windmill capable of producing clear, renewable wireless energy. Wireless energy in the middle of the Common sounded too crazy, thought Baynard in disbelief, but that was something he expected from the eccentric business tycoon. Baynard was sure Sir Alberon's press conference with the media, after lunch today, would bring who knows what other surprises. To further complicate things, the protest near the Repeater meant he had to increase security or at least advise Alberyx Enterprises to do so. Baynard knew a well-known group of locals was dissatisfied with the winds of change Julian Alberon and his company wanted to bring to Wimbledon. He and Sergeant Jeremy had had to do some crowd control on more than one occasion when this group of protesters decided to manifest against the plans for the new windmill and for any new construction on the only pieces of green left in Wimbledon, especially when it came to Wimbledon Common. At each one of these demonstrations, Wimbledon Police had clashed with their leader, Basil 'Wilberforce' Elders. He was probably responsible for organising and leading this series of insurrectional parades. Charming fellow, though. Polite and eloquent despite the harsh criticisms that came out of his mouth. He knew all the laws and by-laws of Wimbledon, especially those related to the preservation of the Common. And that is why Baynard had been sent here with the Council and Mr Sanders. To make sure this innocuous turret was really as harmless as they said it was.

'…and if you follow me here…' said Richard opening a door leading inside the scaffolding. '…you can see the system works by sending a digital signal to the radar built inside the New Wimbledon Windmill.'

'What's the purpose again?' blurted out Baynard ignoring the fact Richard may have mentioned it already.

'I can explain that in simple terms.' interjected Mr Sanders. 'The Repeater is simply the younger brother of what we built inside the Wimbledon Windmill. It is a smaller version of the machine whose only purpose though is to amplify the wireless electricity signal so that we can carry the current further. Sir Alberon wants to ensure everyone can benefit from the new source of energy all around Wimbledon Hill and beyond. The Repeater is another milestone towards that vision of his.'

'Mmm…alright…' commented Baynard doubtful.

He felt he was just hearing a load of marketing gibberish.

'So, what is the verdict? Anything out of line?'

He looked at the council representative who inflated his chest, the moment it was his turn to speak, as if to feel important at such decisive moment. He flicked through his paperwork and paused for what seemed an unnecessary moment of reflection.

'No, not at all!' he finally said. 'The machinery is not a danger and the Royal Wimbledon Golf Club granted permission explicitly for the purpose applied. I will only file a recommendation for one more inspection when the system goes live. It is in a week's time, did you say?'

'Yes!' confirmed Richard. 'Does that mean we are not under arrest?'

'No, you're not!' blurted out Baynard. 'This was just an official inspection. Mr Sanders, are you satisfied?'

The lawyer nodded.

'Great!' the inspector said returning his gaze to Richard. 'Now, you can resume your work here as normal. Anything to add?'

Baynard turned to the Council representative.

'Thank you for your co-operation.' he replied. 'And please brief your chief engineer, when he finally wakes up from his sleep-in, and ask him to get in touch with the Council as soon as possible so he can sign the report. A copy of the report will be sent to Alberyx Enterprises.'

The inspector left as quickly as he came, followed by Mr Sanders and the Council representative. As they tracked back their footsteps to where Jeremy waited, the silence of nature on this side of Wimbledon Hill became gradually tarnished and was completely gone by the time the three reached the crowd of protesters still chanting at the entrance to the footpath.

'Still here?' commented Baynard while helping the lawyer and the council rep get safely in the car.

'Yes. They don't want to budge!' groaned Jeremy. 'Everything in order down there?'

'Ah yes… All this fuss for what is a giant transmission tower! Listen, I don't see him here. Has he arrived yet?'

'Who?'

'Basil "Wilberforce" Elders.'

'Ah, him! No, actually. Come to think of it, I am surprised he hasn't made an appearance at all to rally the troops as per usual. No sign of him, not even at this early hour.'

'Ok. Please update security staff from Alberyx Enterprises. I am sure they are all over this already but better stay in touch with them. It is an important week, and it is only Monday!'

Baynard looked at his men trying to disperse the crowd. He then frowned. It was unusual for Basil not to show up. Unless he was going to show up somewhere else. Somewhere where he could do more damage.

The Dog and Fox pub was full of foreigners, according to the man behind the bar. Enrico had to ask him twice before he understood he meant people not from Wimbledon. In fact, the pub was strangely busy for a Monday lunchtime, and the reason was on the front page of the copies of the Wimbledon Gazette everyone was reading at their table. It showed a nice big photo of the old windmill and a smiling Julian Alberon signing the papers that months ago had allowed him to start working on his dream for Wimbledon. Journalists from across that big urban mass called London and from the wider UK had flooded in for the double-event scheduled for that day. Already in the morning, they had joined the crowds as the New Windmill was finally revealed to the public. In the early afternoon, Julian would give a press conference to the media about his plans for wireless electricity, and that same evening the British Museum and the Wimbledon Museum were presenting their findings from the Old Rectory. Wimbledon had never had so many events all at once, and the local hotels rejoiced at the large number of bookings they had received. Almost all pubs and restaurants in Wimbledon were busy for lunch or dinners. Enrico and Viviane were lucky enough to find their usual table, overlooking the roundabout of Wimbledon Village.

'Wine for you. Ale for me.' the Italian baker said as he put down the drinks on the table and sat down.

'I don't get it. Isn't it *aperitivo* time? Spritz, Negroni?'

'*Macché, sei matta?* With this weather? And anyway, I love this pub, and when you're in a pub, you drink beer! So, I will drink beer. And I ordered fish 'n' chips again. Definitely not your *bruschetta* with olives, tomatoes, mozzarella and pesto …*che schifo!*'

'Whatever…' ignored Viviane sipping her wine.

She was used to Enrico's maniacal food principles by now. She dabbed the napkin on the corner of her mouth and adjusted her lipstick using a tiny pocket mirror. Viviane's lips were always a warm red, not too flashy, but enough to accentuate their shape of a peaked cupid's bow. She quickly checked her updo hairstyle and made sure her whole appearance was acceptable.

'I see…All for the journalists, the photographers…' commented Enrico.

'Cut it out!' snarled Viviane half-joking. 'You have been in Wimbledon for less than a year and let me tell you: I never saw Wimbledon so busy and so popular outside of the Wimbledon Tennis Championship. Perhaps, Julian's winds of change are definitely here and that could only mean good for business. Yours and mine, of course. Speaking of which, did you ever get a reply to that letter from the Royal Wimbledon Golf Club? Didn't they ask you something about ordering bread from you on a weekly basis?'

'Something like that.' nodded Enrico. 'No idea what's it about. I am actually meant to pay a visit to the golf club after Julian's press conference.'

'Maybe it is another work opportunity for you, Enrico. Didn't you say you wanted to expand your clientele? You have your bakery, and most importantly you have a job.'

'Shame we can't say that for Quentin…' commented Enrico on a sad note.

'I was just thinking about him. I was really surprised to hear what happened. Poor chap! He did a good job looking after the windmill. He used to run the small museum on the ground floor and the little café next door. The windmill was almost his second home.'

'I think he lost his marbles too.' noted Enrico tapping at his temple. 'He was talking to me about seeing ghosts and he kept blaming Alberyx Enterprises for it.'

'Ghosts, did you say?'

'He chatted about his bizarre theory that wireless electricity makes you see ghosts! He sort of gave me the shorter version to the story and spared me the full conspiracy theory.'

'What kind of ghosts? Headless knights? Hovering blankets with rattling chains?' questioned Viviane in a playful mood.

'Sorry, Miss Viviane. Nothing close to traditional British folklore. Quentin actually mentioned an Earl of Cardigan and a duel on the open field near the windmill. That reminds me I need to ask Dr Watkins about it. He could help me check some of the historical facts.'

One of the barmen in casual clothes came up to the table with their lunches, bringing napkins and cutlery. The two noticed the nice colourful dishes put in front of them and soon started munching away.

'I have not seen Dr Watkins in a while.' said Viviane in between mouthfuls, careful not to smudge her lipstick. 'But he will be at Julian's press conference today. It would be nice to catch up and see what he's been up to. I know he is very excited about tonight's presentation at Eagle House. He has been so occupied with the Wimbledon Museum and the findings from the Old Rectory, spending all these months running between the two places, reviewing any item the team from the British Museum dug up. I am not surprised he and that archaeologist from the British Museum are eager to finally share their discoveries with the public. What's his name again?'

'Simon. Simon Deeley. Have you met him?' asked Enrico.

'Not at all. I only go by what Dr Watkins said to me once, when we briefly spoke. Very meticulous man, apparently. Kept him very busy.'

'I have not met Simon either, but I do believe he has kept Dr Watkins more than busy. You were lucky to chat to Dr Watkins at all. I only saw him a couple of times at the bakery, as he rushed in and out to buy some bread. We did not even have time for a quick chat, and he looked very tired to me. I hope he is not overdoing it.'

'Julian Alberon was kind enough to protect the Old Rectory and give him and the British Museum full access to it. Dr Watkins would not have missed such an opportunity for the world. Wimbledon rarely lands on historical remains of that calibre, and that old as well. What was it, Anglo-Saxon period?'

'I think so. I haven't been there to see what they have done with the place. The Old Rectory is well protected nowadays after what happened. Julian does not want to take risks understandably. Not since that strange night…'

'Don't you start bringing back old fears!' reminded Viviane. 'I don't want to hear about your nightmares. I saw how you were about to mention to Julian about his hand and the glove.'

'Ok, ok… forget what I said! I just hope Dr Watkins is getting some sleep. I know he was struggling last year. The same goes for Julian. I think I saw him tired too, almost drained out, behind all that positive energy of his.'

'What?' exclaimed Viviane. 'Didn't you see or hear how Julian delivered that speech? He definitely has the energy. Look what he built in… what?... Three, four months?'

'It seems to me they have both become hyperactive all of a sudden. Meanwhile, both he and Julian still wear this glove around their burnt hand… and I thought it would have healed by now… I am just worried. That's all.'

'Easy, Enrico. They are fine, they are doing well, and they have doctors that can look after them. Since when are you a doctor? I'll tell you what. Why don't you ask Dr Watkins yourself today how he feels, eh?'

Enrico shrugged and carried on eating. Ever since he had seen that blurred apparition in the Old Rectory, that humanoid shape consumed by the flames, each time Dr Watkins and Julian Alberon were mentioned Enrico remembered the sleepless nights that followed or, when he did actually manage to drowse off, the vivid nightmares he experienced. It had been calmer for a while but still he could not forget the visions of the pool chamber filled with burnt bodies. While everyone had managed to move on, he was stuck with these visions in his head, and he seemed incapable of getting rid of them. He needed some form of distraction and perhaps chatting with Dr Watkins would have helped. He did miss his stories about Wimbledon.

Enrico and Viviane carried on having their lunch and moved to lighter subjects. The pub menu, the cold weather, their respective shops. Yet, in the end their conversation led back to the New Wimbledon Windmill and the

Old Rectory somehow. Perhaps because the pub was bustling with journalists and bloggers shouting about the only topic of importance on that day. Their loud voices boomed from every corner of the Dog and Fox, firing thought-provoking questions one after the other, followed by cheering and arguing and clinking glasses. No Wimbledonian present could ignore them now the future of Wimbledon had quickly become front news.

Nathan Glenn stood at the bar with his lemonade, oblivious of the buzzing crowd. Those who knew him could tell he was not a fan of Alberyx Enterprises. He would not join his peers in celebrating or even enquiring about the horrible metallic windmill that had just been presented. His mind had drifted to the radio conversation he overheard the night before. Security at Alberyx Enterprises was gravely worried about Basil Elders, better known as Basil 'Wilberforce' Elders as the man himself had insisted clarifying many times when called by name or quoted in the news. Nathan had been following the well-known protesters' leader with a detached interest. While he did not see much in Basil Elders at first, Nathan was now convinced that the fact they shared a common enemy could come in handy when exposing Alberyx Enterprises and its dodgy dealings. First, they closed off the Old Rectory without much opposition. Now they had the power to rebuild a Grade II building like the windmill in less than six months, and even build antennas in the middle of the Common. According to Nathan, Basil 'Wilberforce' Elders had the resources to push both of their agendas at the same time. The journalist took a sip of his lemonade. He checked the time on the brass clock above the bottles of spirits. He would leave soon, before everyone else, to get a front row at the press conference. He hoped Basil Elders would make an appearance so he could take the opportunity to interview the man himself.

A journalist walked up to the bar, right next to Nathan. His tag said he represented a magazine in Surrey. He was trying to get the attention of the manager.

'Sir. Excuse me.' he called out.

'Yes. How can I help?' said the manager as he approached.

'Hi. I have a complaint about the room.'

'Are you staying at the Dog and Fox hotel?'

'Yes. I have an issue with my room.'

'What seems to be the problem?'

'The lights and the radio and even the TV no longer work. This morning none of them turned on.'

'OK, will send someone up.'

'Thank you.'

The journalist walked away to join the group he had come with. Nathan looked at the manager. His well-trained ears could not ignore something he had already heard before.

'Lights, radio and TV at the same time?' he questioned ironically.

'I know.' said the manager, almost apologetically. 'And it is the third room reporting it this morning.'

'Third?'

'Yes. Can you believe it? The electrics blew overnight. I know the radio and the TV were a little old in these room but not that old. Our electrician is still trying to figure it out.'

Nathan listened, preferring not to mention his experience with the streetlamps and the digital radio transmitter from the night before. There was some interference and flickering but his transmitter did not blow.

'Has anyone else in Wimbledon experienced this?' asked Nathan.

'Not sure. I didn't hear anything.'

The manager excused himself to make his way to the reception, outside the pub area. Nathan checked the time again. He then drank up his lemonade and found his way out. On the way to the exit, he grabbed a copy of the Wimbledon Gazette lying on a table. He flicked through it, checking even the small articles. As he expected, no major problems to the electric grid had made it into the paper. Even his social media feed failed to mention cases of radio interference or lights flickering. His journalist's intuition however could not dismiss the coincidence. After all, wireless electricity had just been announced that morning by Alberyx Enterprises and nobody knew how harmful it could be. Nathan thought about it for a moment; he then glanced at the photo of Sir Julian Alberon, close-up, black and white, staring back at him under an enigmatic light from the front page of the Wimbledon Gazette.

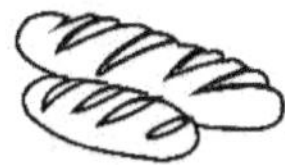

Enrico scratched his head in front of the Edwardian-looking building. The aged red bricks alluded to its vintage charm from a bygone era with the authentic look of an old-fashioned club, despite the random infiltrations from modern times, such as automatic sliding doors or the bright green fire exit signs.

'Is this the one? Is this the famous Royal Wimbledon Golf Club?' said the Italian baker.

'No, that's the Wimbledon Common Golf Course.' corrected Viviane. 'We need to walk a bit further, to Camp Cottage.'

'How many golf clubs are there?'

'Three.' confirmed Dr Watkins showing his three middle fingers. 'All of them are more than one hundred years old.'

The history of golf at Wimbledon was a complicated one, at least for Enrico, as he heard it from Dr Watkins on their way to the Royal Wimbledon Golf Club for Julian's press conference. Golf was a sport the Earl of Spencer had introduced on Wimbledon Common as early as the 1860s. The London Scottish Golf Club was the first club to form in 1865, headquartered near the windmill and organised by soldiers who were members of the London Scottish Rifle Volunteers. However, the civilian part of the club decided to split and form their own club, the Royal Wimbledon Golf Club, in 1882. That was the year when the new club officially opened its premises at Camp

Cottage. However, it was not until 1907 that they were given permission to build its own eighteen-hole course to the south and west of the Wimbledon hill.

'OK, so when was this Wimbledon Common Golf Course built?' asked Enrico pointing at the Edwardian building.

'The year after. 1908, I believe. They share the golf course on the Common with the London Scottish Club. Come on then, let's hurry up or we will be late.'

'Well, that's a lot of golf courses!' commented Enrico.

The three walked further along Camp Road in the cold air blowing north from the Common. After a short walk they came to another building sitting under the shadow of a young maple tree. It was a Victorian-looking cottage with black and grey bricks, and large, well-spaced windows.

'Now, this is the Royal Wimbledon Golf Club!' confirmed Dr Watkins as he approached the entrance.

Enrico noticed how this building also echoed the charms of a British civilisation while struggling to shake off the signs of modernity. Despite its grim exterior look, the refurbished interior was a little warmer and cosy, with pale oak tables and dark blue carpeted floors decorated with pink fleur-de-lis. There was a reception hall and then straight ahead one double-door led to a large dining room facing southward on the golf course. Dr Watkins showed their press conference invitations and then led Enrico and Viviane through. The two had never been inside and admired in awe at the open view of the red flagpoles and green fairways of the golf course outside, stretching away from the main building. The tables of the dining room had been cleared to one side and the rest of the room had been rearranged as a temporary press conference room. There was a large table to one side, backed by a marketing panel with the formal, bright corporate colours of Alberyx Enterprises. In front of the table, rows of comfy padded seats and armchairs had been set out to make it look like an auditorium. There were no more than thirty or forty seats. This had come as a specific request from

Sir Alberon who wanted a more intimate environment with the press and everyone joining him on that day. He was sitting at the table, with a microphone in front of him and a couple of bottles of water. He was chatting with the people next to him while everyone waited for the press conference to start. His lawyer, Mr Sanders, was next to him nodding amicably, adjusting his yellow tie.

There were three more seats at the main table. Next to Julian's other side, in the middle of the table a chubby man with a puffy red nose and plump cheeks nodded eagerly at every single word Julian Alberon said. His attire struck as being rather vintage. He wore a winged tailcoat and a white waistcoat underneath with a gold pocket chain hung across. On the table, right in front of him, there was an old-fashioned top hat. His grey sideburns, thinning hair and aquiline nose made him look like a happy portrait of William Gladstone, and if it were not for the smartphone in his hand, the audience would have thought the man had come out of a Victorian history book. The man in the tailcoat was not alone. On his lap, a West Highland White Terrier lay comfortably with its head on its paws. It occasionally lifted its head to gaze at the audience with its tiny black eyes and wagged its tail as if sharing the same excitement as his owner. The chair next to him was empty and the name tag on the table said 'John Crane, Chief Engineer'. To Enrico, it was a relief and a clear sign they were not late if the chief engineer clearly had not showed up yet. Last person at the table, sitting on his own, was the Chief Superintendent of Wimbledon Police. He eyed the room carefully, nodding casually to the policemen present at random corners of the room. The Chief Superintendent leaned forward to see if Inspector Baynard had arrived yet, only to find no sign of him in reception. He then spotted Enrico as he made his way into the room and through the audience with Viviane and Dr Watkins. The Chief Superintendent gave Enrico the cold shoulder when their eyes met briefly. He was not very fond of the Italian baker and his bad habit of sticking his nose into police matters.

Enrico ignored him and instead joined Viviane who was already waving at Julian from among the crowd.

The trio sat in one of the middle rows, by the large French windows looking out onto the golf course. Dr Watkins picked one of the comfy high armchairs. He wore a nice grey tweed suit and a red and blue tie. His silver hair was nicely combed, and his head slightly tilted back to peer through his glasses at Julian Alberon and the team. Enrico and Viviane sat quietly next to him like students late for their lesson and took the opportunity to get a better look around. At the back of the temporary auditorium, there was a long line of cameramen and the PR team from Alberyx Enterprises. The front rows were packed with journalists scribbling furiously on notepads or photographers constantly aiming at the table to get the best angle. Enrico did not recognise many of the people in the audience. He did not see Baynard either, whom he half expected to be there, considering the strong presence by the police.

There was some feedback from one of the microphones and Julian started tapping to test the volume and get everyone's attention.

'Good afternoon. Thanks everyone for coming.' he said in a composed manner. 'Before I start, I will ask Lord Cotton here to say a few words on behalf of the Royal Wimbledon Golf Club.'

He then turned to the chubby man next to him with a polite gesture.

'Thank you, Sir Alberon.' replied Lord Cotton, clearing his voice. 'We are excited to have you and Alberyx Enterprises here to share with us your future plans for Wimbledon. For those who don't know, this morning was the opening of the New Wimbledon Windmill. It is the first step towards a revolutionary vision which is set to change Wimbledon, and which Sir Alberon will be happy to share with us today. When he approached us for planning permission for his antenna, the Repeater, we were more than welcome to support him in his endeavours after what he's done for Wimbledon. Since then, we worked closely together, and we have come to understand his vision even better. We do hope it will also help debunking some of the misconception we heard over the last few months. Once Sir Alberon has finished, we will open to the audience for some questions, and Miss Halywell in the front of row will ensure everyone is given an opportunity in the brief time we have. So, without further ado, let's begin.'

'Thank you, Lord Cotton. The New Wimbledon Windmill will generate about one third of Wimbledon's energy needs, and it will use non-intrusive technology, safe for the environment. It all started from the idea: what if we could use wireless technology as a conduit of energy? No more cables above or below ground. No more dirty or unsafe, bulky power stations. This is what the New Wimbledon Windmill is meant to do: act as a generator of clean energy. But how? It will use one of Alberyx Enterprise latest patent in quantum technology, designed by our team to harness geomagnetic storms in the atmosphere to convert photons, that is light, into electromagnetic energy. Our system, built at the top of the windmill, will read the tiny particles of light and tap into their high frequency to extract pure energy. Let me show you!'

A screen behind him switched on displaying the Common from a bird's eye view. Three locations were highlighted: the windmill, the golf club and another in the middle of the golf course labelled 'Repeater'. The dot representing the golf club was blinking.

'Behind me you can see the windmill and the Repeater are switched off. The club is currently drawing electricity from the national grid.'

He gave a nod to an assistant at the back of the room and all the lights suddenly went off, switching on the backup lights. The screen behind Julian flickered.

'We've just switched to the local backup generator so that there was no loss of power. You can see the light of the club has stopped blinking. The club currently is off the national grid. We will restore it immediately using an alternative route.'

He smiled and asked a member of his PR team at the table to press a few keys on her laptop. There was a sudden droning sound, and the lights came back up on, brighter than before. The screen behind Julian was now showing the windmill and the Repeater blinking together with the club.'

'We are now using wireless electricity from the windmill!' he announced to the stupor of the audience. 'This is just the beginning of what I consider to be an ambitious plan. Think about the clean energy from our own local power grid. Think of the savings! What I showed you today is a live test while we finalise the last checks and we are ready to scale up. I take the opportunity to thank the Royal Wimbledon Golf Course again for allowing us to use their precious golf course to bring this revolutionary idea to Wimbledon. The Repeater, not far from here, as you can see on the screen, will capture and amplify the wireless electricity coming from the windmill as any transmission tower would do via cables. From here on, it will feed into the Royal Wimbledon Golf Club and connect to the rest of Wimbledon.'

Julian nodded once more at the back of the room and there was a quick change in the lights, less bright as the power from the national grid was restored. The screen behind him was now showing the golf club as the sole blinking light.

'Back to status quo!' confirmed Julian effortlessly.

The press conference proceeded at a softer pace, filled with charts and slides and promotional videos, carefully planned one after the other. Enrico thought Julian and his team had tried their best to simplify what the New Wimbledon Windmill was meant to do. Enrico glanced around to see the audience reaction. They were all mesmerised by Julian's revolutionary idea. One thing that caught his attention was a sporty jacket a few rows ahead of them. It was a shocking pink colour branded at the back with the label 'Club Captain'. It belonged to an athletic, slim woman. She sat still with her back straight and not once did she slouch or fidget in her seat throughout the press conference. She had long, straight brown velvety hair, bound in a ponytail and pulled through the opening at the back of the sports cap she kept on her head. Enrico observed her sportswear curiously and then looked at his own white chef's jacket and the rest of the audience. He grinned upon realising his attire was not as informal as he had thought.

'By the end of this week,' carried on Julian. 'most of the final safety checks will be completed, and we will be in a position to turn on the generators at the New Wimbledon Windmill officially and supply the first few kilowatts. Join me again at the windmill this coming weekend to see this dream come true when I will personally turn on both the New Wimbledon Windmill and the Repeater to make them operational. Please make sure you book your front row seats now for the biggest event in Wimbledon history!'.

Sir Julian Alberon enjoyed a round of applauses before Lord Cotton took the floor to ask the audience if they had any questions.

'Good afternoon, Sir Alberon.' said the first reporter to be given the microphone. 'What has been the response from Putney, considering the windmill is close to the border with their jurisdiction over the Common, and therefore its safety is a source of concern for them too?'

'I spoke to the members of their Council as well.' answered Julian without breaking a sweat. 'We followed protocol in the same way I consulted Wimbledon's. I asked them to approve the planning permission as an extra insurance policy and they are now fully behind the project.'

'I did not know the Common was also Putney's...' whispered Enrico to Viviane.

'Ssssh...' hissed Dr Watkins without turning around, to which Enrico zipped his mouth and carried on listening.

'Hello, Sir Alberon!' followed up a second reporter. 'I am from The Times, and I wanted to ask you about the tremendous work done across Wimbledon in the last few months. The saving of the Old Rectory as an historical site and the salvage of the Wimbledon Windmill from disrepair must have kept you busy. What's your secret?

There was a subtle laughter in the audience. Julian grimaced.

'Sleep well. Eat well. There is no secret, really… oh well, apart from having a great team to support you.'

Julian nodded at his staff at the back.

'And also loving the place you live in. I am doing this for Wimbledon, and it is work I had planned for years. The opportunity came along, and I just found it was the right time to do it.'

Enrico saw Julian looking in their direction. He knew he was nodding at Dr Watkins and his help.

'Since you mention the Old Rectory, let me remind you that tonight we have the presentation on the brilliant work done by the Wimbledon Museum and the British Museum. I am excited to hear what they have to share so please come along!'

After the quick promotion, more questions followed with Lord Cotton picking and choosing as hands went up in the room.

'Hello! We are from the Botanists of London.' another reporter introduced herself. 'What do you have to say to the Wimbledon and Putney Commons Conservators, the WPCC, and their strong criticism towards your plans? I quote: "Alberyx Enterprises in the end is a business company whose only aim is profit, even if it means killing off the peaceful and natural habitat of the Common that lasted for millennia until today". Do you have a first response to share?'

'Let's keep this press conference friendly.' warned Lord Cotton. 'This is not the place for false accusations…'

Julian Alberon raised his hand as if not to worry.

'Actually, thank you for asking that question!' he said. 'I will start by saying Alberyx Enterprises is not here for profit or gain since there will be no charge for the new service we are bringing to Wimbledon. Secondly, the quote you gave me is not directly from the WPCC but rather the personal opinion of some of its members who did not agree with the concessions and the compromises I openly discussed with the representatives of the WPCC. The wireless electricity of the windmill will mean no harm to the flora and fauna of the Common. Yet, I do respect the opinion of my critics, even the harshest ones.'

The reporter sat back down and another hand went up. Lord Cotton pointed at the journalist instantly recognising who he was.

'Nathan Glenn, from the Wimbledon Gazette.' announced Lord Cotton trying to conceal the irony.

'Good morning, Mr Glenn. Talking about harsh critics...' added Julian in amusement.

He was aware of what Nathan Glenn had been writing about his company. He was not surprised to see him here.

'Morning to you, Sir Alberon.' acknowledged Nathan glancing at his notes. 'Readers of the Wimbledon Gazette would like to know what the Lord of the Manor of Wimbledon has to say about all this...'

'Mr Glenn,' chuckled Lord Cotton. 'The title of Lord of the Manor is simply an old noble title on paper, but it has no jurisdiction. The Council decides. I hope you have not wasted your question.'

'Well, may I ask if Sir Alberon has bought the title since it was sold off to an unknown party more than six months ago?'

'Mr Glenn, I don't see what this has to do with what we are presenting today.' reproached Lord Cotton. 'Again, I kindly ask you to put forward another question please.'

'Fine!' replied Nathan curtly. 'You have answered previously that this wireless electricity is unharmful. Would you care to explain how you went about testing? I do not recall seeing signs informing locals about it...'

Lord Cotton and the Chief Superintendent looked at each other. They knew Nathan could be a troublemaker. They still kept a straight face and Lord Cotton glanced at Julian if he was happy to answer. The business tycoon did not seem worried, keeping his self-confidence together.

'Mr Glenn, I can assure you first of all, I do not own the title of Lord of the Manor. I thought it would be polite to answer that question first since it is an easy one. Secondly, all tests were run in a localised manner with panels of cobalt attached to the surface of the scaffolding. There was no need to give any warnings as safety measures were in place and authorised. Unfortunately, my chief engineer, John Crane, is unavailable today due to personal reasons. He would have been able to answer you in more detail. More than happy to issue a statement to the Wimbledon Gazette.'

Once Julian had finished his reply, Lord Cotton fixed his gaze on Nathan, expecting the answer to be satisfactory. The journalist grimaced. He was not satisfied at all. Yet, he was clutching at straws on how to best enquire about the radio interference. He was sure the wireless electricity had something to do with it. He simply had nothing to go on yet.

'That'll be all. Thank you!' he replied sitting down again.

Lord Cotton sighed in relief. However, before he prompted the audience for the next question, a sound of commotion and voices arguing came from the adjacent reception room.

'How may I help…sorry, sir…hey, you cannot walk in there at the moment…'

The high-pitched voice of one of the receptionists could be heard clearly over heavy footsteps heading in the direction of the conference room. A handful of men and women barged in through the large wooden double door. The receptionists struggled to push them back. The policemen stood on alert, hands on their guns, fearing the worst, but the group was unarmed and all they did was take a short step forward into the conference room before making a stop without uttering a single word. They were dressed in jeans and leather jackets, either blue or black over nice white office shirts. The only colour that broke the pattern of their improvised uniform was the colour of their scarves or their hair, or the red letters across their t-shirts saying loud in capital letters 'Wimbledon for the People!'. It seemed they wanted to take a stance and be sure everyone in the open space could see them and read the message on their t-shirts. Their leader was at the front of their rough triangular formation. It was impossible to ignore his presence. He was wearing something distinctive. He was the only one wearing chocolate brown jeans and a faded brown aviator leather jacket. His long, thick flannel scarf was wrapped around the neck two or three times, but one long end hung to one side down to right above his belt. His round gold-rimmed glasses gave him the look of an intellectual. He must have been in his mid-fifties.

'What is the meaning of this?' said Lord Cotton raising his voice. 'Please leave immediately!'

He put his White Terrier down, already growling at the interruption. Lord Cotton stood up and so did the Chief Superintendent with a look of disdain on their faces. Enrico spotted the woman in the sport jacket doing the same.

'Isn't this a press conference, Lord Cotton?' said the leader of the newcomers, smiling broadly to the press with an air of politeness and civic sense that confused Enrico and Viviane.

Lord Cotton was fuming and struggled to find an adequate response to say in public. He had recognised the man. Everyone had.

'Is that who I think it is?' whispered Enrico to Viviane.

'Yes. It is Basil Elders!' noted Viviane a little mortified for Julian.

'Of course, it is a press conference!' replied Julian Alberon to keep control of the situation in front of the press. 'Do you have an invitation?'

He motioned for Lord Cotton to sit down and then turned back to the new arrivals.

'Well, I do.' commented Basil bemused. 'But I left it at home. I think though press conferences like these should be open. You know, free for everyone. Like the Common.'

'By all means.' added Julian keeping it together. 'Please take a seat or feel free to stand where you are, Mr Elders.'

Enrico and Viviane glanced at each other, and then looked at Dr Watkins's worried face which had the same expression as everyone else in the room. The atmosphere was so tense it could be cut with a knife. The Chief Superintendent walked to one of his men, and the policemen quickly shuffled around the room to create a human chain around Basil Elders and his group. The police stood alert and vigilant, exchanging stern glares with the men and women opposite them. They had been clearly instructed to defuse the situation and not to arrest anyone. Basil's group was now still and unarmed. Enrico knew the Chief Superintendent would not want to make a fool of himself and the police force in front of the journalists.

'Basil "Wilberforce" Elders as a matter of fact.' corrected the supposed leader.

He was eager to make a point, more for the cameras than for Julian Alberon's sake. The businessman smiled with calm and gave a subtle nod to Lord Cotton to resume as normal. Enrico could tell Julian Alberon knew cold indifference was the best weapon. Basil 'Wilberforce' Elders was here to put on a show. The Italian baker had barely heard of the man and the marching protests. Most of Wimbledon, including Dr Watkins, were not fond of him. They claimed he was a clever troublemaker and so far, Enrico could not argue with that assumption. However, the ten or fifteen people behind Basil showed he had a following.

'So, we have time for one or two more questions.' announced Julian Alberon as if nothing had happened.

Viviane turned to look at the Alberyx Enterprises staff in the audience and she could see they were scrambling for an exit plan before the conference turned into a PR disaster.

'I have one.' said Basil aloud, defiant.

He looked at the audience when speaking. He ensured the cameras were on him.

'I hear your chief engineer is not here today.' added Basil with malice.

He hinted at the empty seat without looking at it. Enrico and Viviane saw Julian Alberon's face contort for the first time.

'This does not look good!' commented Viviane.

'No, it doesn't. Should we say something?' suggested Enrico.

'Stay put!' whispered Dr Watkins with a hand on Enrico's shoulder. 'Don't make things worse!'

'On the contrary, let me rephrase.' continued Basil with admirable eloquence and pungent sarcasm. 'I have heard your team can't find him since they last saw him yesterday afternoon. That he seems to have disappeared into thin air and he is nowhere to be found. Poor chap! And he was working on a Sunday, wasn't he? Workers' unions may not like that! Am I right?'

'Mr Crane had personal matters to attend to.' replied Julian Alberon clearing his voice. 'He regrets he could not be here with us today.'

He swallowed hard and smiled back at Basil.

'Maybe he was not feeling so well. Working overtime maybe? Is that a given at Alberyx Enterprises?'

The sarcastic comment did not go unnoticed. The Chief Superintendent thought it best to gently push the crowd away and end the press conference. He gave a nod to Lord Cotton and the police constables.

'Poor chap, indeed! Will he be back on his feet for the big day?' he asked again with a hint of irony. 'He is the only one who can fix the windmill, isn't he?'

'That's enough!' interjected Lord Cotton standing up again and tired of hearing Basil's insinuations in his own golf club. 'This is not an inquiry, and we are not in a courthouse. We are ending the press conference here and now, so on behalf of the Royal Wimbledon Golf Club and Alberyx Enterprises, thank you for coming and please leave your contact details on the way out if you wish to attend the launch next weekend!'

Lord Cotton was quick in summoning the staff and asking them to help clear the open space. The audience quickly left their seats, a little annoyed by the uncomfortable scene. Others stayed, cameras still rolling, as the press conference started to descend into a confused mess.

'How about Mr Crane's girlfriend?' shouted Basil louder, towering over the people on their way out and making himself heard over the low murmurs. Some of the journalists ignored him, others scribbled notes on new leads for their article while shots of him were taken. It was obvious Basil 'Wilberforce' Elders was really talking to them, and he had used the press conference to get all eyes on him. He was making the news.

'The session is over Mr Elders!' repeated with authority Lord Cotton.

In a matter of seconds, the policemen joined the club staff to help the audience vacate the room, and with them Basil and his gang. Basil gave a rebellious smile, gloating at Lord Cotton and Julian Alberon. He then spoke to one of his men and before the police had time to push them out by force, the group turned around to join the exodus out of the large dining room and leave peacefully.

Lord Cotton and Julian Alberon composed themselves and took a sigh of relief once the crowd was out of the club and the door had been closed. The dining room of the golf club reclaimed a sudden calm where only the faint cries outside were a stark reminder of what had just happened. A policeman noticed Enrico, Viviane and Dr Watkins were the last audience members still in the room and moved towards them, with the intention to escort them out.

'No, please. They can stay. And so can Dr Watkins.' advised Lord Cotton. 'Please, join us at the table!'

The chubby owner of the golf club walked briskly around the table, and he was joined by his side by the lady with the sporty pink jacket who had also stayed behind. The White Terrier hopped past them and wagged his tail at Viviane and then Enrico, who kneeled down to stroke him.

'Hello, new friend!' he said.

The little white dog barked in agreement.

'I see Little Caesar likes you!' noted Lord Cotton with a pleased smile. 'You must be Enrico LoTrova. It is nice to finally meet you! Viviane, Dr Wakins, nice to see you again. It has been such a long time!'

Lord Cotton's cheeks were still red, probably from the embarrassment of the recent stand-off at the press conference. He had tried to save face by showing how tough he was toward Basil Elders, but contrary to what Enrico thought, his manners were gentle and heart-warming.

'I do apologise for the unpleasant event you have just witnessed.' continued Lord Cotton. 'Allow me to introduce myself. I am Lord Cotton, and I am the President of the Royal Wimbledon Golf Club. This is our Club Captain, Miss Ramona Halywell. Or should I say, my second in command.'

He pointed at the sporty woman next to him. The lady glared back from under her sport cap which she had no intention of taking off. Her cold blue eyes and stuck-up nose summoned the image of a serious and professional woman, picky of whom she mingled with. While Lord Cotton made them feel at ease, Enrico and Viviane felt Ramona Halywell was not pleased they were there. Her stare and posture simply did not budge. Hands behind her back, feet slightly apart, shoulders squared off. To the Italian baker she could have been a soldier if she had been wearing a different uniform. Little Caesar, now busy sniffing around their feet, certainly did not like her. He growled at her from time to time.

'My pleasure!' said Ramona curtly, her hand stretched forward at a perfect angle and at the safest distance.

Enrico shook her hand, firm but non-committal. Viviane did the same, even more convinced there was something about her she was not particularly fond of.

'Club Captain?' asked Enrico, genuinely curious. 'Are you a serious golfer?'

'Oh no! Miss Halywell actually manages the running of the club.' answered Lord Cotton on behalf of Ramona. 'She runs it like a tight ship.'

'I am the best in what I do.' added Ramona congratulating herself almost machine-like. 'Sorry for the inconvenience before. We will review what happened and how Mr Elders and that gang of hooligans managed to just walk straight in here!'

'I am sure you did your best.' noted Viviane, sceptical about Ramona's modesty. 'I don't think I have seen you before. Have you always worked at the club?'

'No. This is my second job, so to speak.' replied Ramona with a hint of impeccable snobbery. 'I also work for Alberyx Enterprises.'

'Do you run a tight ship there too?' joked Enrico absent-minded.

He regretted it the moment Ramona's big round blue eyes glared at him as if to convey every single thought she had about Enrico without uttering a single word. Ramona came across as a woman who knew where she stood and knew what she wanted.

'I work in tech. Mr LoTrova. Data analyst to be correct. Surprised, eh?'

Enrico and Viviane were taken aback by her attitude. She acted as if she was entitled, taking every opportunity to gloat. Little Caesar growled again at her feet, and then started to bark.

'What's the matter, Caesar?' said Lord Cotton with a cute voice.

He picked the little white dog up and gave him a cuddle. The dog found it comforting and surrendered reluctantly to his owner's caresses.

'Now, I am glad you are here, Enrico.' continued Lord Cotton. 'I believe Ramona has been trying to get in touch with you.'

'Oh, has she?' replied Enrico.

'Yes, Mr LoTrova.' added Ramona, unimpressed. 'We sent you a couple of letters to ask you to come to the club. Did you receive those?'

Viviane cleared her voice loud enough for Enrico to hear. The Italian baker recognised her gentle reminder of 'I told you so' and was glad she did not nudge him in front of Lord Cotton.

'Yes! Yes!' replied Enrico enthusiastically. 'That is why I came here. To find out more.'

'Very good.' noted Lord Cotton. 'This is actually an idea that came from a chat with Dr Watkins, last time we spoke.'

Dr Watkins nodded with satisfaction at both of them, knowing what was coming.

'Enrico,' interjected the curator. 'I think you will like what the golf club has to offer. Lord Cotton, would you care to do the honours?'

'Absolutely delighted!' answered Lord Cotton over-excited.

The club owner seemed to have found a renewed conviction. Miss Ramona did not smile at all, not even a smirk to show whether she agreed or disagreed. The woman was as cold as the weather outside, thought Enrico.

'As you know, Mr LoTrova, we are so happy that your bakery, *The Wynnman*, opened in Wimbledon. Fresh bread and the occasional coffee and pastry is what this town needs. Here at the Royal Wimbledon Golf Club, we value tradition and high standards. I may be interested in considering your bakery as one of our main suppliers. This would mean a regular order of bread for our kitchens here. What do you say?'

Enrico was gob smacked. He could not believe his ears.

'*Bellissima idea!*' he rejoiced. 'I think it is a great idea. I'd love to work with you.'

'How about lunch tomorrow at the Fox and Grapes pub to go over the proposition?'

Lord Cotton was moving fast. Enrico's eyes widened. A business opportunity just landed at his feet, and a pretty big one. He glanced at Viviane, and she looked happy too.

'*Fantastico!*' exclaimed Enrico again. 'Tomorrow works for me!'

'Good. Then it's a date!' joked Lord Cotton patting Little Caesar's sleepy head.

The two men shook hands under Dr Watkins's pleased smile and Ramona's impassionate stare. Even Little Caesar woke up briefly to bark and join the celebrations for a new business partnership.

'What have I missed?'

Julian Alberon joined the group, his cordial smile beaming at them. Viviane, though, who admired the business tycoon the most, knew Julian was keeping up appearances. Some of his spark of enthusiasm had faded.

'We were just celebrating Lord Cotton and Enrico's potential partnership.' said Viviane.

'Wonderful!' added Julian.

'Are you ok?' asked Viviane with her supporting smile.

Julian blinked his eyes before staring into Viviane's. He tried to hide his broken smile.

'Yes, yes.' he sighed again. 'Press conferences are hard work. You can never please everyone!'

'I do apologise Sir Alberon once more.' repeated Lord Cotton. 'Ramona and I will find out what went wrong.'

'That's fine, Lord Cotton. I like to look forward and put the past behind me pretty quickly. This man has some issues with the work my company does. It is his opinion and I respect that, but we can't stop progress for Wimbledon, can we? Dr Watkins, I trust to hear what you think. Am I doing something wrong?'

'I don't think so.' replied Dr Watkins. 'You are not butchering Wimbledon's landscape the way it has been throughout history. I have not seen the windmill myself, but I have seen the pictures. It is nice not to see it in ruins anymore.'

'Who is this Basil Elders exactly?' asked Enrico to the group.

'Basil "Wilberforce" Elders, to be precise.' mocked Viviane, mimicking the leader's group.

'Didn't he used to be a scout ranger and member of the WPCC?' gossiped Lord Cotton talking to Dr Watkins.

'He is a teacher at Octagon School down the road, but I know he was a part time scout ranger on the Common. Up to six months ago or so. Then the Rangers' Home was closed as part of the windmill restoration project. That is when he started opposing Julian's plans in most of the WPCC general meetings. He finally left the WPCC, dissatisfied, and created his own movement, Wimbledon For The People.'

'Why the "Wilberforce" middle name?' asked the Italian baker.

'Funny story, that one.' Dr Watkins grinned. 'William Wilberforce is a British politician who was responsible for pushing many reforms, such the abolition of slave trade. He focused on improving workers' conditions, and alleviating poverty by supporting free education. He lived in Wimbledon at Lauriston House in the 1780s.'

'So, Basil Elders is a descendant of this Wilberforce?' commented Enrico.

'Not at all.' explained Lord Cotton bemused. 'He just added it himself to sound important. Just a playful reference.'

'A clever one.' added Dr Watkins ready to draw more historical facts as he was accustomed to. 'Wilberforce was responsible for creating the first school here in the village, called Wimbledon Free School, and contributing to the early widening of public education. He and John Cooksey then built what is now known today as Octagon School, not far from the Royal Wimbledon Golf Club, and it is still a school as of today. Basil "Wilberforce" Elders teaches there. I guess he wishes to bring reform to Wimbledon. His way, of course!'

'Well, if he wishes to do so, it's fine as long as he remains a law-abiding citizen, otherwise he will be treated as a criminal!' condemned the Chief Superintendent.

He joined the group, barging in with Mr Sanders to his side. To Enrico, he seemed to act in the same arrogant way as Basil Elders had just done. He looked at Julian and Lord Cotton. They did not seem to mind, he guessed.

'We should not give him more attention than he has already attained here. Sir Alberon, I have spoken with Mr Sanders and reviewed security arrangements for tonight at Eagle House. We should be better prepared in case Basil Elders wants to drop in on us again like today. On behalf of Wimbledon Police, Lord Cotton and Sir Alberon my sincere apologies for today's events.'

He gave a polite nod of apology. His stern, hard face then turned to the Italian baker.

'Mr Letrova!' said the Chief Superintendent, making it clear to Enrico the man took the same bad habits after his subordinate, Inspector Baynard. 'Your fame precedes you!'

'LoTrova! And thank you.' Enrico nodded to thank for what he thought was a compliment.

'I understand your bakery business is doing very well.' added the Chief Superintendent. 'I do recommend you keep it that way and profit from the success. Your obstruction of justice is renowned at Wimbledon Police Station, in particular with me and Inspector Baynard. Please keep out of this delicate matter with Basil Elders, if you don't mind, and I do hope your presence here is purely coincidental. Don't start stirring things up, will you?'

Enrico was speechless and taken aback by the comments. If it had been Baynard, he could have slipped in a joke, but he was not on the same terms with his boss who he had met only once.

'I wasn't even thinking of...' the Italian baker muttered.

'Good!' the Chief Superintendent interrupted turning back to the others. 'I will be on my way, Lord Cotton. I am holding a security briefing with Baynard after this morning's protest and will let you and Sir Julian Alberon know our plans to support you tonight and for the rest of the week.'

Lord Cotton gave a warm thanks to the Chief Superintendent, who in turn waved goodbye with a quick glance to each of them. The last was for Enrico, and he narrowed his eyes to remind the Italian baker of what he had said and who was in charge. Then yelling could be heard once more outside, followed by loud chants of protest. It was not a good sign.

'What on earth is that?' exclaimed Lord Cotton with suspicion.

The group went through the double door into the reception to see what was happening. The entrance doors to the club were wide open. Outside, in the car park, Inspector Baynard was barking commands at his police constables while looking over his shoulder and pointing at the car entrance. Enrico and Viviane and the rest of the group looked at each other puzzled.

The chanting grew louder. They finally walked out into the car park and stopped under the maple tree, together with staff from the golf club. Along Camp Road, cutting across the view from the golf club entrance, they could just about make out the crowd of protesters through the trees, forming a long line of black and blue leather jackets, with a larger group clustered at the entrance of the car park. They swarmed around like crazy flies oblivious of the cars piling up.

'Get these protesters out of the way! Now!' cried Baynard before dismissing the police officers.

They joined the rest of the force forming a line of defence at the car entrance and slowly pushing the crowd of protesters out. Basil 'Wilberforce' Elders did not come to the conference with just a handful of his friends. The rest of his followers had been kindly waiting outside in incognito, and now a party of fifty or sixty people blocked the narrow stretch of the country lane, shouting in protest 'Wimbledon For The People' and even waving banners bearing the same motto.

'This is ridiculous!' complained Lord Cotton, aware of club members pouring out into the car park a little shocked by the Basil Elders's theatrics.

'Sir Alberon, we'd better get going.' advised Mr Sanders. 'I have the car waiting just here.'

'I agree.'

He then turned to Dr Watkins.

'Best of luck for this evening, Dr Watkins. I hope we will have a better chance to catch up with you and Simon. Enrico, Viviane, hope to see you there too.'

'Of course!' confirmed Viviane, shouting over the protesters' chant.

The farewell was quick and furtive as if Julian has been planning an escape. Enrico waved as he watched him dash off, with Mr Sanders next to him and the Chief Superintendent accompanying him to the car, as if to ensure his safety against the cries of protests. Julian was indeed the most important man in Wimbledon.

'We'd better find a way out as well.' commented Dr Watkins, worried at what he was seeing. 'I've never seen anything like this before.'

'I don't know' replied Lord Cotton in dismay, hugging Little Caesar tighter. 'Someone needs to put a stop to Basil Elders. Ramona, let's check that no protesters invaded the golf course.'

'Sure.'

The sporty lady disappeared into the club bringing a few staff members with her. Lord Cotton turned back to the curator.

'I will see you tonight, and Mr LoTrova, tomorrow we will have more time to chat in private. I will ask reception to call you a taxi.'

'Looking forward to it!' replied Enrico.

Lord Cotton disappeared inside the club. The trio looked back at the scene. The police had quickly cordoned off enough space to keep some sort of buffer zone between them and the tough crowd of protesters at the entrance and along the side of Camp Road. Inspector Baynard led their way, his icy stare unmistakable among the crowd, shouting orders to the left and to the right one after the other. He held a speaker and used it to warn Basil of his actions a few times.

'Stand down, Mr Elders.' he warned. 'This protest has not been approved by the Council or the police, so I ask you again to stand down and walk away before things get worse.'

The journalists who had stayed behind after the conference pushed out into the car park and the patch of green separating them from the police line. They walked up and down to observe and report without getting involved, like avid bird watchers or keen train spotters. They took picture after picture of the unannounced confrontation that would certainly hit tomorrow's headlines. The noisy scene was a dark blotch against the tranquil and idyllic surroundings on this side of the Common. Enrico did not have to glance at Lord Cotton or the Chief Superintendent, or even Julian himself to know none of them would be pleased about the bad publicity caused by this new stunt from Mr 'Wilberforce' himself.

A saloon car drove out across the club's car park towards the crowd. The police lines changed formation to open a safe passage for Sir Julian Alberon's car. They pushed hard to force Basil's protesters to move up to one side. As the car slipped by, Enrico could not see Julian through the tinted windows. Julian was probably watching the scene with horror, maybe causing him to think twice about the decisions he made. The image of Basil 'Wilberforce' Elders just a few inches from the car, above the heads of his followers, struck everyone. His austere, arrogant eyes behind the gold-rimmed glasses scowled at the car, as he pointed at the tinted windows with one hand and pointed towards the sky like a preacher with the other.

'Time to get back what belongs to Wimbledon! This wireless electricity is not safe!' Basil shouted fearlessly at the car. 'We ask you, Sir Alberon, to tell everyone where his chief engineer is, to tell us what happened when you tested the wireless electricity, to tell us the truth behind the infernal machine that is the New Wimbledon Windmill!'

A loud cheer from the crowd followed. Once the car managed to get through the crowd undisturbed, the protesters gradually lost interest and their chanting decreased in intensity. Still, they waited for Basil Elders to give the signal and the protesters finally broke up into smaller groups. Still, it took about an hour to disperse the crowd, including passers-by and journalists who had stopped by to follow what was another piece of sensational news in Wimbledon.

'We'd better go.' said Viviane pleased to see their taxi finally approaching after being stuck in the traffic jam. 'This scene has upset me.'

'Hey, don't worry.' reassured Enrico. 'Everything is going to be ok. I am sure Julian is handling the matter as he should by ignoring Basil's accusations.'

The Italian baker heard himself saying those words and he thought they were the right things to say to her, if he were to consider Julian a friend. Deep inside though he was worried. He shuddered in remembering his technophobia, and for a moment he wondered how much trust he could put in these metallic towers Alberyx Enterprises was building on the green meadows of the Common. He decided it was better to keep his mouth shut, not to upset anyone, and smiled as he opened the door for Viviane and Dr Watkins.

The events of the day had rocked Wimbledon Village more than anyone had expected. As the winter evening dropped its dark, cold mantle over the busy streets and crowded pubs, the security staff of Alberyx Enterprises and a dedicated team from Wimbledon Police had doubled their efforts to cordon off a wider area around Eagle House than planned, in anticipation of the long-waited presentation by the Wimbledon Museum and the British Museum. Inspector Baynard thought historians and archaeologists may prove to be a less dangerous crowd. However, the mere presence of Julian Alberon as sponsor and guest was enough to make Baynard, the Chief Superintendent and Mr Sanders nervous about what could happen. Nobody wanted a repeat of what had happened outside the Royal Wimbledon Golf Club with the risk of tarnishing the image of Wimbledon further as more people from London made the journey to the south-western part of the capital. It was not just historians and archaeologists as Baynard had originally thought, but also reporters and vloggers from history magazines who had suddenly become interested in this small village upon Wimbledon hill.

Eagle House stood at the northern end of the high street, right next to the Rose and Crown pub. No traffic was allowed through this part of the village; it was either diverted at the roundabout by the Dog and Fox or at the war memorial. Pedestrians were allowed through, as long as they passed some simple security checks. The black gates to Eagle House led directly into a wide square area. The main building was further back, away from the road, allowing visitors to admire the odd architecture as they walked towards it. It was split into three blocks, narrow and tall, rising up to the same level and ending with a decorative border. The middle section had the small stone statue of an eagle on top, with its wings slightly open. The sloped roof was barely visible. The pale blue tint of the façade changed colour constantly because of the suffused orange glow coming from the nine wide windows. The original brickwork under each window had been kept, hinting at the historical heritage hidden behind the modernity of Wimbledon Village.

'I am curious to hear the history of this building!' confessed Enrico dropping an olive into his mouth.

He eyed Dr Watkins curiously, knowing he would catch the bait. They were standing at one of the many buffet tables, where some light finger food had been nicely laid out on tables on three sides of the large hall while a podium and a screen had been set up at the other end.

'Well, I can definitely tell you Eagle House hasn't been used for presentations in a very long time.' commented the curator using his glass of sparkling wine to wave at the large hall they were in. 'The room upstairs are apartments but most of them are empty at the moment. However, Eagle House was a school when it was first built, before becoming a private house.'

'A school? Wow!' exclaimed Enrico, amazed at how Dr Watkins could still surprise them with his stories.

'How come you didn't pick the hall back at the Wimbledon Village Club, like we always do for WAIS meetings?' asked Viviane, as she quickly refreshed her red lipstick.

'I don't think we would have fit in.' explained the curator. 'Simon had quite a few guests coming from the British Museum tonight. I haven't met them personally.'

They scouted the room. Somewhere they glimpsed at Lady Cannizaro from the Duchess Hotel and Reverend Green from Saint Mary's Church. Yet, between the few faces they recognised from Wimbledon, there were many Enrico and Viviane had never seen. Most of them were dressed in tuxedoes and long cream dresses; they had definitely made an effort in dressing up for the occasion. Viviane looked at her red dress, checking it was not too tight. She glanced over at Enrico, and she knew she did not have to worry.

'I hope you at least changed your chef's jacket.' pointed out Viviane making a note of Enrico's favourite and only dress code. 'I thought I would see you in a suit for once.'

'Hey, this is freshly washed and ironed. Just for the occasion!' retorted Enrico.

'Well, let's hope they don't confuse you with one of the waiters.'

'Ah, Enrico!' Dr Watkins laughed. 'You are such a character!'

There was a sudden commotion in the room. Faces turned towards the main entrance, and as expected, Julian had just arrived. He was on his own if you did not take into account the three bodyguards at arm's length. He made his way towards the nearest table, shaking many hands along the way, pushing through as quickly as possible.

'I don't see him enjoying that.' commented Viviane. 'He has too much attention for his liking. First fame, now threats from these psychos.'

'Are you referring to the group led by that Basil "Willibie"? What's his name again? The man from the WPCC.'

'Basil "Wilberforce" Elders is not the WPCC, Enrico. Don't make that mistake!' warned the florist as if she had just heard a blasphemy. 'The WPCC does great volunteer work to fund and look after Wimbledon Common, ever since… how long Dr Watkins?'

'1871.'

'1871, see. They are not savages like Basil's group. Some of his men are ex-WPCC members, yes, but they are miles away from what the WPCC believes in. They are just a bunch of rogue rebels!'

'You have to admit he has a point, though.' Enrico dared to say grabbing another olive.

He was toying with the thought he had earlier that day. Viviane and Dr Watkins turned to him, doubtful.

'What do you mean, Enrico?' said Viviane worried.

'Don't get me wrong. I mean, you heard Quentin. He lost his job as guardian of the windmill. Dr Watkins said this Basil Elders lost his part time role at the scout ranger's house. Now it makes sense why some people may be suspicious about things being built around the Common unless they are newly planted trees and birds' houses. Did you hear some of the reporters' questions? Especially, that Nathan from the Wimbledon Gazette.'

'Oh no! Quentin Plainstraw?' commented Dr Watkins shocked. 'Oh dear. I didn't know…'

'What are you getting at Enrico? Are you blaming Julian?'

Viviane's voice faltered under the emotions. She tried to keep it down.

'No, Viviane. I mean the company. Alberyx Enterprises. Perhaps they need to be more tactful. That's all.'

Viviane snorted unconvinced. She picked a new glass of sparkling wine and turned to look at the room again.

'Oh, look who's here!'

She pointed to a space not far from the podium. Lord Cotton and Ramona Halywell were mingling with a group of friends. The chubby golf club owner and the slim sporty woman stood by each other, and Viviane wondered what brought such opposites together. He was always laughing while holding a worried Little Caesar under his arm, paws in the air and the little black eyes darting in all directions. She, instead, stood tall and still, with her arms crossed, and a pursed, reserved smile hidden behind sips of champagne. Her round, blue eyes carefully observed who was talking. Her hair was free from the sports cap this evening, showing her hazelnut mane pulled back in a long ponytail. Her hair was pulled back too tightly to the point it had no shape.

'Something tells me you are not fond of Miss Halywell?' whispered Enrico close to Viviane's hear.

The florist leered at the Italian baker and took a sip of her sparkling wine, gazing intently into his eyes.

'Is that your kind of woman?' she teased.

Enrico blushed. He gazed in her direction.

'They are an odd duo, I must say.' he commented. 'She's too cold for me, if that's what you are asking…'

'Enrico, Viviane, it is time!' exclaimed Dr Watkins who had now turned his attention to the podium.

Simon Deeley had been practising his speech one last time in a back room near the kitchens used by the catering company. He knew waiters would not be staring at him, busy as they were in bringing canapés out in the large hall. Everyone outside, Wimbledonians and London folk, were curious to know what he had to say. The aura of mystery he and Dr Watkins had kept around his presentation was something Alberyx Enterprises had requested, to better raise funds and sponsorship. Simon did not mind; in the end what he had found in the Old Rectory was worth much more. He ran through the intro lines once more, and then adjusted his tuxedo in a nearby mirror. He ran his hands over his African buzz hair and twisted his jaw to ensure his face looked impeccable as there would be plenty of pictures.

'Aye, yer can do this!' he told himself in the mirror with a hard Scottish accent he normally kept quiet.

The hall was fuller than expected. The lights were dimmed the moment he was announced, and he walked the short journey to the stage area, under the bright spotlights. He waved at the faceless audience and then checked both the presentation screen behind was ready showing the title.

ANGLO-SAXON WIMBLEDON
(ca. VI-VII Century)
The Legend of the Wynnman

There was a thick murmur in the audience as they took in the subject of this evening's presentation. Then silence fell over the room, but the vibe of excitement was still palpable. It was for Dr Watkins and Simon Deeley; even if they could not see each other, they both knew very well this was the result of their work.

'Good evening, everyone!' he commenced with his cheerful Scottish accent. 'Normally, a presentation of 'is kind is usually offered with some comfy seats as the topic can cause even th' toughest historian tae doze off.'

The audience laughed. Simon nodded, building up his confidence.

'However, it was our intention to show you the true value of what has been discovered under the Old Rectory aboot six months ago or so. After many long, extenuating months, and thanks to the generosity of our sponsor, Alberyx Enterprises, we have reached some important conclusions we are ready to share. It goes without saying, for some not deeply familiar of history or archaeology, that Anglo-Saxon relics are rare across Britain and what we have discovered does not come in the form of writings or descriptive text as it is the case most of the time. Hence, we hev to work extensively with the clues we have to draw a picture of what we are looking at.'

Simon proceeded to bring up many references of previous work done by the British Museum. He paused and took a sip from his glass of water. The presentation screen switched to a series of photos of the site discovered under the Old Rectory.

'The Old Rectory is indeed Wimbledon's first and oldest manor house dating back to the 1500s. However, we know a previous house was there in the Middle Ages, held by the church to manage the estate; and before that time, it must have been a grange or farm as part of the Anglo-Saxon village known as 'Wimbedounyng'. It is before this time, probably before the arrival of Christianity, that we believe the Pool of Elixir found under the Old Rectory was built. The chamber with the round pool inside has its name inscribed in the runic inscriptions we discovered, and the writing, one of the rare Anglo-Saxon findings we have ever come across, explains that it was a sort of sacrificial fountain. Its location remains a little unusual, and there is no evidence it was buried underground when first built. The runes inscribed on the eagle-like statue you see on the screen give details of how the sacrifice was made, by burning human flesh and blood inside the pool. German Saxons did carry out human sacrifices although not with such complexity. When it comes to Anglo-Saxons in Britain, there is little to prove such practice apart from the habit of cutting up body parts and setting them on stakes after winning a battle. The more we researched, the clearer it became that this Pool of Elixir was for personal and individual use. It had nothing to do with the public rituals that may have been carried out by the small village of Wimbedounyng, which let me remind you all was more a cluster of huts on the hill far from the main Roman roads into London.

'Who did this Pool of Elixir belong to? History here becomes blurred with legends, and the only reason I am not dismissing this lead, is because of what we were able to interpret on the rest of the inscription. The runes are written by different pairs of hands, perhaps a group of people wishing to leave something for posterity; and they do tell us an interesting story. It is the story of a sorcerer who was able to "move seas and mountains", and apparently control nature at his own will. We believe the sorcerer was so feared by the villagers for his seemingly unlimited knowledge. The Pool of Elixir may have belonged to the sorcerer himself, and it is where he would have carried out his own work. In the inscription the sorcerer is given the name of 'Wynnman'. This mention is the first hard evidence we have on the origin of the name 'Wimbledon', which we knew meant 'Wynnman's hill' but until today could only guess who the Wynnman was historically. Perhaps the locals in the room may recognise the name from the local legend, which is also part of the runic inscription. One night the sorcerer lost control. He shook the hill, so the writings say, as he tried to move seas and mountains to become an all-knowing, all-powerful god. The villagers hid inside a fort nearby praying their pagan gods for protection. A group of men, perhaps local warriors, decided to break into the Wynnman's hut and steal his magic spells to use it against the sorcerer.'

At the mentioning of the word 'spell', there was some giggling and muttering in the audience. Simon pictured members of the British Museum twisting their nose at the mention of magic and supernatural. The archaeologist soldiered on.

'The Wynnman was somehow tricked into falling into the Pool of Elixir. Details are scattered. All we know is what the second half of the inscription tells us. The sorcerer was burnt alive by his attackers, and parts of him were cut off and imprisoned into seven relics. The villagers subsequently hid these relics in fear of the Wynnman returning. They believed all seven relics brought together would allow the sorcerer to come back to life, unleash his revenge and seek the power taken away from him. Where these relics are hidden, if they really existed, is not mentioned. There are no drawings either; there is only a list in the inscription, written in a curious, exact order.'

Simon proceeded to show the runes on the screen, depicting each relic and a black and white drawing of what it represented.

'We start from a flower, similar to an azalea. Then we have an urn or jug, perhaps containing water or mead or some other liquid. We then have an ivory dagger, a fruit of some sort, and a gemstone. The last two are a bit vague and we labelled them as golden coins and a long stick like a spear or a sceptre. Seven relics, and each is meant to represent a part of the Wynnman's body that was imprisoned. The flower is the sorcerer's mind; some form of azalea or rhododendron. The urn is his flesh and muscles. The dagger is his blood, and the fruit is the breath of life. You may interpret this last one as the soul or perhaps life-giving oxygen. The gemstone is his eyes, and again we had difficulty in interpreting what the coins and the stick meant. Probably, they stand for power and war lust, if we run parallels with similar iconography from other sites, although the link is not strong. The explanation I have just given you is a great example of Anglo-Saxon symbolism, and the Old Rectory is definitely a great source to understand culture and society, of the Anglo-Saxons as a whole but also locally, considering Wimbledon had little or no evidence of Anglo-Saxon settlements. Whether the legend is true or not, we don't know but we do know a sorcerer of some sort really existed in the Wimbledon hill area around the sixth and seventh Century.'

There was another clamour in the room. This time it is more one of shock and awe.

'Unfortunately, we lose all evidence of Anglo-Saxon Wimbledon from the late seventh Century onwards as the Christianisation of Britain took over, wiping out centuries of paganism. Whether the horrors of the Wynnman forced Christians to destroy anything that remained, it is hard to say. It is sufficient to mention the first Christian church was built not far from the Old Rectory around this period. Possibly as a way to cover up the Pool of Elixir and hide away its heretical nature.'

Simon noticed a few people leaving the hall as he mentioned this last part. He knew fellow members of the British Museum would find his conclusions about magic spells and mythical relics too far-fetched. He carried on and went on to talk about the other findings collected from the small chamber and the basement to the delight of the less conservative archaeologists left in the room. Enrico's mind though was lured back to the legend of the Wynnman. It was too obvious to ignore the coincidences. He remembered when he found the black azalea. That was a sort of flower. Then the cracked urn he stumbled upon with Viviane in the tunnel. That was the second relic, perhaps. The Italian baker glanced at Dr Watkins and was curious to know if the curator had made the same connection as he had just done. He was standing by the table checking his speech cards. It would be his turn soon.

Simon finished his part of the speech and introduced Dr Watkis with a heartfelt invitation, calling him onto the stage to run through the last part of their presentation. The curator looked up as the heads in the hall that knew him turned to cheer him on. He made his way nervously through, with his white wavy hair softened by the dimmed lights and then shining bright under the direct spotlight.

'Thank you, Simon.' he said, taking over the microphone. 'I must say Mr Deeley is one of the brightest minds I have ever met. It was a pleasure to exchange theories with him, and we do hope he has felt the support the Wimbledon Museum and the whole Wimbledon have given him and his team. He is a meticulous Scotsman.'

The two nodded at each other in gratitude and the audience clapped their hands once more. Dr Watkins then moved on talking about rock foundations and architecture.

'…as you can see from Slide B and C, we were able to look at the soil from both the basement and the chamber, and ultimately determine that the construction of Saint Mary's Church and the Old Rectory may have been, sort of, "planned" by the Church. We know how the Church may have taken pagan sites and repurposed them in the very Early Middle Ages. Temples turned into churches, for example. In the case of Wimbledon hill, we believe the reason was to seal the pagan site forever as a form of protection. Early Christians started to land on British shores from the late sixth Century onwards and the first church on Wimbledon hill is of Anglo-Saxon period, dating back to the seventh Century. The clash between the two cultures here on the hill is very likely to have pushed Christians to bury the past, leaving only traces of the Wynnman as a legend…'

A more detailed section followed, running through the findings from geological reports of the area and comparing them with older reports from the Wimbledon Museum about Saint Mary's. Dr Watkins spoke eloquently, putting forward facts not fiction, making each of his words count. Enrico could see the curator was convinced of his findings, no doubt of that.

The speech ended with a promise of further exploration of the site as the team planned to dig further into the natural rock. Despite a few sceptical heads shaking in disagreement, the audience cheered Dr Watkins once the presentation was over. The lights went back to normal, and a soft murmur resumed in the hall while a representative of the Council joined the stage to thank him and Simon Deeley for their efforts. Shortly after, Dr Watkins and Simon returned to the table where Enrico and Viviane greeted them with open arms.

'*Bravi!*' exclaimed Enrico. 'Well done!'

'That was educational.' rejoiced Viviane.

'Thank You.' replied Dr Watkins. 'Let me introduce you finally to Mr Deeley.'

Simon leaned forward to shake hands. First Viviane, and then he stretched his big hand towards Enrico. The Italian baker felt his strong grip and noticed how his solid physique made Simon's tuxedo look like an unbreakable armour.

'Mr LoTrova! Th' baker!' exclaimed Simon. 'Glad tae finally meet ye! I heard so much about you.'

'Nice to meet you too!' replied Enrico.

'We enjoyed your presentation.' said Viviane. 'It was like listening to one of Dr Watkins's stories about Wimbledon.'

'I guess we were right in the end, Dr Watkins.' chortled Enrico. 'There is some fact in fiction.'

'Don't you start, Enrico!' replied Dr Watkins rolling his eyes. 'A legend is still a legend!'

'He is referring to the Wynnman I suppose?' chimed in Simon.

Dr Watkins nodded.

'Aye. Then we should have mentioned the rest of the Anglo-Saxon legend!' humoured the archaeologist.

He laughed complicitly. Enrico and Viviane looked at him puzzled.

'Oh dear…' moaned Dr Watkins. 'We discussed about this, and we felt we should keep our feet on the ground. I'd better go and thank the rest of the audience for coming, so at least my ears don't have to listen to more fairy tales! See you later!'

'Hey Dr W! Are ye going to speak to Lord Cotton?' asked Simon grabbing the curator by the arm.

'Maybe…' replied Dr Watkins.

'Don't forget tae ask!' hinted Simon, referring to their conversation about Caesar's Camp.

Dr Watkins swallowed hard. He had no intention of bringing that argument up, not tonight; though he knew Simon would not let the matter go that easily.

'I'll see if I can.'

The curator smiled and merged slowly into the crowd. The hall was still busy as most of the audience took the opportunity to mingle and chat over one more glass of sparkling wine.

'What was he referring to?' noted Viviane. 'I mean, about the fairy tales?'

'Just another part of the legend Dr Watkins felt was n'all much, and I kind of agreed. It is about th' seven relics.'

'What about them?' asked Enrico, curious.

'All together they are supposed to free the Wynnman from his prison. However, there is more. Whoever finds all seven relics will be able to, and I quote a part of the inscription here, "feel the power and revenge of the Wynnman, to move the seas and the mountains, to shape the world as they pleased".'

'What does that mean?' quizzed Viviane.

'No idea.'

'Does this have anything to do with the black azalea and the crimson liquids?' commented Enrico.

'The what?'

'The lava rock, you know. The one shaped like an azalea. And that bottle from the cellars under the Old Rectory. Didn't you analyse those?'

The frown on Simon's face hinted at Enrico and Viviane the archaeologist was unaware of what they were referring to.

'Didn't you receive some items from Dr Watkins to analyse recently?' added Enrico, explaining further.

'We received a lot from the Wimbledon Museum. Plus, all th' remains we dug up in the Pool of Elixir. Don't think I remember a lava rock and… what did ye say?... A bottle of crimson liquid?'

Enrico nodded. Simon shrugged his shoulders.

'I need tae check. Where were they found?'

'Well…'

Enrico glanced at Viviane. He could not put into words what they had been through this last year. The way Simon talked about them in a trivial manner left him speechless. It was still his guess. He could not be certain the lava rock and the bottle were really remains of the relics. Yet, the fact Simon did not acknowledge them sounded strange.

There was a sudden change in the lighting of the hall. Quick shadows appeared on Simon's and Viviane's face, and everyone else in the room, bestowing a sinister look upon them. The lights flickered, out of control. The spotlights that were used to light up the stage suddenly became much brighter and then blew up with a bang that quickly fizzled out. The hall fell into darkness for a moment as all the lights flickered again and then went out. There were cries of panic and Viviane heard people stumbling nearby.

'What is going on?' shouted Viviane.

'No idea…' replied Enrico.

Before he could add more, the lights turned back on, and the atmosphere in the hall returned back to normal as if nothing had happened.

'Weird…' commented Simon. 'Glad it did not happen while I wis presenting.'

The three chuckled. They exchanged glances with the people nearby. Everyone was as surprised as they were. It was not long though before the calm was interrupted again by a constant shouting coming from one corner of the hall, not far from the main entrance. Simon strained to look over the heads of those in front of them. Enrico and Viviane did the same. Everyone did, and they were in shock to see a man being dragged away by security. He was wearing a black jacket and jeans. The white shirt he had on bore a slogan in red capital letters. However, nobody in the room needed to read it to understand what it was saying. The man himself was shouting it at the top of his voice as he was being dragged away.

'Wimbledon for the people! Wimbledon for the people!' cried out the protester.

Enrico glanced over towards Lord Cotton. His look of disdain said it all. He then scanned the rest of the room and saw Julian on the opposite of the hall. He looked annoyed and for once he did not show calm or patience. Mr Sanders was next to him blabbing into his ear. Julian then looked down and a sense of worry seemed to take over.

'These protesters again?' sighed Viviane.

'They seem to be everywhere.' noted Enrico.

The protester's cries carried on until the police arrived to help take him away. Baynard came through the main entrance and signalled a reassuring gesture to the audience that was now getting more angered and agitated. His inquisitive stare stood its ground, although he wondered how the protester had managed to get inside. Baynard held the door open for his men to take the man away and then closed it behind him. The shouting faded away.

'Baynard is being kept busy lately!' added Enrico.

'Exactly, so let's try not to make more trouble.' relished Viviane in reminding Enrico. 'You heard the Chief Superintendent today. I don't think they would be happy to hear you getting involved in all of these political protests.'

Enrico groaned. He was known for his curiosity going too far. The label of *ragazzo curioso* was stuck on him, apparently.

'I hear ye are a troublemaker, Mr LoTrova.' joked Simon.

'I would not say that. I think Viviane exaggerates.'

'I do not!' retorted Viviane.

The two exchanged a few playful bickering words to the amusement of Simon.

'Ye two act like a couple!' he teased.

Both Enrico and Viviane pulled a face at Simon's ridiculous comment.

'But I am no troublemaker, so we'll leave you to it.' added the archaeologist with a raise of his glass and quick nod to announce his exit. 'I hope tae see ye around soon.'

He smiled and walked away. From afar, his square, broad shoulders, nicely fit in his black tuxedo, stood out in the crowd as he pushed his way among the other tuxedos in the room. His confidence took the room by storm as if he were still on the podium; he shook hands with conviction as he met and thanked supporters along the way. Wherever he was, he stood out.

'I can't believe he is an archaeologist. He looks more like a celebrity.' commented Enrico.

'You can be one, Enrico, too. That offer from Lord Cotton could help!' chimed in Viviane.

'Something tells me you want me to focus on my bakery, eh?'

'Just saying.' replied Viviane with a shrug. 'You don't want to cross paths with Baynard again!'

Enrico sighed. He had no intention to do so, except his hands had started to prickle with the need to make some bread. He knew what it was. After hearing about the legend of the Wynnman once more in fine detail, it was haunting Enrico again, and it brought back those visions he wanted to keep at the back of his conscious mind. Simon seemed to have ignored the two strange items they had found, and even Dr Watkins had not bothered to mention them together with what they had witnessed in the Pool of Elixir. The Italian baker wondered whether Eric Quercer, looking for the black azalea, or Toby Claymore, pretending to recreate human sacrifices, had all been tomb raiders in search of the relics.

'Shall we go?' suggested Viviane. 'I think people are starting to leave.'

'Yes, sure. But first I need to go to the gents.'

'Ok, I'll wait for you in the car park.' replied Viviane rolling her eyes.

The hall had started to empty slowly. Enrico dashed through the handful of people who were breaking away from the crowd into small group and heading for the exit. He was looking for signs to the nearest toilet and he doubted whether one was available. He went through a side door and stepped into a long corridor. Turning left without a clue where he was, he walked briskly passed a few doors. The corridor continued round a left corner leading to a locked door and a flight of stairs up to the second-floor apartments. Enrico spun around. He should have asked for directions. The voices from the hall were distant. Yet, he could hear chatter nearby quite distinctly. He looked around him and then spotted one of the doors he had passed was ajar. Someone was talking inside with a harsh voice. Enrico's curiosity pushed him towards it, and through the gap he saw Julian Alberon talking to Mr Sanders in what seemed a vacant office. The business tycoon was red with anger, barking mad at his lawyer.

'I can't believe it!' Julian blurted out. 'I've had enough of Basil bloody "Wilberforce" Elders! That man has no respect for the work I am doing for Wimbledon.'

Enrico was taken aback by hearing Julian curse for the first time.

'Even here they manage to persecute me and make a fool of me! How did that protester get in? Where the hell was security? And how did he manage to tamper with the lights? Someone could have been hurt!'

'We're not sure if he tampered with the lights.' corrected Mr Sanders, patiently. 'You need to calm down, Sir Alberon. This is not you. Stress is getting you all riled up. We will deal with it, beef up security and all.'

'I am furious! This has to stop! You tell the security and the Chief Superintendent. We cannot afford more theatrics from Mr Elders and his "cultist group". Something has to be done.'

Julian used the word in the most disparaging way possible. The image of Basil Elders kept flashing before his eyes and Julian's hate for him was plain to see.

'You need to rest, Sir Alberon.' advised Mr Sanders.

'It could have all gone better if John Crane, our chief engineer, had turned up today at the press conference, and shut the mouth of that good-for-nothing accusing us of causing harm to Wimbledon. Where the hell is Mr Crane anyway?'

'We are still looking for him. Security is a little baffled he hasn't checked into his living quarters at Warren Farms. The same goes for his girlfriend, Fran Dudley.'

'This is a conspiracy; I am telling you. Industrial espionage, maybe.'

Julian spoke with accusing eyes.

'Let's not make rushed decisions.' advised Mr Sanders. 'This is not the image we want to show Wimbledon.'

Mr Sanders patted the businessman's shoulder, whose chest heaved with deep breaths fuelled by anger. It took a while for Julian to calm down. His cheeks turned to a lighter, more soothing colour and he left with a debilitated look.

'I'm tired, Mr Sanders. Let's wrap up and go home. We have to review the schedule.'

'Certainly, sir.'

Enrico thought he could barge in and reassure Julian as a friend that everything would be alright. He then retracted the idea and thought it best not to get caught eavesdropping. He took a few steps back and walked briskly away. He pushed hard not to break into a run and make a noise. He was about to turn right back into the hall when he bumped into a familiar face.

'Enrico! Glad to see you!'

It was Reverend Green from Saint Mary's Church. He was in plain clothes for the evening, beaming his peaceful gaze as the good-natured man of the cloth he was.

'Father! Long time, no see. How are you?'

'Can't complain.' he smiled.

'Did you enjoy the presentation?' asked Enrico.

He hoped this conversation would dispel any suspicions about him if Julian passed by.

'Certainly. Mr Deeley and Dr Watkins have done a fine job. Nice to hear more history about our church.'

'Even the bit about the Church and the pagan site?' added Enrico light-hearted.

'Folklore and legends, Enrico.' he chuckled. 'Stick to history like Dr Watkins does.'

'He makes sure we do.' hinted Enrico.

'By the way, did you speak to him tonight?'

Enrico nodded.

'Did he look alright? Remember, it's better if he does not get too excited about tunnels and Wimbledon history! We want to ensure his health comes first.'

Enrico was surprised Reverend Green was checking on him. He knew the priest had Dr Watkins's health at heart after the accidents in the tunnel. After all, they had been friends for years, decades. Enrico though could not grasp why the need to keep tabs on him.

'Relax, reverend. We hardly saw Dr Watkins so we hardly discussed the subject.'

'Will you do me favour, though?'

'What's that?'

'Check he is not too tired. Make sure he gets some sleep. He trusts you. You and Viviane.'

'Is there something you want to tell me, reverend?'

'I am just worried he may not listen to me. That's all.'

'Will do.' replied Enrico

He appreciated the trust he was being given.

'I must go as it is getting late. See you at the next market fair at Saint Mary's.'

They both waved goodbye and Reverend Green disappeared back into the hall among the last standing visitors. Enrico stood by the door. He glanced over his shoulder and noticed Julian had not come their way. He then looked back into the hall. The reverend had left for good and for a moment the Italian baker had the impression Reverend Green had been looking for him on purpose. Check on Dr Watkins, he said. Enrico could only oblige.

Nathan sat in his office studio in front of the digital radio transmitter once more. He had lost count of the number of evenings he had done so. He had been carrying out research all afternoon, especially after hearing Basil 'Wilberforce' Elders shouting at the top of his voice during the press conference. Nathan admired the man for his conviction. He knew they both shared the same goal: expose Alberyx Enterprises for what it really was. Basil Elders's storming of the golf club would hopefully come up in conversations with security this evening.

The journalist fiddled with the transmitter once more, hacking into the digital air waves of Wimbledon, and more specifically those belonging to the Warren Farms compound. It took a while before he could hack into the encrypted channel and tune in on a clear signal. The same two security guards from yesterday were already in conversation.

'…Where did he go then?' the first guard was saying. 'He is not anywhere on the compound. We will need to get the police involved soon.'

'We won't.' opposed the second guard. 'We have clear directives from the boss. We need to find him…like now. Or the whole launch happening next weekend goes pear-shaped!'

'I mean, we've checked every single corner of Warren Farms. John Crane was meant to come back to the compound on Sunday evening and he never did. If something happened outside of Warren Farms, it is a case for Wimbledon Police!'

'Yes, and then we have more journalists on our back and more protesters to take care of. Did you see the stunt Basil "Wilberforce" Elders pulled off today?'

'He is gutsy, though. Come on, you must admit.'

'He's an idiot.'

'That's not what my friend at the Rose and Crown said.'

'Whatever. We need to start searching again, and also look at the area of the Common straight off the Warren Farms compound. John Crane and his girlfriend could not have just disappeared into thin air!'

Nathan bit his lip. There was indeed a serious problem with John Crane. His absence today at the press conference was not down to a personal matter. The man responsible for the tech inside the new windmill had actually disappeared, together with his girlfriend. Nathan was aware Alberyx Enterprises staff who worked on the windmill and the Repeater were living inside the Warren Farms compound. They had been recruited from different parts of the UK, not only London. It would be days before a relative would enquire about their disappearance. The question then dawned on Nathan, about how Basil Elders had acted as if he knew about John Crane's disappearance. He had challenged Julian Alberon on the specific whereabouts of John Crane. The leader of the protesters knew something. He had to check it out, approach Mr Elders somehow.

'Do you think they ran away?' asked the first guard.

'Don't speculate. We need to organise another search.'

'What if they were killed?'

'By who? Listen, do me a favour. Shut your gob and get on with it before our bosses start breathing down our necks. Not that they aren't already doing so…'

The voice of the second guard trailed off. Another surge of interference came on the digital radio transmitter. The guards' voices became metallic, distorted. The loud static Nathan had heard the evening before returned. Then Nathan's own desk lamp went on and off. The journalist looked out of the window, and again, the streetlamps outside were also flickering wildly, car alarms were wailing, and even some of the lights in the windows of the detached houses across the street were out of control as if a child inside was playing with the switch. The interference was having a bigger impact this time and again it was short-lived. The digital transmitter resumed playing the guards' voices to Nathan.

'Again! What is this interference?' said one of the guards.

'No idea but I am not happy about it. We need to do a system upgrade on the security channels. Was it at the same time as yesterday?'

'No. It is later than yesterday. Whatever it is, we'd better check the power generator too. Let maintenance know.'

'Yes sure…hold on!'

'What is it?'

'I got a notification from the team at Eagle House. Something happened.'

'What now?'

'One of Mr Elders's followers just fiddled with the lights. Fortunately, after the presentation.'

'Did they catch him?'

'Yes. Just now.'

The second guard took a sigh of relief.

'It can't be him causing all this interference, can it? What the heck is going on?'

Nathan turned the transmitter off and checked his phone. The event at the Eagle House was indeed all over the local social feeds. A protester scared the audience with a game of flickering lights. Quite juvenile as a form of protest, thought Nathan. Regardless, he knew his next step. After all that had happened, interviewing Basil 'Wilberforce' Elders one-to-one was probably the best way to learn more about the dirt the protesters claimed to have on Alberyx Enterprises. Perhaps he could have an informal chat and befriend the man almost everyone in Wimbledon hated. A nice article on the Wimbledon Gazette would give him a competitive advantage above the rest of the journalists going on about windmills and wireless electricity, worshipping them as if they were gods. Nathan sipped his tea. He knew where to find Basil Elders. He then started drafting a set of questions in his head.

That Monday night darkness fell on the Common once more. Harsh and cold, and dark. The Common, like all commons across England, was a wild patch of green growing unruly, and for that reason it had never seen the artificial light of a streetlamp along its intricate network of footpaths. It had always been pitch dark in Wimbledon Common since the dawn of time, but now, towards the north end, a halo of floodlights organised in a nice perfect circle beamed down at the New Wimbledon Windmill, making the new modern structure and its hazy aura visible from all directions. Two security guards looked at it and wondered if it was visible from space. They were both getting ready to start their security routine for the seventeenth time; they had been doing so since restoration works started on the windmill. Alberyx Enterprises had given them a temporary office in the low building by the windmill. From there, on the hour, they would walk out in the car park and follow an imaginary perimeter around the windmill anti-clockwise until they made a full circle. They would then reach the entrance to the windmill; check each floor twice where the machinery was silent, dormant. The top floor was locked and off-limits, and the two guards had to check each time the security lock had not been tampered with or review the log entries to see if there had been any unauthorised entry since the last tour. It was a routine set by the chief engineer, John Crane, who was the only one allowed up there and the logs showed his last entry on Sunday evening. The routine concluded with their exit from the windmill, an inspection of the empty car park and then back inside the low building to enjoy some warmth before the next security tour.

The top floor of the windmill had one tiny oval window facing south. The moon in the cold, starless sky, beamed through it as the only source of natural light. A bearded man leaned towards the window to read the instructions. It was important not to turn on the only two neon lights present to avoid catching the attention of the security guards as they walked past below. He even had to keep his flashlight turned off, which made his work even more complicated. He scratched his head under the black beanie and glanced at the ominous machine covering half of the tiny top floor of the windmill. It was bigger than anything he had ever seen, even bigger than their previous feat. The bearded man shivered at the thought. The complexity of the 'brain' of the New Wimbledon Windmill scared him and even the mysterious name printed on the surface in between controls and touchscreens reinforced his distrust towards it.

THE OSCILLATOR
Alberyx Enterprises Ltd.

With a deep sigh, he read the instructions and held the USB flash drive in his hand in front of him. He had done this once already and yet he had to be sure he was doing it properly again. John Crane had been an unfortunate spanner in the works, with everyone wondering what had happened to him. The bearded man himself knew he could no longer mask log entries to the top floor with a copy of Crane's badge; now that the chief engineer had disappeared it would look highly suspicious, and he did not want Alberyx Enterprises to beef up security more than they had already done. Alternative means of entry had to be found. The bearded man stretched. His shoulders still ached from the way he had managed to access the top floor of the windmill a few moments ago.

His boss, Lord Awlthorp, had hoped Crane would be well away from the effects of the Oscillator, and yet the chief engineer had been hit, including his girlfriend, Fran. Lord Awlthorp's first hack of the Oscillator had worked as expected but their cover for the week ahead had been seriously compromised. Lord Awlthorp had hardly contained his displeasure with the bearded man when they met earlier that day. His corvine eyes did not betray his annoyance at the collateral damage he would have to deal with. Those eyes looked different; they were darker each time the bearded man looked into them. An uneasy feeling of viciousness seemed to brew in the depths of Lord Awlthorp's soul.

The bearded man shook his head and focused on the matter at hand. He read the instructions once more and then moved to the Oscillator control desk which was beeping colourful dots in the quietness of the room. He turned two knobs then slid his index finger upwards on the left side of a touchscreen. The prompt asked for the USB flash drive and the bearded man put it into the slot below the touchscreen as requested. The shiny maroon colour of the USB casing had a sinister look and a strange feel to the touch. It was not plastic or any other metal but a thin and rubbery material, dry and grainy to the touch. The bearded man had struggled to recognise it. The moment he inserted it, the rows of characters started running wild across the screen by themselves. The man watched the program run its course and checked his watch. He had to make the phone call soon; timings were of the essence for the program to work. Lord Awlthorp had insisted on following this protocol by the letter. The bearded man had agreed, knowing the litany by heart before they had even completed the first test. Yet, he had no other choice but to do what he was told.

The phone vibrated in the back pocket of his black slacks. It was the boss, unexpectedly.

'Yes sir?' he answered.

'Almost done there?' hissed Lord Awlthorp, impatiently. 'Do not engage the thrust until the guards are back in the low building!'

'I can't see them from here. You should have let me drug them, so I could focus without a worry.'

'And raise more suspicion? Everyone's eyes are on the windmill now since they revealed it today. Don't waste any more time, Reggie, and tell me when you are ready!'

The nickname he hated resurfaced, and Reginald Bosham had to swallow his pride.

'As far as I am concerned, I've done what was asked of me: I pressed the button. I don't understand any of these letters on the screen, and to be honest I'd rather not know. Let Operator One carry on with it once I've made the call!'

'Don't wash your hands of the matter, Reggie!' warned Lord Awlthorp. 'Careful what you do, or you can say goodbye to your paid parole!'

Reginald imagined Lord Awlthorp's eyes, now narrowed to a slit, pointing at him with severity. He swallowed hard hoping not to upset him any further. His employer, Lord Awlthorp, had become worse since the last time he worked for him. Paranoid, obsessed, distrustful, checking every single thing he did, casting a heavy shadow over him, all-present, all-powerful, all-evil. Reginald brushed his long beard, a reminder of his time in jail. He had not shaved it since he stepped foot in prison, and even now he was hesitant to do so. Lord Awlthorp had bailed him out somehow before his sentence was over. Reginald had been jailed for being an accomplice to what the Claymores did and the lawyers had done a good job to minimise the sentence, but Lord Awlthorp needed him. Reginald could not say no to the opportunity to get out of prison. On second thoughts, though, his boss was no longer the same as he was the last time he saw him. Something had changed.

'Time to start the treasure hunt, Reginald.' said Lord Awlthorp interrupting his thoughts. 'Call Operator One at the Repeater. Everything is now online. You know we are finally close!'

Reginald did not know, really. He did not grasp any of Lord Awlthorp's convoluted plan. If the first two attempts had been the first steps towards something, Reginald had not seen any change whatsoever. He deemed Lord Awlthorp to be a dangerous madman, and he did not trust Operator One. He was bothered that another person, conveniently called Operator One, was involved in their plans. Reginald was not fond of the idea; the earlier he got out, the better.

'Yes, sir!' confirmed Reginald without thinking.

'Report back once done!'

Lord Awlthorp ended the call. Reginald sighed and listened for any footsteps on the lower floors. He heard a creak from the second floor. The guards were right below him. He waited. He then played with a few more buttons and a few lights blinked and flashed. Then the characters on the screen stopped self-typing, and the Oscillator made a low buzzing noise which finished with a loud ping. Reginald froze. Footsteps carried on below, a bit uncertain, a bit undecisive, until they faded away. Reginald gave a sigh of relief. He forgot about the loud ping. He then grabbed his phone again and called Operator One.

'It's ready!' said Reginald. 'I started the Oscillator and all is ready for you to complete the process.'

'Not even a "hello"?' mocked Operator One on the other line. 'You need to improve your social skills!'

'This is not a courtesy call, Operator One. I trust you are ready to run your part of the computer code?'

'I am.' confirmed Operator One with a curt reply, suddenly void of emotions.

'Good. I connected the USB, and the programme is all set. Ready?'

'Yes, I am. My own USB is ready too to upload the commands.'

'Then go!' ordered Reginald.

He ended the call, and the windmill was still quiet. Reginald knew Operator One had done what was meant to be done when he saw shadows scrambling around the room and an electric spark from the top of the windmill lashed at the starless sky outside. Reginald pulled his black hoody over his head, looking for safety. His eyes glinted with fear as the Oscillator came to life at the top of the windmill.

Ken was late. He was seriously late. He had been playing rugby all evening and realised it was later than expected. His mum would not be happy. She was never happy when he came home past the curfew of ten in the evening. He had to take a serious gamble and take the quickest route home. Either walk down Copse Hill to Coombe Lane and wait for the bus that would take him all around the hill or cut through the Common up to Robin Hood Way and then across until he reached West Hill, where he lived. The latter was much quicker, and he could jog or even run it once he was on Robin Hood Way. He was fit enough. He looked around the rugby fields by the Beverly Brook river. They were empty now and his teammates had already disappeared beyond the fences to the south, down the slope that would take them to Coombe Lane. A soft mist had risen above the rugby grounds and the clouds gave a patchy view of the half-risen moon. It was cold, bloody cold. Ken picked up his gear and walked to the northern border of the fields, crossed a tiny bridge over a minor stream and stepped into the overgrowth of the Common, under the thick foliage of the high oaks, maples and beeches. The open space of the rugby fields was soon a distant memory as Ken walked deeper into the Common. He took the path alongside the eastern shore of the Beverly Brook river, finding comfort in the gurgling sound of water giving him company. He took his flashlight out. Even though the path was clear and well beaten, the last thing he wanted was to trip over something.

The mist had followed him from the rugby fields. It had now spread to this part of the Common and it had thickened around Ken's feet. Ken wrapped his coat tighter feeling the cold humidity rising all of a sudden. There was a gust of wind from the east. The branches shook lightly and the leaves trembled. Ken shifted his thoughts to something else, the rugby, that cute girl from his class. He walked a bit further and then he heard horses neighing. It was a faint noise, but it grew louder with the sound of a gentle trot. Horses were not allowed as far as this side of the Common, especially at night. Maybe they had escaped from the riding school in Wimbledon Village. He looked around and all he could see was trees, dead branches and mist.

By now, the mist had become an impenetrable fog and Ken's flashlight struggled to pierce through it. Half-swallowed trees and branches vaguely emerged through it, as if they were dying arms of drowned men and women crying out to him for help. Ken shivered. He picked up his pace, feeling scared. He flashed the light ahead where he was hoping to see the crossroad with Robin Hood Way at any moment. The neighing was still there in the background, somewhere deep in the woods. Suddenly, Ken felt something funny going on in his hair, as if being pulled and standing on its own. Some kind of static electricity wrapped itself around him, on his light skin hair, on the fabric of his winter clothes. The fog intensified, and Ken's flashlight became useless against a grey wall of fog rising well above his head. Ken panicked. He had no idea what was going on. The horses he kept hearing had now broken into a fast gallop, and they appeared to be in front of him, coming his way through the same path at rushed speed. Ken stopped and steadied himself. He was about to flee back to where he had come from when a group of men on horses jumped out of the fog.

'What the…?'

Ken flashed the light onto them. They wore weird clothes, bulky around the upper body, with a mantle wrapped over their shoulders, and a greyish tunic running mid-length to just above the knee. Trousers were of the same dull colour ending with a pair of short brown leather boots filthy with mud. The horses were running fast, like crazy, but the riders pulled their reins just in time and the horses raised their front hoofs a few inches from Ken's incredulous face. The riders also looked puzzled, surprised to see the boy in the middle of the path, wearing a strange puffy cloak over his torso and arms. The strange light coming from his hand scared them and they quickly shouted angry words at Ken who could not pick up or understand. The neighing of the horses drowned all the sounds. The horsemen looked at each other feeling threatened. They held bows in their hands and without hesitation they took one arrow each and aimed at Ken, shouting even more incomprehensible words.

'Don't shoot!' Ken pleaded.

The boy feared for his life and pleaded with the strange men not to hurt him, but the riders' hard faces were not listening. They barked angrier words and for a moment Ken thought they spoke some kind of variation of the English language that sounded more like German, but still beyond recognition. Then the arrows were released onto Ken despite his pleads of mercy, and he screamed at the top of his lungs. He was hit by a sudden hot wind in the face before falling into oblivion.

Richard looked at the superposition manometer under the headlight fixed across his forehead. It was an odd device he had never seen before. An invention of Julian Alberon's and his scientific team, he supposed. He did not know what the manometer did, but he knew perfectly how to tune it according to the specification received earlier that day. What he did not take into consideration was how long it would take to adjust. His colleague, Phil, had been smarter and left bang on time after five o'clock, leaving him with the brunt of finishing the work John Crane was meant to do. Typical, thought Richard. He glanced at his watch. It was almost ten o'clock. He yawned as he twisted and turned the mechanism into the required settings. He was almost done. It was getting late though and knowing it was night outside, made him even more scared to be stuck alone inside the tight scaffolding of the Repeater. Alone. He told himself he would be on his way home soon, able to get back to his living quarters on Warren Farms and perhaps enjoy a quick beer before bed.

He ran one check, two checks. The manometer was fine. John Crane's notes were clear enough. There was no chance of error, although he would have preferred it if the chief engineer had been around to do it himself and sign off the changes. John was the man of the hour, but on the key date when everyone needed him at the Repeater, he did not turn up at work. He actually had not turned up for any of the events he was meant to attend. Only in the early afternoon had Warren Farms told them he was off sick. How convenient, Richard thought. He then sighed. He was just a trainee mechanical engineer. Nobody would care to listen to his opinion. For now, he wanted to get things done and go home.

He grabbed his tools and climbed down the short ladder to the exit door at ground level. A few of the machine components buzzed and fizzled. Richard stopped and looked around. He found it odd. The noise and the strange electrical activity. He waited. Nothing. He shrugged and switched the light off before stepping out of the scaffolding into the cold night.

Once outside, Richard fumbled in his pocket but found it empty. He could have sworn he had picked up a torch light from the office. He cursed under his breath and pulled up his coat collar to keep the cold out. He would have to follow the hazy green light from the fire exit sign hung above one of the temporary pop-up offices. The short journey across already appeared treacherous as the fog seemed to have devoured the patch of rough grass between him and the nearest office. He treaded carefully so as not to stumble and fall. His mind ran through the lockup procedure before leaving the site. The keys. The alarm. Yes, he had not forgotten the pin. The lights. He glimpsed into the hazy distance. There was a faint light next to the fire exit sign. A desk light was on inside the office, coming through the window. It had not been the case before, Richard wondered. He frowned trying to remember. He heard some static, followed by the low murmur of a voice coming from inside. He thought he had better check it out before they put the blame on him for leaving the site unchecked and unsafe. There were dangerous people out there, like those protesters from earlier that morning.

The trainee engineer walked the short distance back to the office. The soft mist had swirled around the site in the shape of a hurricane. The top of the shrubs barely peeked out over the mist, almost as if being suffocated. After only a few steps, the mist had grown in intensity, becoming denser, thicker, and Richard's visibility was suddenly so poor he could barely make out the shape of the office a few steps ahead. The faint light from the windows had faded away into the cold, dark fog. He now heard faint cries echoing around him. It sounded as if someone was crying and then realised they were more like cheers. It could not have been a party at the golf club, he thought; he was too far away for him to hear anything. As he walked on, he hoped they were not protesters. The mist turned to fog in no time, advancing relentless, and the world around him soon disappeared. A fuzzy feeling of static electricity pricked Richard's hair at the top and back down to the back of his neck. He rubbed his head, and he could feel goose bumps on his skin. Richard remained baffled. None of the electro-magnetic components of the Repeater were on. He had shut off everything, but the more he tried to assure himself the more he doubted. In the meantime, the cheers in the distance grew louder. They were now coming from the north-west, in the opposite direction from the golf club, but now the cheers sounded like cries. Harsh snarls and muffled growls echoing in the dead of night. Richard shivered. He squinted in the direction of the cries trying to make out what on earth it was but he could see nothing through the thick fog. They sounded as if they were right behind the grey wall of fog.

'Anybody out there?' called out Richard, frightened.

A door slammed shut. Richard looked back, lost and scared. He turned round a few times, then he stopped. He had lost his sense of orientation. He should be right in front of the office, but the fire exit sign had faded away too, and Richard only saw endless fog all around him. Then the cries and shouts materialised in front of him as shadows started emerging from the fog. Rows of men with medium-long hair and short badly cut beards, appeared at the edge of Richard's visibility range. They held rudimental spears made of sticks and stones. There was one row of men after another, but Richard could not see them all. It was a whole army of them. The men looked badly nurtured and unkempt; their constant cheering turned out to be chants of war. They looked like angry warmongers staring at a vicious enemy as they prepared to crush them. More loud cries came from behind Richard. The scared engineer made a hundred and eighty degree turn just in time to see more hordes of savage men, dressed in rags and bearing sticks and stones. They stood on the opposite side of a clearing in a middle of a forest, which Richard did not recognise. The office, the Repeater, they were gone. Then a voice cried what appeared to be call to arms and the horde of savage men raced towards him. Richard looked over his shoulder. The rows of warmongers were still close behind him, spears at the ready, waiting to clash with the approaching enemy. It was a charge; no matter how surreal, it was a charge. Richard waved his hands at them with no reaction; it was as if they could not see him. Richard could not believe it. It is a nightmare, he thought; I must have just fallen and hit my head. He closed his eyes and reopened them. The hordes of warmongers were coming closer and closer. He closed his eyes again and reopened them once more. The last thing he saw was the pointy edge of a spear at arm's distance, but before the mass of warriors crushed him, a strong hot wind hit him in the face and Richard fell into oblivion.

'Turn it off!' ordered Reginald when enough time had passed.

'It is off!' said the voice of Operator One panting over the phone.

'Everything ok? You sound breathless!'

'I was almost caught by the triangulation, you idiot.'

'What can I say? Too slow.'

There was mockery in Reginald's voice.

'Shut up!' bit back Operator One. 'I had to be careful not to be spotted when leaving the office. I'm sure I was not alone at the site of the Repeater. There was someone inside the scaffolding.'

'What? Are you sure?'

Reginald was not pleased to hear of more possible collateral damage.

'As much as I can be.' argued Operator One. 'I was not going to stay behind and ask questions.'

Reginald huffed.

'Do you have your USB key with you?' he then asked.

'Yes.'

'Just don't leave traces of your actions.' reminded Reginald. 'Now, follow standard protocol. Over and out!'

Reginald ended the call and waited for a few seconds looking at the graphs shown on the touchscreen of the Oscillator. He wondered which news he would break to Lord Awlthorp first. The results showed the signal had been captured. This was good news. If Lord Awlthorp's crazy instructions made any sense, it meant they now had a better approximation of the location. Another triangulation before the week was over would point out where to search exactly. Reginald could not care less. It was a job like any other. This time, though, he knew that when the job was done, it meant he was getting closer to the day when he would no longer owe anything to Lord Awlthorp and he would finally be a free man.

The burly man stroked his beard. One thing troubled him. If Operator One was right, there may have been another casualty from the triangulation. He darned the poor souls who walked through the Common at this time of night. Reginald hoped it would not complicate plans too much or alter his boss's already precarious mood.

Lord Awlthorp sat in his studio alone, tapping his fingers on the desk while staring at the board in front of him. The scribbled notes and the sketched drawings had multiplied over the last few months, taking over every inch of the board's surface, and at times overlapping old, outdated pieces of information Lord Awlthorp was not willing to throw away. Working with the past had been a treacherous road for him, until now.

The biggest part of the board was a large map of Wimbledon hill, with the village in the lower right corner and the expanse of Wimbledon Common stretching across the rest of the map, until it met the slanted border with the A3 motorway to the north and the Beverly Brook river to the west. Wimbledon Common was the largest heath in London, a wild mix of shrubland and wetland growing unruly across its one thousand plus acres. It laid over the entire Wimbledon plateau rolling down from Wimbledon Village towards the Thames. The plateau was a large mass of clay with an acidic topsoil which had made it hard for cultivation ever since the dawn of time. The Common was indeed a large wasteland, to use the words of the Spencer family and all the medieval books he had found in their vault on the subject. Lord Awlthorp, however, was not interested in geography lessons. For him, the map in his studio had become a sort of treasure map with no directions. The red strings pinned and stretched across different locations on the map were the result of his work in trying to find the third relic of the Wynnman. A dagger of some sort. The archaeologists at the Old Rectory had come to the same conclusion and Lord Awlthorp felt the race was on. Before he knew it, others could be on the trail of the Wynnman. He had to be quick and fortunately he was lucky to have a head start. Lord Awlthorp gave a wicked smile, made even more sinister by the diffused orange glow from the desk lamp.

The dagger was buried somewhere in the Common. Searching for it by using old means was impossible. Lord Awlthorp did not have the time or the resources to dig up or scan the entire Common. Alberyx Enterprises technology had been a God send he had been more than happy to tap into, undetected. The triangulation scan he had been able to hack into had worked the night before and hopefully it would do the same tonight. One or two more triangulations to improve accuracy and the location of the dagger's site would be revealed to him. Lord Awlthorp joined his gloved hands and rubbed them together, savouring the moment as his eyes glinted with greed. Power and revenge. Even Simon Deeley had said it in the presentation at Eagle House: whoever found all seven relics of the Wynnman would have the power to control the world and bend nature to their will. Power and revenge. Revenge for being imprisoned unjustly by an ignorant mass of low-life villagers. Just the thought of that reminded Lord Awlthorp what this would mean for him and Wimbledon.

'Wimbledon one day will regain its glory…' he muttered in the penumbra.

His phone vibrated on the desk. It was Reginald reporting the result.

'Hello, Reggie! Are you the bearer of good news?' he asked maliciously.

Reginald swallowed hard. He had to give the good first.

'Triangulation is done and has just been sent. The results should be on your laptop now.'

Lord Awlthorp opened his small laptop on the desk. The blue tinted screen brightened the room. There it was. The results were promising.

'I can see we are getting closer to the right point in time, Reginald. That leaves us only half of the Common to explore.'

'Well, that narrows it down…' chuckled Reginald, trying to ease the tension for when he had to break the bad news.

'Don't be a fool, Reggie. The state-of-the-art technology Alberyx Enterprises has built has just found a new purpose…other than wireless electricity.'

Lord Awlthorp scoffed at the idea.

'With the help of Operator One, we put into practice a theory deemed impossible by anyone.'

'You mean the theory we also stole from Alberyx Enterprises?'

'Borrowed, Reggie, and do mind your attitude if you don't want to go back to the slammer!'

'Yes, sir' subdued Reginald. 'There is something else.'

'What is it?' snapped Lord Awlthorp.

'We probably have another collateral damage to deal with.'

Lord Awlthorp stayed silent and closed his eyes, channelling his rage. First John Crane and his girlfriend Fran Ludley. Now someone else. The more people caught in the triangulation, the more they would be exposed. He did not need any more obstacles between him and his goal. He would have his hands on the dagger by the end of the week, before the windmill went live and operational.

'Do we know who this person is?' asked Lord Awlthorp.

'No, sir.' replied Reginald.

'Find out, Reginald! Ask Operator Two to investigate immediately!'

'Do you trust Operator Two? In my opinion sir, neither Operator One nor Operator Two are to be trusted.'

'Do you wish to go and find out yourself, Reggie? Go out there and show your face in Wimbledon after what happened?'

The question felt unanswered. Reginald knew he could not walk easily around Wimbledon. His beard and his beanie hat were not enough to disguise him after his picture had been on all the papers.

'Get Operator Two on the case! Now!'

'Yessir! When will the next triangulation be?'

'Wednesday. I need to look at the results more closely. See the patterns.'

The call between the two ended abruptly. Lord Awlthorp stood up and stretched his back. He then massaged one of his gloved hands. He pulled one glove off and stared at the black veins of scars wrapping his entire hand since the accident. He was no longer scared of them. He knew what they meant.

It was close to midnight and time to get the rest he needed. Lord Awlthorp swiftly left the studio to get into his lab. In the middle of it, there was his concentration room, a cubic windowless room. It had always been his place of meditation. Yet, recently, it had become an inner sanctum where he could listen to the voice inside his head. He quickly printed out the results of the triangulation. Laptop or any technological device was no longer allowed in the concentration room. He held the printed results in his hand and then moved inside the cubic room, closing the pressure door behind him. The red candle on the ivory desk was still burning from an earlier session, only melted half-way with hardened drops of wax on the desk. Its flame flickered and the shadows danced erratically against the walls. Apart from the desk, the room was bare. Lord Awlthorp sat at the ivory desk. He put the printed results on the desk and then both his hands flat on the surface. He closed his eyes. He breathed in and out deeply, focusing on the breathing, slowing it down, relaxing every single muscle of his body. He quickly lost sense of the world outside and it was only a matter of minutes before he made contact. The inside of the cubicle went cold, and the candle flickered. A swirl of silvery mist rose above Lord Awlthorp's right shoulder. He knew the great sorcerer was there with him. Then it happened. His hand, scarred by the burns from the Old Rectory, started to throb with pain. Lord Awlthorp gritted his teeth and dropped his head low to endure the pain as he always did. The pain was the sacrifice to be able to speak to the Wynnman.

'Yes...' said a voice. 'Here...'

'The results are here.' said Lord Awlthorp.

There was some silence. Lord Awlthorp imagined the voice looking over his shoulder like a floating silver spectre watching his every move or decision.

'Good…' said the voice. 'You are getting closer…'

'How close? Why not tell me where the dagger is? Isn't that what you need?'

'I am not strong enough…'

The voice faded in and out, still feeble.

'What do you need?'

'I am prisoner, still… The seven symbols hold me prisoner…'

'Do you mean the seven relics? Where are they?'

The voice coughed and left Lord Awlthorp's question unanswered.

'One will lead me to the other…'

Lord Awlthorp had been a believer right from the start and he was living proof the Wynnman's voice had asked him for help. Help to find him. Help to free him. The voice of the Wynnman had started speaking to Lord Awlthorp after the accidents at the Old Rectory, as if part of the sorcerer's spirit had been able to bridge the gap between the real world and an unknown world beyond. And the Wynnman had chosen him, his one and only follower when everything led to believe he did not exist. Now, things had changed. If the legend of the seven relics was true, the black azalea had woken up the mind of the Wynnman and the crimson liquid had resurrected his dead flesh inside Lord Awlthorp as his host. The dagger was the next relic to infuse blood into the Wynnman's flesh and muscles. Lord Awlthorp would slowly bring him to life, stronger than ever, and the Wynnman would reward him with his power.

'Power and revenge.' said Lord Awlthorp.

'Power… Revenge…' repeated the voice, marked with a malicious and vindictive, and yet subdued, fatigued. 'I will… restore… what was taken from me… from Wimbledon…'

'We will restore.' joined in Lord Awlthorp with trepidation. 'You can trust me. What I need to do to find the dagger?'

'The dagger…' muttered the voice of the Wynnman, getting weaker. 'The dagger is close to the source of life… Come and find me!'

'The Pool of Elixir?' guessed Lord Awlthorp.

'No… The source of life…'

The voice became weaker until it was only a faint echo, and then it was gone. Lord Awlthorp opened his eyes and the vivid flame of the candle shone in them. The printed piece of paper on the desk had some dark stains all over it. At a closer look, they appeared to be words written in dry blood. Lord Awlthorp gasped as he saw blood dripping from his gloved hand. He grabbed a handkerchief in his pocket and wrapped his wrist. He found it strange there was no pain, just like the previous times it happened. His hand had been the ultimate sacrifice. He winced at the memory and then gazed at the printed piece of paper. The Wynnman had left another clue for him. A line of unintelligible characters had been written below the printed text. Unintelligible for the untrained eye, but Lord Awlthorp recognised the Anglo-Saxon runes he had learnt to interpret. Another set of coordinates, more complex. He had to hand these over to Reginald and in turn to Operator One as soon as possible so that they could implement it in the computer code. Renewed strength pulsed inside Lord Awlthorp. The closer he was getting to the relic, the stronger his bond with the Wynnman was becoming. Strong enough to win his powers. With the help of Alberyx Enterprises technology, he was about to break the boundaries between reality and a world beyond, between fact and fiction. All for Wimbledon's glory.

Julian Alberon woke up in his bed in a pool of sweat. He thought he had had a nightmare although he could not remember it well. He was being chased by someone or something, before falling over into a crimson river. He turned on the bedside lamp and felt a sting of pain in his scarred hand. The glove he wore at night was a light, silky one. The thought of letting the scarred tissue touch the bed sheets did not appeal to him. He sat on the edge of the bed, holding his hand. There was nothing wrong with it. No swelling, no bleeding. Just a twinge of pain now slowly receding.

The alarm clock showed it was early morning. He needed more sleep after the previous day, which hadn't always gone for the best. Images of Basil "Wilberforce" Elders, the press conference and Eagle House, flashed in his head and almost crashed together in a loud bang. Some form of migraine was about to hit him hard. He needed more sleep. He had to rest. Follow Mr Sanders's advice. He got up and walked to the bathroom to find some sleeping pills in the cabinet. His face in the mirror looked thin and drawn. He had better get some sleep right now or he would not be in best shape for the end of the week.

The lights above the mirror cabinet in the bathroom flickered. Julian popped a couple of pills and looked once more at his face in the mirror. He noticed something had shifted above his right shoulder. Behind him, just outside the en-suite bathroom, the door to his walk-in wardrobe was open. A shape stood in the penumbra.

'Who's there?' gasped Julian spinning around and grabbing the toothbrush holder.

At that moment, fear came over him. If Basil 'Wilberforce' Elders could infiltrate anywhere, there was nothing stopping him or his followers from scaring him in his own house.

'I know you are one of Basil's men…' cried out Julian in vain.

The shadow did not move. It blended in with the darkness, with glints of silver floating enigmatically in mid-air. Julian blinked, unsure if he were just talking to an empty closet. He branded the toothbrush as a weapon, at the height of his chest.

'I am about to call security…' he warned.

'You need to stop him…' whispered the shadow.

'Stop who?' challenged Julian without dropping his guard.

'He will ruin everything…' the shadow spoke again. 'He will destroy you…'

The businessman faltered forward, crossing the threshold of the bathroom door. His eyes tried to adjust to the lighting and still the shadow was a shapeless blotch in front of him.

'Who is there?' Julian called out.

The shadow did not reply.

'I am warning you!' spat Julian, impatiently.

Julian pounced and swung the toothbrush holder as if it were a club. He hit nothing and lost his balance, falling forward against a line of hanging clothes. Julian blinked. There was nobody in the closet. Julian groaned and blamed his lack of sleep for acting in such a stupid way. Nobody was after him to kill him. Yet, the words he thought he had heard rang in his head like a broken record.

He returned to his bed and laid wide awake for some time, staring at the ceiling. His thoughts stuck to the words he had just heard, filled with dread. 'He will ruin everything'. 'He will destroy you'. Julian did not understand what they meant. He thought it best to call his doctor tomorrow.

He did not fall asleep straight away. His mind drifted to the presentation at Eagle House. Julian was pleased to hear what Simon Deeley and Dr Watkins had found through their research. He then recalled the chat with Mr Sanders, trying to calm him down. They had heard someone outside rushing down the corridor. Julian remembered them stepping out of the office and seeing Enrico in the far distance. The Italian baker was always around. Always. However, he thought none of it and fell back to sleep.

Dr Watkins woke up in his plastic resin chair, slouching over the counter. Something had woken him up. Perhaps a dream or a nightmare. He was still fully clothed. He felt a crack in his back as he sat up from the uncomfortable position. He squinted around the white lab. The only light was a desk lamp with its spotlight fixed on books and reports scattered on the counter. To the far left he could make out the shape of the black azalea-shaped lava rock and just next to it the old Cecils' wine bottle with the dregs of crimson liquid. His equipment, his shelves, and the rest of the room were all swallowed in darkness. The curator could not tell what time it was. He had fallen asleep and had lost track of time. Surely, it was the early hours of the morning after probably falling asleep while reading something the night before. It had happened many times in the last few months. Coming back from the Old Rectory always meant catching up on some findings, some reports, some old folklore books. Even after coming back from Eagle House last night, Dr Watkins felt the urge to look up a few topics that had been nagging at him lately.

Piles of old books were stacked up in front of him. In the middle of one pile, one book had been left wide open on a double page about Anglo-Saxon legends and mythology. Dr Watkins forced himself to remember what he had been reading and glanced at the open book on his desk. He thought he could see dragons and warriors beckoning at him from the still pages, framed in the replicas of gilded medieval manuscripts. Dr Watkins chuckled to himself. He had been reading too much about Anglo-Saxon mythology and historical facts. His mind was now invaded with the terrifying fantasies of early medieval folklore. Enrico and Viviane were probably right in saying he should be sleeping more instead of working so much.

Dr Watkins was about to put the book back and call it a night when his eyes fell on a small detail on the open pages. The medieval text and drawings he had been looking at could not have been clearer in telling the story of a 'magic man', a sorcerer who terrorised villagers on the hill. Even though no names were mentioned, Dr Watkins recognised a pattern very much like the myth of the Wynnman he had rejected so many times as a fairy tale and pure folklore and was now forced to support with Simon. In the old book, there was a reference to one of the 'sacred mounds' where the villagers went into hiding from the sorcerer. The images alongside the text showed a man in rags pointing at a wooden fort built on an earth mound. All the elements were disproportionate in size, with no consideration of depth. The fort was in flames with large heads sticking out from small windows, shrieking in pain. The sorcerer looked at the scene with a hand raised at it. He held something pointy in his hand. Dr Watkins took the magnifying glass. It could have been a disproportionate skinny index finger. On taking a closer look, though, he thought it could have been a blade. A dagger. The dagger. The third relic. Dr Watkins sighed in disbelief. He was now a believer. All these years he had scorned at the fairy tale as a made-up story but now he could no longer ignore the evidence rising to the surface. The facts suggested someone very powerful had existed, and such an individual may have indeed left behind what was possibly the largest collection of pre-Christian relics in the Wimbledon area, assuming these seven relics were still intact, and still buried under the acid soil of Wimbledon Village.

The curator raised his eyes, thoughtful. He knew the 'sacred mound' could only be Caesar's Camp. He did not need Simon to remind him of that. Prehistoric evidence had shown burial mounds present in the area of the Wimbledon hill plateau since the Bronze Age as it was common all across Neolithic Britain. These mounds had been used over millennia by later civilisations. The Romans, the Anglo-Saxons, the Vikings and even the Normans; they used it as burial mounds or turned them into the forts. Caesar's Camp was the only one spared by Wimbledon's urban expansion. He could not disagree with Simon's theory but digging up Caesar's Camp was not an easy feat. Lord Cotton and the RWGC would not allow it simply based on a hunch. In fact, Simon's new theory was just that. Yet, the Scottish archaeologist would not relent. Last night already Simon had asked for an update, twice on the same day. Dr Watkins had no choice but to talk to Lord Cotton. He was meeting him tomorrow with Enrico for lunch, and perhaps it would be the best time to do so.

A thud distracted his thoughts. Dr Watkins looked around the silent white lab, shrouded in the shadows.

'Hello?' called out the curator.

No answer. Dr Watkins's imagination ran wild for a moment. His mind drifted back to the drawings, and those scary pictures of demonic monsters, evil sorcerers and brave warriors.

'Is someone there?' he called out again, a little queasy.

The curator remembered something had woken him up. He closed his eyes to think better. He tried to remember the dream he had just had while asleep. His memory was hazy, cramped with visions and other contorted imagery. The tunnels, the crimson river, running, drowning. Whether it was a dream or perhaps a distant memory, Dr Watkins could not tell. He then remembered seeing a human presence. It was a shadow in the background calling to him, with a deep and low voice. Dr Watkins opened his eyes and for a moment he thought he could see a shadow in the deepest corner of the room. He rubbed his eyes, wondering if he were still dreaming.

'Did you find the Wynnman?' asked the shadow.

'Who are you?' Dr Watkins asked.

The shadow stood motionless, and the curator was puzzled whether the voice came from the dark silhouette. A silver halo ran feebly around the outline of the shadow. The lack of light made it more surreal. A spectral vision in the darkness. Dr Watkins shuddered.

'Do you remember?' said the shadow again.

'Remember what?'

'Remember the Wynnman… You need to find him!'

Dr Watkins gasped. He suddenly felt a sting of pain in his scarred hand. It had not hurt in a while and now the pain was stronger than ever, just like days after the accident at the Old Rectory. The curator cowered and held his wrist tight, staring at the scars. It was as if they were pulsing. He was not sure if he was imagining everything. He screwed his eyes up until the pain in his scarred hand receded. When Dr Watkins finally opened his eyes in the solitude of the white lab, the shadow seemed to have gone.

Enrico's first feeling was one of national pride to know his Roman ancestors had come all the way to Wimbledon. Dr Watkins had to correct him more than once and warn him not to be fooled by the genitive 'Caesar's'. The Romans never settled in Wimbledon, as it had been historically proven many times. No signs of baths or forums or even walls like in Bath or Chester. The name Caesar's Camp was actually a nickname dating back to the early nineteenth Century when used for the first time by a London mapseller.

'Is this it?' replied Enrico disappointed after following where Dr Watkins was pointing at.

Not only did the Caesar's Camp have nothing to do with Caesar. The place itself had nothing special about it. If he had walked near it or over it, he would not have even noticed it. All he could see from the footpath running between hole six and seven of the Royal Wimbledon Golf Club was an uneven depression cutting across the fairway and part of the woodlands of the Common.

'Yes. Can you see the rampart, that raised edge over there?' explained Dr Watkins.

'I don't see anything, Dr Watkins. You said a mound is some form of raised hilltop with a ditch around it. I don't see any hill here, just a stretch of undulating terrain.'

'That's because it has eroded over time. It was a large circular mound of raised earth with ramparts all around, of which you can see the shallow signs from one section here. Over the centuries, as the mound flattened and the ramparts were levelled, it had become an invisible trace of Wimbledon's pre-Roman history.'

'How big was it?'

'If you look at the aerial photo I have here, it is quite big.'

The curator handed it over to Enrico. The photo was in black and white, showing a distinct circular moat-like imprint almost carved out of the Common's grounds. Its surface covered an impressive large area of what was now the Royal Wimbledon Golf Club. The mysterious circle was cut in half, right in the middle, by the footpath where Enrico and Dr Watkins stood in. However, if it was not for Dr Watkins's historical wisdom and for a nice stone plaque devoured by overgrown plants, Enrico would have never known of the existence of Caesar's Camp.

'What was it then?' asked the Italian baker tilting his head left and right. 'A fort? A Roman fort?'

'You are not paying attention, Enrico! Caesar never came here so forget the Romans. Even though we found some Roman coins, its shape does not match their military style. It probably acted as some sort of fort in an older past. We are talking about evidence we found here which goes back to the Iron and the Bronze age, around 1500 BC maybe.'

'Wow! And they built a golf course on it?' commented Enrico with a grin. 'Damage to historical heritage. You should be furious about it!'

'That was before my time.' replied Dr Watkins. 'The land was already private property before the Royal Wimbledon Golf Club bought it. Most of the levelling is due to the careless act of John Samuel Drax, owner of the Old Park in the early nineteenth Century, when he had the brilliant idea to build houses here. He was stopped in time, thanks to the newly founded Wimbledon and Putney Common Conservators, the WPCC, but by the time they arrived, Drax had already levelled most of it and there was nothing to be done about it. Drax caused more damage in half a day than natural erosion. Fine example of why today there is a strict regulation in defence of the Common. It justifies the role of the WPCC, safeguarding the conservation of Wimbledon Common since 1871.'

'Ah, I remember. You mentioned it last night. Ok, Dr Watkins, why did you bring me here this morning?'

Dr Watkins smiled with an understanding nod.

'Do you remember Simon's talk about the legend of the Wynnman and the seven relics?'

'Sure. How can I forget that I named my bakery after an evil sorcerer?' joked Enrico. 'Well, it goes to prove that Wimbledon's original name, *Wimbedounyng*, which means 'Wynnman's Hill', is indeed a reference to a person who really existed and played a bigger role than we thought.'

'I find it amusing that you didn't believe in legends a few months ago and now you are all over this. Ok. Wynnman. Seven relics. What does this have to do with Caesar's Camp?'

'Simon thinks there is more to discover. When reading the reference of a local shelter, or fort, where the villagers hid from danger, we quickly thought Caesar's Camp as fitting the bill. Perhaps evidence about the relics is hidden underneath it. We never found anything around here, even though we were never able to dig properly around here…'

'Hold on, Dr Watkins.' interrupted Enrico, wondering what the curator may be suggesting. 'Why are you telling me this?'

'You said you saw a vision in the Pool of Elixir, didn't you?' replied the curator.

The Italian baker flinched. He was not expecting him or anyone to remind him of his experience at the Old Rectory. For once, he did not know what to say. He was not sure Dr Watkins or anyone believed him.

'Maybe… I don't know… Memory is a bit hazy now. What does this have to do with the relics and Caesar's Camp?'

'I know you saw something.' continued Dr Watkins. 'Julian and I barely survived the horrors of that devilish fire. Whatever we saw or experienced, don't you think it is linked to the Wynnman and these relics?'

The Italian baker realised for the first time he was not alone in believing there was a link.

'So, you and Simon want to dig up this part of the Common and the golf course too, because the relics may be under it?'

The curator escaped Enrico's gaze for a moment before admitting what his and Simon's intentions were.

'Do you think the timing is right?' asked Enrico playing devil's advocate. 'This area of Wimbledon is a bit heated right now, don't you think? The Repeater. Basil "Wilberforce".'

'I know, I know. But can't you see what is at stake? All I ask is that today, at lunch with Lord Cotton, you will help me to put our case forward.'

'You put me right on the spot, Dr Watkins. I don't think Anglo-Saxon relics are on his agenda. And I am sure Viviane would probably advise you and me against it! Didn't you just talk about how important the WPCC is and protecting the Common?'

'Yes, I did.' Dr Watkins was quick to reply. 'But if we don't do it, more dangerous people will come to Wimbledon and search for these relics one way or the other.'

'What do you mean?'

'We can't ignore the fact certain individuals have been searching for them already. Eric Quercer, the black azalea. The Claymore brothers, the crimson liquid.'

'You too noticed the similarities when hearing Simon's presentation?' said Enrico stupefied to hear Dr Watkins mentioning it.

'The black azalea is the flower, that is the first relic' Dr Watkins started listing. 'The crimson liquid was found in a container. That is your urn, the second relic...'

'*Piano piano*, Dr Watkins! Hold your horses!' said Enrico to stop the rush of excitement coming from the curator's words. 'Aren't you rushing things a bit?'

'I can't sleep when I think about it.' confessed Dr Watkins. 'What if the power promised by the legend of the Wynnman was in part true?'

'Don't be silly!' cautioned Enrico a little nervous. 'If this is a joke, I won't let you scare me off. It is just a legend, like you told us many times, and I am sure all this is a playful coincidence.'

The images of the pool chamber full to the brim and the shape consumed by fire returned and flashed before Enrico's eyes. The fact Dr Watkins had just mentioned that specific event, had left Enrico unsettled.

'It may be because of the things I've read. All the Anglo-Saxon folklore about monsters and warriors. What if someone else thinks the legend is not a coincidence and was, or maybe, still is looking for these relics?'

'Like who?'

'Someone who would not stop at anything in order to find them.'

'I don't think you are thinking this through properly, Dr Watkins. Who might this someone be?'

'Maybe the same person or persons who hired Eric Quercer, the Claymore brothers and Reginald Bosham.'

Octagon School was the most descriptive name anyone could have chosen. The building was small and made simply of brickwork with little or no decoration. The octagonal shape was not immediately obvious. Coming from either direction onto Camp Road it was easy to notice an odd building, but it would still take a while to realise it was octagonal, and not round or square. It had always been a school and still was, with a modern extension rising behind the octagonal building.

Nathan walked through the open gate and followed the short portico alongside the courtyard until he reached the main arched entrance. He had made an appointment first thing in the morning and Basil Elders was available to see him a little bit before lunchtime. Nathan had been vague about the purpose of the meeting. The journalist though knew his fame preceded him, and Basil 'Wilberforce' Elders was going to be prepared for any questions he may have.

The leader of the protesters was waiting for Nathan in one of the classrooms on the second floor. The tag on the door said 'Advanced Physics'. Nathan rapped gently and went straight in. Basil was sitting at his large desk in an empty classroom. He was not wearing the usual leather jacket he was known to wear at rallies. Instead, he wore a simple white shirt and kept his long scarf wrapped loosely around his neck.

'Mr Glenn, from the Wimbledon Gazette. Is that right?'

He put a book down and stood up to shake Nathan's hands. A firm grip and an arrogant look behind the gold-rimmed glasses put Nathan on the spot.

'Thanks for your time, Mr Elders.'

'Basil "Wilberforce", please.'

'Sure, Basil… "Wilberforce".'

Nathan found it odd to be asked to call him by his name plus his nickname. He was shown a seat by the side of the desk and glanced at the book Basil had been reading.

'Schopenhauer? I was not expecting it from a teacher in Advanced Physics.'

'The two enemies of human happiness are pain and boredom.' replied Basil quoting the philosopher. 'I like to keep my mind busy and active.'

'How come Schopenhauer?'

Basil pulled a face full of derision. He adjusted his glasses and leaned forward. His arrogance transpiring.

'There is one quote that strikes me the most. It is the closest to my field of work. "In Time, all things follow one another, and in mere Space, all things are side by side; it is only through the combination of Time and Space that the representation of coexistence arises".'

'Coexistence? Like you and Alberyx Enterprises.'

'Your sarcasm is feeble, Mr Glenn. Coexistence of Time and Space is a theory I have been advancing myself. Perhaps you should do a better job in your background research.'

His petty comment was typical of Basil, but Nathan had no intention of being belittled. He let Basil carry on with his gloating.

'Talking about research, I assume you didn't know the great philosopher Arthur Schopenhauer studied in Wimbledon for six months. At Eagle House, as a matter of fact.'

'Eagle House, you say? Apt choice I must say. After last night…' teased Nathan.

'What makes you think I am behind every act my followers decided to organise? I say you are quite daring, Mr Glenn.'

'It is my job.'

'I know it is, and you stay true to that vocation. You don't compromise, for sure. I know that from reading your articles.'

Nathan took the compliment in his stride, expecting worse to come from a man who did not hold his tongue back.

'I have very little time, Mr Glenn, and I would like to have lunch before I resume my lessons. What is it you want? If it is an interview you want, I guess you picked the wrong day.'

Basil took his glasses to clean the lenses with the long end of his scarf. He kept his gaze on Nathan. The journalist shifted in his seat, feeling under pressure as if he were one of Basil's students.

'I wouldn't call it an interview, Basil.'

'Basil "Wilberforce". Please.'

'Yes, of course. Basil "Wilberforce".' Nathan corrected himself apologetically. 'I am just trying to make sense of a man who teaches Advanced Physics but has a strong duty as a citizen when it comes to engaging in local…let's say…political activities.'

Basil put his glasses back on and leaned against the back of the chair with his arms crossed.

'I hope you've read my file, Mr Glenn, or whatever you have on me. I don't need to tell you that alongside my PhD in Advanced Physics, I also have two masters in sociology and environmental studies, and I have been a part time scout ranger for Wimbledon Common. As a teacher, though, it is my responsibility to impart lessons of civic duty when teaching the young minds of this school or any school. That same civic duty pushed me to do the same for Wimbledonians, asking them to act before our Common becomes a land of concrete or our beautiful Wimbledon is sold off to the highest bidder.'

'Does that include attacking publicly Alberyx Enterprises?' poked the journalist.

'Ah, Mr Glenn. Weren't you the one who raised those doubts in your article about the Old Rectory? First, we get some anonymous person buying the title of Lord of the Manor of Wimbledon, and then Alberyx Enterprises takes over the Old Rectory, and bit by bit they take over every part of Wimbledon's life, to the point we become dependent on the company.'

'So, what's your goal?'

Basil chuckled.

'The resolution is stopping Alberyx Enterprises in their expansion. Full stop.'

'And will you achieve that by just being vocal about it?'

'You treat me like a revolutionary, Mr Glenn. I like it. If that's the spin you want in your story.'

'I am just curious on what grounds you accuse Alberyx Enterprises, and in particular Sir Julian Alberon.'

'Don't you see what they plan to…no, let me correct myself…what they've done to the Common?'

'How can you be sure that the new windmill is dangerous, or that wireless electricity is a health hazard?'

Nathan had to probe deeper into Basil's motivations and get a hint of what he knew the things he did and how he knew them. Nobody else had raised concerns about health issues but him. Nobody raised questions on John Crane's whereabouts but him. Basil Elders was now giving him a side glance, his head cocked to the side.

'God is a bit like electricity, Mr Glenn. You don't see it. You don't smell it. And yet, you believe it is out there. You believe it exists.'

'I am not here for an existentialist lesson…' groaned Nathan.

'Listen up, Mr Glenn!' he cut off. 'If you play with forces you can't see, you are likely to burn your fingers. Trust me, I am the one who has studied the laws of physics and beyond.'

'Care to enlighten me then on why you think John Crane burnt his fingers, if I can use your analogy?'

Basil Elders smirked. He was expecting a wild card by Nathan Glenn, an unscrupulous journalist who also happened to hate Alberyx Enterprises. Basil thought Nathan could be a useful ally, as a voice to be reckoned with. On the other hand, he had to play tactfully to avoid the police spying on him. Basil thought of a good test.

'I have my contacts, Mr Glenn. My inside people. You probably do too, nosing around where you shouldn't.'

Nathan swallowed hard. He wondered if Basil or Alberyx Enterprises security had learned about him and his transmitter.

'I know John Crane has kind of disappeared.' added Basil.

'Care to explain how he disappeared?'

'I said "kind of". He has not disappeared in the real sense of the world. He just disappeared from the public eye. He is actually in there. Inside that filthy compound that is Warren Farms. You see, the wireless electricity made him sick.'

'Are you sure?' commented Nathan, his eyes widened.

'Surprised?' added Basil with satisfaction. 'What if I told you there are more casualties from this insane experiment Julian Alberon brought upon us?'

'What are your sources?' challenged Nathan, sceptical about Basil's claims.

The teacher was bragging too easily about it. The whole business smelled funny.

'I knew you would not believe me. Hence, let me put it this way. Come down to Wimbledon Police Station this afternoon.'

'Why would I…?'

Basil uncrossed his arms and leaned forward, slamming his hand on the desk. Nathan almost fell off his chair.

'Because if you want your scoop, Mr Glenn, before this mass of blind journalists, who have come here to hear about a windmill and some old rocks found underground, then you'd better shut up and listen!'

A subtle bell chimed shortly after. Nathan heard teenagers chattering as they rushed out of class to take their deserved lunch break. The corridor outside quickly became busy with people.

'Time's up, Mr Glenn. I suggest you consider my offer. If you want that scoop, that is, and achieve the personal success you wish to pursue. As Schopenhauer said, every man takes the limits of his own field of vision for the limits of the world.'

'Is that your philosophy?' teased Nathan, who had had enough of Basil's quotes from the German philosopher.

'My philosophy is to bring down the tyrant and give Wimbledon back to the people. If you excuse me.'

Basil 'Wilberforce' Elders stood up and patted his trousers. He then showed Nathan the door, inviting him to leave. The journalist complied and he heard Basil walking up to the door behind him. He did not turn around as he left the empty classroom. Before he joined the stream of teachers and students to leave Octagon School, he heard Basil's reminder.

'I hope to see you this afternoon.' he called out.

Nathan had somehow got what he wanted. A one-to-one meeting with the most unpopular man in Wimbledon, who had been surprisingly open and offered Nathan the chance to follow him in action. An offer no other journalist would get. He bit his lip wondering whether he should take it or not.

Basil stood on the threshold, watching Nathan leave and nodding at peers and students passing by with a polite smile. Despite his social activity, he was still respected at Octagon School for he was a brilliant teacher. One of the best the school could afford. Basil gloated for the privileged role he had, almost untouchable. He glanced at his watch. He had to make a quick call before going to lunch. He quickly closed the door behind him to be alone once more in the empty classroom.

The Fox and Grapes pub was on the south-western corner of a square block of houses and buildings completely isolated from the residential core of Wimbledon Village. All around the block were parks or forests in one form or the other: Cannizaro Park to the south, the Common to the north and west, and Rushmere Green to the east. It was easy to spot the pub from afar because of its light pink façade and external walls crowned on top with a drape of hysteria and a multitude of colourful hanging just below the roof. Enrico looked at the pub from across Camp Road, leaning on the high exterior wall of Cannizaro Park. He had never been inside the pub. It was a popular place, always busy every time of the day. He looked at the coloured opaque windows blurring the shapes and shadows moving inside. The sound of clinking cutlery and boisterous chatter boomed out of the pub each time a new customer arrived or a satisfied one left.

'Cold, isn't it?' asked Dr Watkins bringing up the weather to break the silence.

Enrico muttered in agreement. He was still brooding on what the curator had said before at Caesar's Camp. His suggestion that all that had happened was linked to the legend of the Wynnman had left him disturbed. Enrico buttoned up his chef jacket and checked his Nokia 3310 to see how long he had to wait before Lord Cotton arrived. He was looking forward to hearing his proposal over lunch. The Wynnman bakery was doing well, staying just above the profit line ever since the first tough months, but an opportunity like this one, with a considerable volume of orders guaranteed for the year, would strengthen Enrico's business further. For once, Enrico wanted to focus on the business offer he was being given, and Dr Watkins's words were distracting him.

'Can we keep the Caesar's Camp discussion for last?' asked Enrico turning to Dr Watkins next to him.

'If you prefer, Enrico.'

'Thanks. I do not want to jinx the whole thing.'

A grey Bentley turned into Camp Road and parked a few metres from the Fox and Grapes entrance. The chauffeur stepped out with grace and went to open one of the rear passenger doors. The Italian baker was quick to recognise Lord Cotton as he climbed out of the car in his usual vintage attire. Tailcoat, waistcoat, top hat, with the addition on that day of a nice walking stick. His small dog, Little Caesar, jumped out of the car and proudly stood by his owner with his little black eyes looking across the road. Lord Cotton smiled warmly at Enrico and Dr Watkins and beckoned them to come over. His lifestyle and appearance came across as posh or elitist, but Enrico had to admire his approachable manner, always stretching out and never keeping distances. It was clear from the moment they sat inside at one of the tables by the fireplace when Lord Cotton did not hesitate to order three full pints of rich ale.

'You need to excuse me, Mr LoTrova.' said Lord Cotton with his jovial, red-cheeked face. 'I like to make my clients and partners alike feel comfortable. I asked around and I know you would prefer a local beer rather than wine or that sparkling version from your motherland. *Prosecco*, isn't it?'

'Oh well, there is more than just *prosecco* if you think of *lambrusco*, *brachetto*, *moscato* and other *spumanti*. But you have chosen well, Lord Cotton, and I thank you for the thought. Beer is fine.'

'Good. And by the way, I like to make the most out of a business lunch. Let's order starters and mains, and then let's see if we have space for pudding. I hope that works for you Dr Watkins.'

'I may leave before pudding as I have some work I need to do at the Old Rectory, if you don't mind.' replied the curator.

Lord Cotton called the waiter. Enrico glanced around while they ordered. The black and white interior of the Fox and Grapes showed an old and new contrast, where the lower half was made in a half-worn wood and stone structure from the early nineteenth century, when it was first called the Union, while its upper half shone with brand new white wooden panels up to the ceiling as if they had been freshly built and painted. The entrance was protected by a thick green curtain to keep the cold out and it opened up to the first half of the pub warmed by a grand fireplace, but which had no fire in it most of the times. There were just a few dining tables and wooden wall benches dotted around. It was one of the smallest pubs in Wimbledon, where the small number of guests allowed in sat cosily close together. The open bar in the middle, split the pub into two parts divided by a small step. The second half had mainly dining tables and looked more modern but still cosy.

'So, Mr LoTrova? Which part of Italy are you from?' resumed Lord Cotton once the waiters left.

He was patting the head of Little Caesar who kept on circling around the table in seek of attention or maybe a bone to gnaw on.

'Centre of Italy. Small village. And please call me Enrico!' replied in short Enrico, always staying vague on the subject to avoid the usual long-winded geographical explanations.

'Florence? Chianti valley?' guessed Lord Cotton. 'All marvellous places! And you have good food! I must say your fame precedes you, Enrico. I have only heard good things about the Wynnman bakery. An apt name too, I must say!'

Enrico blushed at again another shower of compliments. He wondered if this is what fame felt like.

'Now, let's talk business!' continued Lord Cotton. 'We are reviewing our menus at the club for breakfast, lunch and afternoon for the year ahead. The Royal Wimbledon Golf Club has a multitude of suppliers signed up for bread and pastries to the point we now have a different supplier for each service. It has become unmanageable! Putting all our bread and pastry orders through you, locally, would remove most of the clutter and bring food that is fresher and more convenient. How does that sound?'

'It sounds like a great opportunity, Lord Cotton!' agreed Enrico. 'How much volume are we talking about?'

Enrico almost spurted his beer in shock as he heard the quantity. It was a lot more than what he baked currently. Dr Watkins smiled to himself.

'Is that a problem?' asked Lord Cotton, worried.

'Nonononono…' justified Enrico apologetically. 'You just caught me by surprise. I had a different estimate in mind. It is no problem!'

Enrico heard himself say those words. No problem meant full focus on the bakery. Dr Watkins's words from earlier that morning resurfaced as a distraction. He could not let his curiosity ruin the opportunity Lord Cotton was giving him.

The starters came. Home-made Scotch eggs, duck liver pâté terrine, prawn cocktail. The three enjoyed the food while Lord Cotton provided more details on the offer. Enrico had no doubts it was an unmissable opportunity. He also thought the food was exquisite and probably made Lord Cotton's offer more palatable. The mains were even better: one lamb shank with vegetables and one fish and chips, which Enrico did not mind devouring for a second day in a row. By the time they finished, they had both ironed out the details for a new partnership: Enrico would be providing a regular delivery of bread to the Royal Wimbledon Golf Club.

As the three relaxed and dozed a little in a post-lunch lull, their conversation eased off to lighter, more casual subjects. Enrico glanced at Dr Watkins. This was the time to raise the questionable subject of digging up Caesar's Camp. Yet, the curator was hesitating.

'How long have you been at the head of the Royal Wimbledon Golf Club?' asked Enrico hoping to lead the conversation in the right direction.

'It has been in the family for a long time. My uncle was my predecessor, and my family has always been from Wimbledon. We were good friends with the Spencer family when they still owned the title of the Lord of the Manor.'

'So, you are a Wimbledonian, born and bred?'

'Yes. Like Dr Watkins here. The two of us have been friends since we were kids.'

Enrico was surprised to hear that. If they had been friends for such a long time, he did not understand why Dr Watkins could not bring up the subject of Caesar's Camp.

'How's the golf club?' asked Dr Watkins, finally speaking up.

'Well, it runs smoothly thanks to Ramona helping me out. We've had better days though. The way we run the club today is so much different from the way my uncle or forefathers did. Lately, I have not had the chance to meet the new Lord of the Manor. The title was sold by the Spencer family more than five months ago and still no news'.

'How does that affect you?' asked Enrico puzzled.

'The Lord of the Manor is just a title nowadays. However, he indirectly owns some of the land in Wimbledon, which includes the golf club.'

'You don't own your golf club?'

'He does.' interjected Dr Watkins to explain. 'When it comes to the land it is built on, there is still a special relationship nurtured with who owns it. The Spencers sold most of the land but there are still some parts associated with the Lord of the Manor on the paper.'

'It is just common courtesy to know who the Lord of the Manor is.' added Lord Cotton. 'However, nobody seems to know who bought the title.'

Enrico nodded and took a sip of his beer thinking whether it would be apt now to ask about the problems he was facing with the golf course.

'Don't you have any issues with the work being done on your golf course?' asked the Italian baker.

'You mean the Repeater? Not at all. It is great work coming along nicely. For the community.'

'I was referring more to that Basil "Wilberforce" guy. He does not seem to share your opinion!'

'Don't worry about Basil! He always took the side of the anti-establishment and lately stood against the small progress Wimbledon Village strived for. I am surprised the school he works in does not have any issues with his recent behaviour.'

'I was surprised to hear he is a teacher.' added Enrico.

'Yes. Advanced Physics at Octagon School.' confirmed Dr Watkins. 'But Basil was never this disruptive. Nothing that would lead to the sort of civil unrest we have seen in recent months.'

'Is it only recently then?'

To Enrico, the matter was getting interesting.

'Since I made the contract with the Council and Alberyx Enterprises.' replied Lord Cotton.

'Not a fan of Sir Julian Alberon, I suppose. Or do you think it is because Basil lost his job as a scout ranger?'

'That was unfortunate. But Sir Alberon is a man of genius, Enrico. It is what Wimbledon needs.'

'Indeed, he is.' seconded Enrico, unable to ignore the extent of Julian's sphere of influence. 'Do you think we should do more for Wimbledon?'

Enrico eyed Dr Watkins as he posed the question. The curator knew that was his cue. Now or never.

'I think we are doing enough and there is room for more.' replied Lord Cotton with optimism.

'Well, there is something that has come up with Simon Deeley, Lord Cotton.' jumped in the curator.

'What is that?'

'We think the Anglo-Saxon trail may continue to Caesar's Camp.'

'Is that so?' Lord Cotton said, puzzled. 'Last time the Wimbledon Museum searched that area was…when? 1935?'

'Roughly, yes.'

'And nothing was found, if I remember.'

'Yes. Mr Deeley thinks there is something deeper.'

'Deeper?' Lord Cotton frowned. 'You mean underneath it?'

Dr Watkins nodded.

'I am afraid what you are asking of me, Dr Watkins.' sighed Lord Cotton. 'Digging on the golf course will require voting. From our members, from the WAIS. You have my support, as a friend, but you will need to convince others rather than me.'

Dr Watkins had expected that answer. He knew the process himself and his mind rushed to find what to say to Simon.

'Would Julian be willing to support us?' wondered Enrico. 'He has financed the Old Rectory. I am sure he would be interested in financing a new archaeological site at Caesar's Camp.'

Enrico's question went unanswered. Little Caesar barked all of a sudden, jumping on the spot and prancing around, with his muzzle pointed at the entrance of the pub, at something he did not find agreeable. Lord Cotton picked Little Ceasar up, cuddling him a little. The three men then looked up and the rigid, soldier-like posture of Ramona Halywell had just entered the Fox and Grapes. She wore big sunglasses and a pink tracksuit with a furred hoody. Her lips and cheeks hardly moved, sculptured onto her face with heavy foundation and make-up. Her features were shaped as if she were a beautiful statue cold to the touch. She walked over to the table and turned to face Lord Cotton with her back to Enrico and Dr Watkins. The Italian baker could tell how proudly she gave herself importance from reading again the words 'Club Captain' written across her back in a dark rosé colour. She hushed a few words to the club owner.

'Again?' blurted out Lord Cotton. 'What do they want me for?'

'If you remember you need to be consulted and informed each time.' said Ramona. 'It is what we agreed to. It is quite urgent. I tried to call but you didn't pick up the phone!'

The way she spoke got on Enrico's nerves. More than her cold, icy attitude, it was her overly formal and inflexible tone, as if read from a textbook.

'They'd better keep their engineers in check.' moaned Lord Cotton. 'We can't make a fool of ourselves again!'

'What happened?' asked Enrico, his curiosity quick in picking up Lord Cotton's words.

'This is a security concern.' Ramona replied curtly turning to him. 'And last time I checked, Mr LoTrova, you were not a member of the club.'

'I apologise for Ramona's attitude.' interjected Lord Cotton. 'She runs the club like a tight ship!'

'You don't say…' added Enrico under Ramona's suspicious gaze.

The sporty woman did not flinch and then returned to speak to Lord Cotton.

'They asked for you, Lord Cotton.' said Ramona. 'at the Repeater.'

'Who is they?' insisted Enrico.

Ramona did not turn.

'Alberyx Enterprises.' announced Lord Cotton disheartened. 'I am so sorry, Enrico, but I need to address this. Please feel free to stay for dessert or a coffee. I will pick up the tab. My treat, I say. We can meet next week to draft the contract. Ramona, would you be so kind to stay behind and sort the details with Mr LoTrova?'

'How about Caesar's Camp?' questioned Dr Watkins, eager to have an answer.

'Why don't you come with me? We can have a quick chat. My driver can then drop you at the Old Rectory or the Wimbledon Museum. As you wish.'

The two men stood up from the table and bid farewell to Enrico. Lord Cotton put Little Caesar under his arm and nudged Dr Watkins towards the exit. The dog's barks had turned to whimpers as his master walked away towards the entrance. Ramona stayed by the table and took a seat in Lord Cotton's chair, calling the waiter. She asked for the bill but on the side, she also ordered a gin and tonic, with detailed accuracy on how much gin and how much tonic. She then sat comfortably, checking her smartphone. Enrico was still half-standing up. Ramona's oblivious attitude towards him left him dumbstruck and a little out of place. She had not even asked him if he wanted a dessert or a coffee before closing the tab.

'Having a drink on Lord Cotton, I suppose?' he teased.

'Yes.' replied Ramona without looking up.

'Do you need my details for whatever Lord Cotton plans to do next?' hinted at Enrico, sitting back at the table.

'Don't make yourself too comfortable, Mr LoTrova. If it was me, I would not have arranged such a lunch for you.'

She spoke those words very slowly, adamant for Enrico to grasp their true meaning right from the start. Enrico knew Ramona Halywell did not need to be read between the lines. She spelled her despise for Enrico outright.

'What happened back at the club?' insisted Enrico.

The woman ignored him, pretending her smartphone was more interesting.

'Another big show from Basil "Wilberforce" Elders?' teased again Enrico knowing he was pushing his luck.

'You should not meddle with things that do not concern you.' she replied curtly, not budging from her position. 'You're not part of the club yet, and personally I don't think you should be part of it anyway. We don't need your services.'

'Easy! I am only here to help.'

'You are unreliable, Mr LoTrova.' shot back Ramona always ready to have the last word. 'It took you some time to acknowledge our requests for your services. Is that how *you* run a *tight* ship?'

Ramona's mockery was clear for Enrico to see, quoting his own words said to her at the press conference. The club captain was in no way interested in befriending the Italian baker or making him feel welcome. The waiter came with the bill. Ramona looked up from her phone for the first time. She lowered her sunglasses to take a good look at him and gave a fake, broad smile. Her round blue eyes cold and vitreous.

'We don't need you and your stupid chef's jacket.' she added as the payment went through. 'The Royal Wimbledon Golf Club does not need you at all. We can get good bread elsewhere!'

She was not scared to be mean and talk openly about it. Enrico had no intention of sitting back and let her words slap him in the face.

'*Un attimo*...Just a sec. Doesn't Lord Cotton have a say on this?' Enrico asked.

'Ultimately, I decide the suppliers, the partnerships, the price. I basically decide who is worth joining our inner circle. I would not hire someone like you!'

'You should save such attitude for Basil "Wilberforce" Elders. I am sure he would give you the perfect treatment! Anyway, I think Lord Cotton asked to draft a contract, so I am afraid your opinion does not really count.'

Enrico's words hit the nail on the head. Ramona pursed her lips and tensed in her seat. She cocked her head to the side and Enrico thought he heard the bones in her neck crack.

'Listen to me!' said Ramona turning to face Enrico and lowering her sunglasses.

The large blue eyes peered over directly at him for the first time.

'Lord Cotton will give you a contract, for sure, but you will not sign. It's not for you, so stay away from the Royal Wimbledon Golf Club. Do I make myself clear?'

'Not sure what the problem is Ramona…'

'It is Miss Halywell to you, Mr LoTrova. Please make sure you do the right thing!'

'Or what?'

Ramona scoffed and did not give Enrico the pleasure of a reply. The Italian baker stared for a moment as he sat there facing the mean Ramona Halywell, isolated from the cheerful tables with plenty of food and drink. He was not sure what Ramona's real agenda was. He was starting to feel irritated by her nasty attitude and was taken aback by her strong confrontation.

'What happened back at the club again?' he insisted again.

She looked at him and then quickly put her sunglasses back. She stood up, adjusting her furry hoody nicely at the back

'Goodbye, Mr LoTrova! Just remember what I said.'

'Or what?' he exclaimed raising his voice.

People at the tables nearby turned around startled. Even the waiter by the bar looked at them with some concern. The Italian baker blushed and raised a hand in apology.

'Exactly the type of people we don't need…' belittled Ramona as she prepared to leave.

She then called the waiter again.

'Get Mr LoTrova here some herbal tea.' she whispered to the waiter.

She then turned to Enrico.

'See you hopefully not too soon, Mr LoTrova.'

'Goodbye Ramona!' waved Enrico, acting as normal as he could just to get on Ramona's nerves.

He was not going to let her attitude belittle him, especially in public. She disappeared quickly through the green curtain and the cold air from outside seeped in through the open door. A cup of herbal tea came shortly after. Enrico stared at it. He was not fond of herbal tea. It was the perfect insult: Ramona treating him like a child and a worthless baker. I don't need your charity, Enrico thought angrily. He was still baffled by the harsh encounter with Ramona Halywell and thought it best to wash it away with an espresso back at the bakery. What Ramona's agenda was eluded him. Control freak, perhaps. Enrico simply wished Lord Cotton was the one making the final decision, unbiased. Still, he wondered what Ramona would actually do if he did sign the contract.

When he left the Fox and Grapes pub, he felt a little overwhelmed by what had started with Lord Cotton's generosity and ended up with the meanest encounter he had ever had in Wimbledon Village. Camp Road was clear of cars now that lunchtime was over, and the lazy winter afternoon rushed towards winter dusk. Enrico crossed the narrow road and stood opposite the pub for a few minutes thinking about what had happened. Ramona's words did not sound right, and Enrico was finding it hard to forget. He thought maybe he should walk to the golf club right now and make a scene. On second thoughts though he knew he would only make a fool of himself and lose a great opportunity.

Enrico turned the corner to walk south on West Side Common. He recalled the emergency that had unfortunately summoned Ramona to come to the Fox and Grapes. Another accident, perhaps, thought Enrico. Engineers. Alberyx Enterprises. The Repeater. Enrico wondered if this was indeed another of Basil Elders's attempts to bring chaos to Wimbledon. Out of all the weeks, the man had chosen this one in particular, and it had been probably his intention all along. While lost in thought, he did not notice a large SUV car had stopped at the corner of the Fox and Grapes. There was no incoming traffic and yet it stood there waiting for something or someone. The car then turned right into West Side Common, aligning itself with Enrico's path. The person behind the wheel revved its engine and screeched against the dirt track to accelerate towards Enrico. The heavy rumble made Enrico turn and he saw the huge, intimidating bonnet of the car heading towards him without any sign of braking or swerving. The car was now moving at a higher speed, faster than was allowed on Wimbledon Village roads. The Italian baker realised the sudden danger he was in and swerved to the right. The car swerved right as well, tracking his movement. Enrico glanced at the grassy path of Rushmere Green and dashed for it, thinking the car would not follow him there. The large SUV went off the road and bounced onto the uneven terrain, not relenting. Enrico glanced to his right. The entrance to Cannizaro Park was not far off and the gate was half-closed. He changed direction, jumping back on the road. The large SUV lost speed as it swerved on the uneven terrain. It then drove back onto the road and back at Enrico. The Italian baker gasped for air and could feel his lungs were about to burst. The gates to Cannizaro Park were his only escape route. He leaped forward through the half-open gate, throwing himself onto the tarmac. The car zoomed by and almost hit the columns of the entrance before it was forced to swerve back onto the road and drive away from the scene. It had been a close shave. Enrico landed on his side among the curious onlookers of Wimbledonians returning from their stroll in Cannizaro Park. He lay belly up, gasping for air, under their shocked gaze. Someone had just tried to kill the Italian baker with a hit and run.

Wimbledon Police Station was a mess. Enrico and Viviane did not recognise the place at first. Outside, the whole front of the building was already packed with journalists and cameramen.

'What are all these people doing here?' Enrico asked the policeman on guard at the entrance.

'Honestly, I don't know.' said the policeman. 'One minute the road is deserted. The next we see this swarm of journalists grouping outside here, asking where Basil "Wilberforce" Elders is.'

He quickly let them in before turning his attention back to the crowd. Enrico and Viviane were asked to sit in the waiting room. A group of people stood in one corner and they huddled around a woman in her fifties. She was sitting down, her face sunk in a handkerchief wet from her tears. Some of those close to her shared words of support, as good friends do, while others glared with anger at the policeman on duty behind the helpdesk. A man of the same age as the woman, perhaps the husband, was arguing with the policeman about the situation. Enrico and Viviane could not make out the conversation, but they had arrived at a critical moment. Viviane turned to one of the women nearest to her.

'What's all this?' she asked.

'Shocking, my dear!' replied the woman almost hysterically. 'This morning my friend's son was found wandering aimlessly in the middle of Wimbledon Common. He has turned into some kind of vegetable. Doesn't talk or react. Doctors say some sort of brain injury, but others heard the police claiming he may have been attacked last night!'

'Attacked?'

'Yes, by men on horses.'

'Pardon me?'

'Men on horses.' repeated the woman feeling a little on edge. 'What? You don't believe it to be possible? Let me tell you. This town is going to the dogs. Wimbledon Common is no longer safe. Especially after they built those two horrible, hideous pieces of metal...'

Viviane understood she may be referring to the New Wimbledon Windmill and the Repeater. Although they had opposing views, she thought it best not to start an argument. The woman with the handkerchief looked distraught.

'I hear you.' concurred Viviane, not clearly taking sides.

'The police are not allowing the parents to see him yet and they are not telling us what is going on. I think it is outrageous!'

'Don't worry. They know what they're doing. Who is the boy with now?'

'He is being visited by a doctor. Apparently, Inspector Baynard is on the case.'

Viviane could tell there was a hint of mockery in the woman's words. The atmosphere at the police station was tense like never before and the trust in the police force was treading on a thin line. Viviane thought it best not to get involved. She gave the woman some reassurance about Baynard being on the case and asked her comforting words to be passed on. She then took her seat next to Enrico who had been eavesdropping on the whole conversation.

'That's three today!' he commented.

'Three what?'

'Well, first we hear Lord Cotton mentioning a security concern about Alberyx Enterprises engineer, based on what that horrible Ramona Halywell told him. I was then a victim of a deliberate hit and run. And now we find out that a boy has been attacked on the Common. No matter what you say, Wimbledon has seen way too much action in the last twenty-four hours. I need to see Inspector Baynard!'

'Well, calm down. You are not the only one!'

Viviane patted Enrico on the shoulder. The Italian baker still looked a little shaken and extremely nervous. He had barged into her flower shop less than an hour ago gesticulating like a madman. He was clearly upset, and it took a while to calm him down, and put some sense back into him. He had wanted to report the hit and run incident directly to Inspector Baynard and here they were.

'Did you see the car's number plate?' asked Viviane.

'No. The car was going too fast.'

'Did you have a chance to see who was in the car?'

'No. Nothing at all. I bet it was Ramona Halywell.'

'I doubt it!' grimaced Viviane. 'Just because she wasn't nice to you, doesn't mean she wants to run you over. What did she tell you again? I am curious.'

'She threatened me if I dared sign a contract with Lord Cotton. Can you believe that?'

'It is outrageous!' agreed Viviane, shocked by Ramona's attitude. 'Who does she think she is? You should report it at the next WAIS meeting. But, still, I don't think she was behind the wheel.'

A policeman joined them shortly after.

'I have come to take your statement and report your…hit and run, did you say?' he asked after checking his notes.

'Yes! Where is Inspector Baynard?'

'He can't come right now, I am afraid. Can I just ask you a couple of questions so we can look into your case?'

The policeman then spurred Enrico on to tell the story, taking more notes on the location, the time, the make of the car.

'That's all for now!' said the policeman when they had finished. 'Let me look into this and we'll get back to you. You don't have to wait. We can give you a call if we learn anything new.'

'Happy to wait!' grunted Enrico. 'I want to see Inspector Baynard!'

Viviane grinned. She found it ironic that the Italian baker was begging to see Inspector Baynard, especially when most of the time they just happened to bump into each other on the most inappropriate occasions.

'I can't guarantee he'll be available.' apologised the policeman before disappearing in one of the corridors.

Enrico was happy to wait though. He glanced around. The mother with her handkerchief worried about her son. The police constables whispering to each other as they came in and out of the building, followed by the noise of shouting reporters outside calling out for Basil Elders. Tension at the police station had pricked Enrico's curiosity and had temporarily cast aside his anger. Something felt unnatural and out of place. Just like Ramona's interruption at what was a turning point in Enrico's baking career.

'You may think it wasn't Ramona behind that car.' resumed Enrico, his arms crossed. 'But everything was kicking off well until she barged in to alert Lord Cotton!'

'What? Do you think all these events are related?'

'Ramona mentioned something about the Repeater. Now, we have this boy who was attacked last night. Plus, I was almost run over by a car, which is not the first time.'

'That was a van, I think.' Viviane corrected reminiscing Enrico's encounter with Toby Claymore.

'That's not the point! I mean, everything happening on Julian's launch week… Isn't that strange?'

Viviane thought about Enrico's question and wanted to ask him what he meant. However, their attention shifted to some loud cheering outside. The main entrance door to the police station burst open and everyone in the entrance looked up scared, including the policeman behind the helpdesk. A group of five or six men and women barged in and took centre stage in the entrance hall. They were unarmed and wore jeans and leather jackets over white shirts.

'What is the meaning of this?' shouted the policeman behind the helpdesk.

The group of men and women stood still though, without any intention to fight or argue. They then split up to let through the man who had dared to oppose Alberyx Enterprises.

'Hear me, Wimbledonians!' shouted Basil 'Wilberforce' Elders with open arms as dictated by his usual theatrics. 'Another scandal from that vulture company that is Alberyx Enterprises. Another scandal that leads me here to complain to our authorities. More people have fallen sick because of wireless electricity; one of them a poor helpless boy, and there's now a desperate attempt to cover it up! What is the police going to do about it?'

More policemen appeared to take a stance around the group. No weapons drawn.

'Please leave the premises peacefully, unless you have an emergency to report.' warned one police officer. 'Otherwise, we will have to detain you.'

'An emergency to report? Of course!' mocked Basil. 'I am here as a citizen of Wimbledon. It is my right to request for police help. They can guide you where to look. See, we are being fooled under our noses and Wimbledon Police is doing nothing about it. Alberyx Enterprises first takes the Common from us and now human lives are at stake? Who should be really arrested here, officers?'

Basil 'Wilberforce' Elders spoke with a loud, clear and articulate voice. He wanted everyone to listen to his words and let his banter take hold of the listeners' emotions. The men and women cheered after each of his rhetorical questions. Enrico and Viviane heard what was going on outside as even more of his followers gathered, together with the media.

'Mr Elders!' warned again one of the police officers. 'I have orders to escort you out if you do not stop this slander in public. Please let us do our job!'

He took a step forward from the ring of policemen and tried to make a stance against Basil. However, his wimpy looks could not match the leader's impressive stature. Basil looked down on him through his gold-rimmed glasses, like a man observing a flea through a microscope, and then smiled with a scornful chuckle.

'Yes, officer. You do your job. However, you may want to know something dangerous is happening. Two engineers of Alberyx Enterprises have fallen sick. One of our own young Wimbledonians too fell sick.'

Basil looked over the policeman's shoulder and met the eyes of Ken's mother, handkerchief in hand.

'Our health is at risk because something attacked them.' he continued. 'Because of that bloody technology Alberyx Enterprises has forced upon us. We need accountability. Mark my words: justice will be done!'

He turned around on his heels and flung his long flannel scarf around his neck as a sign of dismissal. The cheers that ensued were louder and carried on outside where Basil was welcomed by the flashes of photographers and the chants of his loyal supporters. Another sensational appearance of Basil 'Wilberforce' Elders.

The eerie calm that followed left everyone in the police station in a daze. Enrico frowned as he replayed the whole scene.

'What a troublemaker, that man!' noted Viviane.

'He is. He is also clever.' replied Enrico.

'Because of what he said?'

'Yes. How did he know that we have apparently two engineers and a boy sick? He knows more than we think!'

'Hasn't the news just come out? I think I saw that journalist from the Wimbledon Gazette with him. What was his name? Nathan something.'

Enrico nodded absent-minded. Basil Elders was a charming but suspiciously dangerous character. Perhaps he had run him over. That is a stupid idea, he quickly thought. It made no sense. Enrico knew that for once he had done nothing wrong nor crossed paths with anybody. However, he had learnt a thing or two about dangerous characters lingering around Wimbledon.

'Viviane, I am going to talk to him.' Enrico said.

'Talk to who? Don't you want to wait for Baynard?'

'I have a better chance to get to the bottom of this if I ask the right people some questions. I say we start with the Basil "Wilberforce" Elders himself!'

'Oh no...' groaned Viviane.

Enrico though had already left the police station without waiting for Viviane's response. Viviane gave a deep sigh, knowing well what could come out of it. She knew Enrico's curiosity was playing up. She stood up and ran after him.

Outside, an ocean of chaos greeted both of them as the entire street had been blocked by Basil's followers. Even if their leader had left, they still stood there echoing Basil's protest phrases repeatedly. Enrico turned left, pushing through a mass of journalists taking pictures of what was happening from the side line. He ran down Alexandra Road towards one of Wimbledon's crossroads. Basil had just entered the coffee shop on the corner, with a small group of followers who had joined him inside the police station. He did recognise the journalist with them. Viviane was right. The fact Basil 'Wilberforce' Elders was hanging out with a journalist from the Wimbledon Gazette made Enrico even more curious about it. He crossed the street and peered inside the coffee shop while Viviane caught up with him, stopping occasionally to catch her breath.

'What are you doing, Enrico?' she asked, more as a warning than mere curiosity.

'Mr Elders!' called out Enrico, not listening.

He walked into the coffee shop towards the table where Basil and his group had taken seat. A woman turned around on alert. Basil put his hand on her shoulder as a sign to stand down. He had a surreal blasé expression on his face, quite different from a few seconds before inside the police station. There, sitting on an ordinary coffee shop high table overlooking one of Wimbledon's busy streets, he came across as less over the top, less dramatic. He tidied up his scarf and beckoned to Enrico and Viviane to come over. Most of the people in the coffee shop watched in silence as the scene played out; everyone had recognised Basil 'Wilberforce' Elders who had become a sensation in Wimbledon for good and bad reasons. Enrico knew this is what fame felt like. From the moment he and Viviane sat down, the world around them no longer mattered.

'Viviane Leighwood.' greeted Basil, kissing the florist's hand. 'Your flowers have brightened my day more than once. Although I prefer to see them in the wild of a garden.'

'Thank you.' Viviane smirked.

'And you're the baker, aren't you?' said Basil turning to Enrico.

'Yes…' hesitated Enrico, wondering if Basil recognising him was a good thing.

Basil probably knew more than he led to believe. Peering from behind those gold-rimmed glasses, he looked down on Enrico as if every word he was about to say was always worth gold.

'I have not tried your bread, yet. What is your bakery called again?'

'The Wynnman, sir.' helped one of his followers.

The group of men and women that were with him had sat around the table, ensuring Enrico and Viviane could not leave. They watched Enrico and Viviane's every move as if they were bodyguards, making the whole situation uncomfortable while Basil was trying to make conversation as if he had friends at home for tea. Nathan Glenn sat next to him, notepad at hand. He seemed to be there to record what Basil said or did.

'The Wynnman, yes. Let's get an espresso for Mr…LoTrova, isn't it? And for Miss Leighwood…the same?'

Viviane nodded not really caring. Basil told a man next to him to put in his order.

'Good. So, I hear you are trouble, Mr LoTrova.' resumed the leader.

'It depends on who you ask…' said Enrico playing along.

'I know the feeling.' chuckled Basil. 'I think I saw you at the police station. You ran all the way to talk to me. Did you want to ask me something?'

Enrico felt all eyes were on him, not only Basil's. They looked menacing and Enrico thought he had to choose his words carefully or he would end up in a political argument in the middle of Wimbledon in front of a journalist from the Wimbledon Gazette.

'I heard your speech…back at the station…' he started bit by bit, coming the long way around. 'You mentioned people were attacked… or fell ill… Well, you should know I was attacked too today.'

'Ah, so you too Mr LoTrova believe in my cause.'

'Which is?' challenged Viviane.

'Protect Wimbledon, of course. And tell me, Mr LoTrova, what happened to you?'

'Someone tried to run me over. I was wondering if you knew anything about it.'

Basil sighed and looked out of the window.

'I wish the other attacks had been as straightforward as yours, Mr LoTrova. You see, at least you could see your assailant coming after you…'

'What's that supposed to mean?' replied Enrico.

Basil smiled knowingly. He acted as if he had watched this scene play out before. He knew what everyone would say.

'The people attacked since Sunday are the first casualties of this wireless electricity nonsense that is starting to pollute our air waves…'

'The windmill is not yet operational though…' protested Viviane.

'Miss Leighwood!' grinned Basil, amused. 'Do you think Alberyx Enterprises is waiting for us to see them turn on a switch? Don't you think they may have turned on the windmill and the Repeater already? You are naïve…'

Viviane clenched her fist under the table. Her face hardened, not at all pleased by Basil's attitude. His words also struck at her heart, knowing she was supporting Julian and his company.

'Did you say Sunday?' asked Enrico.

'Yes. And I am sure Nathan Glenn here, from the Wimbledon Gazette, is happy for me to give you the biggest name of all: someone who has fallen sick because of this untested technology.'

Enrico saw Nathan nodding. He knew everything already.

'John Crane himself has fallen ill.' continued Basil with his predicament. 'The chief engineer that didn't turn up yesterday for the famous press conference. How is Alberyx Enterprises planning to keep their technology in check with their number one down? And why don't they come clean about him?'

'Why are you telling us this?' wondered Enrico, amazed by Basil's openness.

'Because you came here to ask me who tried to run you over. Perhaps you'd better look closer to home.'

'Sir Alberon would never approve such a thing!' protested Viviane, not willing to take any more of Basil's nonsense.

'Are you really sure, Miss Leighwood? Let me ask you: who decided to build on the Common when our forefathers had fought hard to keep it safe from house development? As a result of it, who lost his job as a part-time scout ranger because the Ranger's Office had to be moved miles from the windmill to welcome the planned restoration?'

'If that means you, Mr Elders, I am sure it was karma.' scorned Viviane.

'Good. Then again, who lost his job as guardian because his services were no longer required?'

Basil's reference to Quentin Plainstraw touched a nerve Enrico and Viviane could not argue with.

'Well, I am afraid Mr Elders has a point...' mumbled Enrico.

'Whose side are you on, Enrico?' opposed Viviane.

'All I am saying, all these changes Alberyx Enterprises is making to Wimbledon, are having some kind of effect that may not be pleasant.'

'I...I am speechless...' stammered Viviane.

'He is enlightened.' corrected Basil, happy with himself. 'Aren't you Mr LoTrova?'

Enrico felt stuck, between Viviane's subtle glare and Basil's persuasive words. He did not want to take sides and he wished he had phrased things differently. He did not dislike Julian or his company. He simply did not like the news coming out about the Common. He actually felt Julian's plans were in danger.

'Well, I have to go.' said Viviane. 'Pleasure to make your acquaintance, Mr Elders. Enrico, are you coming?'

Enrico faltered.

'Fine. See you later.'

She forced her way out, pushing one of Basil's men sitting next to him.

'Wait, I am coming…' added Enrico.

He leapt up from his seat, straightening his chef's jacket.

'Love your chef's jacket!' complimented Mr Elders. 'Like my dress code, it is a statement, Mr LoTrova. You should use that to your advantage!'

'To do what you do?'

'What do I do?'

Enrico was not sure what to answer but the menacing looks of Basil's followers said he had better leave this conversation to another time. There was one thing though he had to ask before leaving.

'You say people have fallen ill… what did you mean by that?' asked Enrico.

'When people start to have hallucinations and see ghosts, Mr LoTrova, it means something unhealthy is in the air.'

He then glanced over Enrico's shoulder.

'I think your lady friend is waiting for you, Mr LoTrova.' Basil added. 'I think it means goodbye for now, Mr Baker.'

Basil gave an enigmatic smile, which left Enrico high and dry. He was no longer welcome at the table by the looks of it so off he went, his pace uncertain. Hallucinations. Ghosts. He had heard this before. Quite recently actually, from Quentin Plainstraw's lips. Yet, hearing it again from a man like Basil 'Wilberforce' Elders, involved in the current state of affairs, could only make Enrico more curious than he already was. His hands prickled to make some dough. He then looked ahead. Viviane had already crossed the road to get back to the car. He had to catch up with her, make amends and tell her what was on his mind. He had the nasty feeling someone may be scheming against Julian Alberon and his ambitious dreams could be in danger.

Inspector Baynard stared through the one-way mirror. He was mesmerised by this boy Ken, sitting in the interrogation room for his statement to be taken. Except the boy did not talk much. He did not speak or move at all. He just rocked backward and forward, mumbling to himself and staring into space with his eyes hardly blinking at all. He did not seem to hear people talking to him, even if someone clicked their fingers right next to his ears. Strangely, he stood up, sat down, moved, and walked around when they pulled him gently under the arm, but otherwise he was completely absent. The body was there, responding to stimulus like an automaton, but the mind was elsewhere. They had no clue what had happened to him. A doctor had just come into the interrogation room to help with a diagnosis.

'Where did they find the kid?' asked Sergeant Jeremy.

'A man called Quentin Plainstraw found him wandering by Wimbledon Common this morning.' quickly replied Baynard, snapping out of it.

'Mr Plainstraw, the guardian of the windmill?'

'Ex-guardian.' corrected Baynard.

Jeremy widened his eyes, unaware of the piece of news.

'He's in the other room waiting to be released.' added the inspector never looking away from the one-way mirror.

'Is he clean?'

'According to his statement, he was out on his mid-morning stroll when he saw the boy standing in the middle of the bushes, somewhere west of Wimbledon Common, with his gaze empty and transfixed on the murky waters. He said the boy did not speak or interact when he called him or when he stood half-inch away from his nose.'

'Had the boy gone missing?'

'The mother said the boy had not returned home and she was getting worried about his whereabouts. Not sure if finding him in such a state would be a relief to her.'

'What do you think happened to him?'

'His clothes were partly ripped and a bit dirty, perhaps from a fall, but when Mr Plainstraw saw bruises on his neck and his lower arms, he did not think twice about calling the police. Once the boy was identified, we then contacted his parents but held off from bringing them into the room until we had heard an expert's view on the boy's health. Never seen anything like it…'

The doctor left the room and walked into the viewing room to share his point of view on Ken. Baynard's inquisitive stare did not need to spell the question on his mind.

'He is definitely in what we could call a catatonic state, inspector.' explained the doctor. 'I see mainly signs of stupor and catalepsy. No reaction to outside stimuli. Fortunately, there is no complete paralysis. He walks around when guided but his brain appears not to respond. A bit of an odd case this one.'

'Is this injury permanent?'

'Too early to diagnose. It looks like a coma. He isn't really present and there is no way of telling when he may come round.'

'Can he talk at all if we wanted to hear his statement?' asked Jeremy.

'It may be difficult. He keeps mumbling something about men on horses over and over and nothing else. Although his speech function is not paralysed, he seems impaired to communicate or even put words together. He is just repeating the same words every now and then, but he does not speak or answer when prompted.'

'What do you think caused all this?'

'Some form of trauma. Maybe physical pain or drugs. Hard to tell at this stage.'

'Do you suspect any foul play here? What can you tell me about the bruises? Could that be the source of pain causing trauma?'

'The dull leaden-blue colour is similar to bruises or contused flesh as if he had been in a fight but a couple of them are actually recent scar tissue healing from a very recent wound.'

'A wound?'

'Arrows, inspector. Or similar type of projectile. I recognised it from the circular and dot-like shapes. Definitely not bee stings.'

Baynard blinked, bewildered. Baynard's inquisitive stare moved to watch Ken in the adjacent room, still in the same position. Staring across the table. Rocking backwards and forwards. Muttering words that made no sense and showing old bruises that came from nowhere.

'Can you tell when he was shot…with arrows?'

The doctor looked at Ken trying to come up with an answer. He tried to hide a hint of embarrassment.

'What's the matter, doctor?' questioned Baynard.

'Well…It seems those scars hint that he was shot a long time ago.'

Baynard blinked again. His inquisitive clear grey eyes glowed in the dark of the viewing room like those of an owl in the night. Something was not right. He picked up Ken's file from the table next to him.

'We have a statement from his parents, and his rugby friends, who last saw him last night. They both claim he was healthy, no injuries, no scars. Especially no visible signs of wounds or contusions like those we see now. The lads did not have anything to drink. No fights, no drugs. Does this mean Ken was hit by arrows or something last night and the injuries healed so fast in a matter of hours?'

The doctor gave a blank look.

'Ok. Thanks, doctor. May I ask you to leave your statement with forensics? Sergeant Jeremy, could you please check Mr Plainstraw's movements from last night?'

Jeremy nodded. At that point a police constable rapped at the door and rushed straight in before being given the clear. It seemed urgent from the red blush on his cheeks.

'Yes?' asked Baynard.

The police constable caught his breath.

'Basil "Wilberforce"…' he gasped, speaking before he had put his facts in order.

'What about him?' snapped Baynard, unable to stand the name lately.

'We had Basil "Wilberforce" Elders storming into the police station with some of his followers. He put on a show and claimed there were two attacks last night on the Common.'

'Two attacks?' exclaimed Jeremy.

'Who on earth does he think he is?' said Baynard. 'Coming here and telling us how to do our job? You should have arrested him there and then!'

'Yessir!' agreed the police constable.

'What attacks is he referring to?' quizzed Jeremy, worried about Basil's theatrics. 'We have the boy Ken here. What is the second one?'

'Well…' hesitated the police constable. 'We heard Mr Elders blaming Alberyx Enterprises again. He did mention the boy. He also spoke of two Alberyx Enterprises engineers who have fallen sick.'

'This does not sound good…' sighed Baynard. 'What does he know that we don't?'

He looked at Jeremy demanding an answer but all he got was a helpless shrug from the ginger-haired sergeant.

'Right. We need to contact Alberyx Enterprises to find out more. Have they notified the police of anything?'

The police constable and Sergeant Jeremy checked their files and shook their heads. Baynard was clutching at straws on what lead to take. Basil Elders. The boy Ken. The missing engineers. Things could not be worse.

'Sergeant Jeremy, please arrange for Ken to be taken to Parkside Hospital. Doctor, any hopes for full recovery?'

'Not until we have run more tests.' sighed the doctor.

Baynard knew that he was asking an unanswerable question. The inspector could read in the doctor's eyes the gloomy possibility of a worst-case scenario, one where the boy would never recover. He did not want to think about it. He had to stay focused. This could be just the beginning of something bigger. He had to keep order in Wimbledon once and for all.

'Right. Where was this boy found again?' he asked Jeremy. 'West of the Common?'

'Yes. He was last seen by the rugby fields near the Beverly Brook river. He must have walked from there through the Common.'

'He may have walked near the Royal Wimbledon Golf Club.'

Baynard had an idea.

'I'd better go and check the Repeater site first.' he added. 'Then get in touch with Alberyx Enterprises.'

'What makes you think this has anything to do with that tower thing?' questioned Jeremy.

'I don't. But I know someone who could help me out.' said Baynard with a wink.

Lord Awlthorp tapped his fingers at the desk in his studio. The notepad was in front of him, neatly laid out, with his calculations scribbled on it. He had verified them twice. With a calculator. With his tablet. They were correct. The latest computer code installed by Operator One in the USB flash drives had worked, managing to mimic the most complex of algorithms. Lord Awlthorp congratulated himself in the solitude of his study. None of it would have been possible if the spirit of the Wynnman had not whispered to him how to bridge ancient knowledge with the best technology he could get access to. It came at a price Lord Awlthorp was willing to pay. A painful price. He glanced at his gloved hand, reminiscing at the trickle of blood each time the Wynnman spoke to him. He winced just at the thought of the pain the gloved hand caused him from time to time. The blood was the Wynnman's price for the knowledge he shared, until the third relic, the ivory dagger, would give the sorcerer his own blood back.

He glanced up at his large map of Wimbledon Common. The red strings pinned on it had changed positions and now they were clustered around a smaller location. Lord Awlthorp grinned maliciously. Since the code had worked, the Oscillator had finally given him a shorter radius for his search. The signs of older pins had remained on the map. They were a reminder of Lord Awlthorp's previous attempts as he edged closer to where the relic may be buried. Now, he had narrowed down the area to a more precise location which overlapped with Caesar's Camp and the fields immediately north of it, near Thatched Cottage. He knew *where* the relic was likely to be. However, the WPCC would never allow him to dig all over the Common. Instead, he had found a subtle and incredible way to find the dagger. All he needed to know now was *when* it was buried. He laughed to himself at the irony. Months ago, he would have spurned this idea, but the Wynnman, speaking to him from beyond, had entrusted him with knowledge about science and technology beyond his wildest dreams.

Ever since the accident at the Old Rectory, he had started hearing the Wynnman's voice. First in his sleep, then at random points throughout the day. He was quick to learn from the beginning he was not crazy. The voice was talking to him as if explaining or giving instructions; it whispered unpronounceable words and listed strange formulas once after the other. One day he sat down at the table in his cubic windowless room, focusing on the voice as it emerged from the silent darkness. Lord Awlthorp then started writing down those letters and words that at first did not make sense, but as he pieced them together, he understood a message was being given to him. The burning crimson liquid had somehow created a bond with the imprisoned spirit of the Wynnman, and the sorcerer had chosen Lord Awlthorp to show him the way to find and finally release him from his prison. The message dictated to him was in Anglo-Saxon runic language. Through a thorough translation of every single word, Lord Awlthorp became more and more convinced they were instructions of a mathematical nature. Impossible, he had thought. All this time, he expected the Wynnman to share a magic spell or a powerful enchantment, so convinced of the Medieval traditions in magic he had been grown to believe in. Instead, what he was seeing written on the page was an archaic formula close to modern algebra and theoretical physics, centuries before their invention. It depicted how to manipulate the wave currents across natural and celestial bodies, and how Lord Awlthorp could use them to find the next relic. At first, the man in black had been clueless as to what they were for. Then Alberyx Enterprises announced their plans for the windmill and the new technology at hand opened Lord Awlthorp's eyes. The Wynnman himself told him how to put the formulas to the test and use the Alberyx Enterprises technology to find the third relic in space and time. It meant he was a step closer to free the Wynnman, and a step closer to access to a form of knowledge that was not just mere wizardry. It was a source of knowledge so powerful, so advanced he could use it one day to give back to Wimbledon a splendour nobody could ever imagine. All he needed to do was to find the seven relics and complete his quest.

Lord Awlthorp's eyes shone avidly into the darkness. It was time to get to work and think short-term. The dagger was the main priority now, and once found, Wimbledon would have three relics discovered under its mantle. He stood up and took the small flight of steps that led to his research room. The manuscripts lay on the counter where he had left them. They had been retrieved from the vault of the Spencer family, where they had been left for a long time. No one had realised they all portrayed the same thing. He could not resist glancing at them one more time. Each manuscript showed various degrees of aging with the best preserved at the top; each one of them belonged to a different point in time. 1935, a chalk sketch still in good condition. 1663, a Baroque oil painting of the same picture. 1215, the last manuscript written in Old English and still easy to read and understand. The one at the very bottom was well protected by a thin glass case, to protect the faded, thick sheet of paper made of linen rags. It was at least a thousand years old, rough, and worn in most places, with runic characters describing the same picture portrayed over the millennia. It was the picture of a small dagger with a sharp curved blade and an intricate decoration carved around the handle. The decoration showed the scaly upper part of a dragon's neck, head and mouth with its tongue sticking out at the edge of the handle. Lord Awlthorp's eyes glinted avidly at the picture, unable to hide his strong desire to get his hands on the next mysterious relic he had been searching for, wondering what other powers he would inherit from the Wynnman. One of the seven relics of the Wynnman would soon be his.

His phone rang. The sombre ringtone echoed mournfully in the room. He cursed for not turning it off, spoiling the moment he was truly enjoying. He looked at the screen. It was Reginald calling.

'Reporting in, sir.'

'What is it?'

'I am afraid we have two casualties. As I suspected.'

'You said there was only one last night…' challenged Lord Awlthorp.

'Yes, that was an engineer called Richard at the Repeater. However, there was also boy walking on the Common…'

Reginald's voice wavered. Lord Awlthorp's silence on the other end of the line made him uneasy. Reginald could imagine the man in black closing his eyes for a minute, controlling his anger. Then his cold voice came through, enough to cut deep into his confidence and crush it until he was sure it was clear who was in charge.

'This is not what I was expecting. Tell me about the engineer.'

'An employee of Alberyx Enterprises. Operator One is dealing with the cover-up just like last time.'

'I assume we can't do the same for this boy…where is he now?'

Reginald swallowed hard. He knew this would be the hardest part of the phone call.

'Spill out the rest, Reggie!' barked Lord Awlthorp.

'The boy was near The Repeater when we ran the test. We couldn't have known…'

'You couldn't have known?' lashed Lord Awlthorp. 'You and the Operators are meant to know every inch of the Common and keep the space clear when we run the triangulation.'

'Sir…'

'Enough!'

Reginald had worked for Lord Awlthorp long enough to know he was not the merciful type. His anger now though, was different from what he had experienced in recent months. An uncontrollable anger fuelled by madness in finding a thousand-old stupid relic.

'Where is the boy now?' insisted Lord Awlthorp.

'He is currently at the Wimbledon Police Station under observation. I think he is in shock.'

'In shock…how?'

'Based on what Operator Two learnt, he seems to have turned into a vegetable.'

Lord Awlthorp weighed Reginald's words. The boy was not simply under shock; he had walked through the triangulation just like John Crane and also this other stupid engineer had done. This was the biggest risk Lord Awlthorp had to face and yet he wondered what the boy had seen.

'We need to move fast, Reggie! I fear news of the boy has already spread panic across Wimbledon and it will make it harder for us to work undetected.'

'Do you plan to complete the triangulation today?'

'Not enough time. I need one more measurement tomorrow and then by Thursday we can complete the triangulation. Make sure Operator One is ready and ask Operator Two to keep an eye on police movements.'

'Why do you think Operator Two would cooperate?'

'We said we would get rid of his number one enemy: Alberyx Enterprises...' replied Lord Awlthorp.

He grinned relishing in the clever puppet master role he had set for himself. While the others did his dirty work, he would keep his anonymity throughout. He could not risk exposing himself like he had done at the Old Rectory. That had been a mistake.

'I will brief them both, sir.' confirmed Reginald.

There was a short silence. Lord Awlthorp heard Reginald breathing on the other end of the line. He could feel his anxiety building up somehow.

'I sense there is more...' added the man in black. 'What is it?'

Reginald took a deep breath.

'One of the Operators warned me of an old friend of ours.'

'And who would that be?'

'Enrico LoTrova.'

'What?'

Lord Awlthorp hated the name. He thought LoTrova would be out of the picture this time. Instead, the name of that devilish baker kept cropping up again and again, like a curse. How he always ended up crossing paths with Enrico, he could not tell. It was as if fate kept pulling them towards each other. Lord Awlthorp had underestimated Enrico before, and this time he had to stop him in the nick of time. He needed to be methodical in the cruellest way possible.

'What is it with this stupid Italian baker? Who the hell is he?' complained Lord Awlthorp. 'If his name is cropping up, it means he is already up to something. We have to get rid of him once and for all before he can thwart our delicate plans a second time.'

'Operator One took some liberty on that…'

'What do you mean?'

'Tried to run him over…'

'Is that so?'

Lord Awlthorp found Operator One more resourceful than expected. Perhaps a sloppy way to remove a threat, in his opinion. Yet, he needed all the help he could get. An idea dawned on him. He knew a way to deal with that stupid Italian baker.

'On second thought, Reggie, why don't we run the triangulation test tonight?'

'Sir, is that safe? You said there is not enough time.'

'Perhaps not, Reginald, but it is necessary. Get Operator One ready at The Repeater, and you, be at the New Wimbledon Windmill ready to operate the Oscillator. This time our test will be targeted to one casualty in particular. I will find a way to lure Enrico LoTrova to the windmill tonight. Once we know he is close enough, he will not escape the effects of the Oscillator.'

'What about our final test?'

'We could catch two birds with one stone by getting rid of the baker while we push our plans forward….'

Lord Awlthorp smiled wickedly. He was determined to get things done. Reginald stayed silent, unconvinced. He would have preferred to meet the Italian baker face to face to beat him up. He had unfinished business with Enrico; after all it was him who had sent Reginald to prison.

Lord Awlthorp's small black eyes glinted again with a surreal evil flare. He smiled wickedly and almost felt an unnatural power surge in him, stupefied by a vision he alone could only see. Reginald, however, struggled to rejoice in Lord Awlthorp's plan. He understood his plan, having seen the effects of the Oscillator. Yet, he stayed silent, unconvinced. He had no choice but to follow orders or he would end up behind bars again. Soon, though, he would have the chance to plan his safe exit for good when the moment was right. He ended the call and sat alone in his hiding place, caressing his beard; with only the monitors, the electronic equipment and two catatonic engineers to keep him company.

Simon Deeley knocked on the museum door on the first floor of the Wimbledon Society building. The door was ajar, so he walked straight in calling out for Dr Watkins. The place was empty. Simon had never been to the Wimbledon Museum. He walked around the glass showcases depicting the history of Wimbledon. The early Medieval village, the Cecils, the Manor Houses, Victorian Wimbledon. It was fascinating to see how much history about the village could be crammed into such a tiny space. A cup of tea on the reception desk was still warm so the curator could not be far. He called out Dr Watkin's name again.

'I am here! No need to shout.'

The old curator emerged from the closet used as storage at one end of the large room. He was wiping his hands with a cloth and his inquiring expression turned into a welcoming grin as he saw a familiar face.

'Oh, it's you, Simon. What brings you here?'

'Dr W, I ask myself how ye manage to keep everything in here, both in the main room and even in storage. 'Is place is so tiny you must run out o' space at some point.'

'Well, if your presentation last night captured everyone's imagination as we thought it would, then I would expect more visitors to the museum and perhaps I could afford to build an extension.'

'I took a brief walk. Some fine pieces of local history ye hev. I am sure you look forward to adding items from the Old Rectory.'

'It is a modest museum, but it tells a story and I never shy away from showing the latest discovery.'

'Talking about discoveries, I was talking to your Italian friend last night.'

'Enrico LoTrova?'

'Aye. Mr LoTrova. Funny character. He mentioned a lava rock shaped in the form of an azalea, and some bottle filled with a strange liquid. He said you found them in Wimbledon recently.'

'They are on loan still to another museum in Surrey.'

'I saw the empty glass cases, so I figured. No idea when they will be returned?'

'Probably in a few more months. April or May I would think.'

Simon watched Dr Watkins with renewed curiosity.

'Didn't ye notice?' he asked the curator.

'What?' replied Dr Watkins grabbing his cup of tea.

'Th' lava rock is shaped like an azalea. A flower.'

'And?'

'The first relic of the Wynnman is a flower, according to the legend!' he exclaimed. 'It wis in my presentation last night. Don't ye see th' connection that the lava rock could be the first relic?'

'Simon, please.' snickered Dr Watkins. 'First Caesar's Camp. Now this. We are getting ahead of ourselves!'

'Ye shuid let me have a look at the two relics when they are returned. They could be yer most precious items on show.'

'I will when they are returned to the museum.' dismissed Dr Watkins. 'I presume you came to hear about my chat with Lord Cotton.'

'As a matter of fact, I did.'

'Ok. Oh, how rude of me. Care for some tea?'

'Aye. Milk and two sugars, please.'

Dr Watkins turned on his small kettle and threw a coaster on his desk for Simon's mug. He had managed to discuss the topic with Lord Cotton after leaving the Fox and Grapes. It had been a friendly chat and yet not a fruitful one. He sighed as they both sipped their teas thinking.

'Lord Cotton does not have any objections to our cause. He's impressed with what we've done at the Old Rectory in such little time. The problem is that what you are asking Simon must go through an approval process. Three to be exact. The WAIS, the Royal Wimbledon Golf Club and the WPCC.'

'It would take forever. Can't he pull some strings? How aboot asking Julian Alberon? I think we are onto something. Perhaps there are more relics underground than we care tae think.'

'Simon, you are asking permission to dig under Caesar's Camp and last time someone dared to level it for construction, it was John Erle-Drax in 1875. All hell broke loose back then. This is why we need to go through the motions today. Not to mention the fact it is also a sensitive week with the opening of the New Windmill.'

'Tell me aboot it.' chuckled the archaeologist. 'When I arrived at the Old Rectory this morning, I glanced at the social media and fans of that guy "Wilberforce" were blabbering aboot the new Alberyx Enterprises infrastructure and how it can fry yer brain or cause you tae see ghosts. Ghosts! Come on!'

'Ghosts, you say?'

'Yeah. Can ye believe it?'

Simon downed his tea.

'Speaking of ghosts, we had another technical issue at the Old Rectory.'

'The time issue again?'

'Aye. Again. Hours are missing from the data. I checked and it seems an electromagnetic interference hit the circuits. Both last night and on Sunday night. Did ye notice anything on Sunday, Dr Watkins, that could have messed it up?'

'No. Nothing I can recall.'

Simon frowned. He was at a loss on the causes behind it. Dr Watkins watched him from behind his mug as he finished his tea. Simon Deeley was meticulous enough not to relent from investigating anything that was odd. The curator knew that Simon would chase ghosts if he had to prove they were not real.

'I am just worried about losing data or worse.' added Simon, thoughtful. 'Anyway, time to go to the Old Rectory for our daily dose of archaeology fun. Ready tae walk thir?'

'Almost. Let me grab my things.'

'Good. And about 'is approval. Can we get the WAIS to look at it this week?'

'Let's see what I can do. It is only Tuesday and so much has already happened.'

Inspector Baynard parked his car not far from the Royal Wimbledon Golf Club. He wanted to keep his visit low key, so he chose a spot on the small roundabout between Camp Road and Camp View. He waited in the car for a few minutes, reading through his notes, thinking of what he should ask Lord Cotton. He had to find an excuse to get close to the Repeater so he could speak to the engineers present there.

When he finally made an entrance, he found it relatively quiet and empty compared to the large crowd that had attended the press conference. Baynard walked up to the receptionist and pulled the best smile he had.

'Inspector Baynard. I am here to see Lord Cotton.'

'Do you have an appointment?'

'Don't think so. I am sure he will find time for me.'

'Let me look into it. Would you like to wait in the lounge bar?'

Baynard nodded and strolled into the lounge bar. There were a few members lazing around the seated area while others were getting ready for a game. The weather was overcast and cold, but still within the parameters of any golfer wishing to hit a ball or two down the fairway. Baynard sat on one of the stools by the bar and waited, pondering whether to ask for a drink or not in the middle of the afternoon. He probably needed one. Fortunately, temptation was cast away when a female voice called out to him.

'Inspector Baynard!'.

Baynard turned and the slender, sporty figure of Ramona Halywell appeared at the entrance of the bar. Her pink tracksuit and furred hood could not go unnoticed. The pulled back hair, kept in a ponytail for practicality, seemed to pull her face and eyes upwards, arching her dark eyebrows over the cold big blue eyes with a sinister angle. She had a malicious, intense look, heightened by her slim figure.

'Hello, Miss…?'

'I am Ramona Halywell, the club captain. We met a few weeks ago during the security briefings. How can I be of service?'

Baynard vaguely recollected the encounter when they had to ensure the club was safe enough to hold the press conference.

'Nice to meet you. I thought I would be meeting Lord Cotton.'

'Unfortunately, Lord Cotton had to leave in a hurry on business. He is terribly busy this week. We all are as you can imagine. He asked me to fill him in and he does send his apologies.'

Ramona beamed at Baynard as she spoke. Her eyes were so persuasive and convincing. The Wimbledon inspector glanced around as if Lord Cotton were hiding somewhere in the bar.

'I would like to speak to whom is in charge. I can wait.'

'Inspector Baynard, I am Lord Cotton's second in command here.'

'I didn't know you used military terms around here.'

Ramona faked a laugh to ease the tension.

'I help run the place. Lord Cotton is always running around, meeting people.'

Baynard hesitated.

'You came all the way here so it must be important, inspector.' added Ramona. 'Do we need some privacy for our conversation?'

Baynard nodded. He looked around and then followed Ramona's inviting gesture into Lord Cotton's office across the hall towards the other side of the building. It was a plain room, filled with many glass cabinets and shelves crowded with trophies of all sizes. Her desk was the tidiest he had ever seen, compared to his standards at the police station. The framed awards on the wall next to it were just proof of her great efficiency.

'I can see Lord Cotton is in good hands...' commented Baynard, observing each award. 'I see here some from Alberyx Enterprises. Not really sports-related, is it?'

'The work at the club is on the side. I actually work at Alberyx Enterprises, inspector.'

'In what capacity?'

'Data analyst. Been there for quite a few years.'

'Are you one of those smart tech people who understand what Sir Alberon built around here?'

'That is beyond my pay grade, inspector.' grinned Ramona. 'I support some of the more basic infrastructure.'

She opened her slim laptop and put it to the side, ready to draw up any info Baynard needed. She then clasped her hands and leaned forward to give Baynard all her attention.

'So, inspector, how can I help?' she said.

The inspector was wary of her attitude and could not deny the fact she was being cooperative.

'Thank you for your time, Miss Halywell.' replied Baynard. 'I just want to ask a few questions. We received reports of an alleged casualty on the

Common last night, not far from here. An assault to be precise. We were wondering if anyone here at the club noticed something.'

Baynard decided to play smart and leave a few details out on purpose.

'Oh dear.' said Ramona genuinely shocked. 'That is terrible. Last night, did you say? No, I don't think we noticed anything. The club is closed after hours. I hope Mr Elders is not accountable for this.'

Baynard preferred to ignore the comment. He had heard enough of Basil 'Wilberforce' Elders.

'Have you checked with Alberyx Enterprises personnel at the Repeater? We want to be sure their safety is not compromised.'

Ramona shifted in her seat locked on Baynard's inquisitive stare. The inspector thought he saw a flash of uncertainty in the perennial strong and assertive posture of the club captain.

'Our custodians wouldn't have raised the alarm because the Repeater is on the golf course and Alberyx Enterprises has full jurisdiction, including responsibility for security. They would inform Lord Cotton and myself if something happened.'

'How about who comes and goes at the site.'

'The club is not responsible for keeping a register or collecting sick notes, inspector.' sniggered Ramona. 'You should contact Alberyx Enterprises instead.'

'Funny you mention sick notes.' teased Baynard. 'But aren't you notified at all? Surely, you must have a vague notion of…'

'We are obliged to know who is and who is not on the golf course. Health and safety. Alberyx Enterprises is responsible for their staff and for the small area on which the Repeater is built.'

'Of course.' said Baynard playing dumb. 'I wondered if you knew the protocols to save me some time. Which staff are you referring to? Mr Crane perhaps?'

'Inspector Baynard, we play golf here.' sighed Ramona. 'Yes, we lent the land to build the Repeater, one of the most revolutionary thing Wimbledon has ever seen, but as I already told you, Alberyx Enterprises is in charge. You need to ask them about their protocols and their staff!'

'Don't you work for Alberyx Enterprises?'

'I am an ordinary employee of another department. I don't have a role or the authority in this part of the business.'

Ramona very skilfully washed her hands of the matter. Baynard had to admit she knew her way out of things.

'Very clear, Miss Halywell. Is it possible to have a look at The Repeater?'

Ramona was annoyed by the intrusive inspector. She glanced at her watch thinking she had more important things to attend to.

'Do you have a train to catch, Miss Halywell?'

'Not at all, Inspector Baynard.' replied Ramona with one of her cold smiles. 'If you follow me, I can take you there with one of the golf carts.'

'Perfect!'

The Repeater was in the same condition as Baynard had left it when he came to check things out the day before. Coming from the south, the tall, thin scaffolding still gave the impression of work in progress. They drove across the golf course, up and down the gentle slopes, and parked not far from the pop-up offices. This time though only two engineers came to greet him as he hopped off the cart.

'Weren't there three of you yesterday?' asked Baynard curiously.

'Hi, inspector!' greeted one with the nametag Phil. 'Richard, whom you spoke to yesterday, fell sick, so he did not come to work today.'

'I see. It must be one hell of a flu. I heard one of your superiors, Mr Crane, also fell ill. If it carries on like this, there will be a pandemic.'

The two engineers looked at each other uneasy, and then chuckled. Baynard could sense the two engineers were probably unaware. They knew as much as he did about what had happened to Mr Crane and now Richard.

'I hear different accents, by the way. You are not all from Wimbledon or London, right?'

'No, inspector. Alberyx Enterprises staff comes from all over the UK and those who are not locals live at Warren Farms.'

'At the compound half a mile north from here?'

'Correct. We have a whole section allocated to our living quarters.'

'I see. Your colleague Richard must be in there with a nice Lemsip and a warm blanket while you work here in the cold, huh?'

The engineers chuckled again. The inspector then noticed Ramona was starting to tap her feet.

'Does Mr Crane live at Warren Farms too?'

'Yes. He is lucky though to have his girlfriend…sorry fiancée…with him.' commented Phil.

'I can understand. I bet it gets lonely here on your own with this inanimate tower.'

The engineers nodded amicably. Baynard heard Ramona shuffling her feet even more.

'Inspector,' she said. 'I am not sure if you can question the engineers without an official approval from Alberyx Enterprises. I believe Mr Sanders is required to be present.'

'I am not questioning anyone, right boys?' said Baynard playfully talking directly to the engineers. 'Just having a chat. Do you mind if I have a look around? Under your supervision, of course?'

The engineers agreed regardless of Ramona's groans. They let the inspector take a short walk around the turret scaffolding and peer from afar inside the office and the workshop pop-up buildings. Ramona did not leave him alone once. She was being very diligent in following protocol. Baynard found it strange she was showing so much care when only a few minutes before she had washed her hands of any responsibility. He knew though she could have called the lawyer Mr Sanders at any moment and he knew he did not have any search warrant with him. He had to restrain himself not to push it too much.

As he walked over the wet grass, the sky started to become cloudy and a light rain started to drizzle on the golf course. A faint rumble of thunder announced its arrival in the distance. Baynard knew he would be asked to leave soon. The moment Ramona started her spiel on weather, security, and whatever excuse she could find to make him leave, Baynard spotted something on the ground. The grass was slightly flatter in one point as if a big weight had been dropped on it. A boulder, a crate. The shape though was somewhat smaller and had no form, but Baynard swore it resembled a human body. When he was closer to it, he knelt down to tie his shoes and checked the grass carefully. There was a dark purple-brown stain near him. He brushed his hand over the patch of grass and ripped some of it up. He rubbed it between his fingers. He placed them to his nose as if to enjoy the fresh musky smell of the grass.

'Ready, inspector?' insisted Ramona once more, sheltering under the roof of the golf cart. 'It is going to pour down soon, and I need to inform our members all games are off.'

'Ready when you are!' replied Baynard with an unusual jolly attitude. 'The scent of wet grass is nice, isn't it?'

He breathed in heavily. There was something else on the grass. There was an unmistakeable iron smell of dried blood. He smiled to Ramona. He had to keep up appearances for now until he was back at the police station. Baynard realised he may be onto something.

'Come on, Viviane. I didn't do anything wrong.'

Enrico waved his hand in all directions to make his case. Viviane smiled inwardly, enjoying the colourful gestures of his baker friend. She turned right at the roundabout and lined up her yellow Fiat 500 behind the queue of cars waiting for the green light in the centre of Wimbledon Town.

'I mean, that man, Basil, is weird but has a point…'

'Yes, he may have, but you should be careful about taking sides. Do you have any idea what his agenda is?'

'You are not mad at me then?' checked Enrico.

'Well, I am mad at them, not you.'

Viviane did not look at Enrico, she casually glanced up into the sky to see the first drizzle falling on her windscreen.

'So why did you leave so fast?'

'Well, it is good not to stick around with that "Wimbledon For The People" bunch. Don't get into trouble, Enrico. Lord Cotton's offer is not yet signed. Plus, I need to get back to the flower shop, and I think you have a bakery to attend to.'

'Yes, you are right. It's all been a bit strange since this morning…'

'I know you are still shaken after the hit and run…'

'It's not that!'

'Then what?'

'Promise not to get angry?'

'Oh, come on!' sighed Viviane.

'Well, it's about the accident at the Old Rectory. And the vision I had. Remember?'

'Oh no…'

Viviane pulled a face, wishing it had been something else.

'What about it?' she said, noticing the traffic light had turned green.

'Not sure how to say it. But Dr Watkins believes there is some truth in it. And Simon Deeley seems to be of the same opinion.'

'You're joking?'

'Well, Dr Watkins and Simon have been repeating the same thing. That all these relics we have found so far…you know, the black azalea, the crimson liquid…they are the relics mentioned in the texts they deciphered.'

'I hope you told Dr Watkins it was just folklore, right? Like he used to say to us.'

Enrico thought about what to say.

'Enrico?' asked Viviane again, wary of what Enrico may have done.

'That's not the point, Viviane.' replied Enrico. 'Dr Watkins told me he thinks someone may be after these relics. Eric Quercer, the Claymores; he thinks they have come to Wimbledon for that purpose.'

'And? It didn't end well for them, did it?'

'What if there are more people planning to come and look for those relics?'

'As if they exist...'

'Well, according to Simon, they do. Apparently, he has asked Dr Watkins to dig up Caesar's Camp because they may be hidden underneath.'

Viviane turned left up Wimbledon Hill Road. The traffic still moved slowly to get out of Wimbledon Town. Up ahead, the stretch of road climbing up the hill towards Wimbledon Village was void of traffic.

'I think you are still shaken by that crazy hit and run, Enrico. Hopefully, the police will call you back for a statement. Try not to think about it.'

Viviane said those words hoping they would resonate in Enrico's head. She knew too well; Enrico's curiosity had been let loose and she was surprised to hear Dr Watkins now meddled with it.

'Last time something happened, it was someone trying to undermine Julian's work. Remember?'

'I do.' sighed Viviane.

'It is exactly the same now. Julian has put all his efforts into building this futuristic windmill, helping the community, and suddenly you have Basil "Wilberforce" Elders attacking him quite openly, I almost get run over, people start falling ill or disappearing... It is one thing after another. All these events are scary...'

'I am sure Baynard is on top of it all and perhaps glad you are not getting yourself involved.'

'I think we should warn Julian.'

'You think he doesn't know? He has the best security he could find...'

'We saved the day last time, Viviane.' Enrico grinned. 'If we are true friends, we don't want anything to happen to him…again. Do we?'

'I'm going to regret this…' muttered Viviane.

She finally sped up the hill in her little yellow Fiat 500 on the last stretch to Wimbledon Village. The tiny car roared up the hill, showing all its might. Enrico looked out of the window at the shaded tree line on one side of the road. There were a few people out and about, walking under the trees. The thick green foliage was a breath of fresh air after the heavy traffic they had just left behind. The road was still lined with flats and houses alternating each other but the trees and the hedges scattered in between sucked them all into a sea of green to the point the houses almost disappeared. Enrico watched absent-mindedly as the view flashed before him. He suddenly sat up in his seat. He thought he recognised someone walking up.

'Hey, isn't that Quentin… Quentin Plainstraw?' he nudged Viviane.

She looked towards him. The very tall man was hard not to miss, with the same sleeveless jumper as yesterday, and his arms dangling backwards and forwards as he trudged up the hill.

'Yes. That's him.'

'Shall we give him a lift?'

'Sure!'

Viviane quickly found a suitable place to stop the car.

'Hey Mr Plainstraw!' waved Enrico from the car window.

The tall man squinted at him and struggled to recognise the Italian baker at first. He carried on walking. When they were a bit closer, Viviane jumped out of the car and called again.

'Oh Viviane! Mr LoTrova! Nice to see nice people.' rejoiced Quentin upon recognising the two. 'What are you doing here?'

'We saw you walking all the way up. Need a lift?'

'Oh, that would be so kind!' thanked Quentin. 'As far as Camp Road or Rushmere Green would be fine.'

'Is that home?' checked Enrico.

Quentin and Viviane laughed almost together.

'His home is a cottage buried deep in the Common.' explained Viviane. 'There is no road for cars. Come on, let's go!'

The car started up again and Viviane drove through the back streets of Belvedere Drive and Belvedere Avenue to join the main road. Enrico observed Quentin through the rear-view mirror. The odd tall man looked around him as if he were a tourist being taken on a tour of a city he had never seen before. The fact he lived on the Common, one of the most talked about places lately, made him a curious character he would like to get to know better.

'So, Mr Plainstraw.' said Enrico eager to chat.

'Quentin, please.'

'Are you Wimbledon born and bred?'

'I am indeed. I used to hang around with Dr Watkins when we were young.'

'And you always lived on the Common?'

'Always. My father. My grandfather. We used to live on Warren Farms before… you know…'

A flash of anger came over his face. Controlled but still livid. He stopped mid-sentence and looked at the happy strollers on Wimbledon High Street.

'Everything ok, Quentin?' asked Viviane worried, careful to keep her eyes on the road.

She too had noticed something was wrong.

'Isn't Warren Farms the headquarters of Alberyx Enterprises?' asked Enrico.

'Do not name Alberyx Enterprises in front of me!' protested Quentin in the back of the car. 'They are careless vultures! Taking, taking…'

'What do you mean?' carried on Enrico.

'Let's try to be tactful, Enrico. Shall we?' warned Viviane, glaring at him.

'They took Warren Farms to build their stupid headquarters. They took the old windmill I looked after. Now, they even want to frame me for all their bloody wrongdoing…'

'Frame you? What else do they want from you?' wondered Viviane.

She stopped the car at the pedestrian crossing and glanced at Quentin, now looking sad and somehow smaller in the back of her car. Second time she had heard some strong words against Julian's company. It made her wonder too what was going on in Wimbledon.

'I was at the police station…'

'We were just there.' interjected Enrico. 'Are you in trouble?'

'No. I actually did the police a favour. Helped that poor boy, Ken. You should have seen him. It was horrible when I found him this morning there in the bushes.'

Enrico and Viviane remembered the name.

'You found Ken on the Common. What was wrong with him?'

'He looked like a zombie. Muttering to himself, but not talking, not reacting.'

'What did the police say?'

'Well, nothing because the doctors can't even explain why he is like this. Yet, Wimbledon Police does not want me to leave Wimbledon.'

'You're not a suspect, are you?' asked Viviane.

'I am telling you. Alberyx Enterprises put the police on my tracks. Now the police is breathing down my neck, and Alberyx Enterprises has made them believe I did something to the boy.'

'Did they actually accuse you?' checked Enrico, incredulous Baynard would allow such a thing.

'No, but it's obvious. Alberyx Enterprises wants to cover it all up. The wireless electricity will make us ill, messing up our brains.'

Enrico rolled his eyes, knowing where this story led. Viviane glared at him once more. This time to ask him to be supportive. She turned left and drove towards Southside Common, with the green expanse of Rushmere Green to their right.

'Here will be fine, Viviane.' said Quentin.

'Are you sure?'

'I am sure.'

The Fiat 500 came to a halt slowly and then Viviane turned off the engine; the only sound to be heard was the soft rain tapping on the roof.

'Are you sure we can't take you further?' suggested Enrico.

'Don't worry, young man. I have seen all kinds of weather on the Common. This is nothing.'

Quentin readied himself to leave.

'One second.' said Enrico. 'About Ken.'

Quentin turned around, interested.

'Is this related to what you were saying yesterday? About ghosts?'

The tall man, hunched in the back of the small Fiat 500, grinned at Enrico.

'You should have heard Ken. He was muttering about men on horses throwing arrows at him. Apparitions, of course. This wireless electricity appears to make you see strange things. Hallucinations of sorts. Some people prefer to call them ghosts. Still, our health is at risk.'

Enrico had just heard those words from Basil Elders at the coffee shop and hearing them coming from a seemingly more tranquil man like Quentin Plainstraw left the Italian baker confused. It was not just about creative imagination. Something was wrong with Alberyx Enterprises, and it was not simply about their planned development on Wimbledon Common upsetting a portion of Wimbledon. There was more behind it, but he could not put his finger on it.

'Time to go.' said Quentin. 'Stay safe and thanks for the ride! Those heavy clouds in the sky are announcing the arrival of some good old English rain.'

Enrico got out of the car to let the tall man leave and make his way onto Rushmere Green, heading towards Wimbledon Common. Enrico and Viviane watched him go from inside the small Fiat 500. Thunder rumbled in the distance. Later, when Quentin had become just a tiny dot on the horizon, heavy rain started to fall. Enrico and Viviane did not know what to say to each other and glanced at the desolate Rushmere Green under the pouring rain. For a moment they thought Quentin's ghosts had come alive and were looking at them from behind the trees along Southside Common.

Nathan Glenn had stayed behind on his own, drinking a cup of hot chocolate at the coffee shop and brewing over the dramatic news he had just heard first-hand. Deep inside, Nathan found it fascinating that, after months of articles targeting Alberyx Enterprises, his suspicions were not far off from reality. The nice local company looking after the community was actually a bad apple not caring about health hazards. Basil was right. This was the scoop he needed. Yet, how Basil Elders had been able to get such information, eluded him. He must have had some very good inside help, Nathan thought.

The rain had created a layer of grey over the dull buildings of Wimbledon Town, which were not as charming as the village. There was one thing he was not enjoying. As a journalist, whatever the case, he wanted to be independent to report on the facts or the opinions. Basil Elders did not seem to leave much room for that. Letting Nathan join him during his open charade at Wimbledon Police Station was a way to promote his cause in exchange for some juicy info for Nathan before the other newspapers heard about. Nathan glanced at his laptop open on the table. He was happy to see his article about the police station online, being liked and shared by so many; his agenda was building up momentum. He felt cheated though. He had not learnt much about Basil 'Wilberforce' Elders. If he needed credibility, he had to validate Basil as a source. The journalist looked at the bright, blue-tinted screen which seemed to put the rest of the coffee shop in a dull penumbra. He then cracked his knuckles and opened a new tab and searched for 'Basil Elders'.

Nothing. Page after page, the web simply regurgitated the same content over and over. Things he and everyone else in Wimbledon knew. Recognised effort as a part-time scout ranger, saving trees and wildlife. One of the best teachers at Octagon School, with many published academic essays on advanced physics. The journalist grinned. Basil 'Wilberforce' Elders did not look at all like the typical stuffy physics teacher. Leaving 'Wilberforce' out of his search had spared him unnecessary results on the history of Britain. Nathan wondered where else he could find more about Basil's sources. The man was clever and had probably covered his tracks well, in order to achieve a competitive advantage over everyone. Police, Alberyx Enterprises, the Media. The only thing he could think of was that such information was probably not available online but held somewhere close to Basil's chest. On his phone. At his house. In his notebooks. In his office at Octagon School. Nathan clicked his fingers at the eureka moment. Octagon School. This is where Basil said they would hold their next group meeting with the followers of 'Wimbledon For The People'. What if he could sneak inside Basil's office then, Nathan thought. He checked his agenda. Next meeting was tomorrow, Wednesday, and apparently it was a very important one that should not be missed. Basil would not share what the meeting would be about before leaving the coffee shop earlier. He had just looked Nathan in the eye and promised a final sting at Alberyx Enterprises once and for all. The journalist of the Wimbledon Gazette had to admit Basil 'Wilberforce' Elders was a dangerous force of nature. Worse than the pelting rain outside.

From the comfort of his front living room, Julian listened astonished at the news he was hearing coming from the TV. There had been non-stop coverage of Basil Elders's visit to Wimbledon Police Station for the last hour. The newsreader used the word 'storming in' as if it had been an attack on the precinct and showed a reel of Basil's speech captured via smartphone by a member of the public.

'What is this man's problem? Seriously, I try to move on and he keeps pulling me back…' groaned the businessman slamming his drink on the coffee table.

'I would not take any notice, Sir Alberon.' commented Mr Sanders. 'He is an attention-seeker. We should get our story straight.'

The lawyer sat comfortably at the large table with his shirt collar open and his yellow tie loosened. He toyed with his glass enjoying a break from formal meetings. The news had spread fast, and he had been working all afternoon to get the facts straight.

'I mean, is there any truth in what he says?' asked Julian, worried.

'We are checking the details. I have been told by security at Warren Farms that Mr Crane and Mr Sullivan fell ill, but from a common cold or flu. They have been taken to the infirmary. So far, there is no risk to their health.'

'So, this man is making things up, isn't he?' questioned Julian pointing at the screen, unwilling to call Basil by name.

'He is twisting the story, for sure. I will get the PR Team on top of this. You should get some rest and avoid watching the news for a while.'

'What about this boy? Ken, is it?'

'I would not be surprised if we receive a visit from the police or the Council on this. However, there is no link to suggest that the Repeater caused the symptoms to this boy. We should delay launch. Not this weekend; perhaps the next.'

'No!' said Julian with a firm voice. 'I am not backing down.'

'It could turn into a PR disaster.'

'Rescheduling would mean we have something to hide, and we don't. You know, how long I have been planning this?'

Julian sat up on the sofa, glaring at Mr Sanders to get his point clearly across.

'If this man thinks he can ruin my vision, he has another thing coming…'

He slammed his hand on the coffee table.

'Sir Alberon, calm down! You are losing your temper too quickly.'

'Well, I can't do that in public. Can I?'

'Did you sleep ok last night?'

'Sort of. I went for check-up at the doctor's. My hand hurt a little.'

He massaged the light cotton glove he was wearing on it.

'Get some rest. I have this covered. We will have a press statement ready later tonight.'

'Can I see it before you issue it?'

'I'd rather you didn't.'

Mr Sanders stood up and grabbed his jacket. In a few swift moves he tidied himself up and restored himself to some kind of formal order, buttoning up his shirt and redoing his tie.

'I'm going now. Please, Sir Alberon, take some rest.'

The two bid each other farewell and Mr Sanders was about to walk towards the main door. A knock quickly came. Julian turned away from the TV and glanced at the main window overlooking the driveway. Outside, the evening had crept in earlier as the rain drowned the feeble remains of daylight. He could see a small car parked but its colour was not clear.

'Who is that?' he wondered jumping up and putting on his maroon dressing gown. He walked past Mr Sanders and opened the door. They were met by Enrico and Viviane standing on the porch.

'Hello Julian!' waved Enrico.

'Oh hello! Please come in. You are getting drenched out there!' said Julian.

'I hope we're not disturbing.' apologised Viviane. 'Especially this week out of the whole year.'

She stepped into the decorated entrance hall and cleaned her shoes warily on the carpet, wary not to leave marks on the polished floor. Enrico followed, with his chef's jacket soaked.

'Enrico, you need to buy a coat!' joked Julian.

'I told him that.' added Viviane.

Enrico shrugged as he cleaned his shoes. He then noticed Mr Sanders standing by the door.

'Do you have time…?' said Enrico.

'Sorry, Julian.' apologised Viviane. 'Enrico thinks you are free all the time…'

'Do not worry! Mr Sanders was just leaving. See you tomorrow?'

'Yes. Don't forget to take some rest, Sir Alberon!' replied Mr Sanders.

The lawyer put on his raincoat and dashed out to his car. Before long, he merged into the heavy traffic on Parkside. The tree line bordering the Common across the road swayed a little from left to right as the winds blew stronger at the top.

'Are you sure we are not disturbing?' repeated Viviane.

'Of course not.' insisted Julian leading them into the warmth of his living room. 'I have been so busy lately. I need distraction and what best than a chit-chat. At public events you don't get the chance to do that so easily.'

Julian led them into his eclectic and eccentric living room where a sophisticated hi-fi stereo stood next to a replica of a Greek statue of Venus and a black grand piano. Viviane and Enrico noticed it was pretty much the same as it was on their last visit. Julian's taste was a melting pot of culture and gadgetry that never reached low levels of ridicule. He had taste in picking the best of both. Enrico realised then the windmill was his first public attempt to prove that on a large scale. The past and the future as one.

Julian quickly turned off the TV, shutting off the news around Alberyx Enterprises. It was bringing him more problems than he needed. Vivian eyed Enrico but Enrico gave her a sign not to worry.

'Tea? Coffee? Gin and tonic? I have some of your *cantucci*, Enrico, left over from the event.' offered Julian. 'What's new with you two?'

'No thank you, Julian, really!' said Viviane not wanting to be a burden, as Julian was always generous.

However, their host had already asked his staff for a large tray of tea, coffee, juice, mixers, and a couple of spirits, plus the *cantucci*. He did not bother asking what everyone wanted. He preferred to bring choice to the table and let everyone decide.

'Really, Julian! You shouldn't have.' added Enrico, feeling embarrassed.

'We should enjoy life the best we can. Tough day, you know.'

Julian gave a thin smile, a timid one to replace the words he could not find. His eyes softened in the dim lights. Enrico thought he looked tired and yet he did his best to be open and friendly. Enrico swallowed hard since he and Viviane were about to bring up the last thing Julian wished to hear.

'What brings you here then?' started Julian as they sat on the comfortable long sofas. 'Last time I checked the Old Rectory was safe and sound.'

The simple act of self-irony made Julian look more down-to-earth than he already was. Enrico and Viviane felt there and then they could be open with him no matter what they came to say.

'H-how…how was your day?' Enrico forced himself to be nice and polite, not quite sure how to start, but inside he was dying to blurt out danger warnings and cry the siren of alarm.

'Ah, Enrico. You need to practice British diplomacy or perhaps learn to play poker. You don't hide your state of mind so well.'

Enrico blinked. Viviane giggled.

'Don't get me wrong. Your visit is appreciated. But I have a feeling I may already know why you are here. I know about some of the dreadful things that have happened today. I have a PR team for this reason, you know, but you two are probably going to ask more about what has been said on the news.'

'Well, we were at the police station today.' explained Viviane. 'We were there when Basil Elders made his speech.'

Julian sighed and pulled all his strength to cope with the subject of the conversation. He looked for his drink and took a gulp, gazing at his two guests.

'What do you make of him?' he asked.

'A troublemaker.' quickly dismissed Viviane.

'He could be more than that.' added Enrico. 'Someone may be trying to bring you and Alberyx Enterprises down.'

'What do you mean Enrico?'

'Just like the Old Rectory. Someone may be trying to infiltrate your business.'

'To do what? Steal our patented technology? I know industrial espionage is strife but our security at Warren Farms is tight!'

'How did Basil know all those things then?'

'He is twisting the truth, Enrico. We checked and my engineers just came down with cold and flu.'

'Is that it?' sighed Viviane with relief.

'And what about ghosts and hallucinations?' continued Enrico.

'Ghosts? What are you barking on about Enrico?'

'Could your wireless electricity be harmful somehow and have some serious undesired side effects on the brain?'

Julian shook his head.

'If you are referring to the state of this boy, Ken, there is no link between his condition and our machinery, and I am a little upset that you think I would be so reckless. Something would have come up, at least one thing during the many in-lab tests we did on the machine and the circuitry. Our use of mobile phones and wi-fi signals are still deemed dangerous by some people today, even if we have enough evidence to show the impact is negligible. All I am saying is, we can't jump to conclusions with a few unfounded cases.'

Viviane and Enrico read honesty in the way he spoke to them. They knew he was talking without filters, without a PR team behind him, and they rarely saw that in public.

'Are you and your team coming out to counterattack all this supposed fake news?' suggested Viviane.

'We have a statement ready. I doubt it will convince Mr Elders to back down though.'

'Why?'

Julian rubbed his hands. He avoided their gaze for the first time. He started to rub the nape of his neck, thinking whether to share what he knew with Enrico and Viviane.

'The problem is that Mr Elders feels betrayed by the terms of our contract. Pure and simple.'

Julian's cryptic sentence left Enrico and Viviane baffled. Julian knew there was no point hiding it anymore. He knew Mr Sanders would disapprove, but Julian was sure everything happened because of a misjudgement he had made and wished he had not.

'What contract?' they exclaimed simultaneously.

'I am afraid this must remain between us.' warned Julian.

He realised he was about to share something of a company secret that he considered more of a personal sin. He looked Enrico and Viviane in the eye.

'I am being serious. I consider you friends after your help at the Old Rectory.'

Enrico and Viviane looked at each other and then nodded. The Italian baker even raised his hand, with the other on his heart, showing he was happy to swear on secrecy.

'No need for that or Mr Sanders would have made you sign a non-disclosure agreement. You see, all the components of the New Wimbledon Windmill and the Repeater rely on a complex feat of engineering which uses complex quantum mechanics calculations to tap into the invisible movement of tachyons and photons for energy. The geomagnetic forces of our planet and universe play an important source and together with these quantum mechanics calculations they will make it all happen.'

Enrico and Viviane gaped, still baffled by his first sentence. Julian laughed to himself.

'You don't need to worry about the actual physics and mechanisms behind it. However, you should know it was thanks to Octagon School that the schematics allowed advanced physics and engineering to create a match made in heaven. The agreement was in exchange of funds for the school. Mr Elders, though, who led the project as it is his field, did not like the fact we decided to defer the funds promised until the power grid was fully working and large enough to cover Wimbledon. Possible when a second repeater was built.'

'You cut all their funds then?' gasped Viviane.

Julian lowered his eyes, rubbing his finger against the glass nervously. He did not answer straight away. He pursed his lips, wondering how to put his view of the facts across.

'I haven't actually cut the funds.' he replied raising his gloved hand as if under oath. 'I've just had to delay them until Alberyx Enterprises was sure they had a date when they could firmly provide them. The funds will be allocated in due time. Simply not today.'

'Well, to Mr Elders it is still a broken deal.' Enrico put it plainly. 'To him, it looks as if you betrayed the school and the students. No wonder he is trying to ruin your image and your company's, basically everything linked to this project of yours.'

'I am still shocked about how far Basil is going to throw mud at it.' deplored Julian. 'I never said Alberyx Enterprises would not pay. All this slander in public, and even claiming these absentees are victims of my machine. I found it a hit a little below the belt.'

'Good grief!' exclaimed Viviane. 'I knew there was something behind it.'

Enrico thought Viviane took Julian's side too easily. She looked sad for him. Enrico felt some empathy for the friend in front of him, but Julian had some wrongs to right. He had to fix the tiny crack in his brilliant and immaculate career. The fact Julian came clean in front of them is perhaps what he needed to feel redemption or at least a bit of it.

'Could he be planning more than just slander, Julian?' asked Enrico.

'What do you mean?'

'Has it ever occurred to you someone may be after you?'

'I am not following…'

'Like the Claymores.'

'Basil is not a criminal as such, Enrico. He may be a troublemaker, but he is not a criminal. And neither am I. Not sure what his motives would be other than ruining me.'

As he spoke, Dr Watkins's words echoed in Enrico's head about the relics and about this someone who may be looking for them. Enrico had been wondering if what was happening in Wimbledon now was related. A hunch, perhaps.

'If you don't mind, I am little tired for the day.' said Julian. 'Please, don't think less of me, but I am working on rectifying any mistake. Again, though, wireless electricity is safe.'

'We believe you!' said Viviane stretching her hand as a sign of friendship.

She held Julian's hand and Enrico smiled at the gesture.

'I am sure if Basil Elders built your calculations, he must know there is no danger in it.' reassured Enrico. 'Well, this conversation went better than I expected!'

'I think it did. And thanks for being good listeners! Let's keep in touch. Shall we?'

'Definitely!' confirmed Viviane.

A phone suddenly rang. It was Julian's. He excused himself and left the room to answer the call. Enrico and Viviane waited on the sofas, thinking of what they had just learned.

'Well, things are a bit clearer now.' sighed Viviane. 'I guess we need to wait for Baynard or the police to tell us who tried to run you over.'

'Do you also think the attempted hit and run on me is related to Basil Elders and Alberyx Enterprises?'

'Probably not. Maybe they mistook you for someone else.'

'I am not so sure…'

Julian returned, phone in hand.

'It was security at the windmill.' he said, puzzled. 'They said they have found some of your stuff from Monday's event. Baking trays, flower pots, and a white chef's jacket. Does that ring a bell?'

'I thought we had picked up everything?' frowned Viviane.

'Me too.'

'Well, they told me just that. They found other stuff too and they put it aside for people to pick up. Not sure why they called me and not you.'

Julian groaned a little annoyed.

'It's ok.' said Viviane. 'We can go and pick our stuff up now. The windmill is quite near here.'

As they were leaving, they thanked Julian again and promised to get in touch if anything new came up.

'I will see if I can get back on good terms with Basil. It's the least I can do.' promised Julian.

He stood at the door with his drink in hand watching Enrico and Viviane jump into the Fiat 500 and make their way onto Parkside towards the windmill. Julian stood on the threshold for a little while, thinking back at the conversation. Remorse was biting hard at him for the hasty business decision in delaying payment to Octagon School. He knew though Enrico and Viviane understood. He had their support. His eyes were fixed on the dark rows of trees bordering the Common across the road. He could not see anything. He could only hear the rain. His gloved hand hurt a little once more. He cursed it, while rubbing it. He then felt a strong migraine coming back, probably lack of sleep. I should blame the constant fatigue, he thought, for my recklessness with the contract with Basil 'Wilberforce' Elders.

Operator One breathed calmly while going through the check-out procedures. Warren Farms had a strict policy about staff leaving and entering the compound. Alberyx Enterprises had to ensure no confidential material left the premises unauthorised and had to check everyone's identity. Since Monday, the checks had become lengthier and stricter. Operator One though knew how to get through undetected. A simple trick that had allowed Operator One to gain the trust of the security guards and smuggle the USB flash drive in and out of the compound.

The country lane leading to Camp Road had become muddy because of all the rain, and Operator One was not happy to make the short trip to the Repeater. But orders were orders. Orders that Operator One was starting to question. The short trip had always been the same ever since Operator One had started working for Reginald Bosham and whoever his employer was. Thinking back, Operator One's reason for accepting the job was a strong ambition to show skills very few people had, plus a morbid interest in the computer code Reginald had originally requested. At first, rebuilding the strange lines of code he had provided over the last few months looked like the work of any ordinary computer programmer. Yet, having seen the code in action in the last few days at the Repeater, made Operator One realise Reginald Bosham could not be the brain behind the operation. It was clear he did not fully understand any of it. Operator One had done a bit of research with what was accessible at Warren Farms Library and had finally grasped the concept behind the complex formulas, hidden deep in the computer code. It was mind-blowing. The computer code was recreating theoretical quantum physics in the real world, and each time Operator One received an updated version, the results were more and more staggering. Something unheard of, close enough to destabilise reality itself. It was time to think beyond Reginald Bosham and find out who he really worked for and had the brains for such a complex operation.

Operator One took the footpath and cut across the golf courses. The Repeater was close and there was nobody around. It was time to call and update Reginald.

'I am in position.' said Operator One.

'You're late.'

'A bit short notice, Reginald. Don't you think?'

'No names, we said.'

'What should I call you then? Operator Zero?'

'Just don't call me. Is the Repeater closed off? Nobody working there tonight?'

'No…' replied Operator One dryly. 'I don't understand why we need to do another rushed test just like that. I thought the next one would be tomorrow. It is not getting easy to move around the Warren Farms compound.'

'Plans change. You should know what I'm talking about after deciding to run over a certain Enrico LoTrova.'

Operator One scowled while approaching the door of the scaffolding leading inside the Repeater. He knows, thought Operator One; and I have no idea how. The fact Reginald knew Operator One's attempt to run the baker over put everything in perspective about the whole, big operation behind him.

'Cat got your tongue?' chuckled Reginald.

'How do you know?' said Operator One.

'Let's say my boss and I have our sources. Just don't take a risk like that again!'

'There was a bigger risk: he could get closer to what we do here.' said Operator One detached. 'Not sure about you but I don't want to get my feet wet.'

'They are already drenched…' chuckled Reginald.

'I thought you would be pleased about me having some initiative.'

'I would be if you had succeeded in running him over perhaps.'

'What about tonight then?'

'Well, we will attempt to get rid of the baker again, through the next triangulation test.'

Operator One had run enough tests to understand how they were planning to use the triangulation and how much damage it could cause to whoever got caught in it. Operator One took a vane pride in the work done and the lives at stake suddenly did not matter. The computer code was Operator One's great achievement and wanted Reginald and his employer to recognise its greatness.

After climbing up the short ladder inside the Repeater, Operator One put on an earpiece to talk hands-free and started fiddling with the command control.

'I'm in position. Let me get started. Are you at the windmill?'

'Yes'

'Is tonight's triangulation still part of our tests?'

'Yes.'

Operator One struggled to get all the information from Reggie's monosyllable answers.

'Are you ever going to share with me what we are doing this for?' asked Operator One while pressing buttons and typing commands on the workstation.

'Just type away. You are working on a need-to-know basis.'

'I see the results like you do, you know. The output from these triangulations pinpoints different locations on the Common and then each triangulation tries to date them somehow. Are you searching for something? Something buried from the past perhaps?'

'Don't push your luck, Operator One!'

'Or what?'

'I'll break you in two. That's why. You can also forget the promised retribution.'

'Playing hard, I see.'

Operator One stopped talking and focused on completing the setup while ignoring Reginald's heavy breathing. Operator One grabbed the USB flash drive and gave it a curious look. The grainy texture of the encasing had always made Operator One iffy about it. It was not your typical plastic case. It felt unreal, unearthly.

Operator One connected the USB flash drive and ran the code effortlessly. The aerial above started to rotate in the direction of the windmill and a series of multi-colour lights flashed in synchrony inside the scaffolding.

'Done!' said Operator One. 'Is your USB drive connected and the programme all set?'

'Yes.' said Reginald.

'Good. Launching very soon then!'

'Say goodbye to Enrico LoTrova!'

The road connecting Parkside to the New Wimbledon Windmill was pitch black with only the headlights of the Fiat 500 cutting through the heavy rain and shining on the grey tarmac ahead. Viviane kept a steady hand on the wheel as she drove towards the only gleam rising above the tree line. It came from the floodlights up ahead, surrounding the New Wimbledon Windmill, dazzling like those inside a football stadium. The whole of Wimbledon Common was an invisible and impenetrable black mass on the horizon.

Viviane drove passed the windmill small entrance and then parked not far from the low building annex. It was the temporary security office, where Enrico had seen the security guards throwing Quentin out. Once the engine of the small car with its little round bright eyes at the front was turned off, the only sound to be heard was the rain pelting down relentlessly against the car roof, making visibility through the wet windscreen difficult.

'Not a great idea to come and get things now.' moaned Enrico.

'Hey, nobody's perfect!' bounced back Viviane.

'Where are they?' asked Enrico referring to the security guards.

'I don't know. The lights are off inside the security office.'

'Maybe they are out…patrolling…'

'This is not a military zone, Enrico.'

'Well, if you read the news, someone may think it is.'

'Shall we quickly check around?'

'If you insist. Let me get the umbrella from the back.'

The two got out quickly and jumped across the puddles in the car park, hugging close under Viviane's red umbrella. The rain fell heavily, and they were getting wet. They dashed to the security building, only to find the main door was surprisingly locked. If the guards were doing their rounds, they should be back soon, they thought. They opted to try the smaller windmill entrance, only to find it closed shut as well.

'Walking in the rain. How romantic!' teased Enrico.

'Don't get any silly ideas!' replied Viviane playfully.

'Don't you know? Ramona Halywell is more my type actually.'

'Cheeky!'

The two chuckled, forgetting the deluge above them for a moment. The rain slowly began to fizzle out.

'There you said it, Enrico. Our romantic walk is ruined. Anyway, where are these security guards?'

'Something does not add up.'

There was a sudden loud crack.

'What was that?' exclaimed Viviane startled.

'Let's walk round the windmill. The floodlights are bright enough to show us the way.'

They reached the front of the windmill where they had stood to hear Julian's speech the day before. The place was now dead, silent, and wet. Further along there was a cluster of abandoned small white houses built against the windmill. The narrow spaces between them made natural alleys that escaped the strong light from above.

'What are these buildings?' asked Enrico.

'I guess they are the ex-offices of the Scout Rangers and the WPCC.' replied Viviane a little sad.

'Oh…'

'I think they've moved them down to Camp Road.'

'Temporarily?'

'Don't know.'

They moved on, walking around the new shiny windmill towering above them until they came across a nice cottage with a sloping roof. The sign above its entrance said 'London Scottish Golf Club' and through the closed glass door Enrico glimpsed at the bar inside, with plenty of beers on sale from Wimbledon Brewery.

'Another golf club? Seriously?' whispered Enrico.

Viviane chuckled.

'This is actually the first, original golf club in Wimbledon.' she explained. 'Apparently, Dr Watkins said it was the first in England to have 18 holes.'

'Wow! There is something to learn in every corner here.'

'Well, why don't we come and visit during daytime perhaps?'

'Please. Let's go back to the car. I've had enough.'

Another sound startled them. The creaking sound of rusty metal came from behind them, followed again by another creak, maybe wood this time.

'Someone's here.'

'Of course, the guards.' insisted Viviane. 'I think they are behind us. Let's circle back and go home. I am cold and wet.'

They walked back, passed the cluster of white houses, and stepped onto the grassy area south of the windmill in the hazy aura of the floodlights. The Common stretched outwards beyond the safe circle of light into a block of black nothingness. There was nobody around. Enrico and Viviane scratched their heads, shifting uncomfortably under the umbrella. In the meantime, the haze from the floodlights was becoming a little thicker and harder to see through. It was a strange effect. Enrico looked up from under the umbrella at the cloudy night sky and the mighty windmill, and then at the ground at their feet. A strange mist had started to settle on the ground layer upon layer, gradually getting thicker and thicker until it rose up to their knees.

'What on earth is this? Is it fog?' wondered Enrico.

'Feels like it but it's a bit too sudden though.'

Enrico stepped out from under the umbrella only a few paces away from Viviane to get a better look around. The mist was rising up fast, like steam from the ground. The Italian baker wrapped his chef jacket around him. He put his hand out. The rain had stopped completely.

'Did the rain just…?'

Enrico turned but a wall of fog had quickly risen between him and Viviane. He could see the faint shadow of a red umbrella fading away as light struggled to pierce through.

'What did you say? Where…?'

Viviane's voice echoed back, trailing off. Enrico traced back his steps to her but found nothing. Viviane should have been only a few paces away. The fog wrapped closer around him, swallowing up the night sky. He wondered where Viviane had gone, or whether he had walked in the wrong direction.

'Viviane?'

He called out a few times without any response. Then, there was a rumble of thunder approaching, angry and fast. Enrico feeling baffled, decided to make his way back to the windmill entrance and the car park but he soon realised he could no longer see anything beyond a few inches in front of his nose. The windmill or any point of reference had disappeared. The landscape of the Common and its black shadows had disappeared too. Everywhere around him was now a block of grey nothingness. Enrico could only feel the soft, wet grass below his feet. He felt lost. He called out to Viviane again. Nothing. The world he knew had disappeared.

Viviane saw Enrico stepping out into the rain and she was about to warn him he would get wet when a strange humming noise behind her caught her attention. She turned around to see a faint glint in the darkness of the Common, gradually fading behind this sudden strange mist. She squinted through the cold, humid fog, unable to make out what kind of light it was. She then heard Enrico speak but his voice had a strange echo and every single letter seemed elongated beyond comprehension.

'What did you say? Where are you?' she called out.

As she turned around again, the windmill, the Common, even the faint glint she had just seen, had disappeared, swallowed by the wall of unexpected fog. Wimbledon rarely saw fog this thick and this quick, she thought. She stamped her feet on the grass, it was still wet and humid, just to feel something real and familiar to reassure her of where she was. She then put her hand out from under the umbrella. The heavy rain had suddenly stopped. It felt weird.

'Enrico?'

Nothing. Then a rumble of thunder came, and a crackling sound of lightning which made Viviane panic, frightened. She put down her umbrella hoping she would see the sky above. Instead, there was only fog. Viviane realised something strange was happening and dashed back to the car, or what she thought it was the way back. She walked for a while without ever coming across a tree or a fence. Not even the hedge leading to the entrance to the windmill. Even the towering windmill itself was gone. She started to panic.

The humming noise returned to her ears or perhaps confusingly she did not realise it had been there all along. The faint glint she had spotted before was now in front of her but still at a distance, although she thought she had left it behind to her right. I must have spun around or changed direction, she thought.

The humming noise grew louder and started playing in a loop, picking up speed, until it turned into a louder roar. Viviane froze, not sure where to turn. The eerie sound seemed to come from all around her. She tried to stay focused on the light which had now become a larger dot, getting bigger by the minute as the sound grew louder. Viviane decided to run toward it, and as she moved closer, it became clearer the sound came from the beam of light itself. It sounded like the roar of an engine accompanied by the puffing of steam and the clang of steel. Viviane wondered if what she was really hearing was the sound of a train. It can't be a train, she thought. They were miles away from the nearest tube or railway station and surely steam trains no longer ran on the local railway tracks. I am hallucinating, she thought as panic rose. She stopped running and bent over to gasp for air. She shivered from the cold and the fatigue from running on the muddy, uneven terrain. She looked up. The beam of light was still there, right ahead, coming towards Viviane at a fast speed. She could now distinctively recognise the sound of a steam train engine. She froze, speechless, unable to grasp what was happening. She then felt the prickle of static electricity on her neck, and it pulled her auburn hair up. Then a hot wind picked up from behind. Its warmth gave her a temporary relief. She then saw a black steam train, one of those small ones from the old days, emerge from the fog rushing towards her. And before she could feel the hit against the metal monster, she fell into oblivion.

Enrico heard a scream, or he thought he heard one. He spun around in the fog, lending his ears for anything he could catch coming out of the lifeless fog. The screams turned into cheers, and from cheers they became an indistinct loud uproar. To his right he felt a large crowd was present, somewhere out there beyond the fog, no matter how crazy it sounded. He listened closely and he could also hear a multitude of feet marching, boots clacking and stamping on the spot. Enrico swore they could have been right there behind the fog. He stretched his hand out and waved it in a desperate attempt to dissipate the fog. He felt he was losing it. He wondered where he was. He called out to Viviane again. Nothing. At some point the circle of visibility around Enrico expanded a little and with the corner of his eye he saw rows of soldiers or footmen marching by at the border with the fog. Five rows turned to ten. Ten turned to fifty. All marching past Enrico in the opposite direction to where he had come from. They were all men, wearing waxed moustaches and their uniforms looked rather vintage. All the men held rifles resting on one shoulder, their barrels pointing upwards. A crowd cheered somewhere, perhaps to the riflemen themselves. Enrico did not know what to make of it all. The men were not turning their heads or even acknowledging his presence.

'Hello?' he shouted.

Nothing. In an instant, the air became filled with static electricity, and he could feel it pulling his wavy hair. He felt goose bumps rising on the nape of his neck and on his arms. Enrico was stunned. Shortly after, a voice hidden in the fog spoke loud with authority. A general or a commander, perhaps. The marching stopped and the voice spoke again ordering the rows to clack their boots and turn clockwise to their right to face Enrico. The men's faces were blank. Enrico waved his hands at them, but he was simply a ghost to them. The commander's voice called out another order and all the soldiers aimed their rifles straight ahead at Enrico. Enrico gasped.

'*Non sparate!* Don't shoot!' he shouted in panic.

Enrico took a few steps back as the loading clicks from the rifles played one after the other. Each soldier was ready to shoot at once. There were some gasps from the invisible crowd, the ghost audience hidden in the fog. Sounds of awe from far away hinted they were still there, watching the cruel show. There was nowhere for Enrico to hide. To him, the whole scene was surreal. He froze in shock and then a hot wind blew on Enrico's petrified face. He shut his eyes, and when he heard the rifles shooting, he drifted into the oblivion of a deep sleep.

Simon Deeley and Dr Watkins were both working late, busy wrapping up the work done that day by the team at the Pool of Elixir.

'Glad we have your team at hand, Simon.' huffed Dr Watkins. 'I am not sure we could have done it all by ourselves.'

He carried the last box of remains to the basement and put it on the table where Simon had stacked the rest. He now stood by the table, checking the latest measurements on his laptop, and comparing them with the portal tablet.

'What's in there?' he asked Dr Watkins without looking up.

'This? They are mainly broken pieces from glass and pottery we found nestled in the rock walls. It took time to take each piece out without breaking them further.'

'Great.'

The scarce enthusiasm in Simon's voice made the curator stop what he was doing and peer at him over his glasses.

'Is that it? Great?'

'What's that?'

Simon was not paying attention to the routine work they were carrying out. Something else was on his mind.

'You are still thinking about Caesar's Camp, aren't you?'

'Is 'at a crime?' sighed Simon, putting the tablet away. 'Most of these remains we already hev here tell us a story we already know. We are now simply logging items, Dr W.'

'So? Isn't that what we do?'

'Aye, it is, unless ye know the rabbit hole goes down a little deeper. And this time I have some evidence for you.'

Simon turned to the laptop and slid it so Dr Watkins could see the screen clearly. The curator edged closer, curious to know. There was a photograph of a chunk of stone, cracked in two to show the linings inside. It was accompanied by a second picture, whose colour tones were more of blues and purples.

'The stone of the pool chamber,' explained Simon. 'I mean the half I believe to be older than Anglo-Saxon times, has these imperceptible fluorescent bluish lines running across. A UV scan is able to show them more clearly.'

'Impressive. Is that a natural glow?'

'Possibly. They are bluestones, small volcanic rocks that ye find in Western Scotland, left behind by ancient volcanic activity. Now, how did the stone make its way here?'

'They brought it down…?'

'Again, possibly. This is where I realised I had read aboot a similar practice when visiting Stonehenge and I started to connect some dots.'

'Yes, I think I remember. They carried the megalithic stones from afar, across rivers. But what does this have to do with Caesar's Camp?'

'Most of the stones were transferred to be erected on mounds. My feeling is that Caesar's Camp is a prehistoric mound with a secret underneath.'

'Such as?'

'We may find the bluestones. And why not, we may find th' truth behind the legend of the Wynnman.'

'And what is that to you, Simon?'

Simon raised his hands and was about to wriggle his fingers mid-air drawing mystical signs as if he were a magician. Then the lights in the basement and the chamber flickered. Simon was stunned, and even Dr Watkins, who had experienced it before, could not hide his shock.

'What the heck…?' cursed the archaeologist.

The intermittent lights were followed by a strange buzz from the chamber. Simon dashed inside, worried in case there had been any damage to the equipment. The stone of the pool was shining with random streaks of silver appearing across the dull stone, as if some form of electrical current ran across its veining.

Dr Watkins rushed to get a closer look and a sudden pang of pain in his hand forced him to drop onto his knees. It had not hurt that much since the accident in this very place. It felt as if his hand was about to break away from his body.

'Dr W, are ye alright?' cried out Simon.

And then the strange electrical interference stopped. The lights went back to normal, emanating their golden glow in the chamber. The stone lost all its sparkle as if it had never happened. Simon stood incredulous. He edged closer to the pool. The stone was cold to the touch. Impossible, he thought. He could not understand what he had just witnessed. Dr Watkin gasped for air and grabbed onto the wall closest to him to help himself up.

'Let me help ye.' cried Simon. 'What th' hell was 'at?'

'Interference?' coughed Dr Watkins.

'From what?'

'This is what happened on Sunday evening…'

'Sunday evening…' repeated Simon. 'Wait here!'

He disappeared into the basement and looked for the tablet. He unlocked the screen and quickly searched the timeline report. As expected, they had just lost two hours of data. Gone, completely. Dr Watkins appeared next to him, still a little shaken, massaging his hand.

'What happened?'

'You tell me…'

'I don't know…'

'Well, either the electric grid can't support our equipment, or something is interfering with our work. Something or someone.'

'It is just a power surge.'

Simon looked at Dr Watkins with a raised eyebrow.

'And what was that you were mumbling back in there before the lights came back on?'

'I was in pain, Simon. It was my bloody hand.'

Dr Watkins raised his gloved hand to remind him.

'Ye were actually saying something.'

'Probably screaming because of the pain.'

'No. Ye said something like "power and revenge". Does it ring a bell?'

At eight a.m. of Wednesday morning Inspector Baynard was waiting eagerly under his umbrella as the rain poured down over Wimbledon. He was leaning against the bonnet of his police car and munching one of his chewing gums to pass the time. In front of him, the tall iron gates of the Warren Farms compound towered high and stood on the defensive in the morning rain, emanating an aura of mystery and secrecy. The gates were locked and the security guard in the little cabin to the left had been clear to Baynard: until Mr Sanders showed up at the entrance to the compound, he could not let the inspector or anyone else inside. Baynard, a law-abiding citizen, agreed and understood. After all, it had been the agreement between Wimbledon Police and Alberyx Enterprises ever since the company bought

Warren Farms to build their private headquarters, one of the exceptional kind. It meant that police had no jurisdiction on Warren Farms and any access had to be agreed and signed by Alberyx Enterprises's own legal team. When it came to security, Alberyx Enterprises managed their own security, and the entire compound was guarded by a high fence using the latest technology. The gate in front of him was the only way in and out.

The inspector remembered when Warren Farms was a gated community with a few residential homes. Beyond the gates, Baynard could now see the large, flat office buildings and warehouses that were typical of an industrial estate. Yet, the clean serpentine paths across the nicely cut lawns made it look more like a campus. He had never been inside Warren Farms. However, every Wimbledonian had a vague idea of what Alberyx Enterprises used the compound for. Julian Alberon had not shied away to promote the core activity of their headquarters as a key driver for his business. From nanorobotics to biotech, from product development to high-tech security, Warren Farms researched and prototyped across a multitude of industries, including government contracts. Julian Alberon's creative freedom and entrepreneurial leadership had allowed him to turn ideas into reality, and as the company grew, confidentiality around projects became mandatory. Warren Farms became a well-protected area for Sir Alberon to guard his ideas jealously. Still, the self-made businessman had showed good business acumen from the start, working with the law and the community to make sure Warren Farms existed in harmony with Wimbledon. Until recently perhaps. The precarious balance had started to come under threat by Basil 'Wilberforce' Elders. The Chief Superintendent had asked Baynard to follow up on the man's claims about missing people immediately. The inspector would have preferred to wait for forensics to hear their views on the dry blood he had found the day before. He had not yet told the Chief Superintendent about that. He would not until he had something more tangible to go on.

A man in a suit popped around the corner of a building not far from the gate, right inside the compound. Baynard recognised the formal and stiff presentation of Sir Alberon's lawyer, Mr Sanders, with his yellow tie. He waved at him from where he stood.

'Morning, inspector. Early bird, I see?' he said nodding at the guard to open the gate.

'I like not to waste time, Mr Sanders. I think you received the note from the police station.'

'We did, although I don't think you should have bothered to come all this way.'

'We couldn't take Mr Elders's claims lightly, Mr Sanders. You are aware of his accusations towards Alberyx Enterprises.'

'I am. Believe me, the company couldn't stand idly by. We issued a statement last night re-confirming that our engineers are simply off sick for normal reasons.'

'Hence, I am here. The Chief Superintendent would like me to verify that. For the sake of Wimbledon.'

'Sure. You can park your car just over there, in the visitors' car park.'

Baynard drove through the gate and then Mr Sanders led him on foot through the main artery of the compound, a wide avenue that wound around the buildings and through small self-contained squares. Side roads broke off from the main avenue, connecting it to more and more buildings as far as the eye could see. At each intersection, signposts vaguely referred to the purpose of each building: Plastics Distribution, Marketing, Living Quarters, Aerodynamics Centre, Goods Depot, Bar, Nanomanufacturing plants, Restaurant. The list was endless and Baynard failed to grasp how big the place really was.

They walked until they reached a large white house with a red cross painted on it.

'I assume that is the hospital?' guessed Baynard.

'Yes. We call it "Infirmary".'

'I see. I read "Living Quarters" back there. From what I understand most of your workforce works and sleeps here. Is that correct?'

'Yes. We turned a series of barracks into apartments, mainly for those not local to Wimbledon. We have all the facilities here, from food halls to entertainment and sports, as a way to keep their commute to a minimum. There is more space for expansion if business goes well.'

'Are all staff contractors?' asked Baynard.

'Most workers are. We also hire permanent staff when we need specific expertise, like Mr Crane.'

'I understand. Where are you going to put all the people once you start expanding?'

'We've already thought of that.' Mr Sanders said pointing his finger to the ground. 'Two underground floors have been built with more to come.'

The lawyer smirked at Baynard's surprised look. The place was bigger than he had ever imagined.

They walked into the Infirmary where they were immediately greeted by one of the nurses who had been waiting for their arrival. Baynard glanced around. Nothing out of the ordinary. White and clinical, with the pungent smell of disinfectant, and with nurses and doctors running around with clip charts and stethoscopes around their neck.

'We have the best medical staff here to serve the thousands of employees.' explained Mr Sanders. 'We don't want to put a burden on Parkside Hospital. I am sure you understand.'

'I do.' nodded Baynard, wishing Mr Sanders's marketing presentation of Warren Farm was over soon. 'You said Mr Crane was hired for his expertise. What kind of expertise is that?'

'He has worked on quantum computing and electromagnetic energy. Sir Alberon thought he would be a great resource for the wireless electricity project.'

'How about Mr Sullivan?'

'He is an assistant engineer at the Repeater. Maintenance, mainly.'

'Do you foresee delays in this weekend's planned launch?'

'Not at all, inspector. We have faith the system will work, and by then Mr Crane will be as fit as a fiddle.'

A room had been prepared for Baynard and Mr Sanders to welcome the two patients. The inspector found it a bit over the top; it made it all look like prison during visiting hours. There were a couple of plain tables and chair and a television fixed high in one corner. No windows; only the bright artificial neon lights against the aquamarine colour of the walls. A man was sitting at one of the tables wearing hospital nightclothes of the same colour. He was in his late twenties with predatory eyes looking tired and weak. He was watching TV and looked up when he saw Baynard and Mr Sanders coming in.

'Hi! I am Mr Crane.' the man introduced himself.

'Mr Crane!' replied Baynard, taking a good look at him. 'Glad to finally meet you. You have been on everyone's lips lately.'

'So, I heard on the news.' said Mr Crane pointing at the TV.

'Will Mr Sullivan be joining us?' asked Baynard realising the man was on his own.

'I am afraid he is asleep.' said Mr Crane. 'I am told it is the side effects of his morning medications.'

'You caught us off guard, inspector.' interjected Mr Sanders, apologetically. 'If we had known you were coming, I would have ensured he'd be present.'

Baynard nodded with his icy stare. He was not particularly happy with only meeting one of the two. Nothing he could do about it though.

'I won't take much of your time.' he quickly replied. 'We've heard many statements on your account, as you probably know, and we simply wanted to verify these claims. I hope you feel better now and you are in a state to do so!'

'Getting there!' sniffed the chief engineer. 'I just had a nasty cold. Working on the Common at this time of year means a lot of humidity…'

'Can you confirm your whereabouts between Sunday evening and today?'

'I finished work at the windmill on Sunday evening. I felt horrible on Monday. That groggy feeling when you know you are coming down with something. And so, I came to the Infirmary.'

'Let me explain, inspector.' jumped in Mr Sanders. 'We have a company policy where we ask staff to drop in at the Infirmary and spend time here if they feel unwell. To avoid spreading germs, you know?'

'Sounds reasonable. And tell me, Mr Crane, what is your job exactly?'

'I already explained, inspector…' stepped in again Mr Sanders.

'It's ok.' replied Mr Crane. 'I believe the New Wimbledon Windmill has opened so it is no secret. I work at the New Windmill.'

'Talking about the windmill, what is your position on health hazards linked to this wireless electricity?'

Mr Crane motioned to Mr Sanders not to worry. He was happy to provide an answer.

'There are none. It is completely safe. I heard rumours about me falling ill. Nothing to do with wireless electricity. Perhaps I would blame Alberyx Enterprises for not considering weather conditions when asking us to work late in the winter evening.'

The chief engineer eyed Mr Sanders, hinting at an issue which had been discussed many times. Baynard took some notes. It appeared the Chief Superintendent had the good news he wished to receive. The inspector then remembered the chat he had had with the engineer at the Repeater.

'Do you happen to know the whereabouts of Fran Ludley?'

'When? Now?'

'You tell me. Doesn't she live here on the Warren Farms?'

'Yes, she does. She said she had to go back home to look at some arrangements for the wedding.'

'I see. Congratulations! Where is her home?'

'Norfolk.'

'From what I understand, your request was about checking on the health of Alberyx Enterprises engineers, wasn't it?' asked Mr Sanders.

'True.' replied Bayard without flinching. 'I just didn't want to leave any stone unturned on his matter, especially with Basil Elders picking on anything in order to throw mud at you.'

Mr Sanders sneered at Baynard's comment. He did not reply back. Baynard held control of the situation although he had little to go on. So far, he had not spotted anything strange. His work here was almost done. Too easy, though.

'Is it correct you are the only one with access to the top floor of the windmill?' asked the inspector.

'Correct.'

'Anything you can tell me about Mr Sullivan?'

'Part of the support team of Engineers.' said Mr Crane. 'Nice guy. Works a lot. He was responsible for looking after the Repeater.'

'And neither you nor Mr Sullivan have received threats or intimidations in the last few months? Anything at all?'

The chief engineer widened his eyes, taken aback by the question. He gazed around while his memory searched for anything that could be useful. 'Don't think so, inspector. Apart from the usual protesters hanging by the windmill when the restoration was underway, I never experienced threats directed at me.'

'I think that's all.' concluded Baynard wrapping up his notes. 'Thank you for seeing me. Mr Sanders, thank you for your co-operation.'

'Not a problem.' said Mr Crane with a weak smile. 'Happy to help.'

Mr Sanders nodded at him before he disappeared through the patients' door. The lawyer and the inspector left from the way they came in, through the main hall of the Infirmary and out in the misery of the rainy day.

Outside, the sound of the rain was now drowned by loud chatter. The campus had suddenly become busier than before. Workers from Alberyx Enterprises had flooded the footpaths and the small squares as they walked briskly on their way to work. Baynard could see them rushing inside buildings to escape the rain. Workers dressed in all kinds of uniforms: suits, overalls and lab coats. Warren Farms appeared to be a mini town hidden inside Wimbledon Common.

'A lot of people here.' commented the inspector casually.

'True, inspector. So many people, it is hard to meet the same person twice.'

'I can imagine. Mr Sanders, have you ever met John Crane before?'

'Not before today. I was meant to meet him for the first time at the press conference on Monday. I am in the legal department and Sir Alberon handles the engineering team himself.'

The two pushed through the crowds of workers until they reached the visitors' car park.

'If you need any further assistance, Inspector Baynard, please do not hesitate to contact me.'

The lawyer handed over his business card. Baynard tapped his pockets for his, pretending he had run out. He never carried business cards.

'Will do if we need any further assistance.'

'Don't forget to sign when you check-out!' Mr Sanders reminded him.

Once out of the compounds, Baynard drove down the country lane taking him back to Wimbledon. He then parked on the side of the road to gather his thoughts. The overcast sky was brighter, but the rain was not planning to stop any time soon. He sat in his car, tapping his notepad on the palm of one hand in deep thought, then he stopped and opened it to read one of his notes, and then went back to tapping it again faster, more nervously. The visit at Warren Farms had been too easy, or perhaps he had been used to expecting the most complex of cases. Recent events at Wimbledon had made Baynard prepared for the worst. He put his notepad away and checked his phone to see if forensics had notified him. There was only one message. From an unknown sender. Baynard frowned. It usually meant an unsolicited message with a fraud link to click on. He sighed at the fact they even tried to catch out a police inspector. The message though had no link.

A friend

Baynard blinked and stared at the short message for a while, trying to break it down and figure who may have sent this. The message had arrived this morning while he was coming back from the Infirmary. It probably meant to go and check the Repeater now. The inspector was wary it could be a false lead or even a trap. However, he knew yesterday's visit at the Repeater had been overseen by that control-freak of Ramona Halywell. He may have a better chance of eliciting more from the engineers alone and he could play it casually without causing a stir. The problem was he did not have any warrant that would allow him to snoop around; he would have to make up something along the way. He switched the engine back on and quickly turned around. He then parked further down at the beginning of Camp Road, close to the footpath leading to the Repeater. He jumped out and put up his umbrella. He stood there for a minute observing the wet, lush grass of the golf course beyond the fence. He then looked to the left and even from where he stood he could easily see the mast of the Repeater to the south-west of the Common.

The two engineers were working as per usual inside the pop-up workshop. Baynard could see them between the shutter slats. Their skilled hands were focusing on a cylinder full of wires. Baynard hoped two things. Firstly, no interference from Ramona Halywell or any member of the Royal Wimbledon Golf Club. Secondly, he hoped the two engineers would not pay too much attention to the papers he had in his hands when he flashed them in front of the two. At a quick glance they could easily be mistaken for a

233

search warrant, instead of being an old letter of recommendation from the Chief Superintendent, dated from two years ago.

'Morning gents!'

The two engineers looked up, sheepishly.

'Don't stop what you're doing.' he reassured once they recognised him. 'I have a formality here to carry out. Search warrant to act upon, if you don't mind.'

Baynard waved the papers from afar together with his badge. It was enough to get the engineers to comply. The two did not seem to mind or perhaps did not care. One of the engineers led Baynard inside the pop-up office. The inspector did not really know what to expect from this risky, last-minute act of his. Lord Cotton, Miss Halywell, Mr Sanders, could turn up at the door at any moment, and then the Chief Superintendent would not be happy. He pretended to know what he was looking for and checked a standalone file cabinet, then a couple of the shelves. There were only project drawings and engineering schematics. He looked around the rest of the office. There was a small sofa and a table in one corner, covered with magazines and empty mugs. Baynard thought fingerprints here would be too many. There was no computer, on which to nose around, which made his search totally useless. He asked the engineer with him if he could assist him with providing access to the Repeater under his supervision. The engineer complied, still uncertain on how to behave around the inspector. They made the short walk to the scaffolding and opened a tiny door. The engineer led Baynard inside. The tall and slim metal structure towered over their heads. Looking up at the transmission tower of complicated web circuits and wires, Baynard started to question what he was really doing in there. Just because he got a friendly message from an unknown sender, did not necessarily mean there was a case to pursue. Yet, the dried blood he had found here the day before would not let him put his mind to rest, and even after seeing John Crane safe and sound, he still had a young boy who had turned inexplicably into a vegetable and worst of all he had nobody to put the blame on. Baynard did not like to be played. He felt something was brewing and he needed to get his hands on more hard evidence to be sure of it. Hunches don't solve cases, he reminded himself.

'What the heck?' blurted out the engineer stretching his hand upward.

Baynard blinked and found himself staring at a small blank screen. He looked up and noticed the engineer climbing up a small ladder. He pressed a few buttons and pulled out a USB flash drive from a slot on the side panel.

'Everything alright?' said the inspector, suddenly interested.

'Well…inspector…not sure who or why but someone left something here that is not certified as safe to use.'

He climbed down waving the USB in his hand. It was an ordinary USB key with a black encasing.

'Not certified as safe? What does that mean?'

'How can I put it? This is not part of the schematics. It is not meant to be here. It could mean the entire machine has been tampered with. It is like plugging your personal computer into a bank's private network and release a virus or malware!'

Baynard recognised a genuine worried look, and it was clear the discovery was troubling. The inspector jumped at the opportunity.

'Are you saying it was not there before?' he asked. 'And it is not meant to be here in the first place?'

'Precisely. I don't even know where it has come from. It's not mine or the company's'

'When was the last time you checked in here?'

'Yesterday, I think…'

The engineer forced himself to remember.

'Are you sure?' repeated Baynard.

The engineer nodded after a while. Baynard could read concern all over his face.

'Happy to take this to the police station.' offered Baynard putting his hand out. 'We have experts at the police station who can check this out if you are worried about security.'

'Well…I don't know if I should report it to Warren Farms first…I am not clear if the process would allow a third party…'

'You would breach a search warrant!' interrupted Baynard patting the pocket with his face papers. 'That means going to prison for obstruction of justice!'

Baynard had to do it. There was no other way. He felt sorry for the engineers, but it was for a good cause. One the Chief Superintendent would pardon him for. The engineer handed over the USB flash drive reluctantly and the inspector put it in his inside pocket.

'If you see anything strange in the coming days, call me straight away. Here's my number.'

Baynard wrote his number on a piece of paper. He gave a reassuring look at the engineers, knowing they had done the right thing. He then looked up at the Repeater and thought about the message he had received. My unknown sender wanted me to find this, I suppose, thought Baynard.

Dr Watkins knocked at the door of Enrico's bakery. No answer. He cupped his hands to peer better inside. It was late morning and the shelves inside were completely empty. Even on Enrico's most distracted of days, he would still manage to bake a first batch. Something was not right. The curator would have let it pass if it had not been the same across the road. Viviane's flower shop was closed too and Dr Watkins knew she would not miss business hours that easily. Unless she had been following Enrico. The curator frowned at his own reflection in the shop window, and a mild form of panic took hold of him. He had rushed to see Enrico and Viviane and tell them about what he and Simon had experienced at the Old Rectory, and the fact his two friends were not available conjured all kinds of perplexing images.

Power and revenge. He did not remember at all uttering those words while down in the Pool of Elixir, and Simon had looked perplexed by what he had described as a seemingly out-of-body experience. Dr Watkins stared at his tired reflection, pushing Viviane's plants out of focus, and then a prolonged yawn followed. He felt sleepy. He had not slept well. Nightmares were haunting his sleep again. They conjured these underground tunnels with crimson rivers flowing through, and the mere touch of the substance made him feel atrocious pain. A pain that persisted in his gloved hand the moment he woke up, even if just for a few minutes. Worst of it all, the nightmares had been even more vivid during the last few days and the one from last night felt even too real. He dreamt of Enrico and Viviane being hurt by a horde of dragons straight out of his Anglo-Saxon books. The absurdity of it all made it even more frightening.

And then this morning Simon Deeley had called from the British Museum. He wanted to push for a new inquiry into the electromagnetic disturbance as soon as possible. The archaeologist claimed it was for safety concerns. The curator though understood Simon was simply fascinated by the phenomenon and he saw it as another reason to expand research across Wimbledon hill. Dr Watkins could not disagree. Whatever happened, the pool had come to life again somehow, for no apparent reason. Simon Deeley was now on his way to Wimbledon and had requested to join the curator in his chat with Lord Cotton to fast track conversations about Caesar's Camp. Dr Watkins was happy to comply, although his thoughts were elsewhere. Danger seemed to lurk once more over Wimbledon, and now more than ever, he wanted Enrico and Viviane to be by his side. However, they were untraceable. Both Viviane's smartphone and Enrico's Nokia 3310 kept going to voicemail.

The walk to the Royal Wimbledon Golf Club was a painstaking one. While passing in front of one of the newsagents on Wimbledon High Street, Dr Watkins glanced at the headline of the Wimbledon Gazette and was surprised to learn about what had happened to this boy called Ken. He could not resist buying a copy. Absorbed as he was with Simon's discussions on the Old Rectory and Caesar's Camp, Dr Watkins had not had the time to check the latest in Wimbledon. Flicking through the pages as he walked on, the curator read about Basil 'Wilberforce' Elders and his claims about the unhealthy effects of wireless electricity. Wimbledon was getting out of control, he thought. Then, as he left the high street and stepped onto Rushmere Green, all kinds of thoughts and ideas tormented Dr Watkins's mind, fuelled by an irrational fear something bad had happened to Enrico and Viviane.

Simon was already at the Royal Wimbledon Golf Club. He was waiting right by the entrance under his grey umbrella. He waved to Dr Watkins.

'Good morning, Dr W. Are ye feeling ok today?'

'Yes, thank you. Never been better.' the curator lied.

'Oh ok. It's just that after yesterday evening, you got me worried.'

'Nonsense. I think we are working too much, Simon. Now, are you ready to do this?'

'Aye. Always ready.' grinned Simon, pulling his strongest Scottish accent.

He ran his hands smoothly over his hair and then prompted the curator to lead the way.

Inside, the club was busy but not too crowded. A sign at reception warned players about the intermittent rain and apparently there was more to come in the next few days.

'Good morning!' announced Dr Watkins polite as ever.

'Morning, Dr Watkins.' replied the receptionist. 'How are you?'

'I am fine, thanks. This is Simon Deeley. We wanted to see Lord Cotton. I know it is an unexpected visit…'

'Do not worry.' reassured the receptionist, speaking on friendly terms. 'Let me check.'

She scanned the calendar on her screen.

'Unfortunately, he is away on business.' she confirmed.

'Away from the club? Is he in Wimbledon?'

'Oh no. He left London and should be back…erm…I think end of this week.'

'Oh!' said Dr Watkins surprised. 'He didn't tell me!'

'Would it be possible to book an appointment with him then?' stepped in Simon, overly eager.

'Sure! Anything else I can help you with?'

'Is Miss Ramona Halywell in?'

'Later today. Do you want to leave a message?'

'No, that's fine. That'd be all. Thank you.'

Dr Watkins and Simon thanked the receptionist and walked to a quiet part of the hall, far enough so as not to be heard. The curator had a worried look on his face.

'Something tells me ye didn't expect that, Dr W.'

'Well, no. I mean Lord Cotton does travel but he hadn't mentioned anything about leaving London.'

'I guess my plan for Caesar's Camp is doomed from the start…' sighed Simon upon realising fate was not on his side. 'I will brief my superiors at the British Museum, Dr W, and see if I can use their influence and perhaps Julian Alberon's to support our cause.'

'Our cause?' said the curator surprised.

'Don't ignore it!' Simon smirked. 'Ye were as baffled as me yesterday evening. Ye saw those silvery streaks of electrical current in the Pool of Elixir, and you can't deny the electromagnetic disturbance. I strongly think the explanation may be waiting for us under Caesar's Camp. We really must dae more research into it!'

It was the first time the word 'must' had come out of Simon's mouth, and it quickly changed perspective on things for Dr Watkins. He felt confused, disorientated. The fatigue from the sleepless nights started to take its toll on him. He was searching for the rights words to say, when two golf players entered to meet up in the club hall with another couple. The shock in their voices caught his attention. Even Simon turned to listen.

'Again? An attack?' said one.

'I am telling you.' said the other. 'It is another attack by Basil "Wilberforce" Elders, probably.'

'What happened actually?'

'I don't know. All I could see was the police surrounding the windmill this morning.'

'Good grief. Was there any fire or smoke?'

'Nothing but seeing Wimbledon Police spread across the Common always means one thing lately.'

Upon hearing those sarcastic words, Dr Watkins had a funny feeling the news had something to do with Enrico. Then his phone rang. An unknown number.

'Hello?'

'Dr Watkins?'

He recognised the voice. He quickly moved away from Simon, to find some privacy.

'Yes?' he asked surprised.

'You'd better come. There is something you need to see.'

Baynard's inquisitive stare turned into a couple of blinks. He could not believe his ears.

'Come again?' blurted out Baynard. 'The blood I gave you is…what?'

'Old, inspector. As in, it dried and coagulated a long time ago.'

Baynard's icy stare looked at the forensic expert before him.

'Old? How old?'

'Very old. Centuries' old or even more. Where did you find the sample? At the Wimbledon Museum?

'I am in no mood for a joke. How could this be centuries' old?'

'Well, we need time to pinpoint a date, but I have no doubts it coagulated a long, long time ago.'

'How could I have found it on fresh grass?'

'Hard to tell. However, the dried platelets could have been well preserved somewhere and then taken and smeared against the grass. There is risk of contamination here.'

'How about DNA?'

'We sent the results, but it will take some time. Not sure how reliable this will be, though.'

'Ok. You call me personally the moment you have results.'

Inspector Baynard pointed the finger at him and then at his chest to ensure the forensic expert would not forget. The feedback on the blood samples would have sounded ridiculous to anyone. Baynard had witnessed strange things as of late, so he had no intention of dismissing them altogether. It did make him feel uncomfortable though. Perhaps the USB flash drive would bring more light on the matter.

'Another thing. Can you check this out?'

He handed the USB flash drive over to the forensic expert who looked at it more closely, turning it around in his hand. Then he held it up against the light.

'We should have a look at it for sure.'

'Results by the end of day perhaps?'

The forensic team knew when Inspector Baynard proposed a deadline, no matter how casual he put it across, he always meant business and demanded results on time.

'Will try.'

'You do that. Utmost priority. It is linked to that boy's accident, to Ken.'

Baynard went back to his messy desk. Jeremy was waiting by the window. Seeing him made Baynard's heart sink, as he was still unable to predict what else Wimbledon and its mysteries would throw at him. He fell into the chair and his stomach gurgled reminding him of his missed breakfast. He groaned and ran his hands over his face. The inspector quickly restored his cold, inquisitive attitude.

'What now, Jeremy?' prompted Baynard, ready to take on anything at this point.

'You tell me, inspector. What did you find at Warren Farms?'

Baynard looked at Sergeant Jeremy. Even he looked worn out. His ginger hair looked messy and dull. Baynard had no mirror to check himself but undoubtedly looked worse.

'Nothing. John Crane is fine, fit as a fiddle if it wasn't for a cold.'

'So, Basil Elders is lying?'

'I guess so. Or worse. We still don't know what happened to the boy. Do you have any news on him?'

'Not much.' replied Jeremy sadly. 'He is still in a catatonic state, mumbling to himself. Doctors are at a bit of a loss and running more tests. The old scars don't make much sense either.'

'You have another thing coming. Forensics just dropped a bombshell telling me the dried blood I found yesterday is centuries' old. Someone is having a laugh on us and when I put my hands on…'

He gestured a strangling gesture at whoever the culprit was.

'I found something else at the Repeater. I was there just now.'

'Without a warrant?' whispered Jeremy looking suspiciously around the office. 'Does the Chief Superintendent know?'

'Of course not. But it did bring some results!'

Baynard explained to the sergeant about the USB flash drive and how the engineer was worried about a security breach. Finding blood and a USB case on the location was too much of a coincidence.

'Do you think it is connected to the boy?'

'I don't know. Maybe. This is what I thought until I learned that the two engineers are not missing.'

'Well, while forensics is busy, we may have something else to look into...' suggested Jeremy. 'Check your email!'

The sergeant thought it best for the inspector to read it for himself. He noticed Baynard was already moody, and he did not want to be the messenger of more painful news. Baynard checked his emails for the latest morning briefs, and one stood out since it linked to Alberyx Enterprises and Wimbledon Common.

'Attempted break-in at the New Wimbledon Windmill?' he read out loud. 'Last night?'

'Can you believe it? And the thing is not even operational yet.'

'It says here the security guards claimed to have been knocked out at the windmill last night.' read on Baynard. 'Did someone break in? Was something stolen?'

'Well, we thought so but actually nothing is actually out of place.'

'I see. The two guards claim to have lost their senses... Alberyx Enterprises confirm the machinery inside the windmill is not damaged... Nothing missing from the inventory. This is strange!'

'Scroll down. They found a car parked outside the windmill.'

'Whose car is that?' Baynard asked.

'A yellow Fiat 500.' replied Jeremy, raising both his eyebrows.

'Viviane Leighwood's car? Did you get in touch with her?'

'We tried the flower shop and her apartment above it. Nobody has seen her since yesterday evening when she closed shop.'

'Did you ask you-know-who across the street?'

'That is the tricky bit. Mr LoTrova is missing too. The Wynnman bakery has been closed since yesterday evening and nobody is answering the door of his studio on the top floor.'

Baynard was not pleased to hear the news, regardless of what the Italian baker may or may have not done. His mere presence meant trouble.

'Well, we cannot say they are missing until twenty-fours have passed but why was Viviane Leighwood's car there? Are we looking at the CCTV footage?'

'Yes.' acknowledged Jeremy, brushing his hair to the side. 'We are setting up a parameter and we are working with Alberyx Enterprises to confirm everything is ok.'

Baynard stroked his silver goatee listening attentively whilst also focusing on the facts coming up on his monitor. He had hoped the Italian baker's name would not crop up for once. He quickly searched for the name on the police database. A recent entry came up.

'Did Mr Lirtiva come to the station yesterday?' misspelling Enrico's surname as he always did.

Jeremy frowned and leaned forward to look at the screen.

'An attempted hit and run?' read Jeremy. 'That does not sound good.'

'Someone tries to run him over and then he disappears? This does not sound good at all.'

'Hey, he came into the police station the same time as Basil Elders stormed in.'

'I don't need more coincidences, sergeant. See if you can find Mr Lerreva and Miss Leighwood before the Chief Superintendent finds out they may be remotely linked to the windmill or Alberyx Enterprises or even Basil Elders.'

'Yessir!' replied Jeremy.

Baynard returned to the main case page to check the latest details. There was one more section he had not read. It was about the top floor of the windmill, which fortunately had not been breached. It was only accessible by one member of staff and that was the now famous chief engineer, John Crane. There was a picture linked to the section. A man whose face Baynard did not recognise.

'Who is this?' he asked.

'You have some weird sense of humour, inspector.' joked Jeremy.

Baynard looked up at the sergeant. His inquisitive stare glared at him. He was in no mood for laughs.

'You don't recognise him?' said Jeremy, bewildered. 'That's the man you saw this morning. That's John Crane!'

Baynard kept a normal, routine face. His blood though was boiling. He disliked being played, and in plain sight worst of all. Simply knowing that the man he had met earlier that day was not John Crane, had just turned everything upside down. Questions about who and why flashed before him. Baynard wondered if Mr Sanders knew about the scam or if the doctors at the Infirmary knew. He even asked himself who the man he met was. The biggest problem was how to build a case good enough to allow a search of Warren Farms, catch that con man and find out where John Crane really was.

Baynard flinched. Something had dawned on him. He desperately looked for his notepad amid everything on his messy desk. He flicked erratically through the pages. He then found the page he was looking for. There was a statement he had not cross-referenced at all, and he blamed himself for overlooking it.

'Sergeant Jeremy!' called out Baynard.

'Yes sir? I'm here!'

'Can you please get in touch with Norfolk police and ask if they can trace this woman?'

Baynard circled a name and ripped the page from the notepad.

'Who is she?' asked Jeremy, baffled by Baynard's reaction.

'Fran Ludley. John Crane's girlfriend.'

Reginald stopped in the middle of the thick forest, a few miles from the nearest footpath. He leaned against a beech tree, looking carefully around him. The light sound of rain on the dead leaves was the only company he had so far. He glanced at his watch and cursed under his breath. Being late was the last thing on his mind but being out during daytime was a risky thing to do. Damn you, Operator One, thought Reginald; he wondered what on earth could have gone wrong. He adjusted his black beanie hat and resumed his jog along the uneven terrain, his boots crunching on the dead leaves. He clearly remembered the way to the Royal Wimbledon Golf Club and the Repeater, but even in broad daylight it was easy to get lost in the homogenous pattern of trees and shrubs growing on top of one another. An unruly lay of the land.

After a while, the stretch of Camp Road came into view through the trees. He was not far off now. He remembered Operator One's advice about reaching the Repeater. The two engineers had booked lunch at the Fox and Grapes, courtesy of Alberyx Enterprises following the stress and extra work from recent days. They would not return for at least one hour, and the rain had forced most games of golf to be cancelled. It was the perfect moment to meet. Reginald did not like it one bit, and even mentioned Inspector Baynard's nosing around Warren Farms but Operator One insisted over the phone to meet face to face. The burly man could not take the matter lightly, and after having Enrico and his lady friend nosing around, who knows who else was trying to get in the way of their plan.

He crossed the road and made his way down the footpath giving furtive glances in all directions. He walked further down, way beyond the Repeater, and climbed over the fence of the golf course further down the hill. This way he could double-back and reach the Repeater through the wild shrubbery without having to walk in the open. He had to be sure it was safe.

He was not a wanted man, but he preferred to keep a low profile around Wimbledon since he knew stumbling upon the wrong person could mean being recognised instantly. When he came to the small clearing between the scaffolding and the pop-up office, he looked up and down and into the distance. No players around. Reginald moved stealthily behind the office pop-up building and peeked inside. Operator One was waiting for him. He looked around one more time, suspecting the worse; all was clear and so without hesitation he walked through the office entrance closing the door behind him.

Ramona Halywell was sitting cross-legged on the sofa across the room, holding a hand grip that she kept squeezing. She wore a navy blue coat over another of her sporty uniforms of a similar, lighter colour. Her white training shoe dangled at a paced cadence. Her deep blue eyes gazed at the new arrival, hardly blinking. Her whole lean body was poised with a dominant attitude.

'You're late!' she teased.

'Don't you start, Ramona! You play a dangerous game calling me out here!'

'What? No special names, like Operator One and Operator Zero. If so, then it is Miss Halywell to you. Keep it professional!'

'And tell me…why on earth did you force me to meet you here?' asked Reginald.

Reginald stood by the window, nervous. He kept an eye outside in case the engineer appeared in the distance. Ramona bit her lower lip, thinking of her answer.

'I think you know.' she said.

'I don't!' snapped Reginald not following.

Ramona sighed.

'I kind of figured out what we are doing here. All of this plan of yours. The reason I asked you to meet is because I am curious to meet your employer, Reginald. He seems a resourceful man against all adverse conditions, and I think I may understand what his vision entails. I want to know more, Reginald!'

'It is Mr Bosham to you!' retorted Reginald. 'And what makes you think my employer wants to meet you?'

'Well, if I've guessed right about this plan, and what this computer code does to the Repeater. Perhaps you and your employer will need to be careful that I don't inform the authorities or Alberyx Enterprises.'

'You called me here to blackmail me?' chuckled Reginald. 'You have no idea who you are meddling with.'

Ramona scowled. She did not like Reginald making fun of her. It was time to play her wild card.

'What if I told you the USB flash drive has gone missing?' she said.

Reginald stopped laughing.

'What's that supposed to mean?' he said.

'Well, in the rush of yesterday's evening triangulation, when I left to return to Warren Farms, I left the USB flash drive in the Repeater. When I came to check late morning, it was gone.'

'What do you mean gone?' spoke up Reginald, alarmed.

'I mean gone. What do you think? Someone must have found it and taken it.'

'Then you find that USB right now or I will crush you until there is nothing left of you!'

Reginald raised his fist at Ramona. She hardened her jaw.

'You are just a mindless baboon! The stupid muscle in this whole operation!'

'And you are a computer nerd who thinks she can play golf.' spat Reginald.

'What's wrong with that? And for the record, I am a software analyst and engineer for Alberyx Enterprises.' bit back Ramona. 'Unlike you, I can read those lines of code I was instructed to recreate. Have you ever wondered what they do? Something about breaking the fabrics of reality, apparently. Is that what the triangulations are for?'

Reginald hesitated. Ramona sensed his doubts.

'You have no idea how this thing works, do you? You are just the muscle obeying orders. What, do you think these hallucinations on the Common are just an effect of electromagnetic waves?'

Reginald only knew of Lord Awlthorp's plan to pinpoint the location of the Wynnman's dagger on Wimbledon Common. How everything worked, or how they were meant to retrieve the dagger, was still not clear to Reginald. What worried him was how Ramona had managed to guess so much about Lord Awlthorp's plan on her own. Whether she was right or wrong, she was becoming a liability. Worst of all, the USB flash drive had gone missing. He knew a moment like this would come.

'Not sure what you expect to gain from this little speech of yours. Don't expect anything until you find what happened to your USB flash drive! You are here to run that code, Miss Halywell. Play your role and I will play mine.'

Ramona grinned.

'What's so funny?' said Reginald.

The sportive woman gave him an intense look. She was enjoying the moment. She then slipped her hand inside her pink jacket and took out her USB flash drive. Reginald recognised the maroon-colour case, identical to his.

'What games are you playing at?' barked Reginald, hiding his sigh of relief from Ramona. 'You said you lost it…'

'I was testing you, Reginald. Or perhaps I was making myself clear. I could easily misplace this flash drive and expose you, your employer. I could make things difficult for both of you.'

'What do you want?' said Reginald, direct. 'Is it more money?'

'I want more of everything. Money is nothing compared to what this computer code does, whoever designed it. I want to know more about it. I want a meeting with your employer.'

'What makes you think he wants to meet you, Operator One?' questioned Reginald, using the undercover nickname to mock her.

Ramona laughed maliciously. She then stood up and stretched her slim figure as if waking up from a restful sleep. She walked over and stood a few inches from Reginald's heavy-built figure.

'I want what he is trying to achieve. I want to be part of the team.'

Her eyes shined with greed. A greed Reginald failed to comprehend. He barely understood the complex plan Lord Awlthorp had come up with and felt his boss may have found his match.

'You're wasting your time…'

'I can send this USB to the police or the Wimbledon Gazette…'

'Alright, alright, I can speak to him, but with no guarantee. It would have to be after the work is done tomorrow.'

Reginald glared back at Ramona, annoyed by the way she had put him in check.

'I could kill you right now with my bare hands.' he threatened.

'You wish, you brute. But you need me!'

She giggled at him as if they were children in a school playground. She reached Reginald's face with her hand and stroked his hard jaw. The two kept their gaze locked and then Ramona moved away from him with playful indifference which made Reginald more nervous. Reginald could not hate her more.

'How do I know you are not trying to screw us over?' said Reginald.

'You are not my type, Reginald!' teased Ramona. 'Anyway, you don't have much bleeding choice, do you?'

Ramona sat casually on the edge of the desk, tapping her nails on the pale beech wood. Her bluff was working. Reginald was unaware the copy she had already made of her own USB flash drive, including all its contents and without forgetting any explicit references to Reginald she could add. It was already in Wimbledon Police's hands after Baynard had found it as she had wanted him to. The anonymous text message she had sent to the inspector would set things in motion. In less than twenty-four hours, the police would find the breadcrumb trail she had left on purpose for them to frame Reginald. She was one step ahead with her plan.

The two gazed at each other in silence once more. Reginald knew Ramona was a smart woman and her powerful gaze was starting to make him feel uncomfortable. He massaged his jaw without losing eye contact with her. Reginald knew Ramona was challenging him to get to the top. He had always feared this moment would come sooner or later. Somehow, knowing he wanted out, he could not care less. Perhaps he could use this to his advantage to get away and let Ramona take all the blame. He needed to think it through.

'We did the last test last night and I think we're happy with the results.' said Reginald, breaking the silence. 'I guess we are all set for tomorrow night to go live with the final operation. I am going to the windmill tonight to schedule the automated process.'

'Tomorrow is the big day, eh? Do you have the new coordinates?'

'Yes. Here's your copy. Make sure you familiarise them and be ready tomorrow night.'

Reginald put a piece of paper on the table and pushed it over to her. Ramona read it and then she ripped it up.

'I assume you have a good memory.' commented Reginald.

'I do, Mr Bosham, I do.'

Ramona then stood without saying anything further. She thought she heard something. Faint laughter. Voices in the distant. She turned and lowered her head to look through the window. One of the receptionists from the golf club was walking across the golf course towards the Repeater, together with a black man in a faded salmon shirt and khakis. Ramona was quick to recognise the archaeologist who presented at Eagle House.

'Our time is up, Mr Bosham. You'd better move. We have company!'

She kept her cool while Reginald scrambled to make a quick exit and dived through the wild shrubland. Ramona watched him disappear and grinned with satisfaction at how the conversation with Reginal Bosham had played out. She had made her stand, and she now had the upper hand. Hopefully, she would soon get rid of him and find out more about the plan and who was behind it.

'Miss Halywell!' called out the receptionist. 'I thought you might be here. I have been looking for you. There is a man here who wants to speak to you. A Mr Simon Deeley. I'm sorry but he insisted…'

'Miss Halywell?' interrupted Simon.

'It's ok.' waved Ramona to the receptionist. 'Hello, Mr Deeley. Don't think we've met, have we?'

She beckoned Simon to come in. She put her plastic, well-sculptured smile back on, to appear welcoming and gracious for the new arrival. She cleverly concealed her cruel schemes for later.

'Not officially. Hi! Nice to meet ye.'

'Pleasure is all mine, Mr Deeley.'

'Simon, please.'

'Simon, of course. What did you need to talk about? I take it is very urgent.'

'I am looking for Lord Cotton. It is important.'

'Lord Cotton is away on business. Can't it wait until his return?'

'I was told this morning ye'd come to the club later today. I heard you are second-in-command or something.'

'That is a bit of a joke round here. I guess I am trusted well enough to help Lord Cotton in running the club. Anything I can help with?'

She tilted her head in a very child-like but disturbingly sensual manner. Simon watched her curiously.

'I came here with Dr Watkins. He had to leave on an emergency. I wanted to stay and actually ask what I came here to ask.'

'Which is?'

Simon clasped his hands and then rubbed them together as if the words would magically come out. He knew he was not talking to an archaeologist or historian.

'You see over there?' he started pointing somewhere north.

'What? The Repeater?'

'No. Caesar's Camp.'

'Yes. The levelled-up mound. I hear it has some historical value?'

'Well, Dr Watkins and I believe it hides some valuable information about our archaeological excavations at the Old Rectory. I am sure ye're aware of...'

'I am.' acknowledged Ramona suddenly intrigued. 'What do you mean "hides"?'

'Well, our assumption is that more traces of Anglo-Saxon civilisation or even older ones lay underneath. I'm talking aboot relics and artefacts.'

'You mean underground?'

'Yes. Deep underground.'

Ramona clicked. The computer code she had built was an algorithm to determine a location in the first place, even before looking at the more complex quantum calculations. She remembered the co-ordinates Reginald had given her. They covered an area north of Caesar's Camp, smaller than previous triangulations. She wondered whether Reginald was looking for something underground, and if it was the same as what Simon had been enquiring about.

'What exactly are you asking me, Simon?'

'Permission tae dig under Caesar's Camp.'

Ramona burst out laughing.

'I am sure it is easier said than done. I do not have such authority and neither does Lord Cotton!'

Simon was deflated by the mocking reaction. He had just hit another wall. Ramona found Simon's idea more and more intriguing. She tried to remember his presentation. Something about Anglo-Saxon legends. About a sorcerer who was able to move seas and mountains, and control nature at his own will. She made a mental note about this if she ever got closer to Reginald's boss, whoever that may be. She looked at Simon wondering if he was the one. The archaeologist looked lost.

'Simon, Lord Cotton and I can definitely raise the matter with our members. You and Dr Watkins will need to raise it with the WAIS, with the WPCC...'

'Aye! I know that!' cut off Simon, who had had enough of bureaucracy. 'We're already going tae ask the WAIS to approve this week, and I wanted to ask ye if ye could dae the same. Happy tae present my plans to both the RWGC and the WPCC. I will leave a message for Lord Cotton to contact me personally the moment he is back.'

'Sure! Sorry I could not be of more help.'

Ramona, leaning on the door frame of the office entrance, watched him leave. She did not blink or move from her position until Simon had disappeared from view in the direction of Caesar's Camp. She then decided to return to the club and check everything was in its right place.

Ramona's walk back to the club was tranquil in the cool, humid air of winter. She did not meet anyone on the way, so she took her time to fit together some of the pieces she had been wondering about for some time. Reginald Bosham came to her a few months ago requesting her computer programming skills with the promise of a lavish pay way beyond her modest salary at Alberyx Enterprises. She could not say no, but as the months progressed, she became more aware and even more suspicious of what she had been asked to do. She would be at the Repeater at a certain time, receive the call and launch the programme installed on the USB flash drive. She remembered the fog startling her the first time and how she had been told by Reginald to run indoors before it thickened, without explaining why. He himself did not seem to know why. She then heard the rumours about what had happened to the engineers John Crane and Richard Sullivan, and now this boy Ken, who was nearby during the Monday test. She smiled wickedly, not bothered by the impact on human life. She had more important things to think about. Ramona researched some journals at Alberyx Enterprises and understood the fog could be just a cloud of electromagnetic forces working on containing some sort of the quantum superposition. This is what the code said, strictly in technical terms. What was inside the fog and what caused men and women to come out as the media had described, left her perplexed. Nevertheless, Reginald and his employer had built a quantum machine beyond what Alberyx Enterprises could even dream of. She could improve it, re-sell it to Alberyx Enterprises, become famous. Her ambition devoured her. She wanted a bigger piece of the cake and she had tried ever since then to show her potential: she ran the code on time and with precision every time; she tried to run over the Italian baker to get noticed, hoping it would please Reginald Bosham; last night she even helped him drive the baker into madness. She had realised though she needed to change her tactics; up her game if she wanted to come out successful and make a name for herself.

Ramona reached the Royal Wimbledon Golf Club and edged closer to the side of the building towards a green door. She opened it with her master key and sneaked inside. She then walked down to an underground basement. The large vats and generators took most of the space, including a few boxes from the bar dumped there for temporary storage. The loud humming noise from the generators filled the room, silencing everything else. She walked up to a gated door, looked behind her, then grabbed another key from around her neck to open it. The corridor was very narrow with metal doors lined up to the right. She reached the last one at the very end and only then could the faint barks be heard over the noise of the generator. She used the same key to open the metal door and went inside the small cell used to hold the hydraulics system. Lord Cotton could not recognise her through his blindfold, but Little Caesar kept yanking his leash as he barked angrily and growled at the cruel woman who had chained him and his master to the pipes.

'Who's that?' cried out Lord Cotton. 'What's the meaning of all this? Where are am I? Let Little Caesar go at least. What do you want? Money? I can get it!'

He continued with his pleads together with Little Caesar's bark of protest. Ramona did not say anything. She watched in silence. She knew what to do. She would show Reginald and his employer what she was capable of. Ramona was a woman with ambitions.

A cool air kissed Enrico's face waking him up from his deep sleep. He opened one eye. He was lying down on something soft and rather comfortable, staring at a pallid yellow ceiling. From one corner, a subdued natural light came in. An open window let in the cold air that had woken him up. Enrico lifted his head. A strong pain hit him back. His head felt it was exploding. He massaged his temples, opened the other eye then closed it. He needed time to adjust to the light. His headache felt like the worst hangover he had ever had. He swallowed a couple of times to wet his dry mouth. It had a very bitter aftertaste. Enrico could not tell where he was. He looked around him. It looked like a small bedroom with furniture all made from rough, hand-carved wood. It looked very old and shabby. The beige rug on the pale wooden floor was worn out and gnawed at one corner. Enrico could not recognise the place. He tried to remember what had happened to him. All he could recall was the windmill, the rain, the fog. He then moved on to remember the last thing he had seen before waking up. His head still hurt a little as he pictured the rows of riflemen aiming at him. The memory still felt real. Enrico wondered whether it was a dream or was it real. It must have been a dream, but he could not tell when the dream had begun or how he had ended up lying in a stranger's bed. And Viviane, he thought; he wondered why she was not here with him.

He pushed himself up through the pain and peered through the nearby window. The sky was a leaden blue, a typical late winter afternoon. Down below, there was a small garden covered in dead leaves and bordered by a dense line of cypresses. Enrico looked beyond the cypresses and all he could only make out were the trees of a thick forest filling the whole background scene. Enrico could vaguely hear the mellow sound of a gurgling stream. It did not seem far off. The place was, however, unrecognisable. He was considering his next move when the door creaked open and a very tall man in a sleeveless dark green sweater over a light blue shirt walked in. His ruffled hair and extravagant look helped Enrico recognise Quentin Plainstraw, the ex-guardian of the windmill. He was carrying a small tray with a China bowl filled with a steamy green blob.

'Hullo, Mr LoTrova!' he said cheerfully keeping his balance while wedging the door open with his shoulder.

Enrico was startled. He did not know whether to say 'hi' back or jump through the window to escape.

'Easy, Mr LoTrova! You are safe and sound in my cottage.'

'What? Where?'

Enrico looked out of the window again, confused.

'We're still in Wimbledon.' reassured Quentin. 'On the far western edge of the Common.'

Quentin carefully lay the tray on the small bedside table so he could focus his attention on Enrico and his health. He turned on a small bedside lamp and sat next to Enrico. He took Enrico's head in his hands and twisted and tilted it as if under medical examination.

'Your pupils seem alright. Do you still have a headache?'

'Yes...but...'

'Impressive. Never seen a quicker recovery. It must be all that bread you eat.'

Quentin chuckled as he released Enrico's head.

'What? What…happened…? Where is…?' mumbled Enrico pressing harder on his temples and making circular motions to ease the acute pain.

'What happened is a bit complicated to explain. When I saw the fog hovering above the windmill, I ran out of the house and I found you and Miss Viviane near Stag Bog, deep into the Common in a state of shock. You were both sitting by a tree, talking gibberish and with an empty gaze on both your faces. The wireless electricity must have hit you hard! I brought you here to keep an eye on you.'

'Wireless electricity? What? Is Viviane ok?' cried Enrico trying to get back up on his feet before falling back on the bed because of his dizziness.

'Easy, Mr LoTrova. She is fine, sleeping in the other room. I gave you both some of this while you were catatonic.'

He hinted at the green liquid.

'You should have some more.' Quentin continued.

He picked the China bowl and offered it to Enrico.

'Catatonic, you said?' asked Enrico dubious. 'Like that boy Ken?'

He bid his time, not really wanting to drink something he did not recognise. He was not sure what Quentin was playing at.

'Drink first!'

'What is this?' protested Enrico pushing the bowl away. 'Is this why I have this bitter taste in my mouth?'

Enrico refused even as he clenched his teeth to stand the pain. Quentin sighed and lowered the cup momentarily.

'Sorry for being pushy! It is just nettle and mint soup. Traditional family recipe. Fully herbal, vegan, gluten-free, and all that malarkey. It will calm down your nerves and completely remove the effect of the wireless electricity. That is why you have a bitter aftertaste. It is one of the side effects.'

'I don't understand…?' Enrico struggled to stay focused and understand what he was being told.

'See, drink first and ask questions later. Take your time. We will be in the living room downstairs waiting for you.'

'We who? Who is we?

'Dr Watkins, of course. I called him today telling him about you and Miss Viviane and he did not waste any time joining me here. I think we ought to have a conversation on what is happening on Wimbledon Common.'

Enrico pulled a face that summed up his bewilderment and total disorientation. He was not sure why Quentin or Dr Watkins had not called the police in the first place, given the situation. Whether the tall man was telling the truth or not, the painful headache pushed the Italian baker to trust him and take the bowl. He took a first sip. The soup was packed with flavour together with the freshness of mint and the sweetness of onions. It tasted denser thanks to some what seemed like mushy potatoes. Enrico waited for an effect, but nothing happened.

'Well done!'

'Am I meant to feel anything?'

'Your headache should go away soon.' said Quentin taking back the tray. 'I will say it again, Mr LoTrova. I am impressed with your recovery. It just took under twenty-four hours when normally it takes a day or two'

'Recover from what?' grumbled Enrico.

He felt some of his strength coming back.

'Come downstairs, and I will explain.' replied Quentin with a smile. 'As I said, take your time.'

He turned as if he wanted to say something, but instead he shook his head and disappeared. Enrico sipped more of the soup. After a few mouthfuls, the sweetness vanished, and the bitterness returned. Enrico regurgitated some of the soup; it was so bitter it was hard to swallow. He wished he had some bread on the side to cover the taste. The effects were quick though, and the pain had eased a little more by the time he was able to stand and leave the room.

The cottage was small, on two floors. Enrico stepped into the corridor and the aged wooden flooring creaked. There were only two doors to the right before the corridor turned on a ninety-degree angle down some stairs leading to the ground floor. One door was locked, and Enrico could hear running water inside. It was the bathroom for sure. The second door was wide open. He peered in. The window opposite was wide open with the same view, letting the cool air in. It must be getting close to four or five in the afternoon, thought Enrico; I have been asleep for almost a day. Inside the tiny room, two beds were placed one on each side of a common bedside table. One was empty, the bed sheets unturned, but in the other one Enrico could not miss Viviane's auburn hair spread out over the cushion like autumn red leaves. He moved closer and whispered her name, but she did not answer. She was sleeping heavily with a gentle snore that did not diminish her grace. He called her name again, a little louder, but she would not wake up.

'She is in a deep sleep.' said a female voice behind.

Enrico turned. A stout young woman in a dark top and a long tartan skirt with tones of amber and grey, was standing at the door. She had a towel over her arm and her short honey-coloured hair was wet. Her face was plump, with her little eyes shifting between Enrico and Viviane's bed, unsure whether to stare at one or the other for too long.

'She's what?' repeated Enrico.

'She is recovering from the shock.' explained the young woman. 'It takes a long time. She may not wake up until tomorrow morning. You instead are already up and walking. I am impressed.'

'Second time I've heard that today although I don't really know what I have recovered from. Is she going to be ok?'

Enrico was genuinely worried and the more confused he became, the more he grew concerned about what had happened to them last night on the Common.

'Don't worry. She will be ok. Quentin has a way to treat it.'

'The strange green blob?'

'Yes, mint and nettle soup. So simple, huh? My name is Fran, Fran Ludley.'

'Enrico. Enrico LoTrova.' he replied, shaking hands with the woman.

'Oh, you are the baker, aren't you? I think I've heard your name before.'

Enrico gave a brief smile of acknowledgement although he did not feel in the right state of mind to appreciate compliments. It was time to get answers.

'Do you know what happened to us?'

'Yes, I do. It happened to me too a few days ago. It was horrible.'

She lowered her head and touched the corner of her eye, a tear in memory of something awful.

'My boyfriend and I were caught by the fog all of a sudden.' she continued. 'That was on Sunday. Then I saw this steam train coming at us and I remember it was running at full speed before it hit us face on…'

She paused. Her bright eyes could not hide the remains of the traumatic experience. Enrico moved closer and held her by both arms.

'It's ok. It's ok. You look alright to me now.'

The young woman smiled nervously, avoiding his gaze to hide her puffy eyes.

'I don't remember anything after that apart from waking up late at night between Monday and Tuesday with a massive headache and a bitter aftertaste.'

'Did Quentin save you too?'

Fran nodded.

'What about your boyfriend?'

Fran gulped and struggled to hold back the tears.

'I am sorry…' Enrico winced, feeling guilty of touching a raw nerve. 'Is he…?'

'I don't know. He wasn't with me when Quentin found me.' she asked drying her tears.

He patted Fran's shoulders to cheer her up.

'What did you see?' asked Fran.

'I saw an army of riflemen ready to shoot at me. Can you believe it?'

'That is so strange. Did you see the fog too?'

Enrico nodded recalling the strange phenomena he had witnessed near the windmill. The fog, the static electricity, the visions. His mind raced back again at the previous night, trying to understand whether his memories were a dream or reality. He was convinced they were a dream but then the shared experience with Fran struck him as real.

'Oh, I see you already met Fran.' echoed the voice of Quentin Plainstraw from the corridor. 'Glad you did. You two have a lot in common and perhaps we can get to the bottom of this. Follow me! We have no time to lose.'

Quentin beckoned them downstairs. The whole ground floor was taken up by the living room with just a small corner kitchen full of pans and bowls. The walls and the whole decor were filled with warmer colours, from bright yellow walls and a bright red carpet to vases and table runners of a rich green and orange. So much furniture cramped altogether in such a small, confined space. Enrico's first thought was where Quentin Plainstraw actually slept. He then glimpsed at Dr Watkins, perched on the bulky sofa with a cup of tea in his hand and a heavy tome he was reading, on his lap. On the tiny coffee table next to him there was a stack of books of all sizes, miraculously keeping its balance. Enrico rubbed his tired eyes trying to take it all in.

'Enrico! Thank God you are alive!' said Dr Watkins looking up from his book.

He closed it and stood up to hug the baker.

'I was worried this morning. Quentin called me out of the blue and told me he had found you. Glad I can see with my own eyes that you're feeling better. What on earth happened? You do feel ok, don't you?'

Enrico groaned something that resembled a positive answer. He slumped into the empty armchair next to him, his body heavy from just walking down the stairs. He rubbed his eyes a few times to take in the new surroundings.

'Let me get you some coffee.' suggested Quentin. 'It is not an espresso but will do the trick.'

He patted Enrico's shoulder and headed to the kitchen. Enrico yawned. He knew he would not get his sought-after espresso, but he was too tired to complain. The headache was going away though, and he owed it to Quentin. He was dying to know what had happened to him.

'Can…someone…explain?' the Italian baker stammered in a lazy voice.

'Quentin told me how he found you and Viviane in a bad state.' explained Dr Watkins. 'A catatonic state, from which you wouldn't wake up…'

'It's the wireless electricity, Enrico.' complained Quentin from the kitchen. It is conjuring ghosts on Wimbledon Common.'

'Ghosts?' frowned Enrico

Dr Watkins rolled his eyes.

'He kept saying you two had seen a ghost!' added the curator. 'I came here as soon as I could. Quentin brought me to the rooms straightaway. You and Viviane looked like zombies, expressionless, motionless. It was horrible. Then Quentin administered his green soup and then your eyelids gradually closed as you both fell into a deep sleep.'

'Yes, the soup… I still don't know what it's supposed to do…' commented Enrico.

'To help you stop seeing ghosts and not turn mad!' exclaimed Quentin as he brought coffee to Enrico. 'It's the only thing that seems to fight the spectres coming out of the fog.'

'What is this story of spectres and ghosts again? What I saw, I am pretty sure was real…'

'It feels real.' said Fran sipping her tea. 'Not sure it is though… I don't know what it is. But it was scary. So scary I hardly wanted to leave this house and venture into the Common again…'

'Can someone please start from the beginning? First someone tries to run me over with a car and then I… don't know… the fog comes, and I get thrown into an arena full of soldiers…'

Enrico's voice trailed off, struggling how to describe his mishaps.

'Someone tried to run you over?' said Dr Watkins, alarmed. 'When?'

Enrico told them what had happened outside the Fox and Grapes the day before, and also what had happened when he went to report it at Wimbledon Police Station. Upon mentioning Basil 'Wilberforce' Elders, the missing engineers and the boy Ken, he saw a different reaction on everyone's face, ranging from awe to despair.

'Alberyx Enterprises is a heartless company!' blurted out Quentin.

Enrico remembered Quentin's hard feelings with the company. He noticed though Fran was quiet, looking down and dabbing her wet cheeks. Enrico's story had touched her and he didn't know why.

'Are you ok?' checked Enrico.

Fran nodded without looking up.

'What's wrong? Do you work for Alberyx Enterprises perhaps?' Enrico asked her curiously.

'No, but my boyfriend does. I live with him at Warren Farms.'

'Who is your boyfriend?'

'John Crane.'

Enrico's eyes widened.

'Where is he?' he asked without thinking.

'I don't know… I tried to call his mobile number, and there is no answer.'

'Why are you here then?' challenged Enrico. 'Why didn't you go to Alberyx Enterprises or the police?'

Enrico looked at her and Quentin. The two avoided his gaze.

'We were planning to as soon as Fran had come out of her catatonic state.' started Quentin. 'It was meant to be yesterday, on Tuesday, and that is when I found this boy Ken. I know the kid. He is from Wimbledon, nice family. What worried me was that what happened to Fran and her boyfriend had happened again, and I thought to myself I had to alert the authorities. Fran and I decided I would take him to the police station and see if they believed my story. But they didn't! And guess what? I am now a suspect!'

'What about you, Fran?'

'I am terrified! Something out there may have killed my boyfriend. The Common is not safe…'

'It is Alberyx Enterprises. They are unleashing ghosts upon us!'

'Ok, I get it. I've had enough of hearing about ghosts. Can we take a step back please?'

Enrico exchanged glances with Dr Watkins. The curator had been listening, putting his own throughs together.

'Perhaps we should start from what you saw.' noted Dr Watkins. 'Soldiers, did you say?'

Enrico nodded.

'Then let me explain from the beginning. From the wireless electricity.' announced Quentin.

He stood by the bookshelves, toying with the mug in his hand and ready to address the small audience. Enrico was hoping he would not have to hear another of Quentin's crazy conspiracy theories. He glanced at Dr Watkins. The look on his face was sceptical and yet he did not plan to object or leave the cottage.

'I think I asked you once already, Mr LoTrova.' started Quentin Plainstraw clearing his voice. 'I will ask you again: do you believe in ghosts?'

Enrico groaned on hearing the subject crop up yet again. He blew on his hot coffee and let the aroma touch his nostrils to give him the kick he needed. Of course, ghosts did not exist. His conviction faltered though when he tried to explain rationally what he had seen.

'Maybe.' answered Enrico playfully.

'Do you remember what I saw in the green open space by the windmill?'

Enrico felt Quentin was testing him. He quickly jumped to a few days back when he met Quentin for the first time. The duel, he thought.

'You told me about ghosts duelling or something.'

'The duel between James Brudenell, Earl of Cardigan, and Captain Harvey Tuckett, from 1840. To be exact.'

'Is that real history?' asked Enrico looking at Dr Watkins to verify the historical fact he had wanted to check for some time.

'Indeed, it is.' confirmed Dr Watkins, intrigued. 'Duels were a common way to resolve matters or disputes before the police force was introduced, when duels became illegal. Plenty of duels happened in the Common over the centuries, especially near the windmill. It was the perfect location. The one Quentin mentions was the last to happen.'

'Ok, Quentin. Let's agree you saw this…duel. Assuming you did, can we call it an apparition or a vision maybe? Ghosts sound silly!'

'You are one step ahead, Mr LoTrova. I like that!'

Enrico did not follow. He thought Quentin would start talking about hauntings and yet there was still more coming.

'You see, when I saw the ghost duel, it was about a month ago. I remember because that is when the new sails were built, and I was asked to look after the old ones until they came to pick them up the next day. That night it was clear skies. Cold but not a cloud in sight. Then all of a sudden, this thick fog came from nowhere and wrapped itself around the whole windmill. I came out of the annex building baffled by it all and walked right into it. In a matter of seconds, I was lost and wandered round to find my way until I reached a clearing in the fog. There I saw the duellers preparing to shoot. It looked real, very real. The same way these apparitions did to you and Fran.'

'Did they try to shoot at you?' asked Enrico noticing the similarities with what he had been through.

'Not the duellers. I was in the way of Thomas Dann, the miller living at the windmill at the time who had been given the role of constable. He had stepped out to stop the illegal duel from happening. I saw him running towards me with a baton or a gun. He shot at me and I cried in terror before I fell to the ground.'

'But he did not mean to attack you?' questioned Enrico.

Dr Watkins grinned.

'If you know the history then you know what happens or happened.' added the curator. 'What Quentin describes is a historical event clearly documented in Wimbledon history books. These "ghosts" or apparitions are showing things based on how they actually occurred in the past.'

Enrico scratched his head.

'I am lost…' he mumbled. 'Isn't that what ghosts do?'

'Think outside the box, Enrico.' cried out Quentin, his eyes wild. 'Ghosts happen where there has been a tragedy. But we know ghosts don't exist! What we see in these apparitions is normal historical events playing over and over again. Fran, you said you saw a steam train chasing you, didn't you?'

'Yes, but it wasn't chasing us. It simply came towards us, except there were no rail tracks.'

'Did trains use to run across the Common?' objected Enrico. 'Hardly believable. Dr Watkins?'

Enrico vouched for the curator's knowledge to better understand where Quentin's theory was going. The curator wet his lips, an answer already at hand.

'Well, you need to know that one of the original plans was to extend the London and South Western Railway from Putney to Wimbledon through the Common, but it was abandoned due to opposition by the WPCC, as you can imagine. Hence, the current route of what is known today as the District line tube was opened in 1889 bordering the hill across what was left at the time of the Spencer estate. As you can see, the railway was never built. It never happened…'

'A-ha! See that?' jumped in Enrico to spot a crack in the theory.

'…but a train did exist on the Common for a short period of time. It was an experimental railway built in 1845 by William Prosser between the windmill and Thatched Cottage. A small engine rather than a full-sized steam train but still a train, nevertheless.'

'Oh…' admitted Enrico in defeat.

'The apparitions or hallucinations are a window into the past of the Common.' continued Quentin. 'They just appear to be observed without any interaction. Hence, they don't attack.'

'How do you explain the riflemen pointing their weapons at me then?'

'Are you sure they were aiming at you, and you were not just in their line of fire?' asked Quentin.

Enrico did not have an answer ready. Instead, he thought back at the sequence of events. The memory was hazy or selective. He felt everyone's eyes on him. Dr Watkins spared him the embarrassment.

'If we look at the history, then the answer is simple.' the curator said. 'What you saw was something that really happened. It was a squad from the National Rifle Association.'

'The what?'

The Italian baker had never heard of it.

'The UK National Rifle Association was founded on Wimbledon Common in 1860 way before the American version. The inauguration took place near the windmill, which in turn became its headquarters. The purpose was to support the formation of a home defence force and turn soldiers into brilliant marksmen, especially after recent scares that Napoleon III of France would invade Britain. It was an organisation based on shooting sports and they organised big rifle events every year. Queen Victoria came to the opening and audiences would come to watch from all over London to cheer at the skills of the riflemen. The Victorian sovereign came a few times more to witness the big show and the parade, and once even Kaiser William of Germany came as a guest. Probably the biggest event ever to occur in Wimbledon. Before tennis.'

Enrico thought Dr Watkins must have been with him the previous night because of the way he described the riflemen marching and shooting while the crowd cheered at them. He realised he had seen a slice of history of the Common before his own eyes. It was an incredible coincidence, but three people experiencing the history of the Common was too coincidental.

'Do you know what Viviane saw?' wondered Enrico.

'We heard her mumble about a train so the pattern is there.' said Fran.

'And did you hear what Ken was mumbling?' checked Enrico with Quentin.

'It was hard to hear. Something about men on horses…'

Enrico glanced at Dr Watkins.

'Too vague, Enrico. It could be any time in history…' he noted diligently.

'Ok. So, we know we get these hallucinations.' concluded Enrico, happy not to use the word 'ghosts' anymore. 'I assume Fran's boyfriend and the other engineer may have suffered the same. My question now is: how does it happen?'

'Your guess is as good as mine, but I say Alberyx Enterprises has something to do with it.' insisted Quentin. 'What we know is the common effect these hallucinations have on people.'

'They turn you into a zombie…' stepped in Fran.

'Exactly. A catatonic state you can't wake up from…' added Quentin.

'How did you wake up, Quentin?' questioned Enrico recalling his story about seeing the duel.

'Well, I eat this soup often.'

He hinted at a large pot on the stove. Enrico stood up to peer inside. The green dense blob emanated a strange, sweet and sour smell.

'What is it?'

'I told you. Nettle and mint soup. A traditional family recipe. Don't tell me how it helps! I just know it does. I used it with Fran, with you and Viviane. I regret not having done the same with Ken. I thought the police would believe me…'

'You did what you thought was right at the time. You saved us!' Fran reminded him.

Enrico went back to his armchair, lost for words.

'So, what is causing these apparitions? Do we have an idea on that?' asked Enrico.

'It is the wireless electricity, and the electric storms.' Quentin was quick to add.

'Electric storms?' echoed Dr Watkins keeping his sceptical expression throughout.

'The sudden fog was followed by static electricity, wasn't it?' asked Quentin looking specifically at Enrico and Fran, seeking a common understanding.

The two nodded warily.

'I felt the static electricity when I had the apparitions the first time. You probably wonder how I managed to find you and Fran, how come I was nearby. It was the sparks of electricity filling the sky above a specific area of the Common that drew me out of the cottage. It was scary. When I reached the windmill last night, my suspicions were confirmed and I saw sparks of electricity originating from the windmill, rising above the cloud of fog. The windmill was on!'

'The windmill?' said Enrico. 'I thought they would not turn it on until next weekend…'

'Alberyx Enterprises is up to something.' the tall man warned.

He eyed Enrico knowingly. He did not have to say it out loud. He believed the windmill and the wireless electricity it generated seemed to be the source of these hallucinations. There was a common feeling in the room that the health hazard claims shouted out loud by Basil 'Wilberforce' Elders may be true.

'What do you think?' said Enrico turning to Fran.

'Until I saw you and Miss Viviane in the state you came in, I was not ready to believe any of this. Seeing the lightning from my room was a shocking truth. It scarred the sky with the sound of thunder. And when Quentin told me of the rumours he had heard the day before yesterday about my boyfriend, I started to worry that something serious had happened.'

'Do you think he is involved?'

'No! How could you say that?'

'Well, he is the chief engineer. He built the bloody thing!'

'He was hit by the fog like me. He has probably fallen ill because of it!'

'So, Basil "Wilberforce" is right. Alberyx Enterprises has built something that can damage your brain. I wonder why they turned the windmill on earlier than planned…

'Hold it!' exclaimed Dr Watkins.

The curator of the museum raised his hand. He had a stern look on his face.

'Before you all leave here shouting out your crazy theories, let me put your feet back on the ground' he said glancing at Enrico and Quentin dubiously. 'Your claims are not that watertight. Crazy people find comfort among crazy people. This is what everyone will think. Enrico, do you think Inspector Baynard will believe you when you shout out Basil "Wilberforce" 's theories like his followers? Quentin, what will people think when they find out you kept Fran here for a few days without letting her relatives know?'

Dr Watkins's tone was not reproachful. It put things into perspective. The other three stood in silence looking at each other.

'We should be alerting Julian Alberon and consult with him on this.' added Enrico.

'I will never seek the help of that heartless man.' protested Quentin. 'I lost my job because of him.'

Enrico was taken aback by the strong response. He did not think putting the blame on Julian was the right thing to do although the work of his company had become a danger to Wimbledon. One thing though nagged him the most.

'Do you think Julian knows about what is happening?' objected Enrico. 'I don't think he does. The windmill is not meant to be active until next weekend, and he told everyone that. Someone is trying to put the blame on him or his company. What about Basil "Wilberforce" Elders?'

'He is the one who is telling us the whole machine is dangerous.' insisted Quentin a little upset that his cause was not believed.

Enrico knew Julian would not lie to them. Last night he had actually confessed his mistake over Basil Elders and the school contract with Octagon School. Enrico was sure someone else had turned the windmill on without Julian knowing. Someone who wished to frame him. Basil Elders fit the bill. He shared his thoughts with Fran, Dr Watkins and Quentin.

'That gives Basil Elders a good motive.' agreed Dr Watkins.

'Still, it doesn't make Alberyx Enterprises a saint!' complained Quentin. 'We have to stop it!'

Enrico did not know what to believe. Last night, when they spoke, Julian seemed as frustrated and sorry as they were about the whole situation. He then remembered the chat inside the windmill when Julian gave them a tour of the new building.

'There is something that may explain Julian is in the dark on this. He told us he does not have access.'

'To what?' asked Quentin.

'Yes, to what?' said Fran.

'He does not have access to the top floor of the windmill. That is where the "brain" is, or so he calls it. Quentin, if you saw the New Wimbledon Windmill in action last night, someone must have been inside to operate it. What if someone who has access did or is doing something?'

'If not Julian Alberon, who has access?' asked Quentin puzzled.

'John Crane…' muttered Fran upon realising. 'Are you saying…?'

Her puffy cheeks turned a little red. She was flustered by Enrico's insinuation.

'How could you talk about my John like that?' she cut in. 'He wouldn't hurt a fly. Why would he do something like this?'

'No, Fran. I am not saying it's him, but he is the key. We need to find out!'

'But I don't even know where he is…' she repeated, pleading for his innocence.

'Enrico is right!' jumped in Quentin. 'John knows how the whole thing works. The windmill. The Repeater. He is the means to an end perhaps. Conveniently, he is nowhere to be found!'

'So, what next?' prompted Dr Watkins, still sceptical.

'It is almost dark outside. I am going to wait a bit and then try to break into the windmill.'

'Enrico…' warned the curator. 'That is not a good move!'

'I need to get to the bottom of this. Stay here and wait for Viviane to wake up, please.'

'Please find my John!' pleaded Fran.

'I will do my best. I will get back as soon as I can.'

The Italian baker turned to Quentin with a broad smile. He felt his curiosity was bringing his strength back.

'Quentin, you are the ex-guardian of the windmill, right? How could I get to the top floor of the windmill undetected?'

The auditorium at the top of Octagon School was a public hall the school allowed to be booked for public events by local clubs or societies. The school took on a different look in the late evening hours when students were no longer there. It somehow lost its youthful look, kept on by the relentless cries and laughter of teenagers, and the whole structure suddenly became empty, void. It appeared older and out of fashion.

It was not the typical auditorium. The sloped roof of the building made it look like a large-scale attic with an open space in the middle and four sets of seating areas on all sides. The speaker had to have the confidence to speak dynamically with an audience on all four fronts. It was not an easy feat for the unexperienced speaker. Yet, Basil 'Wilberforce' Elders did not have this problem at all. For him, public speaking was natural. Whether in front of his pupils in a classroom, or in front of his followers from the "Wimbledon For The People" movement like in tonight's session at the auditorium, Basil delivered his message with a clear and emotional connection. Nathan observed him carefully, taking notes about the way he stood and spoke. His gold-rimmed glasses captivating the gaze of everyone present. Basil had just started, rallying up those present with more love for Wimbledon and more hate for Alberyx Enterprises. The journalist sat on one of the back rows, a little apart. Although welcomed, he did not feel he belonged to this group. And yet, when he looked around the auditorium, he saw Wimbledonians from different backgrounds, and he could not say Basil's followers belonged to one group only. His movement was expanding, moved by a strong belief in a valid cause. Whether it was a good or bad thing, he put off making any decision until he heard what Basil wanted to tell the crowd. Outside, it had been pouring on and off. The rain had stopped for now, but the dark evening hours made it hard to tell if the sky had cleared or not. Everyone's eyes were on Basil, though.

'This brings me to today's meeting, and why I asked you to join me here. This beautiful school, like any school, is a source of knowledge and civilisation. We need to thank men like William Wilberforce for allowing education to be expanded to everyone. Otherwise, we would live our lives oblivious to corporate greed and corporate irresponsibility. Like Alberyx Enterprises.'

There was a cheer in the auditorium.

'You heard my version of the facts yesterday. You saw how Alberyx Enterprises and even the Chief Superintendent of Wimbledon Police had the courage to say I am a liar. That my claims are made-up stories! Ah! They want to belittle me, belittle us, for causing unrest, causing trouble in the community. Well, let me say, to quote my good old friend Schopenhauer, a high degree of intellect tends to make a man unsocial. Our eyes have opened, and it is time we open everyone's in Wimbledon. We must expose Alberyx Enterprises for what it is. A reckless company who does not have our health at heart. We've been making our voices heard in town over many months. We made our presence felt by those who wish to tamper with our Common. It is now time to act with a louder voice and a bigger show of our courage and determination.'

He thumped his fist in his other hand, looking at heads nodding and murmurs of approval. He had to shake off the last remains of doubt or insecurity among his audience. He has to be sure they would all follow him in his next act.'

'What's the plan?' broke out a voice in the crowd.

'Yes, dear friends.' resumed Basil. 'It is time to show we are more than just a bunch of grumpy people. Who is with me?'

Basil tested his followers again. The majority roared loudly in his favour. Yet, Nathan spotted a few, still quiet at the back, not yet convinced.

'Tomorrow, early evening, we will all meet outside the Fox and Grapes and from there we are going to march en masse through Camp Road, all the way to the Warren Farms compound. We will stop at the gate and demand answers from Alberyx Enterprises, about the safety of our neighbourhood, about the health of our citizens. Think about that boy Ken!'

Basil pushed for a final emotional charge to make sure his speech clicked with his followers. The audience roared and suddenly everyone called out to each other to join in the protest march, encouraging even those who until now had hesitated. Basil grinned with satisfaction. He had to show Alberyx Enterprises he meant business and they should take him seriously. Tomorrow at this time the Warren Farms compound would be under siege. He would force the company and its owner, Julian Alberon, to listen. He then remembered a quote from Schopenhauer.

'All truth passes through three stages.' Basil spoke out loud. 'First, it is ridiculed. Second, it is violently opposed. Third, it is accepted as self-evident. It is time to share our truth once for all. For the love of Wimbledon!'

The crowd cheered. Nathan watched in silence, taking notes. The group was going to meet tomorrow after four p.m. The journalist wondered if he should join. It meant walking down a dangerous path, mingling with Basil Elders. He watched the followers thanking his leader, shaking his hands, and slowly making their way out, cheers after cheers. Nathan waited to be the one of the last to leave, staying where he was, just watching the scene. Basil's most loyal followers joined him to confirm details for tomorrow, and Nathan heard someone talking about banners and flags. The journalist asked himself if such protest was allowed without permission. Basil Elders was able to rally up to more than a hundred people. Months before, he had managed to do so more than once for the peaceful marching protests on Wimbledon High Street, which the Council had approved. Yet, in this case Basil talked about a siege on Warren Farms. It did not sound good, and Nathan wished to understand what drove him to such extreme. He wanted to use tonight's opportunity to get into Basil's office on the floor below and see if he could dig up something.

'Eager to know more, Mr Glenn?' spoke Basil.

The auditorium had emptied itself and Nathan realised he was the only one left.

'Ah sorry. I got distracted.'

He picked his stuff, slid out of the row of seats and walked out of the auditorium. Basil 'Wilberforce' Elders stood by the exit waiting for the journalist.

'I will walk you down. I need to finish a few things in my office.'

Nathan's heart skipped a beat and he cursed under his breath. Now, he did not stand a chance to get into Basil's office. He nodded and walked ahead with Basil. The journalist quickly thought of Plan B, perhaps wait for Basil to finish and leave. He ought to be careful.

'What did you think of my speech?' asked Basil.

'Inspiring…' replied Nathan, not sure what to say.

'Is that all, from a man of words like yourself? Don't you want Alberyx Enterprises to be exposed? We both want the same thing…'

'We do. I am not sure a siege is the best thing though. The pen is mightier than the sword, so they say.'

'True. I respect that.' abided Basil with a calm Nathan still found discomforting. 'However, we've waited for too long and no action has been taken.'

'The police say John Crane and Richard Sullivan are ok at Warren Farms.'

'Lies! Alberyx Enterprises paid them to protect their own flock. What about Ken? Does anyone bother checking what happened to him?'

Basil's response was more like his own. Nathan, however, did not pursue the matter and walked on in silence until they reached the floor of Basil's office.

'See you tomorrow. I hope.'

'So do I.' replied Nathan, non-committal.

The journalist left Basil in the corridor. He pretended to make his way back down to the ground floor and then, when he thought Basil had gone back to his office, he sneaked back up to the upper floors, moving in the dark towards where he thought Basil's office was. The door was ajar and the light was on. Basil must have gone back to his office to finish something for work. He could hear whispering. Basil was talking to someone. The journalist thought he must be talking to one of his followers. He was curious to find out. He was here to find more on Basil 'Wilberforce' Elders and what pushed him to become the number one local enemy for Alberyx Enterprises.

Nathan crept forward. There was a caretaker's closet a few doors before Basil's office. The journalist weighed up his options. He could hide there if necessary. There was only a thin ray of light coming from the office. Nathan kept close to the wall and moved along slowly until he was able to peep into Basil's office wall. The voices now were more distinct.

'Tomorrow we are going ahead with the protest.' spoke up Basil.

'I could not be more pleased.' said another voice.

Nathan did not recognise the voice.

'What is your ETA?' asked the voice.

'At Warren Farms? After twilight. Around six p.m. when it's dark. Will you make sure the police and Alberyx Enterprises private security are out of the way, as agreed?'

'Of course, as agreed. We will keep them busy so that you have the freedom to say what you need to say.'

'And the gates?'

'The gates will be opened so that your march can carry on inside onto the main square of the compound.'

'Our march will still be a peaceful one. No weapons of any kind.' reiterated Basil.

'Sure. This is what we agreed, Operator Two, and I am happy with how you've treated Alberyx Enterprises so far. We hope we've supported you enough in your cause.'

'You have no idea how it feels to be betrayed.' replied Basil bitterly. 'All my work stolen under my nose and Julian Alberon claiming the idea to be his. He still has not agreed to pay after I, on behalf of Octagon School, provided all the theoretical calculations for their research team. The Oscillator is a product of years and years of my own research on quantum mechanics. They should give me a medal!'

'Indeed, Operator Two. Your knowledge in the field has definitely helped us tamper with the machine to our favour. Hence, we hope the intel and the secrets we fed to you from Alberyx Enterprises were satisfactory enough for your revenge. We know you wanted to scratch the good image of the company and expose them for who they really are.'

'Oh, it was more than enough. I cannot believe they still claim their engineers are safe. This is what happens when the good academic research work I carry out is used for some nefarious purpose.'

Nathan listened closely. Someone had been feeding information to Basil Elders and tampering with the New Wimbledon Windmill and the Repeater. He was not able to see well enough inside the office. He was dying to know who the other person was.

'True.' said the voice. 'Wireless electricity is indeed dangerous.'

'What I don't understand is why me?' questioned Basil. 'And what has Alberyx Enterprises done to you?'

'You suffered a terrible injustice, Operator Two. I believe in your cause and Alberyx Enterprises stood in your way. This company cannot be left to do whatever it wants.'

'Exactly!'

'Well then, we may not meet again until after tomorrow so good luck. I'm sure your protest will stir things up a little, make sure people listen.'

There was a further exchange of words Nathan did not grasp. He then noticed a shadow walking across the ray of light. Someone was coming to the door. Quickly, the journalist tiptoed to the caretaker's closet, without making a sound. He left the door open, fearing locking it would make a noise and attract attention. He stood at the back, peering into the darkness of the hallway. A man in black top and black khakis came out. He wore a black beanie, black boots and his face was hardly recognisable due to a long bushy beard. Nathan was not sure if he knew the mysterious person.

'Ah, one more thing!'

Basil called out and opened the door. The thin light widened across the corridor and hit the mysterious man full-frontal.

'Yes, Operator Two?'

'What about payment?' asked Basil.

The mysterious man grinned. Even with the light on his face, Nathan struggled at first to frame the face he had somehow seen before. He had seen this man in plenty of photos, except at the time he did not have a beard. Nathan Glenn was gobsmacked to see Reginald Bosham free as a bird and talking to Basil 'Wilberforce' Elders.'

'Taken care of.' confirmed Reginald. 'For your services, payment will be transferred to you in a couple of days, assuming you push through with your protest.'

'Of course, of course!' replied Basil.

'It is radio silence from here onwards.'

'Absolutely.'

They separated. Reginald turned away and walked back along the corridor. Nathan backed away deeper into the closet so as not to give away his position. His mind was boggled by the sudden revelation. A criminal like Reginald Bosham should be in prison for life, thought Nathan. Somehow, he had managed to get out; and the fact he had returned to Wimbledon, the scene of his last crime, to work with a troublemaker like Basil 'Wilberforce' Elders did not sound good. Their plan involved undermining Alberyx Enterprises and it was now clear Basil did not have Wimbledon's interest as his priority. He was taking revenge against the company instead.

He stood still listening for Reginald's footsteps walking away. Basil dallied on the threshold for a moment and the journalist could see Reginald's shadow cast on the pale corridor wall. He then saw the shape moving and increasing slightly in size. Nathan blinked. He could hear Basil's steps walking out of the corridor. Nathan buried himself deeper among the dirty rags and cleaning products. He then saw Basil's hand stretch across the door of the closet. He saw the hand grabbing the door handle. Nathan heard the key turn inside the lock and understood he would be stuck in there for the night.

The night fell once again on the Common bringing that sense of awe and mystery to the silent black shadows of the treetops and the deserted patches of grass scattered in random places. The Common grew naturally, without constraint, but had maintained its shape over time, concealing its secret and revealing its marvels to those who ventured through it. Enrico had grabbed a flashlight on his way out of Quentin's cottage. The only light accompanying him was the moon in the starless sky. The cloud had parted slightly, giving a break from the rain, and blowing colder air through the trees instead. Another light became visible as the Italian baker reached the windmill. The floodlights had turned on automatically an hour before sunset as they did every night and shone their strong, bright beams at the New Wimbledon Windmill. From the edge of the forest, he saw the patch of grass south of the windmill where he and Viviane had last seen each other. The place looked quiet and peaceful. The air was clear. There was no fog although Enrico shivered even at the sight of his own breath condensing before his eyes as he waited in the freezing cold. Quentin and Fran had insisted on giving him a thick sweater to wear under his chef jacket. It made Enrico look bulkier and stronger. Deep inside, he still felt cold, and scared anything like last night could happen again. He crouched in hiding while he waited. He felt the Common was alive around him. He saw the branches arching over like claws, the bushes rustle as if alive and kicking, small creatures making creepy sounds and the wise owl hooting somewhere up in the high branches. Enrico's memory of yesterday was still fresh and scary. He was a little terrified each time a sound crept in from the dark. He had looked over his shoulder more than once since leaving Quentin's cottage. The eerie calm of the windmill and the area around it did not give comfort either. It was as if a dark presence floated over the Common.

Curiosity had the upper hand and Enrico had to learn what was going on inside the top floor of the windmill, with or without permission of Julian Alberon or his chief engineer. Quentin had tipped him off about an entry point from one of the vents in the old Scout Rangers' office, where the old fireplace used to be. He knew about it from when he assisted in the restoration work. It was a steep climb, but it was the only link to the top floor without triggering any alarms.

Enrico walked along the edge of the thick woods until he was close enough to where he had walked with Viviane the previous night. He turned off his flashlight since he was now approaching the faint aura of the floodlights, which made things stand out from the dark of the Common. He checked the security guards were not around before crossing the gravel path to jump inside a green enclosure. He looked up. He was up against the locked entrance to the London Scottish Golf Club. It was pitch dark inside. Enrico knew the Scout Rangers' abandoned offices were on the other side of this building, according to Quentin's directions. He found a way around the building and came across the edge of the car park. He looked ahead. Viviane's car was still there, not yet towed away. There was a second car, parked right outside the security office. Enrico could make out two people inside but not who they might be. The car itself, slightly bigger than Viviane's Fiat 500, had nothing stuck on it. No signs or labels for easy identification. Enrico understood the windmill was under watch. The Italian baker needed to apply extra care, whoever those two people were, and stay out of sight as much as possible.

Enrico looked around to see where he should go next. There was a small alley which invited him, leading between the windmill and the London Scottish Golf Club. He walked along it until he was among the white cottages that used to be the old headquarters of the WPCC. They were all empty and abandoned. The floodlights high above the windmill played an intriguing game of light and dark among the cottages. The whole scene took on a surreal look and feel. It reminded Enrico of how Alberyx Enterprises had decided to relocate the people working here. The Italian baker did not want to totally dismiss the great work Julian's company had done; yet he could not turn a blind eye to some of the dubious decisions Alberyx Enterprises had made to build the new windmill. Enrico wondered whether Julian knew how dangerous his vision had become. He glanced around, flashing his torch when needed until he spotted an old signpost that hinted at the main building. Inside, the space had been cleared a long time ago. It was now just an empty room with only a fireplace to one side. This was Enrico's way in. Quentin had told him the vent at the back of the fireplace connected to the old chimney passage of the windmill, which then led up to the top floor. Enrico was not sure how wide this passage was and if it would have anything to help him climb it. I will have to play it by ear, he thought.

The vent was accessible through a square grate at the back of the fireplace. He felt the screws on the grate. They were loose. Enrico paused. Someone had been here. Someone had previously climbed up. Someone who also did not want the police and security to know about it. He lifted the grate, but the squeaking made him stop in his steps. In the eerie silence it sounded louder than a siren. Enrico's heart pounded and feared the guards would appear from nowhere to check what the noise was. Enrico froze and waited. Nobody came. He gave a sigh of relief and quickly lifted the grate completely to slip inside. The vent was dark and cold. Enrico felt the metal all around the tight air vent conduct. There was an upward slope. Enrico noticed small metal handles had been fixed to the slippery surface. They were solid enough to act as a support for climbing. Someone has indeed been here, thought Enrico again. He pushed up in the lonely silence. He could not hear the echo of footsteps or voices either ahead or behind. At the end of the slope, the vent turned into a vertical climb to the top of the windmill. Enrico stopped to look up. Going forward, the metal panels did not cover the whole surface. Every half-metre or so, he could feel the rough and grainy surface of old, charred bricks of a chimney, with fixed rusty iron metal handles acting as an old ladder. Enrico put his foot on the first rung and lifted himself up, keeping noise to a minimum, taking one step at a time as he searched for the next bar. Up ahead, he could just see a weak light. Maybe it had reached the end of the tunnel. He tended his ear but heard no sound apart from his heart beating faster as he climbed up to the unknown, hoping he would make it safely to the top without bumping into anybody.

Inspector Baynard rubbed his eyes cursing his tiredness. Jeremy, who sat next to him in the car, was not helping with his occasional yawns. Of all the nights, tonight was the one he did not feel at his best. Everyday had been so busy and the lack of sleep did not help. Sometimes Baynard wished simpler times. Burglary. Commercial fraud. Instead, he faced the most illogical dilemma he ever faced in his years of detective work.

'Why are we here, inspector?' replied the sergeant with another yawn. 'It's getting late, and I am not sure what you expect to find here.'

The two had been there since the floodlights had turned on as per usual. They had parked the car not far from Viviane Leighwood's Fiat 500. They had been sitting in the car, patiently waiting, observing.

'Time?' asked Baynard.

'Just past eight.' Jeremy replied. 'And it all seems normal to me.'

'Patience, sergeant. It is time to apply some patience.'

Baynard said it through clenched teeth, maintaining his inquisitive stare at all times. He noticed the abandoned Fiat 500 in the empty car park. Nothing of relevance had been found inside. Baynard had ordered not to tow it away. CCTV footage from the night before had shown the Italian baker and the florist walking near the windmill before a technical glitch had somehow wiped a lot of other data from the video recordings. The security guards could not explain how they had managed to lose hours of it. Baynard knew fate was against him. However, he now knew Enrico and Viviane were missing. The same way he knew Fran Dudley had not phoned home or messaged her parents since Sunday, after talking to her colleagues in Norfolk. She was not a missing person for Norfolk police or for Alberyx Enterprises. Baynard would not have probably made much of it if it were not for the fact that the photo he saw of John Crane did not match the man he met at Warren Farms. Whoever he met was an impostor pretending to be him. Everything had now taken on a different perspective. Whoever knocked out the security guards at the windmill the night before had something to do with the baker and the florist coming here, and then disappearing. He glanced up at the windmill. The sails, fixed against the starless sky, gave the illusion they turned in the cold breeze. The whole metallic silver structure was silent and emotionless. A silent witness. Baynard frowned and his inquisitive stare turned cold.

'Everything seems to have started from here.' he thought out loud.

'The windmill?'

'Yes. Basil Elders has been more and more vocal since the inauguration date of last Monday. Alberyx Enterprises has been under heavier attack since then. We now have someone breaking into the windmill…'

'What are you saying, inspector?'

'I am thinking industrial sabotage, sergeant. Someone does not want this windmill to succeed.'

'Who would want that? Basil Elders?'

'Basil "Wilberforce" Elders. He is the most likely suspect. A bit too obvious, though.'

'I still don't get why we're here. We should be back at the police station and build a case to search Warren Farms. You were lied to this morning!'

'A search warrant takes time and needs solid evidence to back it up, especially if I am going to tell the Chief Superintendent I plan to search and seize Warren Farms. I was hoping to find something here while I wait to hear from forensics.'

'I am still surprised about what happened at Warren Farms. Why the cover-up, do you think? Why take the risk to present you someone who is not John Crane?'

'I am not sure. Perhaps Alberyx Enterprises is unaware. They are not new to threats from the inside. We've seen how the Old Rectory was infiltrated.'

'That was not sabotage, though.'

'Well, no. However, I am seeing patterns, especially now that stupid baker has gone missing too. Untraceable. It can only mean he is involved somehow, and I think he played with the wrong people.'

'Are you referring to the hit and run?'

'Yes. Did any fingerprint come up here at the windmill?'

'Nothing.'

Baynard put a chewing gum in his mouth and then opened the door.

'Let's get out!' said Baynard out of the blue. 'Some fresh air will do us good.'

Jeremy followed the order. The car park was silent. To one side of the windmill, they glimpsed at the two security guards on the way back to the security office for some warmth. Baynard raised a hand to them, and they acknowledged in return.

'What now?' asked Jeremy.

'Let's go for a walk.' replied Baynard, wrapping himself to stay warm. 'Let's go round the windmill for a short walk. Stretch our legs.'

The inspector did not have a plan in mind. He thought he needed to take a break from the loud noise thrown at him. They moved slowly around the windmill to the south side. The Common was silent, not speaking of what had occurred on these long-standing grounds. Inspector Baynard wished the trees and the birds could speak. He knew the resolution of the case had to start from here. He wished whoever attacked the guards last night would show up tonight. Perpetrators returned to the scene of a crime in most cases. It was in their nature, or at least this is what Baynard hoped for.

He and Sergeant Jeremy walked at a slow pace, leaving a small silent pause in-between their steps on the wet grass. He listened carefully. Nothing. They walked half-way lost in their thoughts, each one trying to make sense of the case. Baynard listened carefully again. Nothing. Then a metallic sound came. He stopped. He signalled Jeremy to do the same. They stood still while the deafening silence filled their ears. Baynard waited. They looked at the windmill and then their gaze shifted to the abandoned white cottages of the WPCC. The inspector was about to move again when the metallic sound returned, faint but easy to recognise as something slamming against the wall. Baynard gestured to Jeremy to keep quiet and drew his gun out. There was someone lurking in the shadows.

Reginald cursed three times under his breath and cursed once more in the name of Ramona Halywell. He disliked the woman. She was a sly piece of work, trying to show off at any given opportunity. Reginald had struggled on more than one occasion to make her stick to the plan, and her unprompted attempt to run over the Italian baker with a SUV had come unexpectedly. She was a loose cannon, unlike Basil who followed orders like a puppy. But they could not do without Ramona. Both Operator One and Two were vital for Lord Awlthorp's plan.

The burly man looked at the windmill from where he stood. He ran through the steps in his mind. He had to get to the white cottages from the south side, to avoid the car park at all costs. He would then climb up through the vent, prepare the Oscillator, and back out from where he came in. If he timed it well, the police or the security guards would not see him at all. He checked his watch. Time to go. He dashed out of the woods and ran across the grassy plain south of the windmill under the watchful eye of the floodlights. He had to be quick and move into the shadows as soon as possible. There was a tiny gap ahead, between the New Wimbledon Windmill and the south-facing side of the London Scottish Golf Club. It was the path leading through the old WPCC cottages that connected to the car park on the other side. Here, the floodlights did not reach everywhere. Plus, the security guards rarely checked this area. This had been Reginald's secret way into the windmill all this time. He found the fireplace, screwed off the grate and pushed himself into the narrow space. His lean, muscled body was a tough match for the cramped vent. It was a tight squeeze, but he just managed to fit in.

The top floor awaited Reginald in ominous silence. Reginald had to be quick. He ran the computer code from his USB flash drive once inserted in the Oscillator. He revisited the latest co-ordinates and set up the automated process for tomorrow's final showdown. One of the screens woke up and beeped feeling the surge of new commands being input. Reginald waited for them to finish. It was only a matter of fifteen minutes to half an hour. He leaned against the wall, staring at the multi-coloured bleeping lights. He ran over the plan and how it would all come to an end very soon. He did not know whether Lord Awlthorp would ask him to follow in what lay next. He could not care less. He had been planning his own exit for a while, whether his boss agreed or not, and by Friday morning he would be on a car on his way out of Wimbledon and out of London. Letting the blame fall on Ramona and Basil for everything that was going to happen, was sufficient enough to make a clean escape. Lord Awlthorp would succeed undetected in whatever mad project he was getting himself involved, and he would probably leave Reginald alone. Reginald would finally be a free man.

Reginald brushed off his relishing thoughts. The command upload had finished. The Oscillator was now scheduled to run automatically tomorrow at the set time. This would be the last time he would visit this infernal machine and soon he would have nothing more to do with Lord Awlthorp's madness. It was getting too much. Too dangerous. Time to go and make a discreet exit, Reginald thought; I am certainly not going to miss this creepy windmill.

Behind him, in one corner of the top floor, a pair of curious eyes watched him carefully through the grate that led out into the top floor of the windmill. Enrico could not believe his eyes. He had to accept the absurdity of the naked truth. Seeing Reginald Bosham again came as a shock. He thought the man was still safely behind bars and instead he was here inside the most secure area of the New Wimbledon Windmill, playing dangerously with its main computer. He watched Reginald's moves carefully, the input commands, the USB flash drive. Enrico did not know what it all meant but it did not look good. Again, this man was tampering with Julian Alberon's property, and Enrico could not help but ask himself why. He thought he should jump out and face him. He then remembered how strong the man was when they had fought in the pool chamber under the Old Rectory. He realised he had better play it safe. That's what Viviane would say. He quickly thought of his friend and the Italian baker hoped she would wake up soon.

Reginald's hurried steps around the room made Enrico realise whatever Reginald was up to had come to its conclusions, and the burly man was ready to move out. Without thinking twice, Enrico dashed back down two steps at a time, down the steep vent he had climbed before. Enrico's heart was beating faster as he tried to keep noise to a minimum. He could hear the grate being lifted above him. He had to be quick and find a place to hide once out of the vent. From there, he would then wait for Reginald to appear and follow him.

Baynard and Jeremy crept up the path between the white cottages. They could no longer hear the metallic sound, and the inspector thought maybe he had been hearing things. They lowered their guns but stayed alert. They reached a small round clearing at the heart of the tiny cluster of white cottages. All abandoned, as they had been for the last few months. There was nothing out of the ordinary. Baynard hinted at the opposite end of the narrow path, suggesting cutting through to the other end where the car park was. Jeremy nodded. They moved slowly scanning the area around. Baynard took a sidestep into the one of the cottages. Empty. No sign of recent movement. As he was about to head out of the building, his eye fell on something on the ground. A piece of white cloth.

Enrico held his breath as he watched the two policemen from his hiding place. Enrico had spotted Baynard and Jeremy just in time at the last minute. After coming out of the vent, he had crouched behind a large bush outside the cottage so as to get a good view of Reginald leaving. The sound of the grate opening and closing had been Enrico's cue to track Reginald. As soon as Reginald emerged, Enrico did not hesitate to follow him. He was about to come out of hiding when Reginald's heavy built figure reappeared rushing back in Enrico's direction. He kept glancing over his shoulder. He seemed suddenly preoccupied. Enrico ducked down again, wondering who was chasing him. Maybe he was running from the security guards, he thought. Instead, seeing Baynard is not what the Italian baker had expected, and it was not what Reginald had expected either.

Once outside in the clearing, Reginald holding his breath hid behind a tree. The floodlights above cast an enormous shadow on one of the other small cottages nearby, enough to hide him from view. He knew though Baynard and his sergeant were right behind him in the middle of the clearing. Even the smallest sound would attract their attention. He did not dare to move, and simply listened to the policemen's footsteps, not sure how long they would stick around for. A close shave, thought Reginald. He had to be very careful at such a late stage in the plan. He hoped the police would not spot him or find out any traces of his presence. He tried to remember whether he had closed the vent properly behind him. The sooner they left, the quicker this was over.

Then, a phone rang. Enrico touched his pocket, fearing it was his Nokia 3310 going off at the wrong moment. To his relief, it was Baynard's phone. The inspector was still looking at the piece of white cloth while answering the call.

'Baynard speaking.'

'Inspector, forensics here at Wimbledon Police Station. Am I disturbing?'

'It depends if you have news I can actually use for my case.' commented Baynard.

Whatever he and Jeremy were chasing was probably long gone.

'We do. However, it is best if you come to the police station.' advised the forensic expert.

'What did you find?'

'We now know the origins of your USB flash drive. However, it comes with some related information you may find odd to hear over the phone. Like the dried blood.'

Baynard admired the cautious approach of the forensics team. Perhaps this was the turn of events he had hoped for.

'We are on our way!'

He ended the call and put his gun back in his holster.

'Who was it?'

'I'll tell you on the way. Let's get back to the station!'

'What's that in your hand?'

Sergeant Jeremy pointed at the piece of white cloth.

'I think I have an idea or two.' grinned Baynard.

Enrico watched the scene and immediately checked his chef's jacket. One of his sleeves showed a small hole that had not been there before. He closed his eyes in disbelief. That piece of white cloth was from his chef's jacket; the sleeve had probably caught on one of the handles inside the vent; and now, it was in Inspector Baynard's hands.

The Italian baker sighed. Not much he could do about it now. The only answer to everything probably lay with Reginald Bosham. Enrico waited until Baynard and Jeremy had left. When all was quiet once more, he spotted Reginald's silhouette coming out of his hiding place. When the time was right, Enrico jumped out of the bushes to follow him. Reginald was faster than Enrico had imagined. Jumping from shadow to shadow, the burly man was quick to reach the wide green expanse south of the windmill. He then broke into a mad run, escaping the floodlights and disappearing into the thick forest of the Common. Enrico kept his distance while trying to keep up with him. There was no time to lose: he had to find out once and for all what Reginald Bosham had been up to.

The chase lasted a good thirty minutes. Long enough to make Enrico tired of running and taking the repetitive precautionary steps he had to take to maintain his cover. His eyes also ached from squinting for so long in the dark. His gaze had shifted nervously from left to right to never lose sight of the beam of light from Reginald's torch. It jumped from one corner of the forest to the other, moving deeper and deeper into the wilderness of the Common, where the stars and the moon struggled to reach. Enrico's legs ached too much from the careful steps he had to take across the uneven ground; he had to stay in sync with Reginald's movements and time them well enough not to raise any suspicion as they both crunched dead leaves and branches with every step.

As the pursuit continued, Enrico wondered which direction they were going in. It was hard to tell where they were exactly, far away from any of the main footpaths and with no building in sight. Then the thick vegetation gave way to an open plain with no trees and very short grass. Enrico kept his eye on Reginald's dark silhouette ahead of him. The burly man suddenly changed direction but kept a steady pace. Enrico moved quickly; he did not want to lose him. He could now see the lights of the houses on North View and Camp Road. The Royal Wimbledon Golf Club, Warren Farms, the Repeater, they were all in the vicinity. Any of these could be Reginald's destination.

The chase quickly returned to the thick woods of the Common where there was no clear path. Enrico had to follow the trail of snapped branches Reginald had crushed along the way. Enrico did not let his guard down and persevered while keeping a safe distance. Another few minutes and they were out of the trees again. Enrico stopped at the edge of the forest when he saw Reginald slowing down, glancing to his left and right. The clearing was a gap between the forest and a long, raised mound, along which a high barbed wire fence had been erected. The security fence ran for miles in both directions. Reginald stopped in front of it. He cast his flashlight up and down the fence and then the beam stopped on a sign fixed on the mesh. There were several copies of the same sign placed at regular intervals along the fence, all stating the same thing.

Of course, Enrico now knew exactly where they were. He wondered why Reginald would come here and what he intended to do next. Cut through the fence perhaps, thought Enrico. Instead, the burly man took a step back, counted a few steps back, and then stamped one of his feet on the ground. The thud of thick metal rang in Enrico's ears. Reginald kept checking he was alone, looking up and down the length of the fence. Enrico crouched down even further and peered through the bushes again to see Reginald kneeling on the ground. The burly man lifted a manhole cover with his strong hands and then lowered himself down into the unknown. The manhole cover closed behind him with the same loud thud. Reginald Bosham had disappeared underground.

Enrico blinked a few times and scratched his head. This man was full of surprises, bad ones. His presence so close to Alberyx Enterprises must have something to do with everything that was happening in Wimbledon. He was probably the one who had tried to run him over with the car. Enrico waited a few minutes before coming out then he walked over to the manhole. He checked the fence in front of him, strangely there was no CCTV. Too convenient, thought Enrico. He was sure Reginald had someone on the inside at Alberyx Enterprises helping him out so he could act undisturbed. The manhole must have led somewhere under the Warren Farms compound, but Enrico knew if he wanted answers, he had to find out how deep the rabbit hole went. He straightened his chef jacket and rolled up his sleeves to lift the manhole cover. It was heavier than Reginald had made it look and it took Enrico all his energy to just lift it and push it aside enough for him to slip through. Inside, there was an old rusty ladder leading down a vertical shaft. At the bottom of it, a few metres down, the bright neon lights showed the start of a well-lit corridor. Enrico knew he was getting closer to something, and he also knew he was trespassing too. His pursuit of Reginald Bosham had led him into the Alberyx Enterprises facility. He was getting excited. His curiosity was again leading him into dangerous, restricted areas.

The whole corridor was a well-established underground passage. It was kept clean and had a fully working ventilation system. It was nothing like the dark, dirty tunnels he had come across before under Saint Mary's Church. Enrico waited for his eyes to adjust to the brightness of the neon lights. More signs reminded him he was on an Alberyx Enterprises property and Enrico painfully ignored the fact that trespassers would be prosecuted. There was no sign of Reginald Bosham. No voices could be heard in the distance and only the buzz from the ventilation system accompanied Enrico on this new journey. The Italian baker was more and more convinced about his suspicion that someone wanted to undermine or exploit Julian Alberon's success. Yet, he was not so sure Reginald was capable of pulling off such a thing on his own. Breaking into the top floor of the windmill where nobody had access. Entering a highly secured compound such as this one from the backdoor, with no security in the way.

After turning a few corners, Enrico came to a solid square sliding door blocking the entrance, and to each side there were narrow windows made from reinforced glass. Enrico peeked through one of them to see a bright room with unfinished grey concrete walls. Temporary glass partitions split the room into three parts: two rooms with glass doors and a continuation of the corridor leading across to another solid sliding door opposite. The partitions were all made of frosted glass, making it impossible to see what may be hidden in each room. There was no movement, no sign of Reginald. Enrico stepped back to look at the sliding door. No lock, no access pad. There was only a red button to the left. He pressed it and the door whirred open without a fuss. Too easy, thought Enrico. The Italian baker hesitated at first, wondering if it was all a trap, and then leaped through at the last minute just before the door closed again behind him. He crept forward. Half-way down the corridor, Enrico's curiosity got the worse of him and he chose to randomly open one of the two glass doors. Enrico picked the one to his right. He swallowed hard. The dead silence and the emptiness of it all seemed to be watching his every move. He dried the sweat from his forehead and leaned forward very slowly to peek into the room.

What he saw left him shocked and dumbfounded. Two men stood in the middle of the room in between two ordinary hospital beds. They seemed to be staring at the blank wall, with their backs to Enrico, both numb, and void of any consciousness or awareness. They did not sway, nor turn their heads or move their dangling arms; no movements at all in fact. Enrico frowned. He did not recognise the two men from behind. The hospital-style robes told him they must be patients of some kind. Enrico scanned the rest of the room. Beyond the two beds, he could see a few metal lockers and basic medical equipment: a medical drip for intravenous therapy, a heart rate monitor and a cabinet full of medicines. Enrico plucked up his courage and stepped forward. He cleared his throat to grab the two men's attention. The two patients did not flinch or even turn. Even when Enrico knocked lightly on the glass partition, he was completely ignored. The two men were zoned out, lost in a complete state of cognitive paralysis. A catatonic state, thought Enrico. The words echoed in Enrico's mind, realising he was simply repeating words he had heard before. The boy Ken's. Viviane's. Even Enrico's himself. Quentin said he had found them all in a similar vegetative state, completely unaware of who they were or where they were. Enrico suddenly had a hunch and started to look for the medical charts. He saw them on a small table near the entrance. The Italian baker tiptoed across the room to get them, trying not to disturb the two patients even though it appeared nothing would catch their attention. Quickly, he grabbed one of the charts closest to him. To Enrico's horror, the first few comments were enough to confirm he knew one of the two patients. By name only. One of the two men was John Crane.

Viviane woke up but kept her eyes closed. She thought she had heard something. Her head hurt like hell, and she would have preferred to go back to sleep again. She wondered though what time it was and for a moment she could not even remember what day it was. Her mouth felt dry, and a bitter taste stuck on her tongue and at the back of her throat. She knew she was not in her own bed. The flower scent that usually filled her apartment was not there at all. Instead, old musty wood filled her nostrils. She was dreaming perhaps, if not wherever could she be. Her mind was sluggish in waking up and Viviane struggled to remember. A train filled her memories. The sound of its engine, the distant whistle, the rising steam, and even the beam of light piercing through to find her. Viviane saw herself scared like a rabbit in the headlights as she saw the train advancing towards her.

'Are you awake?'

Viviane screamed and opened her eyes. She quickly sat up in bed. The room was well lit, but she still could not recognise where she was, and she definitely did not know the stout girl next to her, with a nervous smile but compassionate eyes staring back at Viviane. The girl's hand was on Viviane's forehead, dabbing it gently and drying up the sweat.

'W-Where am I?' Viviane screamed again, pushing the girl's hand away.

'Calm down. You are safe.' reassured the girl. 'My name is Fran.'

Viviane hesitated. She did not let her guard down. She pushed the bed covers back and realised she was fully clothed. Yet, she could not remember how she had ended up here. Last thing she remembered was being with Enrico on the Common, and then all memories faded. The more she thought about it, the more her head hurt, and the bitter taste in her mouth was still there, now even more unbearable.

'W-what have you done to me? What's wrong with me?' panicked Viviane, struggling to remember.

Fran tried to touch Viviane again, but the florist kept her distance, still under shock. The door to the room then opened and Quentin walked in with a tray and a steamy bowl of nettle and mint soup. Viviane's eyes softened and her whole attitude became less hostile upon recognising the ex-guardian of the windmill.

'Quentin?' she babbled.

'Viviane! You're awake!' exclaimed Quentin. 'Thank God! Everything's ok. You are safe.'

Viviane gave an odd look to Quentin and then to Fran and back to Quentin. Things were not adding up.

'I don't understand…' she said.

'Fran and I have been looking after you since we brought you in.' replied Quentin.

'We've kept a constant eye on you. You were in shock!' reassured Fran once more.

Viviane looked at her. Fran's compassionate eyes did not falter.

'I… I am sorry…' apologised Viviane. 'I didn't mean to…'

'It's alright!' said Fran with a shrug and unable to wipe off her shy, nervous smile. 'You are suffering from side effects we are now used to.'

'Side effects? What side effects? What on earth happened to me?'

'Drink this, my love.' advised Quentin as he brought the tray to the bedside table.

He then sat at the foot of her bed, looking at Viviane with earnest attention. He offered her the bowl of soup and Viviane glanced at the greenish steamy liquid with scepticism.

'What is it?' she asked.

'You can call it medicine, Viviane! It has a bitter taste, but it will cure your headache. It worked on Enrico like magic!'

'Enrico!?' exclaimed Viviane, glad to hear his name. 'Where is he? Is he alright?'

'He is fine.' added Fran. 'He is not here at the moment. He is safe, though, after all that happened.'

'What happened? Where am I?' repeated Viviane anxiously, panic surging again through her.

Her head hurt as she struggled to piece together the timeline of what had happened to her in the last hours or days. She had lost track of time. Quentin and Fran took her through the whole story, as they had done with Enrico, explaining how the windmill was more than it appeared to be and how they had found her and Enrico on the Common under the effects of the 'fog'. Viviane's eyes widened as she heard the story, revelation after revelation, incredulous to what she was hearing. She wondered who could plan such a thing and she worried about Enrico and his whereabouts. Fran told her about her boyfriend's name being on everyone's lips in Wimbledon, and how she had not been able to find him after they were affected by the 'fog'.

By the end of the whole story, Viviane's head was spinning. Quentin offered more of his green soup to make her feel better. After a few more mouthfuls, the florist was no longer disorientated, but the strong pain at the front of her skull was not relenting. Now that her memory was slowly coming back, fatigue was taking over; and yet she wanted to get out of bed and run out into the woods to look for Enrico.

'What do we do now?' Viviane pleaded.

'We are waiting for Enrico to come back.' replied Quentin. 'When we get our facts straight first thing in the morning, we will go to the police so Fran can finally report what's been really happening. We've delayed it for too long.'

'What time are you expecting Enrico to be back?'

Quentin eyed Fran and then looked at his watch.

'Well, it's been a few hours already.' he explained. 'To be honest, we thought he would be back by now.'

'Where did he go?'

'To the windmill. He must be onto something. Whatever it is he has found, I think we should wait a few more hours before getting alarmed.'

'Quentin is right.' added Fran, always calm and gentle in her voice. 'It's better for you to rest a little bit more so you gain your strength back.'

As Fran pushed her back into bed, Viviane wished she could fight back and go looking for Enrico. Her muscles though felt weak and even before her head had hit the pillow her eyes had become heavier and heavier, struggling to stay awake. She nodded feebly before drifting back into sleep. A myriad of images flashed in front of her while Fran freshened her face with a cold damp cloth. The bitter taste was still with her and so were the memories of a mad train trying to run her over on the Common.

The Italian baker was stumped by his discovery. He held his hand over his mouth in shock. Inside the room, the two men stood and swayed like lost souls in purgatory, void of any identity. All this time John Crane had been victim of the windmill's strange effects and he was not alone. The man with him, called Richard Sullivan according to the medical chart, had also been diagnosed with the same catatonic state. These were the two engineers Basil 'Wilberforce' Elders had been talking about. It was true: they had fallen sick. Someone knew about their condition and had taken the necessary precautions to lock them in here, away from public eye. The motives though eluded Enrico. It could have been a way for Alberyx Enterprises to contain further collateral damage. If so, it was difficult to pin down Reginald Bosham's role in all of this. Perhaps it was the opposite: an act of sabotage against Alberyx Enterprises to bring Julian and his company down. Enrico's curiosity and imagination started to run wild, blurring boundaries. The Italian baker wondered where Reginald could have gone. He went to check the only other door. There was no red button here. It was completely sealed, and it could only be opened from the other side. Wherever the other side was. Enrico turned his eyes to the second room. He thought he had better check it out and see what else he could find.

The room in front of him had a long metal table. Its contents were covered with a dust sheet. Enrico lifted it. Underneath it was filled with electronic spare parts, from cables to circuit boards, and plenty of schematics on large-sized paper. Some of the equipment looked like unfinished USB flash drives without any casing. The prototypes bore a resemblance to the USB flash drive Reginald had had in his hand at the windmill. Enrico picked up one of the schematics. It explained how to build a custom USB flash drive. There were some equations to one side and strange characters to the right Enrico had never seen before. Enrico scratched his head. He had no idea what they were for. All his life, he had stayed away from technology, unable to understand any of it. Dr Watkins or Viviane were in a better position to analyse it.

There were other schematics under the pile on the table. A couple of them caught Enrico's attention as he flicked through them. One showed a large, tall contraption with mirrors and aerials, together with more equations and Cartesian graphs. What they all meant was Greek to Enrico. However, on the face of it, it looked like the tall machine could have been the Repeater or even the main component of the windmill, the Oscillator. What struck him the most was the signature in the lower right corner. Basil Elders. Enrico scratched his itchy arms, trying to make sense of it. It appeared the teacher was the designer of it all. Enrico tried to remember what Basil taught at Octagon House. Advanced physics, Enrico seemed to recall from his conversation with Julian.

Flicking through more of them, Enrico came across an older coloured schematic with a faint sepia colour. There was no date on it. The page was dog-eared as if it had been folded multiple times. It was the drawing of a blade, full of detail. It was a sharp and curved blade and had an intricate decoration carved around its handle. The decoration showed the scaly skin of a dragon's or a serpent's neck up to the head and mouth with its tongue sticking out at the edge of the handle. There were some notes scribbled around the image. Some were written in English, while others were just a bunch of symbols, very similar to those Enrico had just glanced at in the schematics of the USB flash drive. An old language, perhaps. Enrico could only think of Anglo-Saxon times. The English notes were organised in short paragraphs, annotations most likely, as part of a study of the blade itself, measuring its length, explaining some of the icons sculpted on the handle. It was the imagined portrayal of an Anglo-Saxon relic, stated the unknown author. The unknown author had written in English 'Caesar's Dagger' in the top right corner. Enrico wondered if there was a link with the Wimbledon area known as Caesar's Camp or whether it was just a coincidence. Enrico remembered Dr Watkins's local history lesson and their visit to the location. Question was, to whom did the blade originally belong. Simon Deeley's presentation at Eagle House came to Enrico's mind which referred to the third relic, a dagger, linked to the legend of the Wynnman. Whether the dagger really existed or was ever found, the notes did not say; neither did they allude to the dagger being buried under Caesar's Camp. Dr Watkins's hunch was right though. Someone was interested in it.

Enrico glanced around quickly, knowing he could not stay for long and risk being found by Reginald. Behind him, there was a desk with a keyboard and multiple PC monitors, and above it a flat TV. The desk was a complete mess. Sweet wrappings, old cigarette ends, and odd bits of paper were scattered all over the place. Not at all as tidy as the way the prototypes had been lined up on the metal table. Enrico was convinced this was Reginald's spot. He operated from here for a reason that was not clear. On the other side of the room there were some file cabinets. He weighed the option of rummaging through them.

A loud, high-pitched beeping sound suddenly pierced the silence of the room. Enrico spun around in the direction of it. A red light was flashing above the second metal door in the corridor, the one Enrico had not been able to open. The flashing red light appeared to be announcing the arrival of someone so the door would be opening soon. The Italian baker panicked. He did not want to get caught. Running away to return to Quentin's cottage appeared to be the best way out. To his horror, the button did not work. The door would not open. Enrico was worried, not sure who would appear from behind the door opposite. Reginald, maybe. The thought of facing him did not appeal to him. Think Enrico think, he thought. Then, Enrico's curiosity took over, bringing Enrico his much-needed focus. He did not have any tangible clue that proved Reginald's involvement or motives. It was only guesswork. He had to get to the bottom of it, find out what he was up to and to whom this basement really belonged. The metal door made a whirring sound as it started to slide open. Enrico rushed into the patients' room. He first thought of hiding under the hospital beds, but they were too high, and anyone would be able to see him from a mile away. Enrico was running out of options. His only possibility was to hide inside one of the metal lockers instead. Fortunately, they were open. The two patients stood passively as Enrico struggled to fit inside the locker and fiddled with the locker door at the last minute to close it shut without locking himself in.

Just as Enrico settled himself into his cramped position, the solid metal door finally slid open. He peered through the eye-level grate in the door. He wondered how long he would have to stay hidden in there, like a packed sardine. He was glad though the door had taken this long to slide open. Very unusual. Condensed air had swept into the room due to depressurisation. Enrico scratched his head, trying to conjure up what lay beyond that door. Two people walked in. Enrico saw their blurred shapes through the frosted glass partition. Enrico's heart suddenly raced. He had managed to find a hiding spot in time, but he hoped the new arrivals would not find anything out of place in either of the rooms. There is not much I can do about it now, Enrico thought. The Italian baker focused on his breathing, urging himself to calm down and make no audible sound. Whoever had arrived must not find out he was there.

'The Oscillator is ready, sir!' said one man.

Enrico recognised Reginald's voice, curt and tough.

'Good!' answered another voice.

Enrico did not recognise it. It was deep and austere, yet vaguely familiar. The two men moved into his line of sight in front of the open door. The man with Reginald Bosham wore a dark cloak and a black hood that concealed his face.

'What is the status of the patients?' asked the man in black.

Reginald walked in to check on John Crane and then Richard, checking their eyes and their reflexes. He was no doctor, and only knew the routine Lord Awlthorp had told him to follow.

'It seems the effects of the superposition are wearing off.' said Reginald. 'The antidote we gave them is working.'

Lord Awlthorp walked into the room and watched carefully without lifting a finger to help. To Enrico it was just a pitch black mass where his eyes and mouth should have been. Whoever this man in black was, he did not want to be easily recognised.

'Give them a larger dose and make sure they are ready to be reinstated in the Infirmary. We won't need them anymore for what we need to do here, and when they wake up, it will all be just a bad dream.'

'How about the police?' asked Reginald. 'They came to Warren Farms this morning. I took a big gamble with John Crane's body double.'

'You did well. Almost clever, I'd say.' Lord Awlthorp smirked. 'From tomorrow it won't be our problem anymore, Reginald. The trail will only lead where we want the police to go. All in check with Operator Two?'

'Yes, Basil is ready.' confirmed Reginal forgetting the code names for a moment.

'Good! How about Operator One and the set up at the Repeater?'

Reginald nodded. He kept quiet about Ramona's threats. Better not say anything as long as the commands are in place for the Oscillator to work.

'Perfect. Time to share the final details of our plan for tomorrow!'

Enrico watched them move into the other room. He had left both doors open, and he watched them move between the metal table and the desk. He pressed his ear against the grate not to miss a word.

'This room by tomorrow morning has to be cleared too.' demanded Lord Awlthorp. 'All these prototypes must be destroyed. And clear your stuff up too. It's disgusting!'

'Yes, sir.' nodded along Reginald.

'We need to ensure by tomorrow this whole basement... disappears!' remarked the man in black.

Reginald nodded submissively and started throwing a few bits of rubbish away from off his desk. Enrico understood who was in charge.

'What exactly is happening tomorrow?'

'In due time, Reginald. When is Mr Elders getting started with the protest?'

'After six p.m.'

'That will give us two hours.' concluded Lord Awlthorp. 'The Oscillator and the Repeater will kick off at eight p.m.'

'Then what, sir?' asked Reginald.

Lord Awlthorp smiled, knowing he had the perfect answer for that, like he did for so many things.

'Tell me, Reggie. What do you think we've been doing?' he asked point blank, with a condescending tone only accentuated by the nickname Reginald hated so much.

Reginald scratched his head. Ramona's words echoed in his head, bullying him about his lack of brains. She seemed to have understood more about Lord Awlthorp's plan than him.

'Looking for the relic... Aren't the triangulations meant to tell you where you are supposed to dig?'

Lord Awlthorp gave out a fake laugh, half expecting the wrong answer.

'No, my dear Reginald. See, when I heard about the technology behind the Oscillator, and found out how Alberyx Enterprises had ripped it off Basil Elders, I took some time to read Mr Elders's theories in more detail.'

'Wireless electricity. We get it!'

'Not quite. The Oscillator is simply using quantum computing to generate the electro-magnetic forces needed to generate this stupid wireless electricity. I looked under the bonnet, so to speak. The technology built by Alberyx Enterprises is advanced enough to play with quantum mechanics and in particular the idea of superposition. Are you following?'

Reginald blinked. Enrico did too, not fully understanding what he was hearing.

'Why do I bother explaining?' sighed Lord Awlthorp. 'You will never understand. Operator One certainly does!'

'Try me...' insisted Reginald, as if he had to prove he was as intelligent as Ramona.

'Superposition includes all the possible quantum states of matter and reality. We normally see these states distinctly. Dark, light. Cold, warm. Dead, alive. Past, future.'

'What does this have to do with the triangulation?'

'Nothing at all.'

'What?'

Reginald looked baffled.

'Digging up Wimbledon Common to find what we are looking for would be such a long and winding procedure. Knowing where to start digging was the issue.'

'But then how do you plan to...?'

'Don't think where but when!'

Reginald blinked again, thinking he was losing his mind or maybe Lord Awlthorp was.

'What are you saying?' he asked, to the point of bursting out laughing in Lord Awlthorp's face. 'That the Oscillator is some sort of time machine?'

'No, you idiot!' reproached the man in black. 'I was able to implement my own formulas and I hacked the superposition manometer built inside the Oscillator and the Repeater to bring all the states of time to one place for a brief period. By leveraging the quantum technology, we will generate enough power to open a temporary window into the fabric of a past reality. A portal to peek through time itself!'

Reginald could not fathom his master's plans. What he had just heard was enough to warn him that madness was creeping in, and it would not be long before Lord Awlthorp asked him to do insane things.

'This is ridiculous…' he muttered.

'You have no faith. You, with your little brain! What do you think we've been doing all this time? All these tests, with the fog?'

'I am not following.'

'Each time we ran the triangulation test, we opened a temporary window into the Wimbledon Common of years past. To see if the technology was working.'

'What about the fog?'

'It is not really fog, but a side effect of the electromagnetic energy created by the Oscillator as it overlaps the past onto the present, so they coexist for a short while. Can't you see? We can re-live what happened a long time ago. We will be able to find out where the third relic of the Wynnman was actually buried!'

Enrico froze. Lord Awlthorp's words made him remember the fog. He then remembered the visions and the National Rifle Association's parade from more than a century ago. A portal to peek through time. He swallowed hard in disbelief; transfixed by what he was hearing. What shocked him the most was that it even made sense, especially when linking the visions in the fog to real historical references Dr Watkins had mentioned. It was all so unbelievable. It was crazy. Yet, it explained what was happening. Lord Awlthorp was the man behind such a Machiavellian plan. The Italian baker listened on.

'What I saw is a fog that swallows up men and women, and then spits them out like those two vegetables.'

'And what you saw was men and women seeing a moment of Wimbledon history almost for real. And tomorrow, I will be taking my own peek into time! At eight p.m.'

'What?' stammered Reginald.

'What we've done here, Reggie, is how to locate Caesar's Dagger. The third relic. Tomorrow, I will find Caesar's Dagger and take it before it is buried forever under the hill.'

'How…How do you plan to get through this window or portal without being affected by the fog?'

Lord Awlthorp gave away a malicious smile. He did not leave anything to chance, having seen the effects of the superposition on the human brain. The random people caught during the triangulation tests had been tremendously useful. It confirmed no man could go through the fog unscathed. Mankind was not built to survive a phenomenon like the superposition of time. He, however, had the Wynnman to guide him. Lord Awlthorp pulled a vial of green liquid out of his pocket and showed it in his open palm for Reginald to see.

'What's that?'

'Drink some of this before the fog appears, Reginald. It will help you cope with the effects of the Oscillator, and I will be able to go through the portal unharmed.'

Lord Awlthorp put the open vial in front of Reginald. He sniffed the content.

'Is that mint?'

'A mint and nettle concoction. Prevents and cures damage to the brain caused by the superposition. Fascinating!'

Enrico frowned with suspicion. Mint and nettle were the same ingredients as Quentin's soup. Putting two and two together, he suddenly felt sick. The man in black could only be Quentin Plainstraw, Enrico thought to himself.

He hated Alberyx Enterprises and had motive to hack their technology. He wondered what Quentin would gain from taking such a dangerous risk, and why he was searching for the Wynnman relics. This did not add up.

'Where did you learn about this, sir?' asked Reginald, hinting at the vial.

'It is of no interest to you, Reginald.' replied Lord Awlthorp putting it back in his pocket. 'Our time's up. Let's go through the plan again.'

'Ok.' sighed Reginald. 'Operator Two will start the uproar after six p.m. at the main gates of Warren Farms.' Reginald started repeating. The Oscillator and the Repeater are scheduled to run at eight p.m. Operator One will ensure the Repeaters turns on as expected. Shall we meet at the well?'

'Yes. That's the location confirmed by the last triangulation. Meet me there right before the portal opens.' confirmed Lord Awlthorp.

Enrico made a mental note of the time and location. Tomorrow, eight p.m. at the well. He did not know about any well in Wimbledon. He had an urge to escape and alert Viviane, Dr Watkins, and even Baynard.

'Are we sure nobody will follow us?' checked Reginald.

'Everyone's attention will be on the Alberyx Enterprises complex. Before they realise what is happening, we will have disappeared without a trace.'

'And what do we do with Operator One and Two after everything is done?'

'Keep them on stand-by until I have new instructions for them.'

'What makes you think they will not turn against us, especially Operator One?'

Lord Awlthorp chuckled and gazed at Reginald. He peered at him from under his hood, with a creepy, knowing smile.

'Whose face they have seen, Reginald? Yours or mine?'

Reginald's jaw hardened. He knew this would come; he was the only link to Lord Awlthorp's doing. Then Lord Awlthorp broke out into a deep, unconstrained laugh, meant to mock Reginald.

'You worry too much, Reggie!' he added. 'We will ensure the evidence points to one man in particular!'

Lord Awlthorp glanced at his watch.

'Time to make a move!' he said. 'We won't meet again until tomorrow evening. Keep a low profile until then.'

Enrico remained cramped inside the metal locker, watching the two men's movements. Shortly after, Lord Awlthorp took out a small remote to open the door and let themselves out. Condensed air blew in again because of the depressurisation. This time it rose quickly to the ceiling and for a moment Enrico could not see anything. He heard footsteps in the corridor, and then they died out as the door closed once more. Enrico strained his hearing once more, impatiently waiting until he was sure he was alone again.

However, Reginald had stayed behind. He was hunched over the desk, tapping away on the keyboard. Enrico waited and waited. He had to get out and get back to the cottage to face Quentin. He was sure he was the man in black. He hoped Dr Watkins and Viviane would believe him. Unfortunately, he had no solid proof with him about the man in black's absurd plan and his involvement in Wimbledon's troubles. Reginald did not even mention his name; he only referred to him as 'sir'. All Enrico had was a time and a place: eight p.m. at the well. Taking hold of his nerves, the Italian baker pushed the locker door wide enough to peer outside. He prayed the door would not squeak or make any unexpected noise that would catch attention. The two patients still stood in exactly the same place, still staring blank at the wall. Enrico now understood what had happened to them. He knew they had to come back to save them.

With all eyes on Reginald, Enrico crept slowly back down the corridor to the square door he had come from. He stood in front of the red button, hoping this time it would work. He calculated how much time it would take before the door would be open wide enough to slide through, before Reginald caught up with him. He had an idea. Enrico focused on the sound of Reginald's hands on the keyboard. The Italian baker hovered his hand over the red button, taking long deep breaths. And then go, he pressed it. The door whirred into action. Then, he heard a chair scraping against the floor. Reginald was on the move. Enrico squeezed through the gap as the door opened, and immediately pushed the red button again so that the door changed direction and started closing instantly. Enrico looked up and Reginald's angry eyes were on him.

'You!' he shouted. 'I thought we got rid of you.'

Reginald was almost at the door, and it was time for Enrico to put his plan of escape into action. He waited for the right moment and then started pulling off the circuits, smashing the red button to bits with his bare hands until the door came to a halt, leaving only a tiny gap before it closed completely. Reginald slammed against the door.

'I will get you, crazy baker!' shouted Reginald. 'And when I find you…'

He stretched his hand through trying to grab Enrico, but he could not reach him. The Italian baker watched him defiantly, safe on the other side of the door. He then ran away as fast as he could, fleeing down the corridor and back to the exit. Reginald's angry voice echoed behind him. Reginald knew Enrico was after him. Soon the mysterious man in black would know too. Time was now running out.

'You'd better have some very good news!' repeated Baynard.

His inquisitive stare clearly stated he was not asking politely. If forensics had called him urgently, then he expected a good reason to drop everything at the windmill and come down to the station.

The forensics team at Wimbledon Police Station worked better at night as they ploughed through the heap of clues that had piled up during the day, from fingerprints and blood samples to filaments of clothing and swabs of saliva. It was usually a less busy time, a time for them to breathe. Not tonight. Baynard had left specific instructions to be called day or night the moment they had something. The forensic expert in charge that night was quick in gathering all the information they had on the disappearances around the Common before Baynard stormed into the forensic lab, weary-eyed and yet decisive with his inquisitive, cold stare.

'We certainly have, inspector.' said the forensic expert, grabbing one of the many files he had at hand. 'Here's what we found. First of all, the dried blood sample did not come up in our database when cross-referenced. Whoever it belonged to, he or she is without a criminal record.'

'Or maybe he died a thousand years ago!' teased Baynard. 'What else?'

'About the blood, not much. We have news though about the USB flash drive. That's why we called you urgently!'

The forensic expert prepared himself and quickly pulled up the relevant file. He scanned it and jumped to the latest findings. He could feel Baynard's inquisitive stare fixed on him, as the inspector stroked his silver goatee waiting for an answer.

'Here it is, sir!' the forensic expert confirmed nervously.

'I am all ears.' added Baynard.

'Inside it is an ordinary flash drive. Yet, the contents are some command files we were unable to interpret. We know they are meant to execute something. What that is, we are unsure of.'

'Don't we have software analysts here?'

'It's not that, inspector. They are formulas unheard of. Nobody has ever seen anything like this.'

'Ok. Stop telling me this flash drive comes from another world. Why did you make me come all the way here?'

'Because we know where it's been made, inspector! I was about to get to that.' replied the forensic expert, flustered. 'We have a code of origin from the manufacturer.'

Baynard's eyes widened as the forensic expert flicked through the report while checking the online database on a computer screen.

'It was only spotted half an hour ago.' he added. 'We thought we'd call you first, inspector. We have not searched it yet.'

'Then what are we waiting for? Let's do it now! Whoever made this is likely to have answers.'

Baynard felt he was getting closer to an answer.

'Let me type it in.' confirmed the forensic without questioning Baynard's inquisitive stare.

The loading icon on the screen rotated for a while, testing the patience of both men.

'Inspector!' boomed Jeremy's voice in the silent forensic lab. 'News from the Chief Superintendent.'

Baynard held up his hand, giving Jeremy a sign to wait. He looked at the forensic hoping for a sign. The blue tint from the screen masked any reaction from the forensic.

'Database is a little slow. Not sure why. Please hold on.'

Baynard sighed. He then turned to Sergeant Jeremy to hear what he had to say.

'What does the Chief Superintendent want now?' he asked.

'He is asking for an update on the whole media frenzy around Basil Elders, and his false accusations.'

'False accusations! We know perfectly they are not.'

'I know. I am just passing on the message. You'd better tell him what we found.'

'I don't know. We have scattered evidence. In some cases, circumstantial. If only I could set foot in Warren Farms…'

'Then the Chief Superintendent would not be happy. You know how he feels about bothering Alberyx Enterprises. I was told he was a bit on edge about hearing Enrico LoTrova's name.'

'Funny you mention that. The piece of white clothing I found at the windmill is from a chef's jacket. Not many of those in Wimbledon. At least, for outdoor wear.'

'Do you think the Italian baker has something to do with this?'

'I don't see the connection. But I wouldn't be surprised if he has tried to find something out and got burnt!'

'What should I say to the Chief Superintendent?'

Baynard knew he would be cornered soon, having to answer questions like why Wimbledon was once again under attack by crazy individuals. Eric Quercer, the Claymores. And now, he did not know who he could blame. Basil Elders. Maybe. Enrico LoTrova. Not sure although he was the common denominator. Ever since the Italian baker had set foot in Wimbledon, strange things had happened. Baynard was not sure if they were related but he could not deny the coincidence.

'Well, that's strange.' concluded the forensic, without looking up.

'What is?' asked Baynard.

'This USB flash drive is only a year old.'

'Great! Happy Birthday!' commented Baynard, unable to hide his sarcasm. 'Built where?'

'It does not make sense…'

'I need a name!' repeated Baynard, anxiously.

He had enough of the non-sense.

'Here it is!'

The forensic hesitated and both Baynard and Jeremy noticed he was not comfortable with the answer. He turned the screen around so they could have a look for themselves.

'Here's the name.' said the forensic, incredulous.

The two police officers squinted at the screen and read the search findings a few times. They too were incredulous.

'Not possible…' muttered Jeremy.

'This changes everything!' added Baynard. 'Sergeant, get started on a search warrant. We may have a window opportunity to find a conclusion to this mess.'

On the screen, the code of origin showed Wimbledon as the location where it had been built. It was part of a batch of electronics produced at Warren Farms by the one and only Alberyx Enterprises.

The knock on Quentin's solid wooden door came out of the blue. It almost knocked him off his chair. He was quick to realise he had fallen asleep. The clock showed it was way past midnight. The knocking persisted. Dr Watkins put his book away and calmly got up from the sofa. Quentin too dragged himself out of the armchair and followed the curator. He was still half-asleep and he stumbled across to the door.

'Oh, it's Enrico. Finally!' said Dr Watkins peering from one of the side windows.

'Let me open the door.' said Quentin.

The messy chef jacket of the Italian baker, covered in mud and dirt, was the first thing they both saw as Enrico barged in even before they had had a chance to open the door. He rushed into the middle of the tiny living room and started pacing up and down, hands on hips.

'Enrico? exclaimed Quentin, glancing at the state of Enrico's chef's jacket. 'What on earth has happened?'

'You tell me!' snapped the Italian baker.

Enrico was catching his breath. He looked at his feet crushing the flowery theme embroidered on the carpet, which reminded him of the miles of grass and leaves he had crushed in the dark after he had left the underground corridor and dashed across Wimbledon Common. Images and words from earlier were still vivid in his mind. He remembered Reginald Bosham's angry face. He remembered the blank, lifeless stares of John Crane and Richard Sullivan. He remembered what the mysterious man in black had said about the Oscillator and his plan to find the relics tomorrow at eight p.m. He glanced at the clock. Being past midnight, tomorrow was today. Of all these things, though, one thing stuck in his mind the most. The nettle and mint concoction. Enrico looked up at the tall man that was Quentin, with his worn sleeveless sweater, with his faded old shirt, with his messy hair. He knew about it too, like the fog and the strange events around the windmill. He could not believe he had been behind this the whole time. He scowled.

'You don't look well, Enrico.' said Quentin, worried. 'Everything ok?'

'Did the fog catch you again?' added Dr Watkins closing the door behind him.

The curator had never seen Enrico so spaced out, so nervous and erratic. Something was on his mind. Enrico stopped walking all over the place and glared at Quentin with a narrowing, unfriendly glare.

'Nettle and mint.'

'Yes? What about it?' followed up Quentin.

'Where did you learn to make that magic soup of yours?' asked Enrico.

'I'm not sure I follow…'

'How do you know the recipe?' insisted Enrico.

'My recipe is a family tradition. It has been with the Plainstraws for generations…'

'But where does it come from?'

'I have no idea!'

Quentin was puzzled, lost for words in hearing Enrico's questioning.

'Is this all an act, Quentin? Do you think we are idiots?' attacked Enrico, raising his voice.

'What is wrong with you?' reproached Quentin, flustered by Enrico's eruption of anger.

'Ssh! You are going to wake up the girls.' warned Dr Watkins. 'What's all this Enrico?'

'You may want to ask Quentin. Where have you been all night?'

Quentin frowned. He was confused and annoyed by Enrico's erratic behaviour at such a late hour. He made a step forward towards Enrico, standing up to him with his fists to his side.

'Here, if you are asking.' he said proudly. 'I've been here waiting for you. Viviane woke up earlier on and she is better. I thought you'd be pleased to know.'

'*Bugiardo!* How do you know the recipe?'

'Of nettle and mint soup? Again? I told you. It is a family tradition. My father taught me, and his father taught him too, I suppose. Herbal medicine for when you have a headache.'

'Stop lying!'

'He's not lying, Enrico.' stepped in Dr Watkins.

He moved to Quentin's side.

'Quentin was here, Enrico' he added. 'Asleep, but he was here.'

'How…?' mouthed Enrico.

'How do I know?' pressed on Dr Watkins. 'Because I was here too. We were waiting for you to come back.'

The curator gazed at Enrico, taken aback by his finger-pointing attitude. Quentin did not flinch or budge from where he stood, as if to challenge the Italian baker. Enrico looked straight into Quentin's eyes. Doubt was stamped on the Italian baker's face.

'Who else knows about the soup?' he said almost to whisper.

'The nettle and mint soup?' quizzed Quentin. ''Enrico, how am I supposed to know? I didn't patent it.'

'Enrico, what is going on?' asked Dr Watkins immediately. 'This isn't you. What happened out there?'

Enrico looked at Dr Watkins, then Quentin, and then his gaze moved across the small living room. He spun around confused, missing a step, and almost losing his balance. He grabbed the back of the sofa to hold himself steady. He saw the man in black standing before his eyes holding the green vial. If Quentin had been here all this time, then he could not possibly be the man in black.

'Er…I am sorry…' said Enrico, blushing in embarrassment.

He sat on the sofa and put his hands on his face, maybe to hide his confusion, or maybe to close his eyes in order to grasp what was happening.

'Enrico!' cried out a female voice from the stairs.

He looked up. It was Viviane, wearing a nightgown over her clothes from the day before. The florist dashed across the room to hug him, and Enrico jumped up to do the same. Fran followed shyly behind and stood aside, watching them in their embrace with a happy smile.

'Viviane!' rejoiced Enrico. 'Are you ok? Did you get some rest?'

'Yes, I did. Bit of headache but a lot better. Enrico, are you ok? What is going on? Why are you blaming Quentin?'

'I'd like to know that too, since you barged in accusing me of lying…' protested Quentin, arms crossed.

'I saw someone tonight. Someone who had a green vial of nettle and mint soup.'

Viviane heard Enrico's voice breaking off and saw his body shudder. His body felt cold, agitated. The look on his face had changed. Less hard and defiant. Viviane watched him carefully. She knew something odd was up with her friend. She wondered if the fog had done more damage that they thought.

'Who was it?' asked Dr Watkins.

'I am not following…' added Quentin. 'Who could have it? First time I've heard of someone else using my family recipe.'

'Why don't you take a seat and tell us what you have been up to all night?' suggested Viviane. 'Fran, put the kettle on. I think we'd better sit down and hear this.'

Enrico edged towards the sofa, choosing his words as if learning to walk and talk together for the first time. The Italian baker found it hard to explain what had happened. He was still processing it all himself. He was scared that what he saw, had been a figment of his imagination and he was turning crazy again, like those two poor men stuck in that basement. He remembered their blank faces. Then, he remembered the man in black and his absurd plan to hijack the windmill to find the relic. Tomorrow at eight p.m. another Wimbledonian may suffer the fate of John Crane, or Richard Sullivan, or that boy Ken. He had to go back and save them. He had to save Julian's company. He had to save Wimbledon.

Enrico's story did not follow a very linear explanation. Scatty at times, Enrico told the events as they came to mind, jumping back and forward. By the end of it, his small audience had their heads turning and they frowned at each other.

'Alberyx Enterprises and their infernal machine. I knew it!' blurted out Quentin at the end.

'Alberyx Enterprises has nothing do with it, Quentin.' noted Viviane. 'Someone has been using Alberyx Enterprises for their own gains, and they re-hired Reginald Bosham, of all people.'

Deep down she was glad to hear Basil Elders's slander was unfounded or perhaps misguided. Mentioning Reginald's involvement stirred Viviane's memories and she could not hide her shock upon hearing the burly man was back on the streets.

'Exactly!' pointed out Quentin. 'If Alberyx Enterprises hadn't bothered building the new windmill or ripping off Mr Elders's work on this physics things…suprasomething…'

'Superposition!' corrected Enrico.

'Sounds gobbledygook to me!' insisted Quentin. 'God knows what Alberyx Enterprises are up to in that huge compound of theirs.'

'That man was not from Alberyx Enterprises.' repeated Enrico. 'He and Reginald want to make everyone believe the company is behind all this so they can deliver the plan.'

'A portal to peek through time?' repeated Viviane, struggling to grab the concept.

'He was serious and scary when talking about it.' added Enrico, unable to hide his fear for the man in black. 'Whatever he has planned will take place in less than twenty-four hours.'

'And you didn't see his face?' asked Viviane.

Enrico shook his head.

'A peek through time…' the curator muttered, as if still catching up with the conversation.

'You don't believe me…' said Enrico.

His heart sank.

'We do believe you, Enrico.' Viviane comforted him. 'What you are saying, though, sounds a little too far-fetched…'

'What about you, Dr Watkins? Weren't you the one suggesting someone may be looking for the relics of the Wynnman? The same person who looked for the first relics in the first place?'

Viviane turned her gaze to the curator.

'What is he talking about?' she asked.

Dr Watkins had been quiet most of the time, listening to Enrico's every word. His theory was becoming true. Someone was looking for the third relic and in the most bizarre of ways.

'Whether real or fantasy, we have criminals out there trying to profit from Wimbledon's history at Wimbledonians' expenses.' explained the curator. 'The relics could be worth thousands, if not millions of pounds, on the black market, especially now that Simon and I made them known to the world after our presentation at Eagle House.'

'Who could be behind such a thing?' questioned Viviane.

'I don't care who is behind it all.' protested Fran with a trembling voice from the back of the room.

She had her head down and her long curly hair fell in front, hiding her face from the others. She had been crying in silence, letting her sobs go unheard.

'John is stuck down there.' she pleaded, her voice breaking. 'We need to do something. Get him out!'

Quentin moved towards her. He gave Fran a small hug. Viviane did the same, upon realising the human value that was at stake. Her boyfriend was in danger. While they were trying to figure out who to blame, two men were locked away in a basement, sharing the same fate as Ken where nobody knew if they would ever wake up.

'I have an idea…' murmured Viviane.

'What's that?' sniffed Fran, wiping Fran's tears before they wet her cheeks.

'Enrico, you said Reginald saw you.'

'I am afraid so.' he shrugged.

'You'd better lay low. If Reginald is in Wimbledon, he and this other man could be looking for you.'

'I can lay low but tomorrow night…'

'Fran, Quentin and I will go the police and show Fran is alive and well. We can then tell Inspector Baynard the whole story. We can then ask the police to search Warren Farms and find John.'

'I don't know…' hesitated Quentin after his last experience at the police station.

'Trust me!' Viviane told him.

'What about these evil people Enrico talks about?' sniffled Fran.

'We follow them to where they said they would meet.' reassured Enrico with determination. 'It is the only way to catch them red-handed. They were talking about a well. Any ideas?'

'There are two wells, in Wimbledon, Enrico.' noted Dr Watkins, rubbing his chin.

'Two wells!?' exclaimed Enrico.

'Dr Watkins is right.' added Quentin. 'One is in Rushmere Green. Can't remember the name. The other is on the Common. It is not far from here, and it is called Caesar's Well. Obviously, Caesar never came to Wimbledon so…'

'Yes, we know that side of the story.' cut off Enrico. 'My gut feeling says Caesar's Well is where Reginald and this mysterious man will put their dangerous plan together.'

'What do you think will happen at eight p.m.?' asked Viviane.

'I don't know…'

'You'd better warn Julian.' she advised. 'We have to tread carefully and be sure who to trust. Julian needs to know there are some rotten apples lurking inside his business.'

'Enrico and I can do that.' prompted Dr Watkins. 'But only once we know you have Baynard on your side! Hopefully we can put a quick end to whatever this madness is!'

Viviane checked her smartphone. It was almost two a.m. Only eighteen hours left to go. It seemed a long time and nobody knew what to expect when the time ran out. Whatever was going to happen at eight p.m., lingered on like a fastidious itch. Too bizarre to accept and too disturbing to ignore altogether.

Thursday morning brought a clear sky layered on the horizon with the pale colours of a cold winter sun. Wimbledon was starting another ordinary day. Shops opened, people went to work, traffic picked up pace, locals took their dog for a walk. For most Wimbledonians it was a day like any other. However, for a handful of them it was a day of reckoning, knowing this Thursday would be a very different one. By the time the day was over, the beloved village would change forever in ways they could not yet imagine, not even in their dreams.

Ramona Halywell woke up at her usual time, cosy in bed inside her studio flat within the living quarters of Warren Farms. A surge of excitement and anticipation ran through her before she had even gulped a sip of her morning coffee. She was eager to see this day come to an end. Tomorrow was going to be her last day under Reginald's control. She had seen and heard enough from that idiot that was Reginald Bosham. It was time to push him aside and finally find out who his mysterious employer was.

She opened the curtains and stared at the Alberyx Enterprises employees going on their business first thing in the morning. Warren Farms was a town within a town, where the working bees were well looked after, carrying on their lives day after day. Ramona did not want to be a working bee anymore. She was aiming higher, and she was convinced she had found her match. The person Reginald worked for, the person behind the triangulation test, and those complex calculations about superposition and quantum mechanics, had the mind of a genius. It strangely captivated her imagination and ambitions. For her, it meant more than just number-crunching and checking boring software code for days on end. She had done her homework and she knew the Oscillator was being used as a radar reading through space and time. This was years ahead of what technology Alberyx Enterprises planned to build. It was her opportunity to become someone. She put on her pink tracksuit and sports cap, while adjusting her high ponytail in the mirror. She smiled pleased with her reflection. Ramona had always been left on the bench, off the playing field, when it came to the big projects. This was about to change.

Her plan was ticking along nicely. The Wimbledon police inspector had believed the text message she had secretly sent to him yesterday, and he had been quick in finding the duplicate USB flash drive she had left at the Repeater. It was only a matter of time before the police would start tracing its origin and turn up at Warren Farms. Reginald would know by then someone had betrayed him. Time was going to be of essence from this point onwards if her plan was going to work.

Her next stop was the golf club. She left her studio flat and jogged to the main gates of Warren Farms, carrying out her routine as she did every day.

She knew she had to stop and check in with security before she could continue her run out on the Common.

'Quite early today, Miss Halywell.' commented the guard.

'A few errands to do after my run.' explained Ramona. 'Mainly for the golf club.'

'I see. They keep you busy. Where do you find the time to get through all this work?'

'Well, I am efficient, you know.'

The guard laughed and pointed at the metal frame used to scan anyone who entered or left the compound.

'Apologies, Miss Halywell. Everyone's nervous lately. A lot of talk about industrial espionage, so we are checking nothing is coming in or out.'

'It's alright. You can never be too safe nowadays.'

Ramona walked right through without hesitating. The buzzer went off. Another guard present gestured at her to come forward. He hovered the scan across her legs and arms. He then moved to her torso and a high-pitched noise went off.

'Do you have anything metal here?'

'My bra wire, I suppose.' joked Miss Halywell.

She leered at the security guard who was thinking fast whether it would be appropriate to check under the pink hoodie.

'Let her through.' said the security guard that had welcomed her. 'Last thing we need is to ask Miss Halywell to undress on this cold morning. It's not the first time her bra rings!'

The security guard let Ramona through and off she went past the main gates. She put the distraction behind her and thought of what she had to do next, while running down the country lane. The Royal Wimbledon Golf Club had just opened for the day and there were not many people around. On any normal day, she would go to Lord Cotton's office to check the mail or run through boring admin she was meant to sort out. Not today.

She passed reception, scanning the hall with her deep blue eyes, and exchanging her cold, formal smile with those she instantly recognised. She went into Lord Cotton's office and locked it. She unzipped her pink hoodie and reached with her hand under her shirt. The USB flash drive was lodged inside her bra to the side. It had been uncomfortable carrying it and running at the same time. Ramona looked at the thin dark red casing and quickly put it in her trouser pocket. Leaving Warren Farms undetected had been a success. She put the USB drive in one of her drawers and locked it up for later that evening. It was now time to plant the evidence that would forever put Reginald out of the picture.

Ramona walked out of the office, past the large dining hall and onto the fairway of the golf course right outside. She then followed the perimeter of the building until she reached the usual green side door. She opened it with her master key and sneaked inside down to the underground basement. The leaking pumps and buzzing generators vibrated emitting a loud noise. The bark of that annoying dog was barley muffled by it. She found it unbearable once inside the small cell where Lord Cotton was chained. The dog had probably been barking all night and still had enough energy to carry on. Lord Cotton on the other hand looked exhausted when she walked into the cramped space where she kept him prisoner. The collar of his white shirt was wide open, and he had taken off his jacket to ease the heat in the sweltering cell.

'Who's there?' he shouted upon hearing the banging of the door. 'Help! Help!'

His voice was croaky and tired. Ramona did not give him the joy of a reply.

'I will make you pay for this!' cursed Lord Cotton with the little strength he had left. 'People will soon realise they have not seen me for a while. They will come looking for me!'

Little Caesar barked as if in agreement. Ramona would have loved to kick the little dog out of the way, but she restrained herself. She needed them alive.

From another pocket, she took out her smartphone and looked for the audio file she wished to play. She stayed quiet and let the audio file play out in its entirety. The recorded voice of Reginald Bosham echoed in the small cell. Lord Cotton listened carefully to the first voice after two days of solitude. He tried to memorise the voice, which was suddenly talking about the Repeater, about the ransom he was going to ask for Lord Cotton's life, and about his plans for sabotage against Alberyx Enterprises.

'What is the meaning of this?' rambled on Lord Cotton once the recording had ended. 'Whoever you are, you will pay for this!'

His words fell on deaf ears. The room around him was empty once again, with only Little Caesar left barking at the locked door. Ramona had already left and put the phone back in the pocket of her pink hoody. Recording Reginald Bosham's voice had been easy, and with a little audio editing she had created the perfect confession of his crimes. Everything was set to frame him. The race was on. All she had to do was turn up at the Repeater before eight p.m. and setup the USB flash drive. However, before the triangulation would run for the last time, she would have to make one important phone call.

Nathan Glenn had hardly slept at all, waiting for Thursday morning to come. Locked inside the closet, he laid on the floor thinking over and over about his discovery from the night before. He could not believe Basil 'Wilberforce' Elders was working with a criminal like Reginald Bosham simply to get back at Alberyx Enterprises. The image of a revolutionary leader was all a show. He was nothing but a pompous, selfish man who did not have Wimbledon's interests at heart. All he cared for was to avenge what was taken from him by Julian Alberon's company. He did not share Nathan's same wish to protect Wimbledon from the abuse. Basil 'Wilberforce' Elders was as bad as Alberyx Enterprises.

The journalist spent most of the night with this hot piece of information he could not share with anyone. Not until the school caretaker opened the closet with a dumbfounded look at seeing Nathan sitting there. He rushed out, happy to be free. The journalist felt he had to warn someone fast. Basil 'Wilberforce' Elders was planning something big by marching towards Warren Farms later today. The police station was the only place he could think of. He ran down the high street and past the roundabout onto Wimbledon Hill Road, not stopping once, running until he had no breath left in him. As he dodged Wimbledonians strolling up and down the pavement, Nathan thought about what he would say to the police and who he would say it to. Inspector Baynard seemed the only good choice. He arrived at the crossroad in Wimbledon Town and turned left towards the police station. He ran past the coffee shop where only yesterday he had been sitting next to Basil 'Wilberforce' Elders as a blind follower. The teacher in advanced physics was nothing but a cult leader, spreading falsehood across Wimbledon. Disappointment and resentment ran through his veins as he ran faster towards the police station. Inside, the building was eerily calm.

'How can I help you?' asked the policeman on duty at the desk.

'Inspector Baynard. Very urgent!'

The policeman did not flinch. Nathan was not sure if the policeman had recognised him.

'What's it about?' asked the policeman.

'I have information about an illegal march by Basil Elders, happening today.'

'An illegal march?' repeated the policeman in doubt.

'Yes. I need to warn Inspector Baynard.'

'The inspector is very busy at the moment. I can take your statement.'

'But it's urgent. Basil Elders wishes to sabotage Alberyx Enterprises and attack Warren Farms!'

The policeman chuckled. He put a hand on his mouth to conceal his grin.

'I understand. I know you don't like Alberyx Enterprises in the first place…'

'That's not the point!' snapped Nathan.

He realised the mistake when the policeman's face hardened.

'I presume your matter is as urgent as storming inside a police station to cause unrest, isn't it?' added the policeman.

He eyed Nathan, not leaving any room for misunderstanding. He knew Nathan Glenn and remembered him from when Basil had made a scene at Wimbledon police station. The look on his face was enough for Nathan to understand he was not on his good books, and the journalist suddenly found himself on the other side. Having spent only a short time in close proximity of Basil 'Wilberforce' Elders, was enough to label him a conspirator or a traitor. It was even worse now that he knew what Basil was up to.

'I was here as a member of the press. Nothing wrong with that.' justified the journalist.

'Not at all. All I am saying, Inspector Baynard is busy so please take a seat.'

'I'll wait outside, if you don't mind.'

Nathan stormed out of the police station. He could not believe the absurdity of the situation. He paced up and down near the corner of the building, glancing at the entrance from time to time. He wished he did not have to wait. A couple of minutes passed. Alexandra Road was busy with morning traffic. Nathan was not paying much attention and did not realise a car had parked on the kerb in front of him.

'Need a ride, Mr Glenn?' a voice called out to him.

Nathan spun around. He was quick in recognising to whom it belonged. Basil 'Wilberforce' Elders was behind the wheel. He stared at him across the passenger seat of his beige compact car. He had his confident smile, framed under his gold-rimmed glasses. For once he was alone.

'Mr Elders! Hello!' stammered Nathan. 'How are you? I'm ok.'

'Are you sure? I am on my way to the school at Octagon School. I can give you a lift.'

His pleasant smile unnerved Nathan, knowing behind that look hid a dirty, secret agenda. He had to act cool.

'No worries. Just waiting for a… friend.'

Bad excuse. Nathan thought he saw Basil frowning. He shuffled his feet, looking up and down the road. He thought he should leave or get back inside the police station.

'I'll see you later, I suppose.'

'Four p.m. rendezvous at Fox and Grapes?'

Nathan doubled-back as if he had not heard.

'Forgot already, Mr Glenn? Today's the day! You will be the only reporter on the front line!'

'Ah yes. About that…'

Nathan looked for an excuse. He could read Basil's suspicious glare.

'I'm not sure I can make it…' Nathan stammered on.

'I think you will!' replied Basil, glancing at the traffic in his rear-view mirror.

'I don't think…'

'Let me tell you a story. I was just on my way to the police, actually. But maybe I don't need to. You can help me make that decision.'

Nathan focused on Basil's words. He suddenly had his attention.

'You see, I happened to come across some suspicious activity at Octagon School.' continued Basil. 'It appeared someone broke into my office and hid inside our caretaker's closet. Naughty stuff!'

Basil paused for a moment. He smiled to himself.

'To make matters even more bizarre, my sources tell me there has also been some suspicious activity on the security network of Alberyx

Enterprises. Someone eavesdropping on guards' conversation. What people get up to these days!'

Nathan swallowed hard. His mind raced. How Basil had found out was beyond him, and it was clear the teacher-turned-leader had more aces up his sleeves than he had imagined.

'I don't know what you are talking about…' denied Nathan.

'You know, Mr Glenn. You know it very well. I think Baynard and his men would be happy to see the evidence I have against you.'

'You don't have…'

'Why don't you hop in?' interrupted Basil. 'Winter is cold this year and I don't think it is gentleman-like to have a discussion this way.'

'I'm alright standing here…'

'Get in!' snarled Basil. 'Or I swear I'll make sure you are the one ending up in prison before the day is over!'

He pointed a finger at Nathan. His face had darkened and was more intimidating than ever. The journalist hesitated. He then noticed Basil nodding. It was not at him though. It was at someone behind him. A man and a woman, dressed in the usual leather jacket and jeans, joined him at his side. One opened the front passenger door and nudged Nathan into the car. They then took seat in the back seats and Basil locked the doors.

'Good boy, Mr Glenn! Now, where were we? Oh, yes. Why don't you hang around with us for the day? Build up momentum for today's event?'

'You can't keep me against my will…' protested Nathan.

'I can, actually. I have proof of you tampering with your radio transmitter. Listening in on what Alberyx Enterprises security guards were saying. I have proof of you being at Octagon School last night. Locking you in was not that innocent, but I had to be sure what you were up to. Seeing that you came here to Wimbledon Police Station, I had to ensure you didn't make a fool of yourself…'

'We, Wimbledonians, are the fools who believe you!' Nathan replied back.

He turned to the man and woman behind.

'He's lying to you. He just wants his money…'

Nathan did not finish his sentence. Basil slapped him hard on the cheek. His skin was almost burning. The woman in the back seat pulled out a gun.

'Be quiet, Mr Glenn!' warned Basil. 'You wanted to know all about our group. Well, now you will see it to the end, whether you like it or not.'

There was conviction in his words. Nathan could read it in his fiery eyes. He did not know what was more frightening: the fact he was technically their prisoner with no chance of escape, or the fact he did not know what lay at the end of this journey.

Inspector Baynard rubbed his eyes and cheeks. He felt rough and the sting in his blood-shot eyes was already an unbearable reminder of the little sleep he had had. He had stayed at the police station all night and the idea of going home anytime soon seemed like a dream. He could not even remember the last time he kissed his wife and daughters.

He rinsed his face in the sink and looked closely at his soaked reflection in the mirror. It had been tough to stay awake, even while his mind raced constantly to process all the evidence he had on the case and build any perspective he could use to his advantage. From what he had been able to conclude, Alberyx Enterprises was involved, probably indirectly. The USB flash drive had been manufactured at Warren Farms, but the content may have been a computer virus or a malicious code. A mole was acting from the inside to break what Alberyx Enterprises had built. Whatever the motive may be, a search warrant was the best way forward.

Baynard stepped out of the toilets. The Chief Superintendent was waiting outside, leaning against the wall. He was clean-shaven and perfumed with cologne. His refreshed morning look was the opposite of Baynard's.

'Any news?' asked the inspector rubbing his hands with anticipation.

'Is this necessary Baynard?' sighed the Chief Superintendent.

Baynard stopped in his tracks. He knew it. His boss was going to be extra careful when it came down to Alberyx Enterprises. He took a good look at him, stroking his silver goatee.

'You asked me to bring back order, chief.' reminded the inspector. 'I am afraid the answer lies inside Warren Farms if we want to stop the spread of rumours, fears and chaos. Something Basil 'Wilberforce' Elders has had on his agenda for a long time.'

'We don't want to rub Alberyx Enterprises up the wrong way. They are one of our biggest employers and benefactors. You are not attacking the company or Julian Alberon, are you?'

'I won't attack anyone, sir, as long as I am given access to the proof I need. I was lied to when I went to meet the fake John Crane. Isn't that sufficient enough for the warrant?'

Baynard was adamant to get to the bottom of it.

'Let's not barge inside Warren Farms looking for a conspiracy, Inspector Baynard. Get in, look for John Crane, and if you can, find this mole. We must show cooperation.'

Baynard was not interested in political correctness at this stage.

'How long before we have approval?' asked the inspector.

'We have the first approvals in. I can't sign it in full though yet.'

'Why?'

'We need witnesses. What about this boy Ken, and what about this girl…what's her name?'

'Fran Ludley. I still haven't managed to make contact with her. About the boy Ken… Hopes that he will wake up soon are rather dim.'

'We need witnesses on board to make the whole thing stand.'

'I am trying…'

'Try harder.'

The two parted ways and Baynard returned to his desk. What the Chief Superintendent asked for was impossible. Ken was still in a catatonic state, unable to communicate, and Fran Ludley was nowhere to be found. He sipped his coffee, knowing he was going to need it. He had already had three. Sergeant Jeremy sat not far away from him, busy sorting all the evidence from the case. The ginger-haired sergeant looked tired too, after the long night.

'Bad news?' asked Jeremy.

'Sort of…' muttered Baynard bitterly. 'The chief needs more witnesses…'

The phone then rang on his desk and the inspector picked it up. Jeremy noticed Baynard's expression lit up all of a sudden.

'Are you sure?' he asked to the other end of the line. 'Ok, bring them to one of the interrogation rooms.'

Baynard hung up and got up on his feet.

'What was that?' asked Jeremmy curiously.

'Ah, Jeremy. I was ready for anything that could bring the case to a close. Do you remember the missing woman?'

'Fran Dudley?'

'Correct.'

'What about her? Did we find her?'

'Well, she found us. She's here at the police station!'

Baynard and Jeremy exchanged the same mixed look of surprise and delight. They both wasted no time and quickly made their way to the interrogation room.

Fran Ludley sat timidly at the metal table. The inspector looked at her through the one-way mirror, to see how she looked. What he did not expect was the fact that she was not alone. There were two other people with her, which Baynard knew well. Quentin Plainstraw, who had been at the police station only two days ago, and Viviane Leighwood, who seemed to have disappeared completely in the last twenty-four hours. Now, all three had turned up to speak to him.

Inside the room, Viviane went through things in her head once more repeating how they wanted the conversation to go. While Fran was behind her all the way, Quentin had been sceptical ever since they had left the cottage.

'I think we are making a mistake…' he moaned next to her.

'Why? You have nothing to hide!' she reassured him.

'I am a suspect.' he whispered, worried about how the police had treated him when he brought in Ken.

'You're not!' said Fran. 'I am here, Quentin, and I can tell the truth about what happened to me. Besides, this is the only way I can find my John!'

Viviane smiled at her. She admired how Fran had not lost her faith in finding her boyfriend despite the odd circumstances. Viviane too had wondered where Enrico was the moment she woke up in one of Quentin's bedrooms. She could not deny she was becoming attached to the crazy Italian baker, and for once, Enrico had not been the one looking for trouble. Yet, trouble seemed to have found Enrico as always.

Their thoughts were distracted by the door opening. They found Baynard inquisitively staring at each one of them. The inspector knew this would be interesting and he was ready for anything.

'Miss Fran Dudley!' he welcomed her pulling a weak smile. 'How glad to meet you! You are someone hard to find…'

He shook hands with her and did the same with Quentin. Baynard then turned to Viviane and gave her a crafty look. He had learned one thing lately. Wherever Viviane showed up, he was sure the crazy Italian baker would not be too far behind. However, for the moment the baker was nowhere to be found. Baynard wondered what he was up to.

'Miss Leighwood. Glad to see you too. We found your Fiat 500 abandoned and were wondering what had happened to you. I hope that friend of yours, Mr Larteva, is fine as well!'

'LoTrova!' corrected Viviane knowing Enrico would have done the same.

Baynard did not pay attention to her comment and returned his attention to Fran.

'Your parents have been looking for you, Miss Dudley. Are you ok? Do you need anything?'

'I am ok.' Fran nodded. 'We are ok. We came here straight away. To tell you what happened.'

Baynard's smile gradually returned to his inquisitive stare. He could see Fran trembling like a leaf. Yet, her appearance and clothes did not show as if she had been under any form of physical duress.

'And what exactly has happened?' Baynard asked eyeing all three of them.

Fran widened her eyes at Quentin since it was his cue. He was fumbling with his hands, mumbling a few words about what he had to say. Viviane prodded him. They had had little time to rehearse how to tell the story, but they were confident it would make sense. Viviane knew Baynard would see through it.

'Erm…Thank you for your time, inspector.' stammered Quentin. 'I was the one… erm… the one to find Fran in the woods. She was in a state of shock and disorientation. I kept her at my house to look after her, to cure her...'

'Excuse me!' interrupted Baynard. 'Are you saying you abducted this woman?'

'No no no no no!' pleaded Quentin, shaking his head. 'She was sick, see. I cured her from the catatonic state she was in. I wish I had done that for Ken… I was scared…'

'And I can confirm everything, inspector.' jumped in Viviane. 'I fear this boy Ken and Fran's boyfriend John Crane may have suffered the same.'

She explained the story of the fog and the hallucinations, of how she, Enrico and Fran had suffered its side effects, and of Quentin's miraculous nettle and mint soup. Baynard was perplexed but listened. Viviane was careful to leave Enrico's part out of it. Until he and Dr Watkins managed to alert Julian, it was better to wait so that the mysterious man in black and Reginald were given the impression nobody was after them.

'Nice story.' commented Baynard when she had finished. 'A clever one too. Now, what do you want me to do about it?'

'Something's wrong with the windmill, inspector.' added Quentin. 'It is causing this fog and hallucinations…'

'I suppose this would work in your favour, Mr Plainstraw. After all, they were the ones to let you go, make you lose your job, weren't they?'

'Sure, but that's not why we are here.' protested Quentin. 'We wanted to alert the authorities about these serious health issues…'

'And get a fat cheque for damages from a large enterprise like Alberyx Enterprises, right? Did Basil "Wilberforce" Elders push you to do this, perhaps?'

Quentin frowned. He tensed in reaction to Baynard's provocation. He did not like being accused a second time in less than a day. Viviane was swift in holding him back and keep the situation calm.

'Inspector Baynard, We just want to help.' she said. 'Fran would be in Ken's shoes right now if it weren't for Quentin. All we are saying is that we may be able to help Ken too. Everyone must be horrified to see him in that soulless state…'

'Miss Leighwood, I am just getting my facts right.' interrupted the inspector. 'Before I can accept all your statements as possible evidence, I need to ascertain their validity. For example, where's your friend the baker?'

'He's at home.' lied Viviane. 'He is still resting from the side effects of the hallucinations. All three of us experienced the same horrible experience. Why don't you believe us?'

She gazed into Baynard's light grey eyes. The inspector did not flinch. He was not going to accept their version of facts that easily. Some of it rang true, but it needed to be watertight if he were to use it in his case towards getting the search warrant signed.

'Inspector Baynard…' spoke Fran with a quavering voice.

Baynard blinked at the sudden interruption. He had been calm and strangely sympathetic. Fran's puffy cheeks turned a pinkish hue, and she pulled some hair behind her ears as a nervous gesture to draw up all the courage she had to. There was a brief silence before the uncertainty wore off.

'I remember something happening to me, inspector.' Fran resumed. 'But you are right. I could have been dreaming. All we ask is that you confirm our story and at the same time give that boy Ken a chance. He may wake up and prove us right or wrong in all of this. If you do that, it may give me hope to save my boyfriend John.'

Fran's voice cracked and she turned away to hide her sadness. Baynard listened carefully. She had looked shy but found the guts to stand her ground. He could only respect that. Normally, he would have ignored such ludicrous type of evidence and yet he had seen enough strange things in the last couple of days and even months. It dawned on him that having Fran here and waking up Ken would give him the two witnesses he needed for the search warrant.

Dr Watkins set foot in the museum slightly before lunchtime, carrying a couple of tomes he had stopped to pick up at home. He dropped them on the desk and went into the back storage to check himself in the small mirror above the tiny sink. His whole appearance was in disarray. He still wore the same light blue suit from the day before, and his grey shirt was all crumpled and not at all presentable. His eyes looked puffed and tired, and no matter how much he stretched his aged skin in front of the mirror, he could not hide the sleepless night at Quentin's. He splashed some cold water against his face. Sleep was slowly catching up with him. He could feel it. He blinked a few times and then gazed at the shelves to his left.

There was a brief moment of loss, of disorientation. The back storage disappeared before his eyes. His mind quickly recalled the vivid nightmares he had been having, the Anglo-Saxon stories of sorcerers, dragons and potions jumping off the page, and then Enrico's tales of a man in black looking for the Wynnman himself. He had been right all along. Someone believed in the infamous fairy tale and was looking for the relics. Who that someone could be, escaped him. Suddenly, a sense of dread mixed with anger and jealousy filled his heart. Power and revenge. The words echoed in his mind. The same words Simon had heard him saying in the Pool of Elixir while in a trance. He came to realise the relics of the Wynnman themselves promised power and revenge, and Dr Watkins knew he had to get hold of them before anyone else would. Something deep inside told him this is what he had to do.

'Dr Watkins!'

The voice came out of nowhere and brought Dr Watkins back to reality with a gasp. His heart was beating fast. His gloved hand was throbbing. Dr Watkins winced and held his hand tightly until the pain receded. He quickly dried his face and walked back into the main hall of the museum. The slim figure of Reverend Green stood by the desk, glancing with curiosity at the tomes Dr Watkins had brought in.

'Oh, there you are!' he exclaimed, hearing the curator's footsteps. 'I thought you had popped out for lunch.'

'Not yet. Not yet.' Dr Watkins rushed to reply in a dismissive tone.

'What happened to you? You look a little rough.'

'It's nothing.'

The reverend knew well his friend the curator. His appearance was unusual, and one he had not seen in a long time.

'Still not sleeping?' he asked worried.

'Yes, I am afraid.'

The curator was quick to admit the only thing that could give him an alibi. He did not want to get the reverend involved in what he was up to with Enrico and Viviane.

'You need to slow down.' insisted Reverend Green. 'This work with the British Museum is going to damage your health. I see you still wear the glove on your hand. I thought everything had healed.'

'Almost. Just keep it for a while longer as a precaution.'

Reverend Green gave the curator an unconvinced look. He could tell Dr Watkins was up to something. He had seen it before, and the title references of the tomes on the desk gave a hint.

'I see you are digging deeper into the Wynnman folklore. I heard your presentation last Monday evening. Is this your follow-up research with Simon Deeley?'

Dr Watkins nodded. He found the reverend's questions a little odd and perhaps more meddling than usual. He knew the reverend cared for him as any old friend would, but this was not the time or place. He had to grab a few things and then go get Enrico at Quentin's house to warn off Julian Alberon as soon as possible.

'Is there anything I can help you with, Reverend? I am sort of in a rush.' the curator quickly added.

'I am sorry.' replied Reverend Green with a deep sigh. 'I just came to ask if you had seen Enrico. The bakery has been closed for two days now. A few people from the congregation were talking about what had happened. I went to buy some bread this morning and the bakery was still closed.'

'Enrico is not well, unfortunately.'

'Really? I rang the bell of his studio apartment on the floor above. No answer.'

'He was probably sleeping. He had a bad flu. It is the season, you know.'

'I understand.' smiled the reverend complicitly. 'Well, do send him my best wishes for recovery.'

'I will.'

Reverend Green headed for the door, taking a good look at the museum as he did so. The curator showed him the way out, pressing him to leave in the most discreet way. He did not expect the entrance door to open and see Simon Deeley standing in the doorway.

'Thir ye are!' exclaimed the archaeologist. 'I hev been looking for ye.'

'Hello Simon! What's new?' replied Dr Watkins casually.

'You tell me.'

He stepped inside, nodding at the reverend. He then took a good a look at Dr Watkins.

'You look as rough as hell.' he added. 'Where were you yesterday afternoon? You left so mysteriously.'

'Just helping a friend.' replied the curator vaguely.

Dr Watkins was conscious of Reverend Green's presence, listening to every word. He had to find a way to dismiss them both, as subtly as possible.

'Reverend Green was leaving and so was I. Can this wait tomorrow?'

'No, it cannae.' replied Simon point blank.

He gazed at him with a firm expression and tried to hide his surprise at the curator's evasive answer.

'I was expecting ye at the site.' he added.

'Oh sorry. It must have slipped my mind!' said Dr Watkins, in part truly mortified, although he knew he had another lead on the Wynnman to follow.

'That's ok…' added Simon, still unconvinced. 'I hope ye can join us today. I think I found the source of those words you spoke out loud.'

'What words?' interjected Reverend Green, showing curiosity.

Simon gave the reverend a tight-lipped smile. He was taken aback by the man's prompt. He wondered what the two had been talking about. There had been a sense of unease from the moment he opened the door. It was the feeling he had interrupted an odd conversation. He was starting to think Wimbledonians acted funny.

'Power and revenge.' continued Simon, looking at Dr Watkins. 'Those are the words spoken by the Wynnman the moment he was imprisoned by the villagers! I found the detail in the last bit of text inscribed on the eagle-like statue in the Pool of Elixir. Strange how we had missed it. I swear it wasn't there a week ago though...'

'Brilliant, Simon. You'll need to show me. Now, if ye excuse me...'

'Hold on, Dr Watkins. How could ye just leave like 'at? Don't you remember how ye fell in a trance in the chamber? That's not normal.'

Dr Watkins felt goosebumps on his skin. Despite Reverend Green being turned towards Simon, unable to see Dr Watkin's face, he could imagine it twisting into a suspicious frown. Until Simon arrived, he had tried to show the reverend everything was ok, including his health.

'Trance, you say?' repeated the reverend with a surreal ominous voice.

'Aye.' said Simon. 'When we had that power surge again, which by the way, is really messing up my instruments.'

'It must be the tests prior to the launch of the wireless electricity, don't you think?' suggested Dr Watkins.

'Maybe I wish someone would help me resolve it.' added Simon.

Dr Watkins struggled for words. He was confident about what had caused the power surge now that he knew the Repeater and the entire machinery at the New Windmill were being tampered with. He could not share that information. Not yet, at least. Reverend Green turned towards Dr Watkins. He had a cruel and caring look on his face, one the curator could not interpret.

'Dr Watkins, you really ought to go easy with your work at the site.' advised the reverend.

'I will, reverend. And Simon, I can definitely join you later and we can maybe find a way to fix the problem.'

'Please come this time, instead of leaving me high and dry, waiting for ye. We also have tae catch up on my proposal for Caesar's Camp.'

'I think we've been through this...'

Dr Watkins felt Reverend Green's stare upon him. It felt strange. He was not sure if perhaps he was feeling a little embarrassed that the usual private conversations he had with Simon, had suddenly become public. Reverend Green though was a friend, and yet he felt a strange opposition in his gaze. He took a deep breath and stared back at him to explain.

'Mr Deeley here wishes to dig Caesar's Camp for further investigation on Anglo-Saxon remains.'

'I see.' replied Reverend Green perplexed. 'I am sure you two already heard Wimbledon's position in general about this.'

He turned back to Simon Deeley who was not impressed by the response. Having spoken to Ramona Halywell the day before in Lord Cotton's absence, he was facing a dead end. He had to draw this matter to the attention of the British Museum and Alberyx Enterprises somehow.

'We have to find a way.' said Simon. 'Let's chat later at the Old Rectory.'

Dr Watkins nodded in agreement, knowing perfectly he may miss the appointment considering a ghastly plan was under way for eight p.m. that night. Suddenly, the urgency of it all made the curator panic. He had to make haste and let Reverend Green and Simon Deeley be on their way.

'I really need to leave now.' he was quick to add. 'Simon, let's meet later. And Reverend Green, please be assured I am ok. I will get some rest tonight.'

Dr Watkins eased the two towards the entrance. He felt bad for Simon but most of all felt bad about lying to one of his old friends, the reverend. He felt his legs giving way under the weight of his insincerity. He knew perfectly well Reverend Green would not be satisfied with his answer and would be back sooner than he thought.

He almost pushed the two out of the museum, pulling a fake smile just to get rid of them despite Simon's protest. He heard them outside for a while and then going down the steps to the ground floor. Dr Watkins leaned against the door and took a deep sigh of relief. He closed his eyes for a moment and gathered his thoughts. His prolonged tiredness still gnawed at him, whispering to him the comfort of a good sleep. He fought hard to shake his tiredness off. He had to get going, catch up with Enrico, meet Julian Alberon, stop who was after the relics of the Wynnman…

The dreamlike state he had experienced moments before returned gradually without Dr Watkins noticing. He saw the museum hall fading and the curator enjoyed the sensation of being in a lull, moved by the breeze. He opened his eyes and was back in the tunnels of the Old Rectory. He stood there in the cold and damp wind blowing out of the darkness. This is where it had all started, thought Dr Watkins. He then looked at his hands. In one he was holding the black azalea and in the other a bottle of crimson liquid. He did not recall how he had got hold of them. He looked up. A silver glow shone far away like a tiny star in the cloudless night sky. The relics were somehow calling him. For what, he did not know. Power and revenge, he thought. It was time to act. It was time to bring the relics home.

The boy Ken sat still on a chair, looking out of the corner window of his room at Parkside Hospital. He appeared to be staring across the driveway of the hospital, and across the road that was Parkside, towards the high wall of trees that announced Wimbledon Common. He did not blink. He did not give any signs of emotion. He did not even stir or shiver when watching Wimbledon Common, a stark reminder of where his mysterious arrow wounds had been inflicted. Ken did not show hate or distress, nor even peace.

Ken's mother held his hand next to him, hoping he would turn around any minute. She too appeared to have fallen into the same frozen, catatonic state. The longer she stared at her boy, the more unaware and negligent she became of what was happening around her. The doctor's words fell from his mouth without being heard. Standing next to her, he was going over the patient's chart with Inspector Baynard and even the inspector was intimidated by how the mother had preferred to join her boy's infinite silence. She had probably heard the doctor's words too often in the last forty-eight hours, and the doctor himself had been honest with Baynard: there was little to go on to explain Ken's condition.

Baynard had given his heartfelt apologies upon arrival. Viviane, Fran and Quentin had done the same, faced with such a sad scene; they preferred to stand a little further back to give some space to Ken's mother until Baynard deemed it appropriate to come forward. Baynard did all the talking, from asking permission to see Ken to briefing the doctor about the recent developments. The inspector was not sure how doctors would take Quentin's herbal treatment. He did not care. Saving the boy's life was key to the case, and he could not let any trail go cold at this stage. If the herbal treatment had worked for Fran and Viviane, there was reason to believe it might work for Ken too. Perhaps what Ken had seen could help Baynard make an even stronger case for getting the search warrant approved in the next few hours.

Viviane exchanged glances with Fran more than once. Ever since leaving the police station with Baynard, she had wanted to say how brave the freckled girl had been. Her compassion, free of anger, appeared to have moved Baynard. The inspector made it clear he needed to verify their claim but, while he could not guarantee anything, he still offered his support. Both Quentin and Viviane could not ask for more. Now, only the doctor stood in their way before they could finally learn what had happened to Ken.

'…and as you can see, no reflexes, no cognitive awareness or reaction to stimuli of any kinds.' carried on the doctor. 'Applying stronger doses of medicines acting as stimulants have not worked and we are waiting before we decide to move forward with any type of surgery to the brain. The diagnosis is, I am afraid, incomplete.'

'And what we are suggesting, how different is it from your standard medication?' prompted Baynard, pushing the doctor to give the answer he was looking for.

'What you are suggesting, inspector, is fundamentally not based on scientific research and the results are unpredictable. The administration of an untested medicine, like a home-made herbal mixture, on hospital grounds is considered risky by the hospital administration.'

'True. I completely understand that. Aren't we running out of options though when you say it yourself you cannot tell me or his mother what the problem is?'

'Inspector Baynard, if you intend to go down this route, myself and the hospital cannot be held responsible for the side effects this herbal drug of yours may have. I would leave it to the mother to decide and sign off her approval.'

Ken's mother finally looked up as she heard the burden of responsibility falling a little heavier on her. Her eyes were tired and scared. She held the doctor's gaze and then Baynard's before returning to look at her beautiful boy lost in a world remote from hers. Baynard could not tell what her opinion was and had to tread carefully not to push too much. The woman could just crack under pressure and simply forbid anyone to test on her semi-paralysed son. He quickly gave the mother and the doctor a nod to excuse himself and hinted at the three behind him to join him outside the room. Once the door closed behind him, Baynard faced the three anxious stares of Viviane, Fran and Quentin.

'You heard the doctor.' he said. 'If you think administering this green medicine is the only way, you need to convince the mother!'

Viviane bit her lower lip and glanced at Quentin, whose eyes summed up the helplessness they all felt. His mint and nettle soup was no official drug; it was a grandmother's recipe whose adverse effects he had no clue about. Quentin played with the small vial he had with him. The green, thick slob sample from his last batch of soup was more vivid in colour when looked through the glass. Viviane and Fran knew it held the key to Ken's health and the answers they desperately needed. Even Baynard, a little dumbfounded at first by the whole story, glanced at it with avid eyes. The stories about hallucinations from exposure to this strange fog plaguing Wimbledon went beyond the inspector's basic understanding of logic and facts. However, the history imbued in the hallucinations Viviane and Fran had described in fine detail made him think of Ken's odd arrow wounds or the old, dried blood. While he could now explain them through Viviane and Fran's story, at least in theory, he knew it sounded utterly ridiculous. The Chief Superintendent and the entire police force would laugh at him if he dared bring this forward. It was enough to say the New Wimbledon Windmill had become a health hazard. If it was causing all these hallucinations because of some rogue agent acting on the side, then his search warrant against Alberyx Enterprises was more than justified. Yet, he had to get that warrant signed and approved today.

'So, are you sure you want to go through with this?' asked Baynard to the three of them.

'I recognise the same symptoms, inspector. No doubt about it.' commented Quentin.

'I agree but we need to convince Ken's mother, not Inspector Baynard.' reminded Viviane.

She then looked at the inspector, her knowing smile crossing his inquisitive stare.

'Perhaps you think we need a woman's touch in there, inspector?'

Baynard shrugged and then gazed at the rest of the group. Viviane understood.

'Fran, do you mind joining me inside?' asked Viviane.

She then held out one hand to Quentin to claim the vial and with the other she beckoned Fran to say 'yes', reminding her she had asked rhetorically. The shy girl pulled a lock of hair behind her ear, her eyes looking elsewhere in search for the right answer. Viviane was counting on the one person that had suffered Ken's condition first and had come out of it unscathed. She knew Baynard would let her in to convince Ken's mother, but she needed Fran with her so she could tell her story.

Viviane softened her eyes at Fran, to convince her of her bravery and that she could do more to help. Fran fiddled with her hands, feeling a little nervous and anxious with the group staring at her. She took a deep breath, closed her eyes and the nod that followed was barely visible. She then opened her eyes and found strength in Viviane's smiling face, giving her a constant flow of confidence.

'Ok…' re-confirmed Fran. 'Let's go inside!'

Ken's mother did not acknowledge the two women straight away. It seemed as if she had not moved at all in the last five minutes. Arms and legs were still in the same position. Maybe she acted in such a way to share the pain with her son who had not spoken or blinked in days. Maybe she hoped to talk to him through her prayers. Viviane thought of this as she approached with Fran, being mindful not to break the invisible bond between mother and son. She asked the doctor in a low voice if they could have a private moment and he nodded with an expression that was more confounded than convinced. Once Viviane and Fran were alone with Ken and his mother, they took a seat by the windowsill, sitting right across them. Viviane spoke first, in the hope she could win Ken's mother over.

'We know how hard it is, ma'am. We really do. We just want to help.'

The mother lowered her eyes, a sign that she heard her words, but no words came out of her mouth. Viviane searched her thoughts to find the right words.

'My name is Viviane. I am the florist in Wimbledon Village. And this is…'

'I know who you are…' said the mother. 'Please leave us alone.'

Viviane hesitated. She could not let go.

'Sorry to bother you. We just wanted you to know, myself and the girl here, Fran, were both in the same condition as your son. But look at us! We are here talking to you now…'

'Please…' insisted the mother.

'We might be able to help you…' rushed Viviane to add.

The mother looked out of the window and let out a deep sigh. She struggled for words. Viviane was about to try something else, but Fran grabbed her arm before she spoke again. It was not a firm grip; more of a gentle squeeze not wishing to hurt anyone. Viviane turned to her and met Fran's saddened eyes. They held each other's gaze and Viviane did not understand why she had blocked her or what her intentions were. Before she knew it, Fran spoke up instead. The quivering, little voice gathered all its strength to find the courage to speak up.

'We are not… here to hurt you!' she said. 'I… I lost someone too, ma'am, or at least I think I lost him. My special other half, you know. We were meant to get married back in my hometown after he had finished his work here in Wimbledon. I still don't know where he is or what happened to him. Something attacked us both in the Common, and only a few days later I woke up from the most horrible nightmare. If it weren't for Quentin who found me in the same state as your son, I wouldn't be here talking to you…'

Fran paused a second to hold her emotions. The mother still looked out of the window, not flinching.

'Yet, I still can't heal!' Fran continued, eyes swelling with tears. 'I can't find my love and I don't know if he is safe. Your son Ken perhaps can help.'

Fran leaned forward and picked the vial from Viviane's hands. She then leaned forward and placed it within reach of Ken's mother. For a brief moment, she looked at Ken, staring into a void nobody could see, and then his mother's.

'I… I…' resumed Fran. 'I know my boyfriend John made me happy and bubbly. Since everything that has happened and since he went missing, I am lost. I don't know what to do or where to turn. Please help me find him. Please…'

Fran then leaned back without saying anything else, not even explaining what the vial contained. She nudged Viviane to stand up and walk out of the room. Viviane hesitated, astonished by Fran's words.

'We'll now give you some time alone.' Viviane said. 'Thank you for listening.'

When the door finally closed, and Ken and his mother were alone once again, a soothing calm filtered out the solitude. It came in the form of words that creep into the hearts and minds of fellow human beings, to remind them that we share emotions and purpose, like love and family. Upon thinking that, Ken's mother shed a tear before picking up the vial and opening it.

Enrico rubbed his hands in the cold, cursing under his breath. Where Dr Watkins was, he did not know. For hours, he had waited for him at Quentin's house and the curator had never showed up. He texted him, called him, but no answer. Alone in Quentin's cottage, the Italian had become impatient and could no longer sit back and wait around. Enrico came to realise the more time passed, the quicker time was running out. He had to warn Julian Alberon himself as planned.

It was late afternoon and the light was slowly dying on the Common. Enrico had left Quentin's cottage in a rush and was now heading across the Common to reach Julian's mansion Parkside on foot, dodging the wild branches dangling across his path. Enrico repeatedly thought over what he would say to Julian. He had to be transparent to him just as Julian had been with him in regards to the affair with Basil Elders. Hopefully he would see the dangers and call his security. He then imagined Viviane and Fran would call having successfully convinced Baynard to look into the matter. Enrico smiled to himself. Yes, he was convinced this was how things would play out. He heard an owl hooting in the distance. Enrico stopped in his tracks. The vast Common around him was crowded by the unruly wildlife and yet it felt empty with no human soul in sight. Despite what remained of the natural light, the Common stared back eerily at Enrico and it looked scarier than when he usually crossed it at night. He quickly rushed forward, not looking back, and wrapped his dirty chef jacket closely around him and close to his neck to fight the bitter cold. He hoped the fog would not catch him out.

And indeed, it did not. For what seemed hours to Enrico, he finally heard the sound of traffic coming through the trees. Must be near Parkside, he thought. The Italian baker picked up his pace. He finally reached Parkside and crossed the busy street to reach Julian Alberon's mansion standing tall and ominous with its Gothic turrets stretching up in the sky where the sun had started to fade away. The warm lights coming from Julian's living room seemed to be inviting Enrico in to save the day and save Wimbledon. He hoped so. He then thought of Dr Watkins, wondering if the curator was alright. Perhaps he had been held up. These last thoughts crossed Enrico's mind as he knocked once again on Julian's door and a sense of déjà vu overwhelmed him. He rushed to remember what he was meant to say to Julian, hoping he would believe him, and the door finally opened.

'Enrico?'

Julian opened the door himself. He was wearing jeans and white shirt unbuttoned at the collar, showing a casual business flair about him. His hair was a little out of place and his eyes squinted to get a better look at Enrico.

'Enrico? What are you doing here?'

'Sorry, Julian.' answered the Italian baker frantically. 'It is very urgent. Can I come inside?'

Julian was slightly taken aback. He rubbed his eyes in the process.

'Sure! You don't have to apologise. Late meetings with the United States last night on the latest tech so I slept in this afternoon. If I don't rest, I won't be able to keep my eyes open on the great day this weekend!'

He smiled weakly, re-adjusting his hair.

'Did we have an appointment?' he then asked.

'No, I am afraid not. A last-minute decision, Julian!' justified Enrico. 'Something urgent I wanted to talk to you about.'

'Urgent?'

Julian saw Enrico's worried face directly under the light of his porch. The shadows around his eyes and cheeks made him look more alarmed. Julian recognised it was something serious.

'Sure! Come in!' replied Julian beckoning him to come inside.

One of his staff appeared in the hall and Julian reassured he would handle the new guest.

'Do you think we can talk in private?' added Enrico stepping inside.

Julian did not like the sound of Enrico's suggestion. The Italian baker was wary of his surroundings, a little on edge.

'Is everything ok?' he asked.

'We think you might be in danger…'

'Who's we?'

'Me, Viviane, Dr Watkins.'

Julian frowned. He usually would not normally answer the door to a crazy man warning of danger ahead, but he knew Enrico well enough to know something was not right.

'We can talk upstairs in my studio.'

He led Enrico to the second floor. Inside the studio, he asked Enrico to take a seat on one of the plush couches by the window overlooking Parkside. He fixed himself a drink. Enrico opted for a glass of water. Julian checked the door was closed and went to sit opposite Enrico.

'What is it then?' he asked getting straight to the point.

'It is about the New Wimbledon Windmill and your entire operations.' started Enrico, forcing himself to remember the talk he had put together in his head. 'Well, we think someone has been tampering with your machinery at the windmill and they infiltrated your compound at Warren Farms somehow.'

'What are you saying, Enrico? That's impossible. Our security standards are top class.'

'I saw it with my own eyes.'

Julian's face straightened. Enrico knew he had his attention.

'Last night I followed a man who has been infiltrating your windmill and one of the basements at Warren Farms.'

'Please, Enrico!' the businessman frowned. 'Is this a joke?'

'No. It's the truth!'

'Are you saying you broke into my own facility?'

Enrico did not see that coming and recalled the trespassers' sign on the fence.

'No-no-no-no-no!' rushed Enrico to ensure he got his story straight. 'I simply followed this man…'

'Who is this man you are talking about?'

Enrico realised he had not broken the big news yet. He gulped before doing so.

'I am sure you remember Reginald Bosham.' said Enrico.

The name could not be ignored; it was still fresh in everyone's mind.

'That vilified crook? Of course, I remember him! He tried to meddle with the Claymores at the Old Rectory!'

'He is the man who has broken into the New Wimbledon Windmill and the Repeater.'

'I beg your pardon?'

Julian thought he was reliving the same moment when Enrico and Dr Watkins had warned him about Reginald Bosham and the Old Rectory. He could not believe it was happening again.

'Are you sure, Enrico? Reginal Bosham is behind bars. You seem a little agitated. Are you sure you don't want some tea or a strong drink?'

'We don't have time, Julian. I have proof Reginald is free as a bird and he has been working with someone to tamper somehow with the New Wimbledon Windmill and the Repeater.'

'What do you mean when you say "tamper"?'

Enrico gulped down his glass of water.

'Do you remember the research findings from Dr Watkins and Simon Deeley? The legend of the Wynnman and the relics?'

Julian chuckled, nervously.

'Seriously, Enrico, is this a joke? I have no idea what this has to do with my windmill, but I think we agreed the legend is just pure folklore, told through some old rocks in the ground…'

'Dr Watkins and I don't care if it's real or not. We believe someone cares though, and they are trying to find and steal the relics. At this very moment, I know Reginald and his accomplice are looking for the third relic. The dagger.'

'I keep my company in check, Enrico. These are serious allegations. And how can they use my windmill to find a relic when we don't know if it really exists? I am curious to hear.'

'You'd probably explain it better than I ever could!' said Enrico, preparing himself to describe what he had seen. 'From what I could tell, it looks like the wireless electricity of your windmill has been re-engineered to generate…erm…suprapartition….no…supraposit…'

'Superpositioning?' exclaimed Julian, bewildered.

'I knew the word would make sense to you.'

'It does. It's a component of the Oscillator but I don't understand…'

Enrico went on to explain what he had heard the man in black saying. About the fog. About the plan to use the quantum technology inside the Oscillator to create a portal that would lead them into a point in time. It was the second time he heard himself explaining and it still sounded far-fetched.

'…so we need to stop them before eight p.m. tonight. You have the power to search the facilities before it all comes out into the open and we involve the police!'

Julian's face was stern at first. As Enrico said those last words, he burst out laughing.

'That is rich, Enrico!' he said, wiping his tears of laughter. 'I must say we both dream of the impossible. I didn't know you had it in you…'

'The impossible?' echoed Enrico, a little disappointed.

'Correct. What you are saying is impossible. Someone tweaked my new windmill to do what…look back in time? Even if my company has built the most advanced technology so far, the scientific know-how you are talking about is simply not there yet!'

Enrico was lost for words. He had been building up hopes that he was onto something, but Julian had been quick to bring him down to earth. He who believed in innovation did not seem to see the story as credible.

'Then prove me wrong.' insisted Enrico. 'People have been claiming your windmill is a health hazard until now, and I have seen what the fog does to you…'

'My windmill is perfectly safe.' scoffed Julian. 'Have you been hanging around with Elders's crowd?'

'You don't want something else to ruin your vision, Julian. What if people find out you knew about what the fog really was? I can imagine what damage it may do if people also found out about how you have been ripping off Basil Elders…'

'I didn't rip him off. What is that supposed to mean?'

'All I am saying is help me get to the bottom of this. Help me find out who is working with Reginald Bosham. Help me save John Crane.'

'Save him? He's just ill with fever.'

Enrico smiled. He had picked the right track. Enrico knew the people who had been affected by the fog were the only witnesses he could rely on. John Crane was held hostage without anybody knowing. In hearing what was happening to him, Julian would not be able to dismiss his claims about criminals causing harm to Wimbledonians. The Italian baker knew perfectly well this piece of information would win Julian's heart.

'John Crane has more than just a fever. When I followed Reginald Bosham and his unknown accomplice, I saw him. He is imprisoned in this basement directly under your compound. And he is not alone. He is with another of your engineers. Richard or something. They were both in the same state as that boy Ken found in the woods. I am telling you, Julian, it is not a fever. It is something worse, and it is a side-effect coming from the New Wimbledon Windmill. Your New Wimbledon Windmill.'

'Stop saying that!' moaned Julian, irritated.

There was a pause. Julian's face was stern and looking behind Enrico at the window where the early evening had slowly descended over Wimbledon.

'You mentioned Reginald Bosham has this contact inside. Did you get a look at him?'

'No, I am afraid not. He wore a black hood and I could not see his face. All I heard was they will put their plan into action tonight at eight p.m.'

Julian stared back at Enrico. His jaw had hardened as his worries and doubts turned into a firm resolve. His eyes narrowed; his whole body tensed. His friendly smile was no longer there. Enrico thought Julian was about to lash back at him with a raging rant against those who wished to bring him and his business down. Instead, he took a deep breath; he then relaxed his shoulder and flexed his neck with a gentle crack of his collar bone, before breathing out all the tension.

'Julian,' added Enrico to reassure his friend once more. 'I came here because we know you'd care to hear this.'

'I do, and I can only thank you.' spoke Julian.

His tone had become a little colder. He had detached from the emotions swirling inside his head and focused on the business at hand. Whether what Enrico had said was true or not, Julian knew he could not risk putting his planned launch day in jeopardy, which was only a few days away.

'What does Dr Watkins say about all this?'

'He was meant to join me to warn you. He agrees with me. We believe Reginald is trying to get hold of all the relics of the Wynnman. It may explain why Reginald tried to get into the Old Rectory...'

'I'm going to stop you there, Enrico. Let's put this fancy idea about the relics aside. You said two members of my staff are in danger and this boy

Ken is suffering because of what Reginald Bosham is up to. Therefore, they will be my priority!'

'Sure, Julian!' nodded Enrico eager to get going.

'I will call Mr Sanders straight away and warn the head of security at the compound.' explained Julian as if giving instructions to a large audience. 'I don't like this one single bit and I prefer to look into it before Wimbledon Police is involved.'

Enrico realised Viviane may have already involved Baynard and his men. He thought it fair to warn Julian as this could get more complicated than they thought.

'One thing about the police. Viviane went to see…'

Enrico's sentence was cut off by a phone ringing loud somewhere in the room. Julian excused himself, forgetting Enrico, and went to pick his phone on the desk. As he answered, he turned his computer screen on and quickly browsed it. Enrico only heard a faint noise on the other end of the line, but whoever the caller was, they seemed to be giving Julian instructions and the businessman had his undivided attention, keen to follow those instructions. Enrico saw he was opening the site of the Wimbledon Gazette and Julian's cool-headed expression faded back to a stern, worried look. He scowled at the screen and then looked at Enrico. His eyes scared him. Enrico had not seen them like that before. They bore doubt, suspicion, directed straight at him. Enrico shrank on the couch with the uncomfortable feeling he was not welcome.

'Ok. How long ago?' said Julian on the phone. 'Deal with it as soon as possible! I will get to Warren Farms to deal with the hunting party. What is their claim?'

Enrico did not hear the reply. Julian's actions were sufficient to tell him something was not right. Julian closed his eyes and put his thumb and index between his eyes. He tried hard to stay in control; he knew life was testing him. Things were slipping away out of his hands at every turn no matter how carefully he planned. Elders. Bosham. And now the news he had just heard was the last straw. He felt a twinge of pain in his gloved hand.

'I am on my way!'

He ended the call and walked straight back to Enrico. The Italian baker was quick to notice the friendly face he knew was no longer there in the room. The disapproving tone was unmistakeable.

'What game are you playing, Enrico?' asked Julian bluntly.

'Sorry…' faltered Enrico.

'I shared my little sin with you and Viviane in complete confidence. As friends. And what do you do?'

'*Non capisco*! What…?' stammered Enrico too, not following.

'The Wimbledon Gazette just published online an article written by Nathan Glenn. In it, he talks about how I ripped off Basil Elders of his ideas and theories to advance my agenda. There is even a nice picture of you at a coffee shop talking to Basil Elders. I wonder who told them about it. Nobody knew except you and Viviane. Who have you told, Enrico?'

Enrico swallowed hard under the weight of the accusation. He knew he had not spoken to Nathan or any journalist. The picture in the blog had probably been taken the other day when he chatted with Basil at the coffee shop about something else. Yet, he could not shed the guilt off completely about giving away Julian's secret. He remembered telling Dr Watkins, and Quentin, and Fran.

'I… I…' continued Enrico, lost for words.

'And our head of security said Wimbledon Police just issued a search warrant for Warren Farms. Inspector Baynard is there right now! Did you know about this too?'

Julian spoke as if he had been double-crossed. He was standing in front of him, arms crossed, clearly upset and requesting an explanation.

'I may have told Dr Watkins…' Enrico tried to explain.

It was the beginning of the impact this news would have. Yet, Enrico had no idea how Nathan Glenn had found out. The journalist would not be so rash to take just Basil Elders's word for it and publish it.

'I understand your concerns about Wimbledon and my business. The last thing I expected was to have to defend myself from my friends or people I trust. Not sure what your game is, Enrico: if Mr Elders is paying you to draw me into a trap, or if you need fame for your bakery. You came here to warn me about danger and public opinion, and you had already called the police. Did you call the police?'

'I didn't...'

'Liar! Apparently, Baynard is on his way with your friend Viviane Leighwood in his car. Guess who else is with them? Quentin Plainstraw. Someone who doesn't really have Alberyx Enterprises at heart. And John Crane's girlfriend, Fran Ludley. Now, what is she going to do? Sue the company because her boyfriend fell ill?'

Julian's voice was hysterical, seeing enemies everywhere, including Enrico in front of him. The Italian baker could only guess Viviane's meeting with Baynard had proved more successful than expected, although badly timed. Enrico wondered how she had managed to convince the inspector and hoped he could do the same with Julian.

'We are all on the same side, Julian.' said Enrico. We have found John Crane's girlfriend and she told us what the hallucinations did to her...'

'But you didn't think to bring her here first. What did she do? Go to the police? Just another bait for Elders and his vulture news. I don't know what you were thinking, but coming to seek my help, for the sake of my company, and then at the same time smearing my name with cheap journalism, and letting the police walk over the compound before I can give a meticulous look into the problem, doesn't give me much warning.'

'Julian, I think this is getting out of hand...'

'You'd better come with me right now to Warren Farms, or I will sue you and everyone else for libel. I want to get to the bottom of this!'

Enrico gulped. Julian seemed blinded by anger now. His aggressive look and tone turned every word of his into a direct threat to Enrico. The Italian baker knew he had not done anything wrong. He just hoped he had got his facts right. In the end, he had convinced Julian to search Warren Farms and see things for himself. Perhaps not in the most pleasant of ways. Surely, the basement was not an invention, Enrico thought, and there would be proof John Crane had been there. He was not a liar, and the last thing he wanted was to ruin the friendship they had with Julian Alberon.

Enrico glanced at his watch. Less than three hours to go. A nagging feeling at the back of his mind worried him about invisible forces pushing their fate towards something inevitable. Whatever that may be.

Basil "Wilberforce" Elders counted roughly the number of men and women spread across the north-western corner of Rushmere Green, opposite the Fox and Grapes pub. There were almost eighty people, perhaps a hundred. They were definitely more than the last protest march. Meeting in such an open space was the perfect choice. These numbers on the narrow Wimbledon High Street would have raised concerns from the onset, and Basil thought it would have taken away that element of surprise he loved so much.

He glanced at his watch. There was some time left before they started their vengeful march on Warren Farms. He went through the instructions he had given to the close followers once more. Their march had to be slow and peaceful; they would raise their voices and bang the gates the moment they reached the entrance to Alberyx Enterprises compound. They had strong voices to be heard and banners to be held high in the sky.

The people strolling on Rushmere Green looked curious and confused. Those who had recognised Basil's group wondered what he was up to. Basil did not mind. Everything was under control after the Council had approved the gathering on Rushmere Green. His plans to march to Warren Farms had not been disclosed, and his only worry was if the police or Baynard decided to show up before they were close enough to the gates.

He glanced at his watch once more. It was nearly time. He decided to do the rounds, check-in with the group and keep his followers energised. Some were chatting over a hot thermos full of coffee, keeping warm against the cold wind blowing across Rushmere Green. Others were putting their finishing touches to a poster or a banner. Harsh words in black and red were clearly visible from afar. Basil felt proud of the opportunity that had landed on his lap. He knew it was a chance to claim back what was rightfully his, and at the same time shame Alberyx Enterprises. Cover-up of their reckless technological experiment. Disregard for the beauty of Wimbledon Common. Corporate abuse of Wimbledon will stop here and now, and Basil knew he would have his revenge. All thanks to the evidence he had received from his benefactor, the burly man he had never met before in his life.

Reginald had never given his real name. Basil did not judge him and never asked him who he was. All Basil cared for was to use him to extract the information and the secrets he craved for to get the compensation he claimed. Basil knew what Alberyx Enterprises had done to the school and its students. The cause was good enough for him. The truth had to come out and he was happy to get it finally done with this protest march. There would be no violence; just the power of words.

He glanced at his watch one last time and then looked to his right. Nathan Glenn stood rigid by his side. One of his men was next to him, close enough to let Nathan feel the gun in the pocket.

'Are you ready, Mr Glenn? It is the final showdown!'

Nathan felt sick. He just wanted to spit at Basil in the face.

'You can't keep me hostage!'

'Of course, I can.' Basil laughed heartedly. 'And believe me, it is better for you. You are as rotten as I am with your cheap journalism. Everyone can see that!'

Nathan grunted. He recalled what Basil had shown him on his phone. Both his blog and his opinion column on the Wimbledon Gazette were now the most viewed sites in Wimbledon. Everyone had rushed to read the slandering online article Basil Elders had forced him to post on the Wimbledon Gazette website. He did not have a choice. He was in Basil's grip until the day was over and who knows after that. He had wanted to get closer to Basil 'Wilberforce' Elders and now he had got too close to the point he was an accomplice. His career could go to ruin.

'I will make sure Wimbledonians hear the truth!' he retorted.

'I doubt it.' replied Basil not at all affected by Nathan's words. 'People will want to hear what they want to hear. They will be judge of our actions. Not the police or the courts.'

'And you are a teacher, for God's sake!'

Basil pulled a serious face. He was not amused by Nathan's last comment. He turned to the journalist.

'This conversation is over. Just remember, you try to run away from us and something bad happens to you. Time to march!'

He nodded to a group near him, announcing it was time to get started. A maxim by Schopenhauer appropriate for the occasion suddenly came to mind, but then his mind went blank. He glanced up. The clouds were returning over Wimbledon. He heard one of his followers mention there was a chance of heavy rain.

Ramona quickly hung up and tapped the phone to her chin, thinking of what to do next. Reginald's voice had confirmed the plan was now in motion. Her work at the Repeater could start very soon, and so could her own personal plan. She thought it over and checked she had accounted for everything. The smallest mistake would expose any attempt by her to cover her tracks.

A quick knock came at her office door. It was the receptionist. She called her in, and the young woman put her head through the door. Something on her face told Ramona she had something pressing to say that could not wait.

'What's the matter?' asked Ramona with a bored look. 'If it's gossip, I don't have the time today…'

'I was trying to get hold of Lord Cotton…'

'Still travelling, I told you. How can I help?'

'You'd better look outside!'

Ramona hesitated at first. She stared at the receptionist. She realised it was no joke or gossip. Ramona walked out of the office to follow her to the entrance. Outside, the trailing end of a marching protest was walking on Camp Road.

'Basil "Wilberforce" Elders's protesters again?'

'Yes, I think so.'

'Are they coming here to bother us again?'

'That's what we thought and were worried we would have to block the entrance. It seems they are directed somewhere else. I thought you might want to know, in case you wanted to reassure club members.'

'It's alright! I will do that. Do you know where they are headed?'

'Not sure. The Warren Farms compound maybe. Some of the protesters had "Alberyx Enterprises" written all over them.'

Ramona took a good look at the crowd again. She wondered if the march outside was a pure coincidence, knowing the plan was about to be set into motion. Something told her it was not, but it somehow fit into the scheme Reginald and his unknown employer had been planning all along. She hoped they were not heading to the Repeater. She was worried Reginald may have an ace up his sleeve against her. She did not want chaos letting loose when she needed to act in the utmost secrecy.

'I need to go and check the Repeater. Please keep an eye on things to be sure they are not planning to invade our golf course.'

Ramona left the receptionist and quickly made her way to the Repeater with the excuse of a security check. The clouds outside were turning a dark grey. Ramona shivered in her pink tracksuit following the path she knew from memory. She crossed the open field of the golf grounds in the direction of hole number seven. The Repeater was empty, as Reginald had predicted. All working staff had finished earlier and been called back to Warren Farms. Ramona glanced at her watch. She had to schedule the superpositioning now, let the machine run and then the rest would be out of her hands. Whether Reginald and his mystery employer had succeeded or not, she would remain untouched.

Ramona entered the narrow confinement of the Repeater. Once inside, she put on a pair of working gloves to leave no fingerprints. She climbed up the short ladder to the raised platform where she was at eye-level with the machine where the USB flash drive had to be inserted. She slipped it out of her pocket with great care and fit it into the slot where the previous one had been. The machine came alive in seconds and the load was ready. Ramona looked up and could see the radar turning to send the electromagnetic signal in the correct direction. She watched the monitor searching the windmill's auto-capture system. A few seconds passed and then the windmill's location blinked on a topographical map on the screen. The monitor flashed a message confirming a successful link. Wave intensity was now steady and the only thing left to do was instruct the Oscillator remotely to open the portal at Reginald's mapped location. Such technology was a piece of cake for her, and she revelled in it as she meticulously carried each step out. Reginald Bosham could not do or understand half of this with that little brain of his. Ramona had to show his employer how clever and resourceful she was.

Ramona gave a boastful smile to a non-existent audience before inputting the last commands. All was set. She waited for a second and listened. The beeping sound was all she could hear at first. Then another sound came to her ears. Drops of rain had started to fall outside. She could hear them hitting hard on the tarpaulin and the flat roof of the pop-up office nearby. The rain would help. It was time for phase two of her plan, before anyone thought of coming over here to nose around the Repeater. She grabbed her phone and ensured the voice-changing application was activated. She dialled the number and the phone started ringing.

'Wimbledon Police Station?' answered the police constable on the other end of the line.

'Hello! I want to report a kidnapping.'

'Who's speaking?'

'Lord Cotton. The basement under the car park at Royal Wimbledon Golf Club.'

Ramona hung up. Quick enough not to be traced and yet assertive enough not to be dismissed as a prank. All she had to do now was wait. She climbed down and found a good spot at the base of the Repeater. She removed her gloves and picked some dirt from the wet muddy ground to smear her face. She pulled her hair in all directions, pretending to have been mistreated, and slapped her face a few times until her cheeks felt hot. It was then time to get the handcuffs she had with her and tie herself to one of the solid metal poles that held the whole structure of the Repeater. She needed to chain herself down indefinitely until someone came. Ramona lay down on the ground and prepared herself to be the victim. She smashed her phone beyond repair and suddenly she was left to her own devices, helpless like a damsel in distress. The waiting game had started, with only the rain keeping her company while the beeping machine started the countdown to an unknown doom.

Baynard's car skidded on the road as he hit the brakes a few metres before the high gates of the Warren Farms compound. The security guard at the gate jumped and dashed out of his cabin with a hand on his gun. He then recognised the car and the man from Wimbledon Police with his silver goatee and his inquisitive stare. Yet, he was not alone this time. A tall man and two women got out of the car and shortly after another police car arrived with four policemen inside. The security guard had no idea what was happening and thought it best to speak through his radio.

'Boss!' he warned. 'You may want to come to the main gate. We have some important visitors!'

Baynard waited patiently for the head of security to come and meet them. He leaned on the car bonnet, clutching the warrant papers he had managed to get signed earlier that afternoon, and did not take his stare off the gates. He wanted to make sure Alberyx Enterprises staff knew he meant serious business this time. They knew he was coming. Again. To Baynard, it was no surprise the head of security decided not to come alone. The figure of Mr Sanders, in his light brown suit and yellow tie, followed close behind. Inspector Baynard turned around and gave a nod to his men. They knew his search warrant was water-tight and yet his inquisitive stare reminded everyone to be careful. There was a chance Mr Sanders would try to wriggle out of it with a legal technicality. He knew Alberyx Enterprises would want to triple check before letting police in on their property.

'Inspector!' spoke the company lawyer again. 'Nice to see you again. I hope still on good terms.'

Mr Sanders hinted at the papers in Baynard's hand.

'Security has just briefed me.' he added. 'We would have appreciated it if the police had given us more time, inspector. Your arrival caught us a little unprepared!'

'Please understand, Mr Sanders, we wish to comply with all the right procedures.' replied Baynard with the utmost effort in diplomacy. 'It is our intention to carry out the search in a civilised manner and we would be grateful if you and your head of security provided the assistance required. This warrant demands access to all facilities in the compound. We believe a hostile individual may be hiding in your compound and we have reason to believe Mr John Crane may be held hostage.'

'John Crane?' spluttered Mr Sanders incredulous. 'But you saw him the other day safe and sound, inspector. What is the meaning of this?'

Baynard knew there was no need to spell it out. He walked towards the corporate lawyer and opened the warrant to the key page. A picture of John Crane was shown.

'Who is that?'

'That is John Crane!'

'Excuse me?'

'You have the same expression I had when I found out the man in your Infirmary is not John Crane.'

'There must be an error. We have so many employees here on the compound…'

'Mr Sanders, we could stay here all day splitting hairs. This is now a police matter, and we believe your facilities, and perhaps even your research work too, may be under threat. There is possible evidence of foul play by someone on the inside.'

'I read the summary.' cut short Mr Sanders, annoyed and still stupefied. 'Mr Alberon is also on his way here. He left home the moment he heard the news.'

'We can't wait for him, Mr Sanders. I expect you to open the gates now and instruct all staff not to leave the compound.'

'Right! Given Alberyx Enterprises has the most advanced security in London, if not the whole of the UK, where would you like to start, inspector? Searching the many square feet of the compound or perhaps interviewing the hundreds of staff in a couple of hours?'

Baynard ignored Mr Sanders's smirk of irony. He did not want to waste any more time.

'We will start from the infirmary, and I demand to speak with the two men you have there under the names of John Crane and Richard Sullivan. Please make haste!'

Mr Sanders sneered at the sarcastic comment. He nodded at the guards and the gates were quickly opened to let the police cars in. Viviane, Fran and Quentin looked in awe at how vast the compound was from the inside. Mr Sanders and the head of security looked at them suspiciously.

'What about them, inspector?' asked the head of security. 'Aren't they civilians?'

'They are with me.' confirmed Baynard without hesitation. 'They are essential to the investigation. You may recognise one of them as Fran Ludley, John Crane's girlfriend. She believes he's missing, and I am sure she would like to see him again. She will be able to confirm whether I am talking to the right John Crane.'

Viviane felt Baynard's pungent remarks pierce the cold air between him and Mr Sanders. The lawyer was in a clear state of confusion and the whole security team appeared to be in disarray at the arrival of the police. Police entering Warren Farms was something they had never witnessed. Viviane wondered if Alberyx Enterprises security was to be trusted. They may be good at hiding their own agenda or perhaps they knew nothing of what may be happening underground around here. She knew though Baynard would see that. For once, his inquisitive stare was on her and Enrico's side. She checked her phone. Enrico and Dr Watkins had not yet called even though she had left a message asking them to join them.

'Quentin, did you hear from Dr Watkins?' she asked turning to the tall man next to her.

'Nothing. Phone goes to voicemail.'

Viviane bit her lip. Something was not right, and even the presence of Baynard and Wimbledon Police on their side was not sufficient enough to feel reassured. The inspector had had a change of heart the moment the doctor at Parkside confirmed Ken had fallen asleep naturally after an hour or so. That was good news for everyone, since Ken had finally changed his fixed posture of days on end and snapped out from his catatonic state. He was no longer paralysed, and the doctors started reading normal levels of brain activity, including normalised breathing and a strong heartbeat. His body pulsed with normality once again and it filled Ken's mother with joy. Quentin's remedy had indeed worked as a miraculous cure and left the doctors scratching their heads. All they had to do now was monitor his status until he woke up. Baynard did not have that kind of time. He realised though he may be onto something. Alberyx Enterprises and their machines were having a strange effect on people and the case of mistaken identity he had at first ignored convinced him there was something suspicious happening at Warren Farms. Fran was Baynard's only hope to recognise the chief engineer who had now become the number one priority for the whole case. Viviane knew that, if the man at the Infirmary was not John Crane, then Enrico had not invented his story. She glanced at Fran, her expression anxious and her mind filled with wild expectations. She was as eager as Baynard to get moving and pressed against the inspector and his men the moment Mr Sanders led the charge.

At the Infirmary, the head nurse was waiting at reception after she had received the news the police were on the compound. She adjusted her uniform ready to welcome the arriving party and to fully cooperate with the police.

'We're here to see John Crane and Richard Sullivan.' Mr Sanders requested promptly.

'Yes, sir.' replied the head nurse without hesitation.

'I will bring two of my men in, together with the three civilians' added Baynard.

Mr Sanders and the head nurse did not object. The inspector then spoke into his radio to update the rest of the team outside and instruct them that nobody was allowed to leave the compound. The head nurse led the group to the same room Baynard had been in last time. Each one of them was eager to see who stood behind the entrance, wondering who they would meet. Each one of them had heard of John Crane but never met him, except Fran. The nurse pushed the doors open and a voice shouted in the room to the top of his voice.

'Fran!'

It came from the back of the room and for a fleeting moment it filled Fran's ears with sweet joy. The recognition was instant. She pushed through the group and rushed to the centre of the room to take a better look at her man waiting for her with open arms. John Crane stood by one of the tables in his lounge trousers, and a broad smile across his face. His light brown hair was a little unkempt. His face and eyes showed he had had little sleep. Yet, Fran could see nothing different in him. He looked normal and unharmed, as she last remembered. Both John and Fran ran towards each other and leapt into each other's arms. It was a long embrace. Fran sank her face deep into his chest, taking in his scent, and hiding her tears of joy. He was her John. She was enjoying the moment before questions started flooding in.

Viviane smiled. She was moved by the scene and even envied John and Fran a little. Glancing at Baynard to her side, she could see his inquisitive stare scrutinising the couple. He scratched his head, completely at odds with the situation. The man before him was John Crane as shown on the picture and he knew he had nothing to do with the man introduced to him as John Crane. He then noticed a second man behind John Crane. Tall and thin, he stood shy at the back, perplexed at the group who had just stormed in. Baynard quickly gestured one of his men to guard the entrance door.

'Nobody leaves the room at this stage.' stated the inspector making a step forward. 'John Crane and Richard Sullivan, I presume.'

'Yes, I am John Crane.' confirmed the chief engineer before the nurse grabbed the medical chart to confirm. 'Who is asking? What's going on?'

Baynard glanced at Mr Sanders. He had also walked forward, eyeing John Crane as if he were a strange human specimen. He thought the corporate lawyer was bluffing but he could see in his eyes that mystified look of incredulity. He too was surprised to see John Crane was not the same man they had met a few days ago.

'Mr Crane!' the lawyer announced before anyone else. 'My name is Mr Sanders. I represent Alberyx Enterprises here legally. Security here at Warren Farms may have been compromised. Inspector Baynard from Wimbledon Police has some questions for you, and also your colleague. Richard Sullivan, I presume?'

'Yes, that's me.' confirmed the shy engineer. 'Can someone explain what this means?'

Richard had walked up to John's side. Viviane noticed no symptoms from the fog in his eyes or John's. They were alive and well, far from Enrico's description.

'Mr Sanders, Inspector Baynard, I am not sure what is happening.' said John Crane. 'We've just been in bed for days with a bad flu, and only woke up this morning. How long were we out?'

'Three days at least.' added Fran trembling in John's arms.

'We are here to clarify a few things.' continued Mr Sanders, unsure what to make of the obvious facts before him. 'As Alberyx Enterprises employees, you have the obligation to answer any questions the police may have. I will be present to assist as your legal representation, if needed. Please proceed, inspector.'

Baynard thanked the lawyer and decided to act fast. He had never liked Mr Sanders and his attitude. The man could pull out a legal technicality any moment. The inspector's mind in the meantime was picking the right questions while eyeing both engineers. They both looked unscathed, in good health. He knew though something was not right. The nurses had brought him a stranger a few days ago. Someone here at Alberyx Enterprises was playing dangerous games.

'You said you both have been unwell, correct?' opened Baynard with his questioning.

'Unwell is an understatement.' replied John, keeping Fran to his side. 'Some sort of bad fever, apparently. Probably down to work exhaustion and cold weather while working on the machinery at the windmill.'

'Apparently, you say? How come?'

'Well, it was so bad we don't remember being ill. We woke up early this morning in bed and our medical chart said we had feverish symptoms, with a very high temperature. We feel better now the nurses have been kind enough to get us back on our feet and inform us we are ready to be released today from the Infirmary. This is before they told us we had visitors. Happy to see Fran for sure, especially after being knocked out for days.'

Baynard frowned. He was not buying it. He quickly eyed the nurse who was nodding proudly at the two patients. She did not seem bothered about the inconsistencies he was spotting one after the other.

'What is the last thing you two remember?'

Both John and Richard hesitated. They gazed around the room aimlessly, searching their memories. Fran looked up at John and could see his smile had gone. He now looked worried, and so did Richard. They both realised they could not remember.

'I just can't tell. I was riding back to the compound after the last checks at the windmill…' muttered John talking out loud to share his thoughts with the crowd.

'Don't you remember cycling with me on Sunday evening, John?' prompted Fran. 'Don't you remember the fog? The train?'

'Miss Dudley, let me ask the questions.' reproached Baynard.

'She's right.' added Richard. 'It must have been Sunday because I was covering for John and doing the last checks at the Repeater on Monday evening. That's the last thing I remember.'

John glanced at Richard and then Fran. His frown grew deeper across his forehead, casting shadows of self-doubt.

'Neither of you two remembers being taken to Infirmary. Perhaps the head nurse can help us clarify that and trace your steps on the day you were taken in.' said Baynard turning to the head nurse nearby. 'First things first, have you met these men before?'

The nurse looked at him and then Mr Sanders for confirmation.

'We have a warrant in effect. Please answer the question.' insisted Baynard.

'It is fine to share the infirmary records with the inspector.' confirmed the lawyer to defuse the tension.

'No, I haven't.' replied the head nurse. But I do recognise now Mr Crane as our chief engineer from the press releases.'

'Did you bring in these two patients?'

'No. A member of staff on duty did.'

'Are they available for questioning?'

'I am not sure, but we have a register stating who brought them in and when.'

'We are getting somewhere. Can you tell me who submitted the two gentlemen to the Infirmary?'

The head nurse nodded and flicked fast through the medical charts. She felt the pressure rising in the room not knowing what the police was expecting to find. Baynard and Mr Sanders though rubbed their sweaty palms, unsure what they would find out. The head nurse flicked back and forth, and then at some point her gestures became more rushed and frantic. She panicked. As she kept flicking through the pages, she realised something was not right and worst of all her expression could not hide it.

'The patients' submission papers! They are missing!' she exclaimed. 'They have been ripped out!'

The heard nurse held the medical charts in front of Baynard and Mr Sanders. Baynard tried to read the genuine shame on her face.

'Let me see that!' interjected the lawyer, incredulous. 'This is impossible!'

He snatched the medical charts to check himself. Baynard kept calm, keeping his eyes on Mr Sanders.

'Since you are doing the checking yourself,' said the inspector. 'perhaps you may try to find out who are the two gentlemen I met a few days ago.'

John and Richard stared at Baynard's icy stare, first pointed at them, and then glancing at Mr Sanders to his right.

'What does that mean, inspector?' asked John Crane.

'I was here with Mr Sanders yesterday and I was introduced to a man referred to as John Crane.'

'I am John Crane, inspector. And I can swear I don't remember…'

'I am sure there is an explanation!' pleaded Mr Sanders scrambling for information in the medical chart.

His forehead gleaned with sweat. Baynard did not flinch. The truth was about to come out.

'Well, it looks like we did meet Mr Crane and Mr Sullivan.' Mr Sanders concluded, satisfied.

The lawyer showed the page to Baynard as proof. The inspector did recognise the surnames. One thing though did not add up and he had just seen it through.

'So, we did meet Mr Crane and Mr Sullivan!' chuckled Baynard.

Mr Sanders and the rest of the group looked at each other. They thought the inspector had lost his mind now that he contradicted himself.

'Inspector, I don't recall meeting you.' restated John Crane.

'I did meet the inspector, though.' added Richard Sullivan. 'On Monday morning. When he came to check the Repeater with the Council.'

'Precisely!' gloated Baynard, causing more confused looks to show.

'Inspector, this is no time for games!' exclaimed Mr Sanders.

'It is indeed a game. A game someone played on me and I only have myself to blame for not checking the answers to my questions. I did meet a Mr Crane yesterday. Except his name initial is different. He is not a John. Would you mind checking what does the Mr Crane from yesterday do?'

Mr Sanders frowned, lost about what Baynard was getting at.

'He works at the windmill.' confirmed the head nurse reading the medical chart.

'True. But that Mr Crane is not the chief engineer, is he?'

'No.'

'Exactly. The Mr Crane you have on record is an engineer but not the one I was looking for. I should have known by the way Mr Crane answered my questions about his role and about Fran Ludley.'

'Is he an impostor, inspector?' asked John Crane.

Baynard thought a second before answering.

'I think there is another Crane in this compound unaware that someone used the similarity to fool me.'

'It is a pure administration mistake, inspector.' explained Mr Sanders checking again.

'Is it?' teased Baynard, knowing very well he had to treat everyone as a suspect. 'Just like the admission papers being ripped out?'

'I beg your pardon!'

'I think we need to be sure this case of mistaken identities is more than just a coincidence. John Crane just confirmed they were informed he and Richard Sullivan will be released today. Do we know who signed their release?'

Everyone waited anxiously to see where Baynard was going. Mr Sanders ran his finger on the last page of the medical charts. He was rushing to gather the facts and minimise the collateral damage this bureaucratic blunder would cause. Viviane saw the look of panic on the lawyer's face. Then, a moment of lucidity flashed across his face. Something finally caught his eye on the medical chart. He turned to Baynard, mouth open, and then the doors to the visiting room slammed open. Julian Alberon barged in, followed by Enrico. He immediately took centre stage between Baynard and Mr Sanders. Baynard first looked at the Italian baker with suspicion. He then looked at Sir Alberon, unsure how to take their sudden arrival.

'Good afternoon, inspector. I came as soon as I heard!' explained Julian.

Julian caught his breath quickly. He then adjusted his hair and straightened his jacket after a wild rush to get to the infirmary.

'Happy to cooperate in any way we can, inspector.' added Julian, once he had regained composure. 'We believe a mole or someone on the inside is working behind the scenes here against Alberyx Enterprises.'

Baynard was taken aback by Julian's confident admission, more open that Mr Sanders had been. He glared at Enrico and Viviane, wondering if they knew something they had not told him and tipped off Julian Alberon before the police.

'Sir Alberon.' Baynard replied. 'Your statement is quite timely. Do you have proof though that could help us?'

'Yes. Enrico LoTrova here shared some evidence with me that may help expose the criminals.'

Baynard glared once again at the Italian baker and then at Viviane. The two together could be good or bad news for him and the case. He narrowed his eyes at Enrico. The Italian baker had finally popped up in the middle of his case.

'Mr Latreva!' greeted the inspector.

'LoTrova!' replied Enrico, ignoring the inspector's sarcasm.

Baynard did not flinch and turned his attention to Sir Alberon, who had exchanged words with the two engineers to check they were in good health.

'And what is this evidence?' asked Baynard.

'I believe these two men were captured by a criminal known to you and me: Reginald Bosham!'

The inspector was taken by surprise. He clearly remembered the name.

'Impossible!' exclaimed Baynard. 'Are you sure?'

'Enrico here has seen him. He is actually roaming free in Wimbledon and he's been meddling with my company's affairs again.'

'Mr Lirtova? Is this true? You saw Reginald Bosham?'

'LoTrova! And yes, it is true.' replied Enrico. 'I saw him hacking the machines at the windmill last night and then entering the facilities here.'

'And when were you going to report that, Mr Larova?'

'LoTrova!' repeated louder Enrico, always keen to make a point. 'That is why we came here!'

Baynard kept his inquisitive stare long enough on Enrico to let him know he did not like being blindsided by undisclosed information. He realised the Italian baker had preferred to warn Sir Alberon first and feared his warrant would be undermined.

'Sir Alberon!' Baynard resumed. 'Assuming your evidence holds true, your lawyer here, Mr Sanders, was about to check who may have tampered with the medical records. We have an issue related to missing persons and perhaps falsified information. Before you stormed in, I had asked to confirm who approved the release of your engineers today.'

'Then let's hear it!' supported Julian, motioning Mr Sanders and the head nurse not to stall any further. 'I would not be surprised to see Reginald Bosham's involvement in this.'

The lawyer stared back. His gaze then floated around the room rather than reading the chart. He met everyone's gaze, looking back anxiously at him to hear what he had to say. What he had read though left him more confused than before. He hesitated, unsure whether the answer he had for Sir Alberon and Inspector Baynard was good enough.

'Mr Sanders?' urged Julian Alberon. 'What's the matter? Can't you read? Who signed the release form?'

Mr Sanders swallowed hard and cleared his throat more than once. Viviane exchanged a quick glance with Enrico. Something did not add up.

'It is you, Sir Alberon. It is your signature!'

The lawyer shared the medical chart with him and tapped his finger on the bottom right corner. The signature, although scribbled and only fairly intelligible, was clear enough for him and Julian Alberon to recognise it. Julian felt someone had pulled the carpet from under his feet. He staggered as he felt everyone's eye on him. He could not believe what Mr Sanders was showing.

'Impossible!' exclaimed Julian Alberon, quick to fill the awkward silence. 'That is not mine!'

He grabbed the chart and looked at the signature more closely from all angles. He rubbed his forehand unable to comprehend what happened, and to Enrico, Viviane and even Quentin, Julian suddenly looked distraught. Only Baynard kept an impassive look, waiting for the drama to play out.

'Your lawyer recognised your signature, Sir Alberon.' commented Baynard.

'This is not my signature, inspector. I mean, it looks like mine, but I did not sign these papers. I would have remembered!'

Julian's words came out strong and determined, fighting back the subtle quaver in his voice. He flicked through the rest of the medical chart, double-checking it was the right one. He could not believe what was happening, and even the nurse and Mr Sanders stood by incredulous.

'My signature is also here… And here…' added Julian.

His voice cracked. He could not deny that what he had in front of him was his own signature. His memory raced back. He had no recollection of signing these release papers in the last twenty-four hours. He tried to remember. He then looked up, and met John Crane's gaze, then Baynard's. At some point, he remembered what forced him to come all the way here. Past Baynard's face, he saw Enrico and Viviane, and his expression of stupor quickly turned to anger.

'You!' he cried out with his finger pointed at the baker. 'You did this!'

Enrico blinked. At first, he thought he had not heard correctly, but when he saw Julian Alberon making way towards him, he was shocked by his quick change in mood.

'You set me up, didn't you?' blurted out Julian. 'You brought me here with the story of an insider just to frame me…'

Enrico babbled. He did not know what to say to defend himself or even explain Julian's absurd reaction.

'It is not true, Julian…' he stammered.

'You said you broke into my property. You said you exposed my dealings with Basil Elders. You are working for him, aren't you? You made friends with that Basil "Wilberforce" Elders who wishes to bring down everything I ever built...'

'Julian, please!' insisted Enrico. 'You're not making any sense!'

'Yes. That is what you and that bastard of Elders wanted. Make me look like a fool, like a crazy man, who can't even remember signing a paper and holding these two men hostages. I thought we trusted each other. Now, how can I do that?'

'This is not how it looks...'

'And how about Reginald Bosham? Do you work with him too?'

'No!'

Julian Alberon and Enrico stepped towards each other, clenching their fists. Baynard stood in their path, eyeing both of them.

'These are serious allegations. I don't want anyone to leave this room or the Alberyx Enterprises facilities. Is that clear?'

Baynard nodded to the head of security, to make sure they had an understanding. Mr Sanders nodded in approval.

'This applies to you, Sir Alberon, and you Mr Lirtova.' added Baynard.

'LoTrova!' replied Enrico, seriously upset. '*Non ci posso credere*! You can't be serious!'

Enrico glanced at Viviane who looked mortified. She did not know what to say. Everything had gone smoothly until that point.

'Inspector!' Viviane stepped to defuse the tension. 'You remember what Fran and I told you. How could Enrico have done this?'

'Hold it right there, Miss Leighwood!' rebuffed Baynard. 'I am going to be very careful with the information you have shared with me in the last thirty minutes. Nobody move or I swear...'

The inspector quicky radioed the police station requesting back-up at Warren Farms and then asked the head of security to work with his men to ensure all access in or out were closed off. He then asked the two policemen with him to take Julian and Enrico to one side. Baynard looked around, wondering if there were more suspects to consider, if they were here with him in the room, and if the ghost of Reginald Bosham was really back to haunt him and Wimbledon as Julian had said. He pursed his lips and thought fast about what to do. Before he could even start formulating the next question, the neon lights of the room flickered. There was a buzz, then simultaneous sparks and the lights went off. Pitch dark came all of a sudden, and a burst from a nearby fuse box echoed in the room. Cries and murmurs of panic filled the room.

'Lock the door! Nobody gets out!' Baynard shouted to the top of his voice.

He was worried the lights would come back on and one of his suspects would be gone. He was in the mid of his sentence when the back-up emergency lights turned on. The less intense glow from one side of the room cast an eerie green light across the room and gave enough light to show everyone's faces. A security guard from Alberyx Enterprises stormed in the room, alarmed.

'The main generator went down!' he cried, exchanging a confused glance with his head of security.

'What?' shouted Julian Alberon. 'How could that be?'

Enrico spotted Julian's hardened features in the weak glow. He appeared different, detached. Enrico was hurt by Julian's words. He tried to make sense of why Julian would accuse him. He recalled the article published by Nathan Glenn and thought someone may be framing him.

'We believe the generator is not the issue.' continued the security guard. 'The power grid feeding the compound was cut off…deliberately! Not sure how to say it, but we are under attack!'

The security guard met the confused faces of Julian Alberon, his head of security and everyone standing still in the semi-darkened room. He knew his words did not make sense because they had not seen what he had seen.

'The entrance to the compound!' he added in panic. 'The entrance is under siege by protestors. They are led by Basil "Wilberforce" Elders himself!'

Julian Alberon was furious upon hearing the news. He could not hide it. He glared at Enrico.

'See, this is your doing! If you hadn't meddled with that man…'

'I did not!' insisted Enrico with his hands clapped together in sign of disbelief

'I ask you to remain calm.' interjected Baynard. 'My men will now take care of the situation…'

He did not end his sentence. Suddenly, the head of security had moved up to him, oddly close enough to feel his breathing on his neck.

'Please inspector. You, your men and the civilians need to come with me and a special group of my staff.'

'Excuse me? We are in the middle of an investigation and I remind you all I am here with a warrant.'

'We are under attack, inspector. Our protocol is to guarantee the safety of all staff on site, guests included. Please come with us!'

A siren wailed outside. Its languid sound sent shivers down Viviane's and Enrico's spine. Fran hugged John tighter.

'What on earth is going on out there?' exclaimed Quentin, worried.

'The group 'Wimbledon For the People' is rattling the gates and the high fence on the sides.' shouted the security guard that had just stormed in. 'I think they are trying to bring it down!'

'Nonsense!' barked Baynard in disagreement.

'We cannot take the risk, inspector.' advised Mr Sanders. 'Our security protocol is being enforced!'

'So what?' protested Baynard incredulous and seeing his policemen had the same expression.

'It means here, on Warren Farms, our security protocol overrides any existing police jurisdiction until the safety of the compound is evaluated. Please follow me!'

'I am not moving.' warned Baynard. 'Nobody does!'

'Inspector!' insisted the security guard.

The guard showed his hesitation at first and then motioned his colleague to start rounding everyone up for escort. Baynard shrugged his hands off him.

'What is the meaning of this, Mr Sanders? Sir Alberon?'

'I am afraid he is right, inspector.' nodded Julian. 'Not that I ever expected this measure to come into force…'

'What?'

'Under the company's protocol a self-defence mechanism will be activated.' added Mr Sanders. 'It isolates the compound from the outside and gives security the necessary powers to guard against the breach.'

Baynard was speechless. Yet, he did not have time to protest further, and he was shunted out of the room, together with his policemen and Quentin. More security guards from Alberyx Enterprises arrived to escort Enrico and Viviane out. Viviane turned around. The others were staying behind. Julian's stare was cold, detached.

'Fran?' Viviane asked.

'We are Alberyx Enterprises staff.' explained Mr Sanders, almost apologetically. 'There is a dedicated safe area for us. We will also follow the security guards' instructions until the situation is deemed safe.'

'What about us?' asked Enrico.

'We have a safe place for non-staff too.'

The siren kept wailing outside. Julian looked up, alarmed by the ominous sound.

'Stay close to the security guards!' advised Mr Sanders.

Enrico did not have a chance to take a final look at Julian. He was suddenly out of the room and out of the Infirmary. The calm of the compound was no longer out there. The paths meandering across the warehouses and staff buildings of Warren Farms were swarming with security guards as if they were a small army, headed towards the main gates. They asked staff to stay indoors and follow the instructions given to them for their safety. There was another noise rising to the clouded sky, coming from a distance. They were cries and chants, shouting all at once.

'What's that?' asked Viviane.

'That's Basil and his followers.' replied Enrico. 'How many are there?'

'Are they really attacking the compound? Is that even sane?'

'I don't know… The little I know about Basil "Wilberforce" Elders tells me he is up to something for sure…'

Their group had merged with the one escorting Baynard and the Wimbledon policemen. The head of security was personally in charge of them and making headway for a safe place. They were being rushed towards the northern part of the compound. The inspector grumbled from time to time, warning the security staff about their potential illegality. They did not flinch. Enrico understood they knew what they were doing. As crazy as it sounded, coming from Mr Sanders's mouth, it appeared Warren Farms was acting as a small independent state within Wimbledon.

They crossed one of the small town-like squares and the cries and chants became clearer. Through a gap between the buildings, they saw the wide area before the main gates filled with security personnel armed to their teeth, with black boots and bulky bullet proof vests. Baynard was speechless. He sneered at the sight.

'I knew we couldn't trust Alberyx Enterprises…' moaned Quentin to himself.

'Look beyond the gate!' exclaimed Viviane.

Enrico squinted to peak through the swarm of security guards. Banners and angry faces were all he could make out of Basil's followers. They were lining the main gate and stretched along the high fence for almost a quarter of a mile. He could not count them all, but their sheer presence was menacing. They rattled the fence, and shouted words of scorn at Alberyx Enterprises.

'This is madness…' muttered Quentin, his head lowered.

They quickly arrived at a large warehouse, and they were led inside an empty office. From the ground floor windows, they could see the action around the main gates. They all watched in silence.

'I need to call the police station.' said Baynard at some point, unable to just sit and stare at the civil unrest.

'Please wait, inspector.' said the head of security.

'The land outside is not yours!' reminded Baynard, who still knew how the law worked in England. 'That is public property and I need to redirect the backup. Wimbledon Police can help stop them from the outside.'

The security guard thought of it. He did not see it as a breach of the security protocol by Alberyx Enterprises. He nodded and Baynard was quick to make the call.

Viviane turned to look at Enrico. He had a beaten look on his face, watching the events unfold before him with a fatigue he could not overcome.

'Are you alright?' she asked. 'Where is Dr Watkins?'

'I don't know. He never turned up.'

'What?'

'I know. I had to get to Julian myself and then…'

'What happened?'

'The Wimbledon Gazette posted an article online that didn't go down well with Julian. He found out when I was there…'

'Is this the one?'

Quentin moved closer holding his smartphone up to them. Viviane grabbed hers to check too. They saw the article and how Julian's misdealing with Basil "Wilberforce" Glenn and Octagon School had been exposed. The picture of Enrico at the coffee shop said it all. Viviane looked closer. She was out of the picture.

'That Nathan Glenn has some guts…' commented Quentin.

'This is not good!' commented Viviane. 'Julian thinks you are against him. Did you manage to tell him about what Reginald and his accomplice are plotting?'

'Yes. He came round and then the news of the article made him change his mind.'

'This is not good at all!' she repeated. 'Did you get hold of Dr Watkins, Quentin?'

'He was not answering before. Let me try again.'

He dialled the number. The Alberyx Security guards stood around them on alert carefully watching their moves. The only colour on their black uniforms was the logo of Alberyx Enterprises on the left breast pocket. Enrico felt he was more of a prisoner. He glanced at his watch. An hour to eight p.m. There was no time to waste. He had saved John Crane somehow. He now had to find a way to get out of Warren Farms and reach Caesar's Well. He was not sure what he would do once there, but he had to do something to stop Reginald's plan at all costs. Outside, Basil's men and women were pushing hard against the main gate and all along the eastern fence, shouting at the top of their voice with rabid anger and rattling the fences as hard as they could until their knuckles were pale white. The security personnel stood opposite them, on the other side of the fence, fending them off without causing harm. The scene looked scary and very fragile. Enrico saddened at the thought of Julian's anger. He felt the situation had slipped out of control without him knowing. The fact Julian thought Enrico had tried to frame him bothered him. It was all lies, and this is what this whole mess was about. Someone had played everyone against each other. The wrong John Crane. The convenient online article exposing Julian. Basil's attack on Warren Farms this evening coincidentally. Someone had been clever enough to frame the likes of Julian Alberon and he knew Reginald Bosham could not possibly have the resources to do so. He glanced around staring at the chaos ravaging Alberyx Enterprises, and an eerie sense of suspicion grew inside him, wondering if anyone he knew was involved, including those near him. Quentin. Basil Elders. Fran. John Crane. Mr Sanders. He could only trust Dr Watkins and Viviane at this stage, and by default Baynard himself. He glanced at his watch. There was still time. If he did not do act now, they would be stuck here for hours, long enough for Reginald and the man in black to carry out their plan and for the fog to take hold of the Common once more; he did not dare imagine what horrors were on their way. What was happening on Warren Farms was clearly a distraction from what was really meant to happen.

'*Allora*, what do we do now?' whispered Enrico to Viviane with a wary eye towards the security guards and Baynard.

'Why the whispering?' Viviane replied with a stiff look.

'I don't trust the situation.' muttered Enrico. 'We have to get out of here and get to Caesar's Well.'

'Are you crazy? We are under siege!'

'It's all a diversion. Basil showing up right now is too much of a coincidence. Maybe he knows something. I would not be surprised if he and Reginald knew each other…'

'A bold statement, Enrico. You really think there is a conspiracy?'

'Dr Watkins is not answering!' confirmed Quentin, ending his third attempt to call the curator.

'Where is he?' wondered Viviane.

'Did something happen to him?' suggested Enrico. 'Too much is happening and waiting around here is not helping…'

'How do you plan to get out?' asked Viviane quietly.

'I was thinking… You, me, Quentin, we climb over the northern fence not far from here to get out. We are then in the Common already. How far to the well?'

'Ten minutes maybe.' said Quentin.

'Are you sure we will find Reginald there?' asked Viviane

Enrico did not respond. It was a hunch where there was so little to go on. He put his hand on Viviane's arm and gave her his warm look of confidence, dampening the cries coming from outside.

'Trust me.'

Viviane replied with a weak smile. She did not question Enrico's hunch. She just looked at him with renewed hope and found comfort in his undying positive outlook on the whole situation. She was about to hug him when Quentin shouted in shock.

'What is that?'

The moment came and went in a flash. Literally. Bright lights burst like fireworks in the middle of the open area by the main gates. They then quickly dissolved into large clouds of smoke, expanding and swallowing the whole compound in an instant. The bursts of light multiplied across the main open area and the smoke thickened reaching deeper into the compound. Some fell not far from the warehouse where Enrico and Viviane were. Visibility dropped too. There was a moment of panic among the security guards. Some ran outside into the smoke. The cloud of smoke was large enough to block the whole view of Warren Farms before them.

'Tear gas!' they cried out voices. 'Stay inside!'

'Tear gas?' echoed Baynard incredulous, while on the phone. 'This is Wimbledon for crying out loud. Not a war zone!'

'This is probably Basil "Wilberforce" Elders's doing!' commented the head of Alberyx Enterprises security. 'He is actually attacking the compound!'

Baynard's icy stare had turned into a livid expression. He was not happy to see his investigation stopped in its tracks at a clue moment. In a chaotic moment like this, key evidence could go missing. Yet, the inspector's fighting spirit was not dead. Reinforcements were on the way to stop the protesters outside the compound, regardless of whether Alberyx Enterprises approved it or not. Outside, the situation worsened and now they all faced this thick wall of smoke which did not appear to be receding at all. It reminded Enrico and Viviane of the fog. It was a reminder of what they had come here for. The Italian baker thought of his chances. The security guards still had their guns in their holsters and no weapons were drawn or pointed at them. He may have the chance to escape, but realised he may complicate things with Baynard, and even with Julian. The Italian baker was impatient and could not bear just hanging around. He knew too well the attack to the compound was a distraction.

'At my signal. Push that security guard against the others.' he whispered to Quentin and Viviane catching her gaze.

'What?' Viviane mouthed.

Quentin frowned.

'Look, it will be eight p.m. soon and I want to get to the bottom of this. I owe it to Julian.' said Enrico.

Viviane bit her lip. She understood where Enrico was coming from.

'Why can't we ask Baynard's help?' whispered Quentin, wary of the security guards.

But they were not listening. They were busy staring at the tear gas attack outside.

'His hands are tied!' argued Enrico. 'Don't you see? He's got no jurisdiction here. That's just crazy! Someone ensured the protocol was activated at the right time, and even attacked Warren Farms.'

'Basil, you think?' suggested Viviane.

Enrico sighed. It was a far-fetched possibility. While Basil was belligerent, he was not the army type. The same was for his followers.

'I think he is a pawn in all of this. The man in black with Reginald is the key in all of this. I need to catch him!'

'Ok. Let's do this...' added Viviane. 'I know I'll regret it...'

'Hold on a minute...' hesitated Quentin.

Enrico did not wait and did not see what was coming. A crash in one of the windows was all he heard. A tear gas bomb had just hit it and landed inside the tiny warehouse office. Everyone gasped and Enrico knew this was fate calling him. He hinted at the security guard closest to Viviane before the smoke was up to their waist. Viviane coughed and quickly pushed the guard with all her strength, letting him fall against the others nearby like a pack of dominoes. The guards lost their balance as they struggled to see and breathe, but it was enough for Enrico to make his move. He acted quickly, pulling the lapel of his chef's jacket over his mouth, and dashed forward to grab one security guard from the back and hold him by the neck. Enrico grabbed the gun ready to draw it, hoping he would not have to fire it. Viviane and Quentin joined Enrico's side. Their eyes were now watery, and the tear gas was starting to have an effect. Baynard tried to make sense of what was happening. His eyes started to burn. He took a few steps forward and saw what Enrico was up to. One of his policemen had a gun pointed at Enrico but struggled to aim in the poor visibility as Enrico, Viviane and Quentin made their way to the exit door with a security guard as hostage. The other security guards had regrouped by now, watching closely Enrico's movement with hands on their guns. The whole group was at a standstill, tension rising. The cries from outside rang louder through the crashed window.

'Stand down!' shouted the head of security. 'We are here to protect you!'

Baynard realised the head of security was standing next to him, but it was only a faded blur. The smoke had filled the room, and everyone was coughing or crying.

'Listen to them, Mr Letrova!' warned Baynard. 'You don't want to complicate things further!'

'And let Reginald Bosham escape?'

'The man has been behind bars all this time.'

'Are you sure? Then ask your men at the station to check. Prove me wrong!'

There was a pause. The Italian baker thought he heard murmuring in the smoke. He kept an eye on any of the security guards getting closer. He followed Viviane with the corner of his eye as she made way to the exit with Quentin.

'You are a fool, Mr Lartova, in taking such a risk!' resumed Baynard.

'LoTr…' Enrico stammered.

He could not finish pronouncing his correct surname. Baynard shouted a new order to his own men.

'Ensure these civilians are not hurt as they are a key witness in this investigation.'

The policemen lowered their guns and then turned to aim at the Alberyx Enterprises security guards.

'I would kindly ask Alberyx Enterprises security guards to step down.' added Baynard.

The security guards looked at each other taken aback. The head of security was not going to have any of it.

'You are on Alberyx Enterprises grounds during a lockdown protocol. We are here to protect you!'

'And I represent the police, here to protect Wimbledon. Don't make a false move!'

He then glanced in the direction of Enrico, more and more a hazy shadow. He spoke out loud to everyone present, to make sure Enrico and everyone heard.

'Reginald Bosham was released on bail a few months ago. The baker is right for once! So, let them go and don't make any silly mistakes. We won't budge until we can speak to Julian Alberon and get to the bottom of this!'

'This is unheard of!' protested the head of security, his role undermined. 'You can't just trust his word!'

'I don't!' corrected Baynard, dryly. 'By the time this crazy day is over, if that crazy baker doesn't bring Reginald Bosham to me, he will go to jail!'

The news sank in. What a relief, Enrico thought. Baynard believed part of his story, at least for now. Yet, he and Viviane could not wipe off the grin from their faces. He could imagine Baynard's icy stare from across the smoky office, still being distant and impartial. Enrico understood the inspector had given him some slack, but Enrico knew they were on their own. He had to find Reginald Bosham.

The Italian baker glanced over his shoulder. They had just come out of the warehouse and the only difference was the cold air. He released the security guard and pushed him back inside the small office.

'This way!' called out Enrico.

Enrico headed north to the outskirts of the compound. Viviane and Quentin rushed behind him, trying to keep his pace. They both thought they would hear guns shooting. Instead, an eerie calm followed as the cries and chants from Basil's followers became a distant echo. The chaos that had erupted at the entrance of Warren Farms became more and more distant as they move away from it. The smoke slowly faded, bringing back the world as they knew it, and the only thing they heard were their frantic footsteps crunching the dead leaves. Rain had started falling and the leaden sky brought the darkness of the evening earlier than expected.

Lord Cotton tried to pull at his chain for the hundredth time. He could not see what he was doing. The rattling of the metal chain and Little Caesar's growling was all he could hear. Even the dog had been trying to break free in vain, pulling his own little chain time after time. The club owner held still for a moment catching his breath. The humming of the water pump and the ventilation system were louder than his own breathing and even Little Caesar's barks and growls. He sighed in despair. Wherever they were, nobody could hear them. He had no idea why he was being held captive, what he had done to deserve this. He recalled the last visit from his jailer that day when he finally heard a voice. A deep male voice. He could not recognise the voice, no matter how hard he tried.

He took a deep breath and pulled his chain again. His shin felt sore, and he had cramps in various parts of his body. He changed position to find a better way to pull the chain. He was about to give it all up, when a clang came from the door. He remained silent. He could hear voices behind it. Little Caesar started growling once the door opened. They were both overwhelmed by an indistinct chatter ringing in the tiny, cramped space. Footsteps approached and Lord Cotton felt hands grabbing him and urging him to stand up. He felt the weight of the chain being lifted and Little Caesar's growling diminished. Once the blindfold was removed, Lord Cotton was pleased to see his dog, safe and sound, but just a little less white from all the dirt and dust. He then looked up at the friendly faces that had come to his rescue.

'Lord Cotton! Wimbledon Police!' said the police officer in front of him. 'You are now safe! How do you feel? Can you hear me?'

Another police officer spoke into the radio transmitter asking the paramedics to come down. Lord Cotton was so happy to see them.

'Thank you. Thank you.' he cried out to the police officers, a little shaken. 'Help me. A man kidnapped me. He wants to sabotage Alberyx Enterprises!'

As he shouted those words, one of the police freed Caesar from his little chain. Lord Cotton was expecting the pet to jump in his lap. Instead, the little dog sped out of the tiny room the moment he was free.

'Little Caesar!' shouted Lord Cotton incredulous.

'Go after the dog!' ordered one police officer to the other. 'I think he caught a scent!'

The police officer by the door ran straight away, alerting his colleagues above in the car park. The little dog ran fast, and the police was worried they would lose track of it in the darkness of the evening. Little Caesar was already up the stairs, about to leave the basement. Three more police officers joined the hunt, wondering where the dog would lead them.

Little Caesar ran with all its might, pink tongue flipping out, the white fluffy hair getting soggy wet in the heavy rain. The scent was still there. Fainter but strong enough to follow it. Little Caesar ran faster, keen to avenge the person who had mistreated his master. The police officers shouted directions and flashed their lights across the unlit golf course, trying to spot Little Caesar's white fluffy shape. It took a few turns through fairways and greens before the policemen understood the dog was heading for the Repeater. The pillar structure looked ominous in the dark, void of colour or details against the black evening clouds. Little Caesar barked as he approached and the policemen drew their guns out, unsure what to expect. They entered the working site area. Nobody was there. Little Caesar went to the service door leading inside the Repeater and started scratching and barking. The policemen moved closer and listened carefully. They could hear a muffled voice of distress coming from inside. One of them pulled Little Caesar away from the door while the other opened it. The little dog kept barking and escaped the grip of the police officer, leaping at a shape lying on the ground. The policemen flashed their lights inside. A woman lay tied up to one of the supporting metal poles.

'Help!' she shouted in panic.

Her eyes were smeared with mascara, and it traced the track of dried tears across her cheeks.

'Help me! I was attacked!' cried out Ramona coughing, pretending to be in pain.

'What happened?' called out one of the police offers.

Little Caesar kept growling at her, not letting go. Ramona hated the little creature. She knew it would lead them there and be a nuisance. She moved her legs hysterically, so the dog would not go for her and ruin her cover.

'Be quiet!' shouted one policeman, picking up the dog and walking outside.

Ramona was glad the darned creature was being taken care of.

'You need to listen to me, officer!' she then pleaded while being freed from the handcuffs. 'Reginald Bosham, the man who did this to me, just did something to this machine. I caught him as he was doing it. Not sure what but there is a countdown on the screen. Perhaps it is a bomb!'

The policeman was confused and alarmed. He could not take a bomb threat lightly. He followed Ramona's hand pointing at a flashing monitor. Before he could make out the numbers reaching single digits, the whole machine turned itself on, blinking all over the place like a Christmas tree. Bright lights turned on at the top of the Repeater. Ramona looked up terrified and so did the policeman, who quickly grabbed his radio and talked to his superior back at the car park.

'Sir, something is about to blow at the Repeater.' he warned. 'We need to get this woman out as soon as possible. She's been attacked. Does Reginald Bosham ring a bell?'

On the other side, his superior struggled to understand what he meant. The policemen did not have time to repeat himself. The USB flash drive inserted into the main computer of the Repeater sent a bright spark through the long, narrow space inside the Repeater. Above, the aerial started to rattle, and bolts of lightning sparked from it in all directions. The USB quickly burst into flames from overheating. Ramona watched in awe. This had never happened during the tests, she thought. The lightning then branched out and jolted in the direction of the New Wimbledon Windmill. Lord Awlthorp's plan had been set into motion.

Sergeant Jeremy drove his car fast down Camp Road onto the narrow lane leading to Warren Farms. Other police cars followed him. They were the police back-up Baynard had asked for. Since leaving the police station with sirens blaring, he could hardly believe the reports that kept coming in one after the other. First, Basil "Wilberforce" Elders had decided to literally attack the Alberyx Enterprises headquarters. Baynard had been very brief on the phone, describing as best as he could how they had been put into lockdown following a siege by Basil's protesters. Then he called again to ask about Reginald Bosham, whether he was still in prison, and the sergeant was surprised to find out he had been released on bail by someone who had preferred to stay anonymous. Baynard had told him he may be the one behind what was happening.

Jeremy thought hard trying to make sense of it, while speeding down the tree-lined lane cutting across the Common. The theories he conjured up in his mind were soon wiped out by the dramatic scene before him. The final stretch towards Warren Farms lay in front of them like a battlefield. At the bottom, where the gates were meant to appear, a deep cloud of smoke swallowed the whole entrance. Jeremy slowed down and then hit the brakes when visibility became so bad that it made it dangerous to drive any further. He and the rest of the police officers jumped out of their cars and lined up in formation. Cries and shouts came from within the cloud of smoke. Men and women suddenly ran out of it, coughing and rubbing their eyes in pain. Some still held posters and banners, or what remained of them; others dropped them on the ground to find a quick escape. Tear gas, muttered Jeremy to himself. He found it hard to believe Basil's followers used tear gas as part of the protest. Any judge in England would be quick to state this was no peaceful protest as originally intended. Basil Elders must have gone mad, or his followers perhaps had got carried away.

'Stay alert! Don't let any of these people get away!' ordered Sergeant Jeremy, already worried some would try to get lost in the woods on both sides of the road.

A young man drifted out of the cloud of smoke, disoriented. He swayed towards Sergeant Jeremy waving his hands in the air. The sergeant squinted at him and quickly recognised the journalist Nathan Glenn.

'Hold it there!'

'I… I… am unharmed.' he coughed.

Nathan did not hesitate to get down on his knees in surrender. He still had not come to terms with what had just happened. Everything had happened so quickly as the tear gas fell around them like bombs during a war. The sound still rang in his ear. He rubbed his eyes. They still stung from the tear gas. He looked ahead with one eye, blinded by the headlights, and saw the silhouette of two policemen approaching to take him away. He was in trouble for sticking too close to Basil Elders, and even if innocent, he knew the circumstances were not in his favour.

'Take him away!' ordered Jeremy.

The sergeant then looked ahead again, looking for other stranded rebels. Suddenly, a familiar figure emerged from the thick cloud. He staggered forward on the road among the fleeing crowd. He seemed disorientated. Jeremy checked twice to be sure it was who he thought it was and once sure he moved forward with caution and determination.

'Hold it!' he called out to the man.

The man stumbled upon hearing the sergeant's voice. He looked into Jeremy's direction. His clothes were covered in mud, as if he had fallen in it a few times. His gold-rimmed glasses were half-broken, and his face was contorted by the sting in his eyes from the tear gas.

'Hold it, Mr Elders!' repeated Sergeant Jeremy.

The sergeant pulled out his gun for precaution but did not aim. The rest of his police officers were running around the area to catch as many protesters as they could. Basil still looked confused and yet he could not help letting out a sardonic smile. Jeremy could not see any weapons on him, but the smoke was not clearing away fast enough, and cries still echoed beyond the cloud of smoke, leading the sergeant to believe danger still hung in the air.

'Mr Elders, please stand down!' warned Sergeant Jeremy. 'Put your hands up and ask all these people to stop running and give themselves up to the police.'

Basil laughed but it was more of a croak. He looked weak.

'We're standing down already, Sergeant Jeremy.' he mocked, barely standing straight. 'Alberyx Enterprises preferred to use hard force against us. Typical! I take it as a complete disregard of the law and of citizens' rights. I rest my case, sergeant!'

'Reports say you launched tear gas at them…' said Jeremy with a doubtful look.

'Us? A pacific protest against those corporate pigs?' scorned Basil.

Despite his conditions, he still had the energy to rebuke authority.

'Look!' he continued waving his hands. 'We are running away in pain. I find it ridiculous you are coming after us and treating us like warmongers.'

'I said stand down, Mr Elders!' warned Jeremy.

'We weren't the ones throwing the tear gas!'

'You can tell us more at the police station. Now, put your hands up and ask these people to do the same. Don't make this any harder!''

Jeremy held his ground while dumbfounded upon hearing Basil's words. Yet, he knew he had to follow protocol and take everyone in as well as finding Baynard in all this mess. He ordered one of the police officers to handcuff Basil 'Wilberforce' Elders and called for more police vans and an ambulance to assist them with the protesters. As they rounded them up and the smoke cleared, the entrance to the compound was bearing more and more resemblance to the outcome of an air-strike in a war-torn country. Jeremy was shocked. He looked around. The first protesters were being taken away into custody. Some were still being hunted down in the woods. Sergeant Jeremy and a handful of police officers made a move towards the gates, barely visible in the thinning smoke. Rain had just started to fall more heavily.

'We're at the gates, Inspector Baynard!' he broadcast on his radio transmitter.

There was some crackling static noise. He tried again.

'Coming out!' spoke the inspector's voice after a few attempts. 'The security guards are escorting us outside!'

The cloud of smoke was dissolving thanks to the drops of heavy rain. Shapes became clearer. The gates. Some protesters stood by them, hands up and waiting for the police to approach. Others were on the ground, groaning in pain after being run down by the stampede of protesters running away.

Jeremy heard the gates opening and a bunch of Alberyx Enterprises security guards came out in a strong defence line to guard the entrance. Shortly after, a group of people was let out. Jeremy recognised Baynard leading the way.

'Inspector, I am here!' Jeremy shouted.

Baynard walked up to him taking in the surrounding chaos. It was a mess beyond belief, and even if things had calmed down, the uncomfortable sensation of the aftermath lingered on.

'What the heck happened?' asked Jeremy.

'God only knows.' replied Baynard bitterly. 'Where is Basil "Wilberforce" Elders? Did you catch him?'

'Yessir! He is in custody, but he claims he did not launch the attack!'

'What?' exclaimed Baynard. 'Why would he say that when everyone in Warren Farms saw his group charging at the gates? He'd better have some answers for me.'

'Did you find John Crane? The real one I mean.'

'Yes! It appears the idea of someone inside Alberyx Enterprises meddling in their affairs is more and more apparent. It is not just the windmill but also the records from their infirmary have been tampered with.'

'What about Viviane Leighwood and Quentin Plainstraw?'

Baynard sniggered.

'Our friend the baker showed up and I had to let him slip out of the compound when the situation heated up. He's onto something and I don't know what it is. We have no time to lose! I want an arrest warrant issued against Reginald Bosham. I need roadblocks in place in and out of Wimbledon. Find him! In the meantime, let's try and clear things up, especially with Alberyx Enterprises. We need to get hold of Mr Sanders, John Crane and Julian Alberon. They are still inside the perimeter of the compound.'

'Are they safe?'

'I hope so. They will have some explaining to do about their bloody security protocols! One more thing…'

'What's that, inspector?'

'We need to find out where that crazy baker of ours went. He'd better be onto something good!'

His inquisitive stare showed his dissatisfaction at the mess all around and he was looking for hope where there was none to be found. He was fuming at how his warrant had turned out and he knew the Chief Superintendent would not be pleased.

Baynard was about to bark more orders, when Jeremy's radio crackled. A rushed voice came through. Neither Jeremy nor Baynard understood what their colleague was saying on the other end of the radio channel. There was a strange interference. Something about being tipped off about a case of kidnapping at the golf course. Something was about to blow. Then the Repeater was mentioned, and when a question about Reginald Bosham's name followed, Baynard knew things were only going to get worse. The sky suddenly groaned, and the clouds churned into large dark grey masses. The air became filled with static and a strong breeze blew through the woods, sweeping across the narrow road and almost knocking people and cars over. Then lightning cracked through the sky and everyone on the ground looked up in shock and awe as the ominous clouds flashed with thunder above their heads. Some thought it was the storm forecast for that night. Baynard begged to differ. Someone had turned on the New Wimbledon Windmill and the Repeater.

Reginald pushed the manhole to one side and lifted himself out onto the clearing just outside the Warren Farms perimeter. The storm had just kicked in and it was now pouring down. He looked around to check the area was safe and quickly closed the manhole behind him, taking cover under the thick foliage of the Common. Lord Awlthorp had been waiting for him patiently there under the cover of darkness. The heavy drops of rain fell hard on his black hood and cloak, and then slid down to the muddy ground, leaving him dry and untouched.

'I saw the tear gas falling. I assume it all went to plan.' asked Lord Awlthorp, with his wicked grin.

'Yes, sir. The distraction we had in mind worked as planned. They all think Basil "Wilberforce" Elders, our dear Operator Two, launched the tear gas attack.'

'Good, Reginald, good. They will now leave us alone. Let's get moving!'

'I saw Enrico LoTrova entering the compound. What if he is onto us and he turns up here with his friends?'

'He won't! Although how he escaped the madness of the fog evades me…' mumbled Lord Awlthorp, slightly annoyed.

'He knows about the bunker so I wouldn't be surprised if he turned up at Warren Farms this evening. Probably to warn about your secret plan.'

'He doesn't know anything! He believes he does. If we move fast, we can get this done quickly before he or anyone realise what is happening.'

'I don't like it. We always cross paths with this baker and he is always a spanner in the works! It is not the first time…'

'Then if you see him again tonight, kill him!'

Lord Awlthorp's face was shrouded in the shadow of his black hood and yet Reginald could feel his evil eyes staring at him, vengeful and demanding.

Reginald nodded at Lord Awlthorp's cold instructions with a sly smile and flashed the gun to show he had it under control.

'It will be my pleasure!' he replied. 'We'd better move quickly north to our position. Countdown is about to kick in!' Reginald reminded him.

'Good. Follow me as far as the small clearing before the slope leading to the well. Don't forget to take the nettle and mint pills! You will need them when the fog appears. It'll spread around the well and then stretch for about half a mile in all directions. You may want to keep sane!'

Reginald gulped at the thought of it. He swallowed the pills Lord Awlthorp had given him. Despite being sceptical about the whole thing, he did not want to end up like the others who had succumbed to the fog. Now, more than ever, he had reservations about following Lord Awlthorp any further. The madness of it all, of all his plans, had taken its toll on Reginald; for all he knew the portal was a fantasy his boss was pursuing blindly without reason. The rational approach he had seen in his boss before was gone. Reginald did not know what awaited them at the end of tonight; he reminded himself though this was his last leg. After tonight, he would not owe anything to Lord Awlthorp once he had the relic he wanted. He would wait for him at a safe distance from the well and lay low. When the time was right and Lord Awlthorp no longer needed him, he would make his exit and leave Wimbledon for good in the early hours of the morning.

Lord Awlthorp wrapped up in his dark cloak, looked back at the vast stretches of the Common behind them, inviting them in to reveal its secrets. Lord Awlthorp smirked. Soon he would have the third relic of the Wynnman, almost half-way to obtaining powers beyond everyone's imagination. He stood silent, wondering if the spirit of the Wynnman would manifest himself, give him the guidance it had been whispering to him since that first night after the accident at the Old Rectory. He knew the more relics he gathered, the closer he would get to resurrecting the Wynnman and bit by bit he would learn where the other relics were hidden. Thinking about what Reginald had said, the image of the Italian baker returned to his mind. He had to admit Enrico LoTrova was a strangely resourceful man. From the beginning, he had always thwarted his plans to unearth each relic. For a minute, he wondered whether the baker had been onto him from the start of his quest. Impossible, he thought. Yet, he wished to know more about who he was, and get rid of him for good.

'All clear, sir!' whispered Reginald doing one final sweep of the area.

'Let's move!' said Lord Awlthorp glancing at his watch.

Enrico, Quentin and Viviane had been watching them closely from behind three large trees not far from the northern fence of Warren Farms. Quentin kept checking to see whether Baynard had not changed his mind or whether the security guards were onto them. Enrico and Viviane instead kept tabs on Reginald and his mysterious accomplice. Enrico was happy to point to the high fence, the manhole, all the elements that matched his story. He himself was happy to know he had not imagined it. He knew it was the same mysterious character he had seen in the bunker the night before. Both Enrico and Viviane tried to take a better look at him. The hood hung loose over his head concealing his identity from every angle; and the rain had become heavier making everything more blurred.

Once Reginald and Lord Awlthorp disappeared into the Common, Enrico was the first to dash out and climb over the high fence.

'Wait!' Viviane tried to stop him. 'We don't want them to spot us!'

She grabbed Quentin and they helped each other climb over the fence. Enrico looked at the manhole and then the Common ahead of them.

'Come on! We're going to lose them!' said Enrico impatiently.

'We know where they are going!' reassured Viviane.

She grabbed her smartphone and pulled a map on the screen, asking Quentin to point where exactly Caesar's Well was. It was not an unknown location to Wimbledonians, but it was remote and hard to pin down if you had never been to the Common. Viviane herself knew about it but she hardly ever visited the site.

'What do we expect to see there?' asked Enrico.

'It's just an old well.' replied Quentin. 'It fell into disuse more than eighty years ago. It was sunken in so I'm not really sure what we should expect. I'd better go and get help. We're going to need it!'

'Find Baynard and Dr Watkins. Tell them where we are.' advised Enrico.

Quentin nodded.

'I hope Dr Watkins is ok.' he said, clearly worried about his old friend. 'You two better be careful! Don't forget this!'

He pulled out a half-empty vial from his pocket. Enrico had never seen the vial before, but the green dense content was familiar. He looked into Viviane's eyes, puzzled.

'Quentin's soup.' replied Viviane. 'We used it with the boy Ken at the hospital and this is what is left.'

'You don't want to lose your marbles!' joked Quentin in face of adversity. 'If the plan of these criminals is real, you will need all the help you can get when the fog reappears. If we get to the windmill, we'll have to try and destroy that infernal machine!'

As he spoke, a strong gust of wind blew from the south sweeping across the Common. The three almost lost their balance and then they saw flashes of lightning cracking against the dark cloudy sky. There was nothing natural about it. The lightning was one long strip rather like a belt across the sky, guided by an invisible hand to the north.

'Oh my God…' cried Quentin. 'I have seen this before. The windmill. The Repeater. They have been turned on!'

'We're late…' said Viviane in shock.

'No, we're not! Let's go!'

Enrico took a sip of the green soup and passed it to Viviane. He then ran into the Common holding his small torch to guide him, Viviane followed. Quentin watched them go until they became an indistinct mass blending in with the shape of the trees.

Caesar's Well was to be found in a depression in the middle of a plateau, somewhere in a secluded part of Wimbledon Common. Even Viviane seemed to struggle to find it, confessing she rarely came this way. The well had been sunken in for more than a century and it lay abandoned surrounded by the overgrowth. The only evidence visible today was the circle of rough-cut stones still maintaining the shape around a hole two metres wide and about one and half metre deep.

'What do we expect to find there?' wondered Viviane as they leapt across the muddy path on their way to the well.

'No idea.' said Enrico. 'I must confess I do regret coming all this way without some form of back up. But we haven't much time left. We have to catch these two criminals before they get away with it!'

'How do we know they have not already accomplished their plan?'

'The fog. I don't see it yet…'

Enrico had been expecting it the moment they had started chasing the two men through the Common. The thought of scary hallucinations from a by-gone era sent a shiver down his spine. He remembered then the man in black sharing the green pills with Reginald. He too had taken a sip of the green soup. He knew he would have to be prepared to run through the fog if he wanted to catch Reginald and the mysterious man in black.

'Caesar's Well is in that direction.' whispered Viviane, looking up from her phone. 'Not far.'

The little map on her screen did not take into account the many alternative paths branching out in all directions across the wide expanse of Wimbledon Common. Instead, what appeared to be one straight walk in one direction turned out to be a long and winding road. The heavy rain did not help, and large puddles had formed making their trek even more insidious. Enrico kept his torch lit on the ground, wary not to give away their position, as they took detour after detour. For all he knew, Reginald could be hiding behind any of the trees around them.

The two suddenly came out on the edge of the woods onto an open space. The sound of the heavy rain was suddenly drowned by the jolts of lightning still crackling in the stormy sky and hitting the top of the windmill far away in the distance. Enrico and Viviane found the scene frightening and mesmerising at the same time. They quickly moved on. To the left, the path led back into the forest down a slope. Here the foliage was less thick, and the ground was covered with slippery dead leaves.

'Over there!' pointed Viviane.

Enrico squinted ahead. He walked carefully down the slope covered in leaves and branches. He then looked closer. Caesar's Well lay before him, unassuming. It was a hole in the ground, smaller than he had imagined, strewn with bits and pieces of litter left by recent passers-by. If it had not been for Viviane insisting they had reached their destination, Enrico would still be asking himself if this was the place they had been looking for. Maybe it was not the place.

'Lost something?' shouted a voice in the dark.

Enrico and Viviane spun around to face the voice and were suddenly blinded by a powerful torchlight coming from behind a nearby tree. Their eyes struggled to adjust and make out the person in front of them. Yet, as the voice spoke again, it became clear to Enrico they were facing Reginald Bosham.

'You again!' spat Enrico.

'I would say the same thing!' replied Reginald. 'You two, especially you, crazy baker, can't help nosing around in matters that don't concern you. We will soon put an end to that.'

Reginald walked up to them and raised his gun to their faces, the barrel easily visible against the light of the torch. The mysterious man in black was nowhere to be seen.

'You won't get away with it!' attacked Viviane, clenching her fists.

'That never crossed my mind!' Reginald threatened. 'You sent me to the slammer once, and that will never happen again!'

'The relics of the Wynnman belong to Wimbledon...' added Enrico. 'I know your plan!'

'You do?' said another voice in the dark.

It rang deep and lugubrious in the darkness of the Common, followed by the crunching of dead leaves on the ground. Enrico and Viviane felt a presence behind Reginald. The strong light from his torch kept the presence in the shadows. It was the man in black. Enrico thought he recognised his voice except something in the tone was different. He craved to push Reginald to the side to be able to grab the man in black and take a look at his face.

'Who are you?' Enrico called out.

'That is not of your concern.' dismissed Lord Awlthorp. 'All you need to know is that your efforts end here.'

He started walking away.

'Where are you going?' shouted Enrico. 'Come back!'

'You're staying here with me!' grinned Reginald, aiming at Enrico with his gun. 'It will be my pleasure!'

Enrico and Viviane felt helpless. Whatever the two men had come to accomplish here was about to happen. Lightning flashed across the dark night sky and cast a surreal light above the tree line. For a moment, in the bright light, Enrico thought he could see Lord Awlthorp's dark cloak disappearing down the slope.

'Enrico! Look!' nudged him Viviane.

The fog had started to curl and thicken at their feet. Reginald gloated at them, knowing what it all meant.

'The fog will make us insane…' lied Viviane, acting scared.

'I am going to enjoy this!' said Reginald. 'I will let you go mad and then probably shoot you both in the head.'

'Oh no…' Viviane played along as the helpless heroine.

Enrico understood Viviane's bluff. Reginald and the man in black did not know they had drunk the green soup and the fog could not harm them. What he and Viviane had to do now was take the gun the moment Reginald was caught off guard. The fog slowly rose from the ground up like a silver spectre waking up in the world of the living. It shrouded their legs with its hazy mantle and then moved up to their waist, feeling cold to the touch. Reginald watched them cruelly, waiting for the fog to take effect.

'Time for goodbyes, Mr LoTrova!' said Reginald with a smug. 'And this time it's for good!'

Enrico did not flinch. All he had to do was get the timing right. Reginald straightened his aim and channelled all his hate for Enrico into the gun. He tightened his grip on the trigger ready for the execution. The fog was now everywhere and the Common had disappeared, leaving Enrico, Viviane and Reginald alone, surrounded by a dark grey void.

'Any minute now!' added Reginald.

Viviane suddenly started shaking and moaning, as if caught by an epileptic seizure. Enrico glanced sideways and found himself staring at Viviane's contorted face with her tongue sticking out.

'Help Enrico!' she moaned, her words half-intelligible.

The Italian baker knew straightaway what Viviane was up to. Reginald lowered his aim, completely taken by surprise by Viviane and the fog. Enrico saw his opportunity. He pushed Reginald's arm up in the sky. The gun fired a shot. Viviane stopped her act and pounced with all her weight against Reginald's heavy figure, knocking him off balance. She then climbed over him and scratched his face with her nails. Reginald groaned and cursed, banging the torch against Viviane. He kept firing the gun up in the sky.

'Get the gun, Enrico!' cried out Viviane for help. 'He is way too strong for me...'

Enrico bit Reginald's hand to force him to release his tight grip on the gun.

'Ah, you bastard!' shrieked Reginald in pain.

The burly man fought back and bashed the Italian baker with his torch. Enrico managed to free himself but stumbled backward. The last thing he saw was Reginald's shadow with Viviane over his shoulder dissolving into thin air. He jumped up and tracked back the short distance, but Viviane and Reginald had already disappeared. Enrico turned around, lost in a thick wall of fog.

'Oh no...' said Enrico. 'Viviane!'

He stumbled left and right. He could no longer see or hear Viviane even though she had been close. He then tried to see where the man in black had gone. Enrico looked on the ground searching for Caesar's Well again. The fog had swallowed everything and only a tiny patch of dead leaves under his feet were visible to him. Enrico panicked. He was expecting something to happen. Surely, the past would come out of the fog to surprise him just like last time. Instead, nothing. Enrico paced up and down. He then heard lightning strike above him, followed by the roar of thunder, and the fog was suddenly whooshed away in outward circles by some invisible strong wind. Enrico put his hand up against the wind, closing his eyes and feeling the wrath of the wind against him.

Then the wind stopped, and the fog receded until it was only a memory. Enrico shivered and opened his eyes. He expected to see the grey, thick fog all around him. Instead, he was staring at a blue sky visible through the leafy branches of the trees above him. The sun had come out and the clouds had cleared suddenly but it was broad daylight. The birds chirped cheerfully as if it were a sunny day in spring or summer. Enrico rubbed his eyes, incredulous. The winter rain, the storm, they were all gone. Enrico shook his head. This could not be a hallucination since he had had a sip of Quentin's green soup. He was somewhere on the Common, but the idea of what time it was eluded him. He looked around, spooked by the whole thing. Viviane and Reginald were nowhere to be seen. And neither was the man in black.

A cry echoed far away in the indistinct mass of green from the woods. Enrico put his guard on. Even in broad daylight, the thick wilderness of the Common was an impenetrable mystery hiding the deepest of secrets. The cry was not one for help. It sounded like a cry of incitement followed by horses neighing. Enrico staggered in the direction of the sound. After a few paces, he recognised the path he had been on with Viviane a few moments before. The neighing of the horses rang closer nearby and Enrico crouched again to hide behind the bushes. In the distance, he saw men on horses scouting the area. He could not make out their traits, but their clothing stood out a mile way. They wore shoddy rags patched together, as if taken from a period drama set in Medieval times or maybe earlier. He shuddered at the thought and quickly became frantic as crazy ideas came up into his head. He wondered whether the man in black had indeed opened a portal through time. Perhaps he was now somewhere else in history. Shut up Enrico, said the Italian baker to himself. Whatever this place was, Enrico was sure the man in black might be there too, looking for Caesar's Dagger.

When the horses had galloped away, Enrico ran off in the opposite direction. He found himself back where he and Viviane had been earlier. The trees were different though. Greener, thicker. Enrico looked down the slope, but he could not see Caesar's Well anymore. The slope led him into the thick undergrowth and Enrico was careful not to crack a dry branch or anything that would alert his position. The neighing of horses was long gone. When he reached a clearing beyond the undergrowth, he saw someone in the middle of it, kneeling by a pile of blue-tinted rocks. Enrico was quick to recognise the man in black's cloak, but his face as always was hidden. Enrico hid behind a nearby oak and noticed his cloak was not black but a deep emerald green. Enrico was curious to know when the man in black had had the time to get changed. The mysterious figure was busy scraping and digging by the pile of rocks, but it was unclear whether he was hiding something or looking for something. The scraping and digging continued for a while, until the cloaked figure finally stopped what he was doing and raised his head. The Italian baker held his breath, worried he may have heard him. Enrico watched him turn his head to the left and Enrico followed the gaze. Across the clearing from Enrico, at the very edge, another mysterious figure had appeared wearing the exact same clothes except this figure was slightly taller, and the cloak and hood were pitch black. The black-cloaked figured stood by another oak contemplating what the green-cloaked figure was doing. He appeared fatigued as he leant against the tree and his chest was heaving as if he had rushed to the place.

Enrico rubbed his eyes, not sure if he was seeing double. The two cloaked figures did not speak and did not give away whether they knew each other or not. The green-cloaked man kept his gaze on the other, unstirring. He then raised his arm and an old, wrinkly hand edged out from the deep sleeves. The fingers were smudged with soil and held onto the blade of what looked like a white and polished ivory knife. It could have been any knife but the ivory colour and the dragon-like detail on the blade were too obvious for Enrico to ignore. It was an exact replica of the drawing he had seen. It was Caesar's Dagger. The green-cloaked figure was offering it to the new arrival, who did not hesitate to stumble forward across the clearing. His pace was uncertain as he walked slowly towards the green-cloaked figure. No words were spoken. The green-cloaked figure stretched his hand further out and the black-cloaked twin hesitated at first. He then took the dagger from the old, wrinkly hand before it was too late. Thunder rumbled in the clear blue sky. Enrico looked up, puzzled, and inadvertently took a step back onto a dried branch. It cracked. The two cloaked figures turned their heads towards Enrico. Their faceless stare, hidden inside the hood, filled Enrico with the same dread he had experienced when he had heard the man in black's voice. He wondered which one of them, if any, was the man in black he had been hunting. His only thought then was to run away. Enrico turned to run, but something else blocked his path.

'Aye! Death to the Wynnman!' shouted a raspy voice.

The scruffy men on horses had doubled back and were now lined up in front of Enrico. He observed more closely. The men looked shabbier, with unkempt hair and yellow, rotting teeth. Each one of them held a spear and only one held a bow in his other hand. They were aiming above Enrico's head at the two cloaked men, with a watchful eye on the odd man in a white jacket next to them, who without knowing had led them to the clearing they had been looking for. Enrico realised these men were not here to hunt him.

'We found you, Wynnman! Now we shall make you pay!' spoke again one of the horsemen.

Enrico froze. The horseman had called out the name 'Wynnman'. The sorcerer's name. If the fog had indeed opened a portal in time, Enrico guessed he was witnessing a moment in real history, which meant one of the two cloaked men was the real Wynnman. Enrico turned to take a better look at the two figures by the pile of rocks. Enrico saw the black cloaked figure was now holding Caesar's Dagger in his gloved hands. Just then, the wind picked up again and clouds gathered once more in the sky swallowing the sun. The horses neighed in fear. Enrico looked at the horsemen. They too had an irrational fear in their eyes, terrified by the two cloaked figures.

'Sorcery!' shouted one of them, brandishing the spear high above his head. 'Death to the Wynnman!'

Enrico thought he had grasped what was about to happen, so he jumped out of the way as the horsemen rode into the clearing. The two cloaked figures stood still, facing the charge. In that very moment, a bolt of lightning scarred the grey sky and Enrico saw the fog rising once again around him. No sooner had he got up to see what had happened to the horsemen and the cloaked figures, than the scene before him melted way and a strong wind blew once more against him.

'Not again!' muttered Enrico, fearing what may happen next.

Enrico stayed face down in the mud until the wind was gone. He then opened his eyes and looked up. The dark woods of the Common had returned to their bleak winter look. It was evening once again, and the rain was falling heavily. Enrico felt cold and confused, unable to say where he truly was. The Italian baker squinted in the dark and realised he was in the same clearing as before, although it looked different. There were fewer oak trees and the undergrowth had almost thinned out. In the middle of the clearing the strange pile of blue-tinted rocks had been replaced by an abandoned well. Caesar's Well. The same well he had been looking for with Viviane just moments ago. Enrico had lost the notion of time; he could not tell how long he had been in the fog. Somehow, though, he seemed to be in a familiar present. He looked more closely around him; he could not see either the horsemen or the cloaked figures. He moved his eyes, slowly getting used to the dark. When he tried to stand up, he realised he could barely walk. It was as if his muscles had hardened and were painful to move. He stumbled and decided to prop himself up against one of the oak trees. He then noticed a black-cloaked figure sitting on the edge of the well, hands on his knees, and he too appeared tired and out of breath.

Lord Awlthorp knew Enrico was behind him. The sudden jump in time had come unexpectedly. Operator One must have turned off the Repeater earlier than expected. He was now back to present Wimbledon, and he knew it would have taken Enrico back too. Lord Awlthorp looked at the ivory dagger in his hand. He could not believe his eyes; he had finally made it. His plan had worked, and he had managed to retrieve the relic from the exact point in time, right before the enemies of the Wynnman had buried it forever. His next move was to escape but first he had to get rid of the stupid baker. He still could not grasp how he had managed to find out about his plan and even survive the fog. He knew too much.

The man in black stood up. His knees were still trembling after the jump in and out of the portal. He had not even considered the sheer effort it would have taken for him to endure the jump. He stepped away from the well as he felt his energy completely draining away. He stumbled forward, unable to walk in a straight line. His eyes fell on Enrico who, like him, could barely stand and walk. They looked at each other in a standstill, breathing heavily.

'You are still here!' protested Lord Awlthorp. 'How did you manage to survive the fog?'

'A little nourishment from a healthy nettle and mint soup. You should know that!' replied Enrico.

'How you know this recipe, is beyond me.' Lord Awlthorp sneered. 'Your persistence is remarkable, Mr LoTrova! Full of surprises!'

'I would say the same thing about you, Mr…'

'If you think I'd give away my identity, you are deluded. That includes your hope to catch me and get out of here alive!'

'Really?' grinned Enrico. 'What makes you so sure?'

'Me!' said someone else.

Reginald growled and jumped at Enrico before he even saw him. His big hands grabbed him by the throat and pulled him up off the ground. The Italian baker struggled to breathe.

'I told you, crazy baker, it was time to say goodbye!' threatened Reginald, tightening his grip.

Enrico looked at Reginald's angry eyes. His whole face had red scratch marks from Viviane's attack. He wondered where Viviane could be and feared the worst. Enrico then looked at Lord Awlthorp. He felt the world slipping away and the dark evening became even darker.

'You...can't...' tried Enrico desperately to speak.

'This is the last time we cross paths, Mr LoTrova.' warned Lord Awlthorp. 'All the relics of the Wynnman shall be mine, but I guess you won't be around to see that.'

'Wh...y?' spluttered Enrico, realising it may be the last word he would say

'You wouldn't understand. As I said, you are not a Wimbledonian. This village has become blind to what it could be. It is time to bring back the power it holds within and restore its glory!'

Enrico failed to understand his words. He tried to wriggle out of Reginald's grasp. Lord Awlthorp grinned. He stood up now that he had regained his strength. He dusted his cloak and adjusted his hood. He then raised Caesar's Dagger and carefully took aim at Enrico as he walked closer.

'It will be my pleasure to kill you!' he said.

'Finish him!' boasted Reginald.

'My pleasure!' said Lord Awlthorp.

Enrico tried to fight back, but no matter how much he kicked, Reginald would not let go. Lord Awlthorp was about to get away, and Enrico knew there and then he had failed.

'Not so quick, you brute!'

Viviane's voice rang in Enrico's ears. The sweet sound of her voice was followed by a gunshot. Lord Awlthorp gasped and bent forward, taking a few steps back. He grabbed his hand in pain and the dagger fell somewhere in the mud. Another gunshot echoed and Reginald released his grip before realising what was happening. Enrico fell to the floor, gasping for air. Reginald cursed in pain and looked at his leg.

'You shot me, you stupid woman!'

He turned around. Viviane had Reginald's own gun pointed back at him.

'Missing something?' she threatened showing it to him. 'Don't move an inch!'

'Or what? Are you going to shoot me?' chuckled Reginald.

Viviane's hands trembled. She knew she had been lucky with the gun so far, shooting at close range to disarm the man in black and then shooting Reginald in the leg. Reginald now hobbled quickly towards her. Viviane focused on him and took aim ready for another shot. Reginald ducked and grabbed her arm before she could even touch the trigger. She felt his strong grip on her, as if he was about to snap her arm in two. Viviane pushed back, trying not to lose hold of the gun. Reginald's face was just an inch from her.

'You will die too. Both of you!'

Enrico jumped back up onto his feet, his head slightly spinning but glad to breathe again. He quickly grabbed the first stone he could find and slammed it on the back of Reginald's neck. The burly man grunted in pain. Enrico hit him again and again. Reginald pushed him back. He then pulled Viviane towards him, still holding her hand, and spun around to face the Italian baker. Reginald now held Viviane in front of him, holding her arm straight at Enrico.

'Ah! I guess she will do the killing for me!'

Viviane felt Reginald's hand forcing her to take aim and press the trigger. Enrico stared at her with the bloodied stone in his hand. He had no chance of escaping the bullet. Viviane thought quickly. There was only one way to fight back Reginald's strength, and so she kicked him in the groin. Reginald immediately loosened his grip on Viviane, and she dropped the gun. Enrico saw his opportunity and rushed forward to grab it. The burly man pushed Viviane away to the ground, but he was too late. Enrico already had his gun pointed at him.

'Don't move!' he shouted.

'You don't have the guts, baker!' Reginald shouted.

He leaped at him, and Enrico pulled the trigger without thinking. The burly man's angry face turned to shock. A large blood stain started to appear on his chest. Reginald put his hand to it and fell on his knees. He struggled to breathe and knew suddenly his heart was about to stop, shot directly through it. He looked up at Enrico, who stared back at him in dismay at what he had done. He had just killed a man. Reginald stared at Enrico briefly. He did not have time to find the words. His dream of getting away once and for all, finishing the job and escaping Lord Awlthorp's madness, ended on that dark evening as his body slumped on the floor. Dead.

'Enrico!' cried out Viviane, rushing to him.

The Italian baker was still in shock looking down at Reginald's lifeless body.

'A... are you… are you okay?' he stuttered.

'Yes. You?'

'I… I didn't mean to…'

'Don't worry! He was about to kill us both!'

Viviane hugged Enrico and gently lowered his arm, letting the gun slip away into the muddy ground. She could feel his heart beating faster, almost as loud as the rain falling all over the Common. Enrico's body stiffened and then relaxed in Viviane's embrace. He took deep breaths and looked down. A few inches away, something shone in the mud. Enrico thought it was a shimmer of light in the puddles of muddy water. On a closer look, he noticed it was something else. He released himself from Viviane and knelt to take a closer look. Viviane followed his actions, puzzled. Enrico grabbed what was shining. It was the ivory dagger.

'Caesar's dagger…' muttered Enrico.

'Oh my God! We've found it!'

'We have…'

Enrico was incredulous. Viviane was seeing what he was seeing. The relic was real and now in his hands after falling out of Lord Awlthorp's injured hand. Yet, strangely enough, it was the least of Enrico's concerns. He was more confused as to how the man in black had managed to lay his hands on it in the first place. He wondered whether he and the man in black had truly gone to the past and back to the present with a thousand-year-old dagger, even though he could hardly explain to anyone what exactly had happened moments before. A wave of questions flooded his mind. Questions that needed answering.

'Where is he?' Viviane said.

'Who?' asked Enrico.

'The man in black….'

They turned around. Lord Awlthorp was gone.

Quentin was running like a madman. He was out of breath, but he had to run. There was no other choice. He was now on the long stretch of grassy meadows heading north towards the windmill. From where he was, he could see the tall structure. The top of it and the metal sails had vanished above the cluster of low clouds churning on top of the windmill, and the lightning kept lashing to the ground nearby, leaving streaks of burnt grass. To Quentin's left, at the edge of the woods, the strange, unreal fog he had seen many times before was rising above the western side of the Common. This time it appeared to be more of a giant cloud, bulging outward and lit by flashes of light from deep inside it. Quentin glimpsed at the weird phenomenon. He could not believe his eyes at what was happening. He had to run and stop the windmill somehow. If Enrico was right, the machine at the New Wimbledon Windmill was the power source to shut down immediately. Without it, none of this could work.

The ex-guardian of the windmill had to reach the vent. He looked across the patches of burnt grass. The lightning had no intention of relenting and had already set one of the small cottages ablaze. Quentin felt he had to save the windmill before it was too late. He plucked up his courage, and covering his face with his arms, he ran towards the small cluster of white cottages. He could hear the bolts of lightning above him, louder than before. Fire and smoke were starting to spread all around the base of the windmill. He had to be quick in finding the vent before it was too late. He finally reached it. However, the climb to the top was easier said than done. His whole body trembled as he squeezed inside the narrow vent. The twisted metal inside the windmill whined as if to shout back at him. It felt it took forever to reach the top. He smashed the grate with his fist.

Inside the top floor of the windmill, a ghastly scene awaited him. The Oscillator was buzzing out of control, and parts of the old wood windmill preserved from after the restoration were already on fire in multiple places. Quentin had to make sense of it all. Dials and charts spiked second after second, already beyond the safety limits, giving the machine a life of its own. Quentin looked everywhere. No switch to press. No mains plug to pull. Outside, lightning and thunder became louder and louder as the fog and the clouds expanded across the Common. Quentin realised the only way to end this nightmare was to break the machine into pieces. It was the only way. To hell with Alberyx Enterprises, he thought. The emergency cabinet was where he remembered it, behind one of the supporting pillars. He reached for it, trying not to trip over the wires, and grabbed the fire extinguisher inside. It was heavy enough to cause damage as a weapon. Quentin hoped he would have sufficient strength to lift it up. As he dragged himself in front of the Oscillator, the whole windmill shook once more. Outside, the ominous skies were dark and impenetrable, more than he had ever seen in

Wimbledon. Across the dark treetops of the Common, in a south-westerly direction, the mass of fog had spread far above the trees, getting bigger and bigger, as if it had a life of its own. Quentin knew it was roughly at the height of Caesar's Well. Whatever Enrico and Viviane were up to, he feared they might have failed to stop the evil plan. By now, he had a firm grip on the fire extinguisher, ready to lift it and lunge forward with one decisive hit. The Oscillator was beeping like mad, processing data non-stop. The electrical noise was random but gradually it appeared to emit the sounds in harmony, as if speaking a secret tongue Quentin could not comprehend. He squinted, trying to shake the thought from his head, but the beeps kept coming to his ears as words. Words that became more and more intelligible as the power of the Oscillator intensified. Something other than electricity was channelled through the wires to create sounds and words so that Quentin could listen to them.

Power and revenge, they seemed to call out.

The machine rattled and vibrated, shaking as if it were alive. No, it can't be, thought Quentin. An invisible force then pulled him towards the machine and the fire extinguisher almost fell out of his hands. The sensation scared him. He squinted again hoping this scary illusion would go away. He tried to pull himself away from the Oscillator. The invisible force though was not relenting. Quentin felt he was about to lose his grip on the extinguisher and even lose his balance altogether. The Oscillator, or whatever lived inside it, wanted to bring him to it and electrocute him. Frightened, Quentin had to act fast. He lifted the fire extinguisher with both hands as if he were holding a cleaver. The force pulled him closer, sliding him across the floor. It took all of Quentin's strength to raise it high enough and charge the Oscillator with one downward swing against the console. The first hit smashed buttons and dials. Quentin felt the force releasing its grip on him. He took the opportunity to try raising the fire extinguisher once more and smash the metal case, exposing wires and circuit boards. At the third hit, the Oscillator had already lost most of its functions. The room went silent. The Oscillator died out and only the fire crackling around him could be heard. Quentin looked out of the window. The lightning outside had stopped. The fog now turned into a docile mist hovering in the distance. The rain was left to pour over the shaken treetops of Wimbledon Common. Quentin hoped it would tame the flames still ravaging inside and outside the windmill. Then the windmill started shaking again. Floorboards cracked open and pipes burst while the Oscillator started to spit fumes and fires. A red light turned itself on above the Oscillator, followed by a high-pitched siren wailing the emergency alarm. Quentin knew it was not a good sign. He had to run before the whole of the New Wimbledon Windmill blew up.

Simon Deeley had waited all afternoon and deep into the evening for Dr Watkins to turn up. In the end, he never showed up at the Old Rectory. He checked his watch, and it was past eight p.m. He knew the curator would not be coming at such a late hour now, and he would not bother calling him for the umpteenth time. The curator had been helpful for months, but lately he had become a little unreliable and evasive. It was not the first time. Simon knew from the start Dr Watkins would struggle at some point to handle everything on his own, especially at his age, and it seems this week out of all weeks had become the living proof. He needed to have a serious word with him and suggest bringing in someone to help. Someone reliable at any time of day, always present, always committed. Starting from his keenness to dig under Caesar's Camp. Up to now, he had faced up to a wishy-washy attitude by Wimbledon with nobody eager to rock the boat too much, preferring to pass the decision-making over to someone else. Dr Watkins, Lord Cotton, the WPCC. Simon understood he would have to turn to Alberyx Enterprises to put forward a business case for the next phase in the archaeological expedition he wished to take on here at Wimbledon. All the corners of the Pool of Elixir under the Old Rectory had been searched thoroughly and they all pointed at other locations across the hill.

He yawned under the dim glow of the lights in the basement. He had finished cataloguing a few items and managed to send his update to the British Museum after the great success at Eagle House. There was keen interest in the findings, minus the folklore spin he had added to the tale. Seven relics. Simon chuckled. Ever since he had heard that baker mentioning a lava rock and some crimson liquid, his mind had been wandering off the straight path of rational archaeology and wondered if the legend was true. The historical importance would be a phenomenal success for his career and for the British Museum. Seven relics hidden under Wimbledon, he thought, imagining the news headlines. In your dreams, he thought to himself. It was getting late and time to go home. He ran a last check on the data logs. He still had not figured out the time gaps and the last time they happened Dr Watkins's trance had freaked him out. They had spent too much time down here. If he could start to dig Caesar's Camp, at least it would be in the open air.

A creaking noise distracted his thoughts. Simon looked up. The basement was silent. He listened for noises upstairs. Nothing. Simon knew everyone had left apart from the guard at the entrance to the Old Rectory. He carried on checking the data logs and then proceeded to turn off the lights across the site. The creaking noise echoed again, startling Simon. He was not sure where it was coming from. He walked into the chamber and around the stone pool. All the fixtures were in place; nothing was loose. He was about to check the basement when something hard hit him unconscious at the base of his neck.

Simon's body fell on the dusty ground instantly. Lord Awlthorp kneeled to check his heartbeat was alright. He then dragged his body to a corner of the chamber before standing in front of the Pool of Elixir once again. He was back here, back to where it had all begun. He moved to the edge of the pool and traced an imaginary line on the stone with his gloved hand. Voices started whispering in his head.

'Power and revenge' echoed one voice, dark and ominous.

Lord Awlthorp tensed and felt pain in his gloved hand. He knew, as he had experienced many times before, the spirit of the Wynnman announced his arrival through the scarred burns on his hand. This time, though, the pain was stronger.

'Did you retrieve it?' said the spirit, with its voice ringing louder in Lord Awlthorp's mind.

'The ivory dagger? Yes…'

'But you don't have it!' boomed the spirit of the Wynnman

'It is safe. It won't leave Wimbledon!' reassured Lord Awlthorp, feeling judged for the first time. 'Where is the next relic?'

The voice did not speak. He looked around in the empty chamber, waiting. Then the pain in Lord Awlthorp's gloved hand increased to the point it was unbearable. He screamed and dropped to his knees by the pool.

'You are not worthy of the rite of passage if you don't bring the first three relics together…' whispered the spirit of the Wynnman.

'I don't understand!' protested Lord Awlthorp, holding his gloved hand in search for relief.

Hail and fire flashed before his eyes as he tried to contain the agony. He did not understand what was happening. The Wynnman's presence had become stronger. He could feel it.

'I did what you asked…' spat Lord Awlthorp through the stinging pain. 'What else do I need to do to reclaim your power… to unleash your revenge on what was done to you and Wimbledon?'

'You are close… But only the three relics combined will point you to the next relic…'

'Can't you just tell me?' said the man in black in desperation, forgetting any form of reverence.

The voice did not answer back. Instead, the pain in Lord Awlthorp's hand intensified. The lights started to flicker. All the equipment in the basement started to go berserk, bleeping and flashing. The eagle-like statue by the pool had started to glow with a shiny silvery light running across its surface and highlighting the runic symbols carved on it. The air around quickly electrified, and Lord Awlthorp's hair stood on end. In front of him, a ghostly figure appeared in a cloak and hood, concealing the face. It crackled in mid-air, cast by the silver sparks of light emitted from the eagle-like statue. The image was fuzzy, but Lord Awlthorp could not mistake the silver spectre rising before him. It was the image of the sorcerer he had just met through the time portal. The spirit of the Wynnman was showing himself to him in the present time. It had one arm stretched out towards Lord Awlthorp, and from under the wide sleeve, a hand emerged tarnished by severe burns and damaged veins exposed to the elements.

'Your scarred hand keeps us connected, as you live what I experienced. I was burnt alive and quartered across seven relics, imprisoned by those who did not understand my power and knowledge. Now, I can feel my strength coming back but I will need the fourth relic to receive the breath of life…'

'Where is it?' sobbed Lord Awlthorp.

The pain was testing beyond his limits.

'I don't know where the relics are… I cannot see them… They keep me prisoner…'

'Where is the fourth relic?' spat Lord Awlthorp, feeling betrayed.

'Bring the three relics together… and they'll show the way…'

The silver spectre of the Wynnman lost its glow and started to thin out. Lord Awlthorp could see through it, and knew it would be gone soon, before his questions could be answered.

'How do I bring them together?' shouted back Lord Awlthorp. 'What does that mean?'

'…they'll show the way…' echoed the voice, becoming more and more distant.

The eagle-like statue by the Pool of Elixir stopped glowing and the image of the Wynnman quickly faded, as if losing strength. Lord Awlthorp lay by the pool on his knees, his chin on his chest. His hand no longer hurt. He checked and no blood trickled this time. No clue had been given. No formula or instructions. With the windmill on fire and the Oscillator probably in ruins, he did not know what he was meant to do next. He wanted to think he had won but realised the ambitious road he had taken was longer than expected.

'I'm not giving up. I will have my power and you will have your revenge!' spoke up Lord Awlthorp, talking to the empty chamber.'

He would not give up. Not now. He knew where to find the three relics, and he would find a way to bring them together.

A noise distracted Lord Awlthorp's thoughts. He glanced at Simon Deeley. The archaeologist lay still on the ground, still unconscious. The noise were steps coming from the basement. Someone was coming.

Enrico and Viviane emerged from the woods and onto the car park only to witness an infernal display. The New Wimbledon Windmill was surrounded by high flames reaching up to the lower sails. The fire had almost devoured everything around it and still burnt intensely.

The Italian baker glanced across the desolate car park. A figure had rushed across it, away from the windmill, and was now kneeling on the ground. Enrico ran towards it, thinking it was the man in black. He and Viviane had raced from Caesar's Well in the only direction they thought he could have escaped.

'Quentin!' cried out Viviane before Enrico had recognised the tall man.

Quentin was coughing and spluttering while the florist helped him to his feet.

'What happened?' she asked.

Quentin had still problems breathing. He pointed his thumb at the blazing fire. There was a mixed feeling of achievement and sadness on his face. Seeing Enrico and Viviane alive meant whatever he had done must have been something useful. However, he could not hide the fact he had destroyed the windmill. For the umpteenth time in Wimbledon history, the windmill would collapse again.

'I think I stopped that stupid machine.' said Quentin. 'What happened back there, in the woods?' he asked.

'We stopped them but...' explained Enrico.

He struggled to explain what he had witnessed in the last hour. He tried to remember what he saw back in the fog. The horsemen, the cloaked man, the ivory dagger. The same ivory dagger was in his hands after the event at Caesar's Well. It was real. Enrico had not yet come to terms with the fact he may have gone through a portal, but he did not have to think twice to guess that the dagger was the missing relic everyone was looking for. The third relic of the Wynnman was in his hands. The relic existed, he thought to himself. The legend may be real.

'I mean, Reginald's dead but his accomplice ran away.' Enrico added, trying to stick to a simpler story. 'We managed though to get what they were after.'

Enrico showed the dagger to Quentin. He then looked at the windmill. The view of the top and the upper sails were hidden behind a pillar of black smoke. It was not long before they heard sirens wail from Parkside down the road leading to the windmill.

'The fire brigade and the police.' noted Viviane. 'What are we going to tell Baynard?'

'We'll tell him exactly what happened back there. We survived the fog and found the dagger before it was stolen. Right?'

Enrico and Viviane nodded at each other complicitly. He noticed she did not seem troubled after coming out of the fog unscathed this time round.

She probably did not witness anything strange. The Italian baker suddenly felt alone with his secret. He wondered if his experience had been real. The horsemen, the cloaked men. It felt real. The blue sky, the neighing from the horses. It was a vivid image he could describe in detail and yet he dreaded the moment he would have to explain things to Baynard, who had trusted him for once, or to Julian, whose trust had shattered in an instant.

'I guess we didn't catch him.' added Viviane. 'Reginald's accomplice.'

'The police will.' said Enrico.

'Do you think he will come back for it? The ivory dagger, I mean?'

Enrico did not have time to reply. The police cars arrived, and he could see Baynard's inquisitive stare before he even jumped out of the car. While the firemen started setting up a parameter in order to tame the half-collapsing windmill, Baynard rushed towards them with Sergeant Jeremy and two other policemen.

'Lartova! Don't move!' Baynard shouted motioning two of his men to apprehend him.

'LoTrova!' sighed Enrico, rolling his eyes.

He did not have strength to fight back and he did not wish to run away either. He had nothing to hide. He let the two policemen grab him.

'What are you doing?' protested Viviane. 'The man you are looking for is back there.'

'What man?' exclaimed Baynard.

'Reginald Bosham…' replied Viviane, handing the gun to them.

She held it from the tip of the barrel, tainted by what she had done.

'Dead, I am afraid.' she added. 'You'll find him near Caesar's Well.'

Baynard looked doubtful. He quickly ordered another group of policemen to go and check the area. He then scanned the expressions of the three suspects before him, seeking an explanation.

'Someone owes me an explanation here.' he said looking at everyone in the eye.

Enrico knew that question was for him alone to answer. Both he and Baynard knew. However, he had tread on his toes when going about explaining the events of the last hour.

'We followed Reginald Bosham and another man up to Caesar's Well.' said Enrico.

'What other man?' asked Baynard.

'I don't know. We could not recognise him. He had his face covered, wearing a dark cloak.'

'Then what happened?'

'Reginald Bosham attacked us.' added Viviane. 'Before we knew it, the other man had run away.'

'Did you shoot Reginald?' asked Baynard hinting at the gun.

'I did… It was in self-defence!'

Baynard cast a stern look at the florist. He was not pleased to hear his priority suspect was dead. He then looked up at the blazing fire.

'Did you do this?' he asked, implying it was Enrico's or Viviane's doing.

'I did.' replied Quentin raising his hand as he was being checked by a paramedic.

'Ah, Mr Plainstraw! I guess that will not go down well with Alberyx Enterprises.' said Baynard with sarcasm. 'I think you three have a lot to explain, apart from making me wonder if I did the right thing in breaking Alberyx Enterprises's security protocol at Warren Farms.'

'Inspector, you need to believe me.' jumped in Enrico. 'Reginald and this other man have been up to something and…'

Baynard held his hand up.

'No need to explain, Lorrova. Leave that for your statement.'

'LoTrova!' corrected Enrico.

The inspector cleared his voice, taking a good look around him as if expecting something or someone.

'Release him!' he then ordered his men, to Enrico's surprise. 'He's not a suspect. I will take them to the station. In the meantime, please go and join the search party. I want Reginald Bosham's body and I want you to sweep the entire Wimbledon Common. We may have another man on the loose.'

He waited for his men to leave until there was only Inspector Baynard and Sergeant Jeremy.

'You didn't hear this from me but…' carried on Baynard, choosing his words carefully. '…we found another witness that confirms Reginald's involvement and corroborate what you said. A woman by the name of Ramona Halywell was found chained to the Repeater against her will. We also found Lord Cotton with his little dog chained to a pipe in the basement of his own club!'

'What?' gasped Enrico.

'Is he alright?' asked Viviane worried.

'He is. They both are. My men are escorting Miss Halywell and Lord Cotton to the station. Mr Bosham has been pretty busy since he was bailed out. We still don't know by who. He's been involved in fraud, kidnapping, extorsion and stealing. He's your inside man at Alberyx Enterprises. I am pretty damn sure!'

Enrico and Viviane were surprised to hear that. He had known about Reginald's involvement, but he struggled to believe he was the mastermind. This is not what he saw when he spied on him in the underground basement of Warren Farms.

'Surely, he could not manage something like this alone.' commented the Italian baker.

'Of course not. Basil Elders helped him stage the whole attack tonight on Warren Farms. He helped Reginald Bosham create the confusion he needed to act in secret. After all, Mr Bosham could not show his face in broad daylight without raising suspicions.'

'Does this mean we're off the hook?'

'I wouldn't be so fast, Mr Letreva.'

'LoTrova!'

'Your way of doing things is not of my liking. It never was! This time, surprisingly, it came to my favour, and I have what I need to hopefully close the case. But I have to warn you. Others may not be as lenient about your behaviour, to put it mildly.'

Baynard's words came as a warning, one that Enrico did not grasp at first. The inspector was hinting at something and before Enrico realised it another swarm of cars had driven into the car park, just beyond the parameter set by the police. Julian Alberon and Mr Sanders were the first to come out of the newly arrived convoy. Their angry faces did not wish well for Enrico, Viviane and Quentin. Julian's in particular was one of dismay as he glared at his New Windmill now beyond recognition if not for its wood and metal frame still standing as it burnt in the night.

'This man!' he started shouting pointing at Enrico from across the car park. 'Inspector, now that you are here, I want this man arrested! And I also want Mr Plainstraw in custody!'

Enrico could not believe his ears. He did not know what was more shocking, either the fact he was being accused of something or how Julian would not even address him by name.

'On what grounds, Sir Alberon?' chuckled Baynard. 'We are in the middle of something here.'

'He's a threat!' spat Julian.

'Hold on…' replied Enrico.

'Inspector, let's be clear!' stepped in Mr Sanders, not letting Enrico voice his opinion. 'Mr LoTrova has breached Alberyx Enterprises security on many occasions. He trespassed the compound, he colluded with Mr Elders, he even shared confidential information with the press if you check the latest news trending on social media…should I go on? As for Mr Plainstraw, he has just destroyed a million-pound project. Look at the state of the New Wimbledon Windmill!'

'It was about to cause more damage than we ever imagined!' replied Quentin defending his position. 'I had to stop it!'

He did not see eye to eye with Alberyx Enterprises, he never had and Enrico for once understood how Quentin had felt when he had been thrown onto the car park by the company. He looked at Viviane. She too was unimpressed with how Julian had just barged in. The disapproving look on his face was miles away from the friendly face they remembered.

'I am afraid the evidence does not point in that direction.' replied Enrico.

'It's your fault! Admit it!' Julian snarled through gritting teeth. 'Look at what you did!'

'What? My fault?' pointing his finger at his own chest in disbelief. 'I tried to save your project!'

Emotions were flying high. Viviane put a hand on Enrico's shoulder to hold back his temper. She was not sure if anyone would do the same for Julian. He was now pointing fingers.

'You were involved in everything that happened. You sought Mr Plainstraw's help. You chatted with Mr Elders and even Mr Glenn from the Wimbledon Gazette. We even found CCTV at Eagle House that you had been eavesdropping on my private conversation with Mr Sanders here.'

Enrico blinked. Everything he had done to protect Wimbledon was turning against him.

'Everything points to you, Mr LoTrova! Don't tell me you are not behind any of this?'

'That is the stupidest idea!' criticised Enrico.

Enrico could not believe his ears. Of all people, he would have expected Baynard to come up with a similar accusation. Instead, it came from Julian.

'You wanted to bring me down, Enrico? You and all the others. Well, I guess it didn't work!'

'Julian… I swear…' stammered Enrico.

'Okay! That is enough!' stepped in Baynard.

He moved in between the two with the help of Sergeant Jeremy.

'Mr Sanders, I would like to remind you we are now on my turf, under Wimbledon Police's authority.' added the inspector. 'You will have to raise this through the civil courts if you want to bring charges to Mr LoTrova here…'

Sergeant Jeremy's radio crackled, interrupting Baynard.

'Inspector! Sergeant! Come in.' called out a policeman on the radio.

'This is Sergeant Jeremy. Over.' replied the sergeant.

'We have reports of a break-in at the Old Rectory.'

'What?' exclaimed Julian.

'Any damage? Any casualties?' continued Jeremy following protocol.

'We have found two civilians.'

'What about the security staff from Alberyx Enterprises?'

'They were called off the premises to join the charge on Warren Farms, apparently.'

'This is ridiculous!' complained Mr Sanders as the news flooded in. 'I don't recall this specific order being part of our lockdown protocol.'

'Who are the two civilians?' jumped in Baynard.

The inspector had become used to surprises blindsiding him at every corner. Waiting for the reply, he was ready to take on anything at this stage. His gaze moved between Sir Alberon and Enrico, wary of their emotions.

'Dr Watkins and Simon Deeley.' confirmed the policeman over the radio. 'They are not harmed but we are assessing the situation.'

'Ok. We will come as soon as we can.' confirmed Sergeant Jeremy.

'Dr Watkins!' exclaimed Viviane.

She exchanged looks with Enrico and Quentin. Hearing about their friend the curator just now deeply worried them. Enrico wondered where he had been all this time when he was counting on his support to meet Julian. If he had been there, he would have perhaps been able to avoid this whole misunderstanding. The radio went quiet and the tension among the group did not relent.

'Do you have anything to do with this?' Julian asked Enrico with an accusatory note.

'*Ancora?* Again? I told you I know nothing about it!'

'I think the courts will be the judge of that!' pressed on Mr Sanders. 'We will find out if you had anything to do with Reginald Bosham!'

'Shut up…'

'Enough!' interrupted Baynard. 'I'd prefer it if this conversation could be carried on elsewhere. You are standing in a crime scene and Wimbledon Police would like to focus on their efforts on ensuring everyone's safety. Now please.'

'Over there, in a glory blaze of fire, is one of our most ambitious projects, Inspector Baynard.' added Mr Sanders. 'Alberyx Enterprises will not stand on the side while this….'

The corporate lawyer was interrupted by Julian, who had put a hand on his shoulder. There was a strange, composed calm in his unexpected gesture.

'Don't bother!' snapped Julian.

'What?' said Mr Sanders, taken aback by Julian's statement. 'Are you sure, Sir Alberon?'

The businessman was not listening to him. His angry eyes had become cold, indifferent, and showed a determination Enrico and Viviane had not seen before.

'I don't know what you have been up to,' added Julian, oblivious of Mr Sanders's advice. 'but we will find out. Until then, it is better if our paths don't cross for a while. You will be hearing from us at Alberyx Enterprises.'

Julian turned to walk away in the rain, giving a cold shoulder to the group. Enrico and Viviane watched him go, almost feeling pity for him. The Italian baker reached out and placed a hand on his shoulder in sign of peace and friendship. Julian shook it off to Enrico's surprise. One of the bodyguards grabbed Enrico and pushed him away.

'Let's take some distances, Mr LoTrova! Shall we?' he snarled once more, half-turning his head to him.

Julian's use of Enrico's surname took everyone by surprise. Viviane glanced at Enrico worried. She found Julian's harsh words hard to digest.

'Sir Alberon...' interjected Viviane hoping to salvage what was a sudden strain in their relationship with one of their key benefactors.

Julian gazed at Viviane from the corner of his eyes. The florist briefly saw the hurt in his eyes. It was a flash before his whole expression hardened, not letting her in. He looked appalled, sickened. He did not say anything and walked away, leaving her and Enrico high and dry.

'*Come si permette?* How dare he?' he cursed through clenched teeth. 'After all we've done...?'

'Don't worry, Enrico! He's an arrogant businessman!' commented Quentin once Mr Sanders had left too to join Julian Alberon in his car.

'I... I just don't... understand how...' mumbled Enrico.

Enrico was lost for words. He could not believe what he had heard. A hint of sadness and a hurt pride hit him at once when Julian gave Enrico one more look of disapproval before he disappeared inside his car.

Viviane put her arm around Enrico. She felt his stiff body not responding to her comforting touch. He had his fists clenched and he frowned at the cars from Alberyx Enterprises, expecting Julian to turn back to apologise. Viviane sensed Enrico's rage brewing. It was the same rage she had felt when Enrico wished he had chased the man in black in the woods. It was the first time, and she knew Enrico was as hurt as Julian. Viviane pulled him closer to her to distract him.

'Come on, Enrico.' she said with her calm, soothing voice. 'He didn't mean it. It's been a tiring day for all of us. We need to take a break and think things over!'

'Miss Leighwood is right. I would go and add that you'd better be careful whose paths you cross, Mr Lerteva.' Baynard advised. 'You don't want your career to suddenly take an unsavoury turn. Take my advice and stick to baking!'

Enrico snorted at Baynard's comments. He broke away from Viviane and rushed past the inspector and the sergeant, walking towards the police cars.

'Sergeant Jeremy!' said the inspector. 'Please take them to Wimbledon Police Station and get their statements. I will stay here to complete the search and ensure the fire is extinguished. Hopefully, we can put tonight's events behind us soon enough!'

Viviane thanked Baynard in a soft voice and rushed to catch up with Enrico. Quentin dragged his feet behind them, with his safety blanket around him, still staring at the burning windmill. The rain had calmed down the fires and helped the fire brigade salvage what was left. He walked slowly past Baynard, walking behind the others. His phone then vibrated. He was surprised it was still in one piece after what he had been through. To his surprise, it flashed Reverend Green's name.

'Hello?' he answered, puzzled.

'Don't say anything and listen.'

Quentin froze.

'Yes?' said Quentin.

'It's about Dr Watkins. It's happening again.'

Quentin was quick in recognising the reverend's concerned voice. Last time he heard it, was many years ago.

Reverend Green hesitated at the top of the basement stairs. The pitch dark made his blood curdle. He walked down the narrow steps into the dark. He called out for Dr Watkins, then Simon Deeley. No response. He was sure the curator had come this way. He had waited for hours outside the museum until Dr Watkins finally came out late into the evening. He had then followed him there to the Old Rectory where strangely enough the security guards had been called away by Alberyx Enterprises. It did not sound right. Nothing sounded right. The curator's erratic and evasive behaviour only fuelled the suspicions the reverend had been having for a while.

Reverend Green was not surprised to find himself back at the Old Rectory. Following Dr Watkins could only lead back to this gruesome place where he knew the curator had spent most of his time recently, together with that archaeologist from the British Museum. The reverend had not liked it one single bit, especially since he knew what had happened to a younger Dr Watkins when he got lost in the tunnels decades ago. Working here, underground, was not a safe place. It was a dark reminder of the curator's past. Reverend Green knew old wounds would come back to haunt Dr Watkins's frail mind, and his recent accident at the Old Rectory had been the trigger. He knew something odd had been going on with Dr Watkins since then. Reverend Green had tried to warn Enrico at the time of the Old Rectory accident and even at Eagle House, but the Italian baker seemed to have taken the problem lightly. Reconsidering, he himself could have been a better friend to the curator and bring the matter into the open. Instead, he had kept quiet while he witnessed Dr Watkins struggling with his sleep more and more, always forgetful about what he had been doing. Reverend Green hoped he was not too late to save his friend's sanity. He did not want to believe his friend was losing his mind. Still, there had to be a reason why after such a long time, Dr Watkins's insomnia and visions had come back.

He reached the bottom of the stairs and the dim light of a desk lamp showed him the way to the end of the basement. Things had been left behind, scattered on the desk and crates, including Simon's laptop. Yet, no sign of the curator or the archaeologist. He lurked forward and peered inside the small chamber. The lights were on. He immediately spotted Simon's body in a corner. He went to check his heartbeat. Someone had knocked him unconscious. He looked around the place in panic. There was nobody else except Dr Watkins. He too was lying on the floor, close to the stone pool. Reverend Green found it disconcerting and rushed to him expecting the worse. He had been knocked unconscious as well. He was alive but his pulse was weak. The reverend had no idea what was going on.

He then noticed a rucksack half-open next to Dr Watkins. It was empty. He looked up and checked the pool in the hope something else may shed some light. At the edge of it, there were two items. One was a lava rock shaped as a black azalea and the other was a small golden urn filled with dregs of a foul-smelling liquid. The reverend had seen them before. Recently, as images in Simon Deeley's presentation, but he remembered the labels on the empty glass cabinets in the Wimbledon Museum. All this time, Dr Watkins had fooled everyone in saying these two items had been lent out to museums around the UK. The seemingly white lie worried him now more than ever. Clearly, Dr Watkins was up to something, and Reverend Green had an idea of what it may be.

Dr Watkins stirred, and Reverend Green turn to help his friend stand up.

'Are you alright, Dr Watkins?'

'What…? What happened? Where am I?'

Dr Watkins gazed around, not remembering how he got there. Last thing he remembered was the Wimbledon Museum.

'What am I doing here?' he repeated, upset he could not answer for himself.

'Are you ok? Can you stand up?' asked Reverend Green.

'Yes! Yes!'

He leaned on the edge of the pool.

'What are you doing here?' questioned Dr Watkins. 'What am I doing here?'

'I would like to ask the same question. What is this?'

Reverend Green pointed at the rucksack and the two relics.

'I… I…' frowned Dr Watkins. 'I don't remember… Why are the relics here?'

Reverend Green frowned at him. That was the cue Dr Watkins was not being himself, as if he were under the effect of something dangerous.

'You don't remember coming down here?'

'No… but…'

Dr Watkins looked over Reverend Green's shoulder. Seeing Simon on the floor shocked him.

'What happened?' cried out the curator, glaring at the reverend.

'He's fine. Did you do that to him?'

'What? Are you crazy?'

'What were you doing here?'

'I... I...'

Dr Watkins traced his steps. He struggled to remember beyond the moment he said goodbye to Simon and Reverend Green at the museum. That was after lunchtime. He had no recollection of what had happened since then.

'I don't remember...'

Dr Watkins was at a loss. His hands trembled. The reverend could see he was panicking.

'What did you come here for?'

'I don't remember! Why are you questioning me like this?'

'Does it have to do with these?'

Reverend Green pointed at the black azalea and the small golden urn and tried to force him to remember.

'You have been telling everyone you lent these to museums around the UK.'

'But... that's what happened...' replied Dr Watkins doubtful.

He felt he was spilling words he did not believe himself. Words that did not belong to him.

'It doesn't look like that to me!' objected Reverend Green, determined to help Dr Watkins face the facts. 'I remember seeing these in Simon's presentation. These are the relics, aren't they? The relics of the Wynnman!'

Dr Watkins froze. A deep howling echoed inside his head. A distant chilling cry as if something had instantly died. He took a deep sigh. These were the relics he had to salvage and save from the mysterious man Enrico warned him about.

'Dr Watkins!'

The curator shook and opened his eyes.

'Yes?'

'Are you with me?' asked the reverend. 'You just drifted off mumbling something…'

'No… no…' denied the curator.

'You haven't stopped looking, have you?'

'Pardon?'

'The legend of the Wynnman. After so many years, denying it as a fairy tale, but you actually never gave up the search, did you?'

Dr Watkins babbled on, unsure whether he had to explain himself or give an answer. Reverend Green's words disturbed him, turning his memory into a broken puzzle where he no longer knew who he really was.

'I never believed the legend of the Wynnman was real until now… with Simon's research...'

'You always believed the legend.'

'What are you saying? That I don't remember what I believe or don't believe?'

'Remember when you went into the tunnels under Saint Mary's Church for the first time?'

'A few months ago?'

'No, Dr Watkins. I am talking about the 1984 speleological expedition.'

'I never went… I was not fit for it, remember?'

'That is what we told you. You actually did go, and we lost you in the tunnels for more than twenty-four hours. We found you unconscious and took you out just in time.'

'What?... I don't remember… I mean, what does this have to do with anything?'

'Why do you think you wanted to explore the tunnels in the first place?'

Dr Watkins chuckled.

'I am a historian, reverend. And Wimbledon's history is everything to me. How could I let the opportunity pass?'

Reverend Green sighed and sat next to the curator.

'You were looking for the relics, Dr Watkins.' he admitted to him, hoping it would help his friend remember. 'The Wynnman was your obsession. It always has been. Since we were kids, you've believed it was real. When the opportunity came to explore the tunnels under Saint Mary's, you were first to volunteer despite your lack of experience.'

'It can't… No… It can't be…' objected Dr Watkins, refusing to accept what the reverend was saying.

'You went inside the tunnels because you hoped to find something about the Wynnman.' carried on the reverend, relentless. 'We never found out if you did. When we took you out of the tunnels safe and sound, you couldn't remember anything, not even going inside in the first place. We thought the worst and preferred to make you believe you never visited the tunnels. Everything changed with the accident here at the Old Rectory a few months ago…'

'What changed?'

'I realised that your obsession really never went away. You insisted again on going inside the tunnels to prove the legend of the Wynnman is real. And because of that, you involved anyone who could help you, just to make a point.'

'How could you say that? We did find something. These relics here… they are the proof!'

'You almost burnt alive here in this very chamber! And now, what on earth were you planning to do?'

Reverend Green hinted at Dr Watkins's gloved hand and then the relics and Simon's unconscious body. The curator looked at Simon and could not even remember what had happened to him, but he feared the reverend was accusing him of it.

'I didn't do anything, I swear.' pleaded Dr Watkins. 'Enrico and I were trying to find out who was looking for the relics…'

Reverend Green burst out laughing.

'Your obsession has to stop, Dr Watkins! Nobody is looking for the Wynnman but you. How long are you going to continue doing this? At what cost? Your health? You don't even remember how you got here!'

Dr Watkins toyed with the black azalea in his hand and put it back. He counted the many times he had felt sleepy and tired, unable to distinguish what was a dream and what was reality. All those nightmarish visions he had about the tunnels resurfaced and took a different meaning. He remembered Hilary Wilson, from Cannizaro House, and how she had written in her diary how the black azalea had influenced her dreams. She was right, and now Dr Watkins feared something bad may have happened and could not even remember it even if he wanted to.

'Tell me!' added Reverend Green. 'Is it worth losing your mind to find a long-forgotten sorcerer?'

'What should I do then?'

'Give it all up! Just leave these relics for Simon to look after.'

'I can't… You're asking too much!'

Reverend Green stood up and went to check Simon. He then stood up and took out his phone, looking for reception.

'What are you doing?' asked Dr Watkins, alarmed.

'I am calling the police.'

'What? You're not going to tell them I did this!'

'Whatever happened here is none of my business or anyone's. You said someone is looking for the relics? Well, they attacked you and Simon, and tried to steal them all. But they failed!'

Reverend Green picked up the rucksack and put the two relics inside. He knew everything had started with the lava rock from the moment Dr Watkins had looked after it. Reverend Green knew the curator would not stop. Acting as an old friend, he had to get rid of the relics somehow and make Dr Watkins give up his obsession. He dropped the rucksack near Simon's legs.

'What's going to happen next?'

'We go back to our normal lives. Back to jolly, good old Wimbledon. These two relics are now a matter for Simon and the British Museum to sort out.'

'What about everything that has been happening on the Common?'

Reverend Green left Dr Watkins's questions unanswered, quick to leave everything behind and expecting the curator to do the same. He placed the call with the police and then took a final look at the curator. Dr Watkins was still shocked by what Reverend Green had been telling him. It made him look back at everything that had happened and for the first time he feared he had been the root cause of everything, making Enrico and Viviane see the Wynnman everywhere, dragging Julian Alberon and his company down a wild-goose chase, blaming criminals like Reginald Bosham and the Claymores as treasure hunters looking for Wimbledon treasure. None of it was real; he wanted to see what his eyes wanted to see. The Wynnman.

'I'm going upstairs to wait for the police.' said Reverend Green. 'You may want to try and wake up Simon, check he's okay.'

'What should I tell him?' asked Dr Watkins.

'Tell him the truth.' teased the reverend. 'You don't remember a thing. It seems you were knocked on the head too!'

'What if he remembers what happened?'

'Then I can only pray for you, Dr Watkins.'

The reverend left without saying anything else. Dr Watkins heard his footsteps going up, and he suddenly felt lost in the small chamber. Everything around him looked unreal, as if he had just woken up from a very long dream. He walked towards Simon and knelt by him. Before waking him up, he took one last glance at the rucksack. The question remained. He could not remember what had happened in the last few hours of his life. He wondered what had happened to Enrico, and Viviane and

Quentin. For a moment, he was sorry for letting them down. Then, all he could think of was if the Italian baker had found any clue hinting at the third relic. Somehow, it was hard to let go.

Outside, the cool air hit Reverend Green's face. The storm had faded, and a gentle drizzle pricked at him in the driveway of the Old Rectory. He knew he had done the right thing. He had helped his old friend, covering whatever he had been up to. He should have done it years ago and the reverend felt the burden of his guilt had finally gone, knowing he had helped Dr Watkins face his obsession. Hopefully, it would be the last time he would hear about the Wynnman.

He checked his phone. Neither Lord Cotton nor Quentin had called back after he had left a few voicemails. He tried Quentin's number again. He had to let him know at least to substantiate the story he and Dr Watkins were about to tell the police.

'Hello?' Quentin answered, puzzled.

The ex-guardian of the windmill sounded out of breath over the phone. There was some noise in the background.

'Don't say anything and listen.' said Reverend Green.

'Yes?' said Quentin.

'It's about Dr Watkins. It's happening again.'

The circus of journalists and bloggers who had invaded Wimbledon for the New Wimbledon Windmill, decided to stay in the village for another two weeks to talk about the scariest explosion ever witnessed in London in recent years. Every media or freelance reporter who had come to witness the launch of wireless electricity, instead spent their time covering how the New Wimbledon Windmill had suddenly become a danger to the community by exploding in a huge blaze. The lightning and the flames were visible from as far as Central London, and it did attract a new wave of curious onlookers brought by the sudden nation-wide media attention. The windmill's mishaps turned out to be the latest sensation as many Londoners from all over the capital made the journey to see the 'windmill that blew up' as the headlines stated. Alberyx Enterprises and its PR machine fought hard to keep their inadequacies under wraps, but it was hard to contain the damage. Despite the big local tech company being the first to issue a statement before anyone had the time to speculate, it was not easy to hide the great fire that had engulfed the new windmill for hours and reduced it to a rubble of ruins. Wimbledon Village became the centre of attention all of a sudden. Pubs, shops and restaurants, were now busier than ever, serving the avid travellers who wanted to hear all about it, from the strange electrical storm and the poisonous fog to the attack on Warren Farms and the hostility between Basil 'Wilberforce' Elders and Alberyx Enterprises.

Enrico waited nervously outside the Fox and Grapes. He glanced at his watch. He was already late for the big lunch Lord Cotton had organised. Waiting a few more minutes would not harm anyone. The Italian baker held a copy of the Wimbledon Gazette in his hands. The headline screamed at him the same thing they had been shouting again and again for two weeks. Industrial sabotage, poor safety controls, bad business. Each time he picked up a copy he hoped the news reported something different, something closer to his version of the story. Yet, the same conclusions by Wimbledon Police dominated the news and by now they had convinced Wimbledonians and Londoners that Reginald Bosham had been the mastermind behind an operation aimed at undermining Alberyx Enterprises and drive down its shares. All the evidence and the clues they could find led to him, how he had planned from the start to provoke Alberyx Enterprises by tampering with the windmill and the Repeater to cause harm to local citizens. Enrico found it hard to believe. He looked up from the newspaper and stared down Camp Road. He recalled his hit-and-run attempt. Reginald apparently had been behind it all. Yet, Enrico was convinced the man in black was the actual mastermind behind the whole affair, just by the way he talked and acted around Reginald. Inspector Baynard had listened unconvinced and searched the Common for a few days, looking for a man in a cloak. Enrico and Viviane's very basic description was not much to go on, and the man in black was nowhere to be found. Within a week, Wimbledon Police was forced to give up the search when it was obvious Reginald Bosham and Basil Elders were the men to be held accountable.

The Italian baker sighed. Images from that rainy night by Caesar's Well daunted him. Viviane had only seen fog while he had witnessed something else he could not describe. He asked himself more than once whether he had really jumped back in time to Wimbledon to a different era. This is what the man in black had boasted over and over, and Enrico had ended up believing it was possible. Now, he was questioning the whole thing, and again he felt alone, unwilling to share the story with those around him for fear of mockery. Perhaps Viviane was right. He had to put a break on his imagination and go back to why he was here in Wimbledon in the first place. To make bread and make a name for himself.

'Hey Enrico!' called out Viviane from the pub's entrance. 'What are you doing out there? Come on, time to celebrate!'

Enrico smiled weakly and pretended he had just arrived, walking briskly across the street.

'Sorry, I'm late.'

'It's alright. We were just having a few drinks while looking at the menu. Dr Watkins and Lord Cotton are starving, by the way, but I kept them at bay. Are you ok?'

'Yes, yes!' repeated Enrico as if to agree to anything just avoid the question.

She saw the newspaper in his hand and gave Enrico a sympathetic look.

'Stop reading that stuff!' she said. 'Smile! Time to celebrate!'

Inside the Fox and Grapes, the warm, cosy air and the scent from the kitchen invited Enrico in with a comforting embrace, teasing his hunger. Dr

Watkins and Lord Cotton's faces lit up upon seeing him. Even Little Caesar's pulled his head up from Lord Cotton's lap to greet him. They were sitting at Lord Cotton's usual table the same table where a few weeks' back he had announced his business proposal to Enrico.

'Here's the famous baker!' cried out Lord Cotton with high-spiritedness.

A few heads in the Fox and Grapes turned upon hearing him and were quick to recognise the Italian baker who had saved the day. Someone clapped in the corner cheering him on. Enrico nodded shyly and sat down, putting the newspaper on the table. Dr Watkins looked at him pleased. He smiled with renewed joviality and Enrico noticed again how he looked more relaxed than he did a few weeks before. It was as if a burden had been lifted. To his side, Lord Cotton appeared in good health once again now that colour had returned to his cheeks. Being held prisoner in the basement had been a shocking experience; he and Ramona had spent the last few weeks giving the police everything they needed to solve the case.

'You two are all in a jolly good mood!' commented Enrico as he ordered a pint of beer.

'You're the hero!' teased Dr Watkins.

'Thanks to you, Enrico, we brought those responsible to justice.' added Lord Cotton. 'You've saved Wimbledon!'

'Have I?'

'Stop being modest!' cheered him on Viviane, raising her glass to him.

Enrico grinned. He found it hard to recognise the sudden admiration from fellow Wimbledonians. His name had not escaped the media frenzy. His name, his bakery, were now part of the stories circulating around the windmill.

'I can't think of a better person to be our supplier of bread and pastry, Enrico.' carried on Lord Cotton. 'I know it was a given, but with everything that has happened, I wanted to at least make the deal official and celebrate!'

He slipped a folded piece of paper to him across the table. Enrico looked at it, puzzled.

'That is a lot of bread!' exclaimed Enrico reading it.

'Wow! You will definitely need to hire staff now!' joked Viviane, leaning against him to read what was written.

The paper was the contract Enrico had been promised. The Wynnman bakery was now the official bread and pastry supplier for all the golf clubs in Wimbledon plus a few other golf clubs in London where Lord Cotton had good connections. Enrico was astonished to read how much Lord Cotton was willing to pay and for how much bread. He was suddenly overwhelmed by the positivity around him and the promise of something good laid out before him. The worries about the man in black had stayed outside the pub, drying up in the cold winter weather, and Enrico was relieved to think they may no longer torment him. The Italian baker realised this was a big step forward.

'I don't know what to say…' mumbled Enrico.

'Well, you can start by being proud of what you've achieved.' congratulated Dr Watkins. 'You've managed to settle in and now you are going to have a pretty robust business. Everyone at the WAIS was thrilled when I told them.'

The curator patted Enrico's shoulder.

'I agree.' joined in Lord Cotton caressing Little Caesar on his lap. 'I recognise good talent when I see it. Don't we Little Caesar?'

The dog raised his head, enjoying Lord Cotton's scratching under the muzzle. His satisfied look could only mean Little Caesar agreed.

'*Grazie! Grazie!*' repeated Enrico. 'Thanks for the encouragement. And thank you Lord Cotton for arranging this!'

'Don't mention it!'

'I noticed Ramona did not join us.' noted Enrico. 'I hope she is ok with this.

The Italian baker remembered Ramona's unexpected hostility. He hoped he did not have to face that again anytime soon.

'Oh, haven't you heard?' said Lord Cotton. 'She left the golf club recently. For good. The experience must have left her a little shaken. The news reported she had been attacked by Reginald Bosham at the Repeater.'

'Where is she now?' asked Enrico.

'Still working at Alberyx Enterprises, I believe. Something about a promotion, I think. We lost a good employee. Oh well, good for her!'

'I still don't understand how she could still work for Alberyx Enterprises, with everything that happened.' noted Viviane.

Lord Cotton shrugged.

'I heard she too is a bit of a local celebrity now.' added Dr Watkins. 'Especially after the role she played to frame that crook, Bosham. If it wasn't for her testimony, and yours Lord Cotton, we couldn't have pinned him for any of the sabotage plans.'

'A horrible man!' said Lord Cotton in disgust. 'Thinking of what he did to me and Little Caesar. I still can't think how he managed to orchestrate everything under our nose. He was foolish enough to talk to me while I was blindfolded, and when the police played an audio recording of his voice, I could recognise that smug voice many times over.'

Little Caesar growled as if to second his master's words.

'He even had you and Simon Deeley caught in his evil plan, didn't he? He knocked you both out. For what? What were his real intentions at the Old Rectory and at the windmill? I am still baffled!'

The Italian baker caught a glimpse of Dr Watkins's expression, half-concealed behind the napkin he dabbed his mouth with. The curator grimaced and massaged his head where he had been knocked unconscious, to remind everyone of how he and Simon had been attacked in the Pool of Elixir.

'Well, we think Reginald Bosham may have been after the Wynnman relics.' explained the curator. 'He was a saboteur and a relic thief. Enrico and I had suspicions someone was after these relics, but I never thought it would be him. It makes sense now; he is the one constant throughout everything that happened in Wimbledon in the past year. Glad we snatched the ivory dagger off his grabbing hands! Again, thanks to you Enrico!'

Dr Watkins searched Enrico's gaze to acknowledge him. His cheerful expression was full of praise and acknowledgement for the Italian baker. Enrico found the curator's rekindled vitality a form of reassurance that he was perhaps sleeping more and better than before.

'Marvellous!' exclaimed Lord Cotton. 'I am amazed by its discovery. What's it called again?'

'Caesar's Dagger.' replied Dr Watkins.

'Of course, nothing to do with Julius Caesar.' winked Enrico. 'Right, Dr Watkins?'

The curator smiled. Little Caesar barked in agreement.

'See Little Caesar?' chuckled Lord Cotton staring into the dog's eyes looking up at his master. 'Everything has been named after you!'

There was a round of laughs at the table.

'Where's the dagger now?' asked Viviane.

'The discovery of Caesar's dagger is an outstanding addition to our latest Anglo-Saxon findings.' carried on Dr Watkins. 'After the Wimbledon Police checked for fingerprints in vain, they handed it back to me and I decided to hand it over to Simon and the British Museum together with the black azalea and the crimson liquid. They will help us determine how old they are, and if they are what we think they are.'

'What do you make of them, though?' probed Enrico. 'Do you believe they are linked to the legend of the Wynnman, and the seven relics Simon bragged about at the presentation?'

'I don't know, Enrico. Maybe we will never know. They are important for their historical value, that's for sure. Whether of Anglo-Saxon origin or perhaps something older, Simon Deeley and the people at the British Museum will have their say now. This is too much for me and my small museum to deal with, but I made myself available as a consultant.'

'That is a sound decision, Dr Watkins!' approved Viviane.

'Time for you to get some deserved rest.' said Enrico raising his glass. 'To your health! I am sure Simon will tap into your knowledge if he needs to.'

'Is Simon Deeley still going ahead with the excavations?' asked Lord Cotton, worried. 'I heard he's been trying to make a case to dig on my golf course, near Caesar's Camp.'

'I tried to delay things, but he is pushing forward with it.' sighed Dr Watkins. 'He raised the matter with the Council and Alberyx Enterprises the other day.' shrugged Dr Watkins. 'I guess we'll have to wait and see, hoping it does not cause another Basil Elders to come out and protest!'

'Basil Elders!' said Enrico with scorn. 'What a character!'

'Well, he's been sent to jail waiting for the sentence so hopefully we won't be hearing from him for a while.' replied Viviane.

'How about Nathan Glenn?' added Enrico bitterly. 'I was not pleased with his article!'

'Hey, today is about celebrations Enrico!' reminded Viviane.

'Don't you think he should pay for what he did too?'

'I think he's been fired from the Wimbledon Gazette and last thing I heard Alberyx Enterprises is suing him for libel. I think he got what he deserved. Anyway, didn't he take the article off the site, saying he didn't write it?'

'Well, someone still believes he did, and that I was on Basil Elders's side all along…'

Everyone at the table knew who Enrico was referring to. Julian had been absent from their lives for days. They had seen him only on rare occasions, at the few PR conferences where he apologised for what had happened and promised something better for Wimbledon. They were not sure whether he was avoiding them, or he was naturally busy with the aftermath of what had happened to his beloved, highly technological windmill.

Their lunch plates were served, and the odd silence was broken by the sound of plates, cutlery, and chatter. The tone of conversation became more casual and the four at the table carried on talking about more mundane things, and sometimes talking about the future.

'Despite all that happened, I have never seen Wimbledon so busy.' continued Lord Cotton. 'This can only mean good for business!'

'I have a feeling it will only get busier.' chipped in Dr Watkins. More archaeologists and historians and journalists and tourists are coming to Wimbledon Village.'

'You'd better get ready with those bread orders, Enrico!' teased Viviane. Viviane gave Enrico a warm, supportive smile. The Italian baker knew what she was getting at with her playful attitude. She kept reminding him how important his bakery was, and Enrico realised for the first time where his focus should be. He had spent too much time brooding about what had happened in the last nine months since he arrived in Wimbledon. He was seeing conspiracy and ghosts everywhere. He now needed to stop and pay attention to the opportunity Lord Cotton had given him. He smiled back at Viviane. His eyes then landed briefly on the newspaper Enrico had put on the table when he came in. The headlines still screamed at him. He turned it over face down in the hope it would not spoil his lunch and so the rest of the day.

Baynard sat in his car with Sergeant Jeremy on the corner between Wimbledon High Street and Belvedere Grove. He had the Wimbledon Gazette open on the main article of the day. Another article on the same subject he had tried to put away for days now. The headlines kept throwing questions about the future of Julian Alberon and Alberyx Enterprises, and the safety of Wimbledon from exploiting criminals like Reginald Bosham. He knew the case was closed and the Chief Superintendent had been satisfied with the swift conclusion. Still, the traumatic effects of that week still lingered on in the press as well as in people's minds. Baynard blamed it on the gossipy bloggers and sensational journalists flooding Wimbledon constantly, asking questions already answered or posing new ones Wimbledonians preferred to avoid in case it would open a new Pandora's Box.

'You are overthinking again, aren't you?' commented Sergeant Jeremy, adjusting his tie in the rear-view mirror and unable to ignore the inspector's inquisitive stare at the street outside.

Baynard let out a grunt, unclear if he meant yes or no.

'I see the news still bother you.' added the sergeant.

'It's not so much the news.' explained Baynard. 'It's like a strange wind has started blowing over Wimbledon, and I have a feeling this town is changing.'

'What do you mean?' grinned Jeremy in an attempt to hide his perplexity at Baynard's sudden deep questioning.

'We had Eric Quercer coming here trying to blow up the Duchess Hotel. Then we had the two fraudsters playing with dangerous chemicals. And now we've had a full-scale sabotage at Wimbledon's number one corporation. Who's going to be next?'

'Maybe that is the end of the road. What makes you think there is more to come?'

'It's a hunch. Wimbledon has become busier, more popular. New visitors will come our way. Just think of the publicity around Alberyx Enterprises, the windmill, and even these archaeological excavations the British Museum has started…'

'What are you trying to say, inspector?'

'I am just thinking out loud. This last case was quite a messy one, and it is a shame Reginald Bosham died before I could ask him all the questions I wanted.'

'But we found good evidence leading to him. I mean, we did find Reginald's fingerprints all over the Warren Farms compound. Isn't that enough?'

'Yeah, probably.'

Baynard watched a mother and baby cross the road in front of them. Then a teenager swung by on his skateboard, hopping from the pavement to the tarmac. He jumped into the roundabout traffic without looking and a few horns blared after him. Baynard did not flinch, lost in his thoughts. For him, scenes like this reminded him of the peaceful rhythm of Wimbledon High Street he feared to lose.

'There are many points in the case I deliberately ignore to stay sane.' said Baynard. 'Like, who was the mysterious friend texting me where to find a clue like the USB flash drive? If it weren't for that, we would still be here scratching our heads.'

'Someone out there knew something and wanted to tip you off…'

'…or pull the strings of the game. Same goes with the old blood from forensics, or the ancient wounds of that boy Ken. What on earth was that?'

'Why are you telling me this? You know, when we stormed the underground basement under Warren Farms, it was clear Reginald Bosham had managed to break in undetected. He had been taking advantage of the latest scientific technology from Alberyx Enterprises. You know the company covers all kinds of stuff. Quantum lasers, heavy machinery, cybernetic prosthetics. They even make synthetic blood and consumer goods like perfumes. It was all part of a trick to make Alberyx Enterprises look like the evil company, using Ken as proof of the physical harm. Think about the tear gas bombs as well. It was Reginald who supplied them to Basil Elders, simply by taking them from Alberyx Enterprises. We had his fingerprints all over the armoury, for heavens' sake!'

'I read the report, Jeremy. No need to repeat it to me!'

'Just trying to reassure you. We got our man! Good ol' Wimbledon is going back to the way it was.'

'I doubt…'

Baynard glanced across the street. The Wynnman bakery stood where it had always been. The shop was still closed, and the inspector was eagerly awaiting the arrival of the Italian baker, praised by many and hated by some.

He sat on the fence on this occasion, not wishing to take sides. He had other plans in mind.

'Have you ever wondered, Jeremy, how things all started?'

'What do you mean exactly?'

'The first case. Eric Quercer and the Duchess Hotel. That was only nine or so months ago and since then we've been busier and busier with the most shocking cases.'

'I don't see a pattern…'

'Well, I do. It all started when that crazy Italian baker came to Wimbledon…'

'Don't be serious, inspector!' sniggered the sergeant. 'You can't say Enrico LoTrova was behind all this. He's regarded as the hero who saved Wimbledon.'

'I don't know. Something about him puzzles me. Who is he? Why did he come here?'

Baynard remembered the Chief Superintendent's words upon finding that Enrico LoTrova's name had popped up again during the investigation. He was not pleased but refrained from placing charges considering Baynard has closed the case, he had preferred a quieter resolution. It had crossed Baynard's mind to consider the Italian baker as a suspect but preferred not to since all the evidence pointed elsewhere. As days went by, he had become obsessed about who the baker was and where he was from. Too many things had happened since his arrival in Wimbledon.

'Is that why we are here, inspector? So, we keep tabs on Enrico LoTrova's movements?'

'Relax. It is nothing like that. I need to ask him something. There he is! With his friends.'

Enrico was strolling down the high street with Viviane and Dr Watkins. They all appeared to be happy and carefree, already oblivious of the dark past events. The way back from the Fox and Grapes had been a pleasant walk-through Wimbledon Village, passing by known places where Enrico could now say he shared memories of with Viviane and Dr Watkins. They walked across the desolate stretch of Rushmere Green, they passed in front of the Rose and Crown and then Eagle House, they stopped by the northern roundabout to take a good look at the Dog and Fox. Enrico had his copy of the Wimbledon Gazette under his arm and not even once did he dare look at it again. Yet, he could not part from it, as if an indelible stain on his clean white chef's jacket. He thought it was all over until they reached the bakery. Baynard's inquisitive stare met his gaze from across the street.

'Is that Baynard?' commented Viviane, looking up. 'What is he doing here?'

'I don't know… I'll be with you in a minute.'

Enrico crossed the street to join the inspector. There had always been an uneasy feeling between the two, and even this time their paths had crossed in the most unusual way.

'Afternoon, inspector. Were you looking for me?'

'Afternoon, Mr Litriva. As a matter of fact, I was.'

'LoTrova!' corrected Enrico. 'And what did I do wrong this time? Or are you here to buy some bread?'

Enrico was conscious Baynard would not just turn up for pleasantries. He searched his inquisitive stare in vain.

'I see you still read the news.' noted Baynard nodding at the newspapers under his arm.

'I am old-fashioned since I am a little technophobic about reading news on a phone. And yes, I keep myself updated on how things are progressing. You know, with the case.'

'The case is closed, Mr Latreva.'

'LoTrova! I know… Then what brings you here?'

'I am here to give you some advice or maybe a warning.'

Enrico swallowed hard.

'What do you mean?'

'It seems you are the man of the hour. I heard people mentioning you when they talk about the accident at the windmill. I shouldn't forget Quentin Plainstraw. He had his share of fame for destroying the windmill, but that's not my point.'

'What is your point?'

'I have seen what happened with Sir Julian Alberon. Not sure what terms you are still are on but...'

'We aren't!'

'Then I advise you Mr Lorrova...'

'LoTrova!'

'...to be careful who you plan to rub the wrong way. I told you already, in all honesty, I dislike you putting your nose in matters that don't concern you. Others may not be that lenient.'

Enrico understood the reference to Alberyx Enterprises. He found it strange that, out of all the people in Wimbledon, Inspector Baynard was the one coming here to tell him to be careful. He was not sure whether the inspector, with his icy stare, was here just because he had to or because he genuinely cares. Baynard was hard to read.

'Why are you telling me this, inspector?'

'I am just curious to know what is pushing you to carry on the way you do.'

'There is nothing odd in what I do...'

'You've been here...how long?... Nine months?'

'A little bit more than that.'

'A lot has happened since you arrived in Wimbledon.'

Enrico blinked.

'What are you implying?'

'I am just saying, it is an odd coincidence Wimbledon has become such a circus since your arrival. You keep finding out things before anyone does, seeing people where nobody else does...'

'I did see a man in a black cloak with Reginald Bosham. I did not invent that! And it was not just me who saw him. My friend Viviane…'

'I re-read your statement many times. Maybe you're right. Perhaps this man was just an accomplice who got away. Anyway, the case is closed: we found who was responsible for it and you're off the hook. Again.'

'You say that as if you're disappointed…'

Baynard snickered.

'I just would like to know what brought you to England.'

'I came here to work, inspector. That is my bakery, if you haven't noticed.'

Enrico pointed over his shoulder with his thumb. He was not sure what Baynard was getting at.

'I have. I hope you'll focus more on baking from now on. Unless you have other reasons for being here…'

'I don't know what you're getting at, inspector, but I think we'll end the conversation here.'

'Before you go and knead some bread, Mr Liriva…'

'LoTrova! LoTrova!' insisted Enrico, bothered by Baynard's assuming attitude.

'…you may want to know we only found two sets of fingerprints in the underground basement underneath Warren Farms. Yours and Mr Bosham's. Apparently, Mr Bosham had infiltrated the compound through the basement and ran his whole dirty operation from there.'

'Why are you telling me that?'

'Alberyx Enterprises has voiced concerns about you, Mr Lereva.'

'LoTrova!'

'Wimbledon Police has put you down as a person of interest. I'm here to warn you to watch your steps.'

'Whose side you're on though?'

Baynard gave an enigmatic smile.

'No-one's. Have a good day!'

And he left to return to his car. Enrico stood in the middle of the pavement, thinking over Baynard's words. A warning, or a threat, or a friend's advice. Baynard was indeed hard to read. The inspector had not thanked him or accused him for his role in the investigation. There was a constant aura of doubt around him. It appeared Baynard did not accept some of the truths that had emerged from the case.

The Italian baker watched the police car drive off and returned to the Wynnman bakery. He opened the door to find Viviane and Dr Watkins sitting at one of the tables. Enrico kept the sign 'closed' facing outside. He was still not ready to resume work. Soon, Lord Cotton's requests for batches of bread would start coming in. His dreams of fame and fortune would finally become true, but he had to put recent events to rest. Forget about Reginald and the man in black. If only he could.

'I heard John Crane and Fran Ludley got engaged.' Viviane said out loud, scrolling on her phone.

'Lovely news for once!' commented the curator, pleased.

'Are you in touch?' asked Enrico moving about the bakery, tidying up things around just for the sake of it.

'Just a few messages.' replied Viviane. 'They moved back to Norfolk. Apparently, John resigned from his position.'

'Oh dear!' commented Dr Watkins. 'I guess he wasn't happy after what happened to him. Does he remember at all in the end?'

'Not entirely.' replied Viviane. 'The doctors confirmed some minor damage from the hallucinations. However, he's fine now. They all are. John, Richard, Ken, they are all back to normal and fully recovered. This is what counts.'

'Dreadful experience!' added the curator. 'Being hostage without even knowing who you are, where you are...'

'Well, because of that, it appears Alberyx Enterprises is abandoning the wireless electricity project for the time being.'

'What about the windmill?' gasped Dr Watkins recently. 'Every time I go for a stroll on the Common, it breaks my heart to see it in ruins again.'

'There's something about it in the paper...' Enrico mentioned absent-minded.

He threw his copy of the Wimbledon Gazette on the table where Viviane and Dr Watkins sat. He did it with disdain, disgusted by what had been written and wishing to part with it for good. Dr Watkins grabbed it, while Viviane looked up from her phone, unsettled by Enrico's moody voice.

'What did Baynard have to say?' she asked as she opened the newspaper.

'Nothing...'

'Are you sure?' insisted Viviane.

Enrico sighed, unsure whether to broach the subject again.

'Do you remember seeing the man in the dark cloak, Viviane?'

'Oh Enrico! Not again!' she said rolling her eyes. 'Yes, I did see a shadow in a dark cloak. This is what I told the police. Why are you insisting Enrico?'

'Why does everyone think I made him up?'

'Nobody thinks that. I just don't think he's the mastermind you think he is. He's just an accomplice who unfortunately got away. All that talk about superposition, or whatever, and portals back in time. All gibberish!'

'But...' hesitated Enrico.

'Seriously, Enrico, do you believe all that?'

Dr Watkins looked up from the newspaper, unable to ignore the conversation.

'You must have an opinion on the matter.' insisted Enrico before Dr Watkins could reply. 'You said it yourself: someone is looking for Anglo-Saxon relics. We've seen it already happening and it is the third time someone has come to Wimbledon to find them.'

'Indeed.' added Dr Watkins. 'And I think it is fair to say Reginald Bosham was the mastermind in all this, trying any means possible to find the relics.'

'He did not have the brains. He had help...'

'Of course, he had. This is what we are saying. Perhaps this man in black you saw is a minion of Mr Bosham's just as much as the Claymores were, and perhaps even Eric Quercer. Reginald Bosham was using them and their specialist skills to his own advantage. Basil Elders fell in the same trap.'

Enrico stuck his hands in his pockets in disagreement.

'Enrico, you said this man had the Caesar's dagger when you found him, right?' asked the curator.

'Yes.'

'And you don't know where he got it from?'

Enrico hesitated. He knew they would not believe him. Perhaps the fog had still managed to make him crazy enough to believe he had jumped back into an older time where the Wynnman lived.

'No.' he lied.

'Then leave it to Simon Deeley and his team to learn more about its origin.' reassured the curator. 'They'll be busy doing studies on the three relics for months on end. If there is more, I will probably know but until then there is no point getting upset. We have the relics: this is what counts!'

'And we're all safe!' added Viviane.

'What now then?' asked Enrico as if pleading for direction.

'Now you have a bakery to run, and I have a flower shop to attend to.'

Enrico snorted and sat down at the table. His eyes flashed in all directions. He was torn inside on whether he should share his surreal experience with his two friends. He recalled the vision he had in the pool chamber, and now sorcerers and medieval nights in the middle of a forest. He was restless and Viviane was quick to put her hand on his. Enrico felt her gentle squeeze. It was her reminder for him to keep his feet on the ground.

'Don't take it personal, Enrico.' suggested Viviane. 'I think you should drop it for now. Take your mind off it for a while.'

Enrico nodded and tried to relax.

'Oh, I found it.' exclaimed Dr Watkins, taking the opportunity to change subject as he found the article. 'Alberyx Enterprises is abandoning wireless electricity. The windmill will be restored to its former glory, exactly how it used to be.'

'Who's paying for that?' asked Enrico.

'Alberyx Enterprises, apparently.' noted Dr Watkins, paraphrasing what he was reading. 'They are covering all the costs. Julian Alberon says he owes it to Wimbledon after relationships have become strained. They are even going to re-hire Quentin as the guardian of the windmill once it is rebuilt.'

The doorbell chimed and a courier in a biker's jacket showed up at the entrance.

'Urgent letter for me Mr Lo… Lor…' he half-announced.

'Thanks! That's me.' replied Enrico snatching it from the courier's hand.

He quickly signed and dismissed the courier with a gesture. He then threw the letter on the table without opening it. Viviane recognised the company logo on the envelope. It was from the Wimbledon Courthouse.

'What is this?' she asked.

'The third time this month…' snorted Enrico, losing his cool once more.

He snatched the envelope and ripped it open, concerned. He took out a nicely printed letter and Viviane glanced at it over his shoulder. She could see Mr Sanders's and Sir Julian Alberon's signatures at the bottom of it, below the magistrate's. She skimmed through the letter, biting her lips.

'A restraint order?' she exclaimed, incredulous.

'Yes.' replied Enrico bitterly.

The Italian baker moved to the large window watching the traffic on the high street. He recalled Baynard's words. He did not have the courage to face Viviane.

'I am not allowed to get close to Julian Alberon or any of his properties within a two or three hundred metre radius.'

'What is the reason behind it?' asked Dr Watkins disturbed by the news. 'Because he thinks you are behind the attack at his company?'

Enrico shrugged. He lowered his eyes and remembered what Julian Alberon had told him in front of the burning windmill. He remembered the flickering of the flames in his disappointed eyes. The accusations played over and over in his head, and he still could not believe them.

'He no longer trusts me…' said Enrico.

'How come he sent you a third letter?' asked Viviane waving the letter at him.

'I have been trying to get in touch with Julian, to explain myself. I wanted to make him reason and tell my side of the story. I even turned up at his mansion. He was not pleased. He has not called the police yet, or sent his lawyer Mr Sanders after me, but these reminders are probably a hint he is losing his patience with me.'

'You stalked him, Enrico?' blurted out Viviane incredulous. 'Why would you do that? And why didn't you tell us?'

'Oh dear…' muttered Dr Watkins, speechless.

Enrico stayed silent. He did not know what to say. Probably he would agree with Viviane that his curiosity had turned into an obsession, and he had unexpectedly pushed people to the edge.

'This is what I was talking about, Enrico.' reminded Viviane, her voice tired. 'You need to let it go and think about your bakery. You don't want to have Alberyx Enterprises against you.'

'Why? Because the company funds everything we do in Wimbledon Village? How can you defend him after the way he treated me? After the way he cheated Octagon School to steal Mr Elders's plans?'

'I'm not defending anyone, Enrico. I'm just being your friend.'

Enrico did not answer. Viviane was the one who kept saying she was his friend, as she always did when they had been through troubling times. He tried to look at her in the glass reflection, but he struggled to find her face against the cars and buses rushing by.

A knock came at the bakery door. Enrico quickly brushed his manic thoughts away and looked up. A young couple in their late twenties stood outside, marvelling at the interior with their hands cupped against the glass. Upon seeing Enrico, they smiled at him in excitement and exchanged a few words between them. Enrico did not take notice. The young couple though knocked again.

'We are closed.' said Enrico.

'I know but we've come a long way.' said the girl excited. 'Is this the Wynnman bakery?'

'Yes.' replied Enrico. 'How can I help you?'

He realised the girl in the couple held a map in her hand and a feverish smile stamped on her face.

'Bread please?'

'I said we are closed.'

'Any bread is fine!' the couple insisted.

Enrico blinked and turned to Viviane and Dr Watkins, unsure how to deal with them. The two grinned at him.

'Yes…' said the girl with the map in a whisper. 'That's him!'

Enrico heard and turned back to them.

'Oh my god!' exclaimed the boy looking at Enrico and pointing his finger at him. 'It is you. Can we take a selfie?'

The baker was speechless. Despite not being that photogenic with selfies, he really did not know what to say. Before he knew it, the girl and the boy turned their backs on him and pulled out a smartphone with the camera pointed at them. The couple kept talking to each other in between takes.

'We followed what the news said about you, and then we found out you were really a baker. We had to come and see it for ourselves!'

Enrico blinked at the strong light from the flash. He glimpsed at his half-smile in the picture they had just taken. He could not deny a visible state of confusion.

'What news?' Enrico asked.

'Don't be silly!' joked the girl, thinking Enrico was teasing her.

'You are a modest man.' said the boy. 'We heard about you, about the windmill and then about these new discoveries here in Wimbledon Village. Roman sites, Anglo-Saxon relics. How exciting!'

'Who are you?'

'Oh, we are both London bloggers, talking about everything from food and history in the capital. We could not ignore the call on this one! Who would have thought about Wimbledon?'

Enrico nodded slowly, a little scared by the couple's excitement. He turned again to Viviane and Dr Watkins who could not hide their laughs.

'Did you plan this?' asked Enrico, looking at them.

'I told you Wimbledon would become busier!' reminded the curator. 'It seems earlier than we thought…'

'Do you happen to know the best way to get to Caesar's Camp?' continued the girl relentless.

Enrico had to think twice before he could put words together again and gave somewhat clear directions.

'Thank you!' said the girl.

They squeezed closer to him and took another selfie. They then rushed off along Wimbledon High Street.

'Hey…' called out Enrico. 'What about the bread?'

Yet, the couple had already disappeared out of view.

'I was right! Wimbledon has indeed become the centre of attention!'

Dr Watkins's words echoed as he pulled the door open and slipped out.

'You don't say…' replied Enrico.

'You have become a local celebrity. Enjoy it while it lasts!'

'You are off then, I presume?'

'Yes, I need to wrap up my handover to Simon. There are a few papers still at the museum. Mind if I keep this?'

He pulled up the copy of the Wimbledon Gazette. Enrico had enough of the subject and did not have to think twice for his reply.

'Keep it! Time to bake some bread!' he replied with a hint of pride.

'Good! We'll catch up soon. You look after yourself, Enrico.'

The curator waved goodbye, and the Italian baker watched him leave. The noise of the traffic flooded the bakery before the door closed shut again, and Enrico was left alone with Viviane and the dreamy chime from the doorbell ringing in his ears.

'That wasn't so bad!' commented Viviane, looking at Enrico in the eye. 'You now have fans!'

'They write blogs about me? I mean, in a good light?'

'Oh, you probably won't see them on your Nokia 3310!' joked Viviane. 'I've seen a few mentioning you and the bakery. There is a lot of talk about Wimbledon since the big accident. The disaster seems to have renewed interest in our village. Everyone wants to come here and see the windmill, see the high street, try the bread from the Wynnman bakery. Isn't that good news?'

She winked at Enrico.

'It is good news! I just… I just didn't realise I'd become popular outside of Wimbledon. I guess you are right: I do have a bakery to run!'

Enrico smiled at Viviane, and she returned the same. He extended his hands and grabbed hers into his. He wasn't sure what to say and then preferred to let the gesture speak for himself. She was being a true friend, one to hang onto to welcome the exciting times ahead. Fame and fortune had finally knocked at his door, despite everything that had happened. He had to seize the opportunity and not let it slip away.

A red double-decker bus passed by, distracting Enrico's thought. He looked out, over Viviane's shoulder, and he thought for a while there were more people on the high street than usual. He imagined swarms of tourists taking over every inch of it. Wimbledon Village was open for business. Enrico knew Wimbledon was never going to be the same again.

Ramona Halywell contemplated the skilful work by Alberyx Enterprises labourers to remove the last falling debris from the ruins of the windmill. The whole area around had been cleared and looked much better. Bulldozers had been busy lifting heaps of twisted metal or bringing down weak walls which swayed dangerously at the lightest gust of wind. Most Wimbledonians were sad to see the windmill in ruins again. However, Ramona did not share the same emotions. She had other things to think about. After leaving the golf club and returning full-time to Alberyx Enterprises with the promise of a job promotion, she had expected someone to get in touch, especially following Reginald's untimely death. She was happy the creep was dead, paving her way to learn the secrets of the windmill. Then came Mr Basil Elders's arrest for conspiring with Reginald Bosham. Such revelations made her realise there may have been other operators, and she wondered if it was not just her seeking the attention of Reginald's secret employer.

The sudden collapse of a stack of charred bricks startled her. She looked at the worker trying to swerve the bulldozer in the right direction and pick them up. Lately, she was jumpier than she had ever been. The more time passed, the more she feared her alibi would collapse. So far, nobody had suspected her. Not Wimbledon Police. Not even Alberyx Enterprises despite her double game with Reginald. The dead man was the only link to her. Forging Julian Alberon's signatures and making a copy of the USB device had been child's play, without Reginald realising all along she had been the one placing his name and fingerprints all over the place for him to fall at the right time. Her copy of the USB had exposed the issues between Basil Elders and Alberyx Enterprises, and how the professor's theory had been used by Reginald for his planned sabotage. Ramona laughed to herself. Everyone saw sabotage where she saw a scientific revolution. Unfortunately for her, all the quantum formulas were gone forever when her original USB drive exploded at the Repeater. She had no idea though what had happened to Reginald's own USB flash drive. She thought of the dubious dark red casing of the original USB drivers. It was the only thing she had failed to make a replica of when creating the copy for Inspector Baynard to find. She had never figured out what the material was, except it gave her the chills for the simple fact its texture was unrecognisable. Ramona shook her head. The plan had gone smoothly, and the proof was her standing here, strolling on the Common as a free citizen who had helped give evidence to the police. However, an unsettling fear had settled in, and Ramona was anxious someone may turn against her and chase her down Wimbledon alleys, holding her responsible for what she did. At every corner she thought Reginald's secret employer may appear and take his revenge on her for jeopardising his plans.

'Miss Halywell?'

Ramona looked away from the windmill. Simon Deeley was standing just outside the charred remains of the low annex at the base of the windmill. He was hearing a safety helmet and a loose yellow jacket. Underneath it, his faded salmon T-shirt against his dark-skinned muscles dazzled Ramona every single time. The Scottish archaeologist had a strange, exotic flair about him, that did not communicate anything related to the stiff air of museums or dust-covered archives. She was keen to know what he expected of her as a new member of Simon's team.

'Mr Deeley!' she waved back.

'Please, call me Simon.' said the archaeologist. 'If we are going tae work together, let's leave formalities out of the way.'

'Ok, Simon.' Ramona agreed.

Her cold blue eyes shone above her broad smile. Simon could not forget her intense, stunning gaze. He found it a little distracting. Ramona's had not been his choice. Alberyx Enterprises had insisted on assigning her to him as a resource. From looking at her resume, he had to admit she had the skills he needed for the work ahead.

'I am glad ye could make it. Sorry, if we could not meet at Warren Farms or elsewhere. The British Museum partnered with Alberyx Enterprises and asked me to determine the damage to th' historical structure of the windmill.'

'Not much left from what I see.'

'The base is still there. Most of the original bricks can be salvaged and restored. I am not that confident about the wooden beams or the sails, though.'

'I believe those have been replaced already in the past.' commented Ramona, showing off the little she had started to learn about Wimbledon's history.

'That's correct. I am positive it will shine again as it once did. But let's get down tae work, shall we? I have the contract in ma car.'

'I am following you.'

Simon showed the way and Ramona followed him to the edge of the car park.

'Dae ye have any questions on the role? Alberyx Enterprises was very quick in filling the position. I must say they are glad for what ye did.'

'Oh…I just did what any honest citizen would do, Simon.' boasted Ramona. 'But I guess they think my computer programming and data analyst skills is what you are looking for.'

'For what we have in mind, aye.'

'And what would that be?'

Simon stopped by his car and paused briefly as if he had forgotten something. He turned to face Ramona. The sportive woman was leaning on the bonnet, arms crossed and her ponytail swaying gently in the soft winter breeze. She waited to hear what Simon had to say and did not hesitate to show her confidence on any occasion.

'I'm sure ye are aware of my application to dig up Caesar's Camp.' he said.

'Of course. I heard you submitted the application.'

'And it is likely tae be accepted.'

'Exciting times. What do you expect to find?'

'Hev ye ever heard about the Wynnman?'

'A little.' said Ramona after rolled her eyes upward. 'Your presentation at Eagle House was very informative. The legend was intriguing.'

'What if I told you it was not a legend?'

Ramona's brow furrowed. She focused on Simon's face, trying to read his expression. He had a knowing smile, wetting his lips from time to time to contain what could be excitement.

'Are you saying the Wynnman is buried down there?'

'Possibly. I didn't say 'at, though.'

'What are you saying then Mr Deeley?'

Simon gave Ramona a sideway glance.

'If ye are going to work with me on the new excavation site, it is important ye know where I stand.'

'I am all ears.'

'What I expect to find down there is something that will help us establish dates. Very important dates.'

Ramona thought about space and time, quantum calculation, and the formulas in her computer code flashed briefly in her mind.

'How do we plan to do that? With a spade and a scalpel?' teased Ramona.

'I am sure the partnership with Alberyx Enterprises can give us and the British Museum more than that. Their help is funding our love for history. However, we hev something of far greater importance.'

Simon said those last words with mystery. Ramona listened carefully. She had come here this morning to simply sign a contract, and it ended up with Simon sharing more than the job specifications did. He was talking about it as if he had to be sure she wanted it. She did, more than anything else. It was an opportunity to feed her ambition and move up in the ranks at Alberyx Enterprises. Lead Data Analyst for Simon Deeley's new excavation site. It rang beautifully in her ears.

'Quit stalling, Simon. What do we have?'

'The three relics.'

Ramona frowned again. She should have been shocked to hear Simon believing legends were real. Yet, her mind raced in another direction. If the relics were real, she thought, then this is what Reginald and his secret employer may have been looking for with their plan of bending time and reality. They had found this old ivory dragger, mentioned in the news, and there were more relics out there. She looked at Simon curiously. The archaeologist appeared under a strange new light. Ramona wondered if Simon knew more that he led her to believe. She dared to ask if he was Reginald's secret employer but held back from making a fool of herself.

'So, you expect there to be more relics underneath Caesar's Camp?' quizzed Ramona.

'This is the plan, Ramona. But it is important ye believe in it as much as I dae, if we are to make 'is work!'

Ramona chuckled, finding Simon's question a little childish.

'Are you in?' insisted Simon.

He was suddenly serious about it and had in his hand the contract he had just grabbed from inside the car. He held it out to Ramona. The sportive woman stopped chuckling. She stood up and adjusted the pink jacket of her tracksuit, looking at Simon in the eye. This was an opportunity she would not miss.

'I am in!' she confirmed, grabbing the contract from his hands.

'Great! You'll be hearing from me the moment the excavation is a go ahead.'

'What makes you so sure it will be accepted? You have the golf clubs, the WAIS, the Council...'

'I don't know. A gut feeling, perhaps. It is as if Wimbledon history had been ignored. We may be sitting on the biggest discovery ever!'

Ramona nodded in agreement, to show she shared Simon's vision. Her mind though kept wondering if everything she had been involved in so far, with Reginald, with Basil Elders, with the Repeater and the Oscillator, if everything were part of a bigger plan.

'Welcome to the team!' added Simon. 'We can then plan things next time we meet. Now, if ye excuse me, I hev to return to my work, and check the workers don't miss anything. Speak soon. Cheerio!'

Simon and Ramona waved each other goodbye. The archaeologist sprinted back to the windmill and disappeared among the bulldozers as quickly as when he appeared. Ramona was left alone with her thoughts. She had had the feeling someone kept pulling the strings, and had somehow managed to place her here, in this moment, ready to work on Wimbledon's next biggest archaeological project after the Old Rectory. Alone in the car park, she immediately felt exposed. The false sense of security Ramona had given herself was starting to crumble, and perhaps the plans organised by Reginald's secret employer were still in motion. She looked beyond the windmill, towards the edge of the car park where the thick of the Common stared back at her. There was nothing where she felt prying eyes observed her every move or thought.

The cold wind blew across the open car park, as if a reminder to Ramona it was time to go home. There was nothing to see here, apart from a derelict windmill unable to explain to her what may happen next. She started walking away along the exit road leading out of the Common and onto Parkside. Her mind was lost, confused. Dreams of ambition and curiosity were mixed with fear and danger. She wondered what she should do next, if she would be able to get to sleep tonight feeling safe. Walking along, she failed to notice the black saloon car driving carefully behind her. It maintained a steady speed to match hers until it caught Ramona's attention out of the corner of her eye. Ramona noticed the black car advancing menacingly and quickened her pace. There was nobody around but her and the car. The black car revved a few times to keep abreast of her. Then the tyres screeched, and the car pulled out and sped ahead and hit the brakes a few metres ahead of her. Ramona slowed down and tried to get a look at the car. Standard number plate, no signs on the back or on the sides. The rear passenger door opened wide. Nobody stepped out. The black saloon car stood still. Whoever was at the wheel, kept the engine running for her. Ramona looked at the rear passenger door. She would have expected some men in black hoods to jump out and kidnap her. Instead, plush black leather interiors seemed to invite her in, without force. Ramona thought she had better turn around, go back, but her curiosity got the worse of her as she wondered who or what may be waiting for her inside the car. She had to know. She saw a shadow in the backseat motionless, waiting. Ramona slowly approached the car like a wary cat.

'Come inside!' spoke the shadow when she was closer to the door. 'You will be in no danger!'

Ramona moved closer to the car door. She saw black boots and black trousers.

'Who are you?' she asked.

The man inside did not reply.

'I thought it was time you met Reginald's employer...' the man teased.

Ramona's body stiffened. She had never thought she would meet him like this, on an idle afternoon in the middle of a side street in Wimbledon. The rush and excitement pushed her forward. She leaned to look inside the car. Ramona looked into the man's face. She blinked. Then she was pushed into the car and the rear door slammed behind her. Ramona panicked and tried to open the car door, but it was locked. Ramona looked out of the car window as the car gained speed again. She grabbed the door handle, wrestling to open it. In vain. She turned to face her captors. The driver stood still behind the wheel, driving away to an unknown destination. She then took a better look at the figure sitting to her left. The man stared at her. He had a thin face and an aquiline nose.

'Let me out!' she protested.

The man again stayed impassive.

'Are you Reginald's employer?' she asked.

The man smirked at her and then burst out laughing. It was an eerie, forced laughter, poorly scripted. Ramona's blood curdled. She looked ahead. The driver did not turn. He stared ahead, focused on driving south towards Wimbledon.

'What is the meaning of this? Let me out!' she protested again, trying to force her passenger door open again. 'Where are you taking me?'

The man next to her had stopped laughing and was now looking ahead. Ramona looked at him more closely. She had never met him. She then gazed out of the car. They were about to turn right, driving at the edge of Rushmere Green. The two unknown individuals did not reply. She saw herself being driven through Camp Road and then the car turned right at Octagon School, finding a quiet parking space on North View Road. A few people could be seen strolling on the flat open space of the Common. Ramona looked at them. They were too far. She then looked out of her passenger window and saw the row of houses across the road, in the hope she could catch someone's attention.

'I swear I'm going to shout!' threatened Ramona.

She then raised her fist, ready to smash the car window, when the driver spoke.

'Don't leave so soon, Miss Halywell!' he said. 'Or do you prefer to be called Operator One?'

Ramona froze and lowered her fist. She then turned to the man next to her, looking at him with renewed interest as the man she had been looking for.

'Who are you?' Ramona asked him

'Oh, don't mind him!' said the driver. 'He's my driver.'

Ramona blinked, confused. The man next to her sneered. He took out his driver's cap and put it on, saying nothing. A bluff, she thought. She saw the real driver unlocking his side of the car and let himself out, exchanging places with the man behind the wheel. Ramona wavered, not sure whether to run or stay. She played with the door handle. Still, locked. She had nowhere to go, and all she could do was stay to find out who Reginald's employer was. The man who came to sit next to her was well-dressed, with a black jacket over a dark grey shirt and a black tie. His corvine hair had a thick streak of white hair above his forehead. Ramona found his face vaguely familiar and yet she could not pin him down. Her mind suddenly felt tired, sleepy, in his presence.

'I am glad to make your acquaintance, Miss Halywell.' stared the man in black. 'You need to excuse me for the arrangements, and my slightly brute force in pushing you inside the car. I had to be sure you joined us today. I am also very careful when meeting new people although we know each other somehow, through common acquaintances now unfortunately deceased. I believe you have been looking for me.'

Ramona watched the man in black closely. She could not help noticing his black gloved hands resting on his lap as he spoke. She spotted scars on the naked part of one wrist.

'My name is Lord Awlthorp.' said the man in black.

Ramona looked closely again at the man's silhouette and felt a little uneasy. She knew she had seen the face before and yet she could not connect to any image in her memory. His voice was deep and indistinct, but she was sure she had heard it before except it sounded distorted like a distant garbled memory. She did not know whether to fear the man or not. His sudden presence had made her feel weak. She wondered if she had been drugged. She touched her arms for the sting of a needle. Nothing. Everything was awkwardly normal and pleasant.

'What is the meaning of this?' protested Ramona. 'Let me go.'

Lord Awlthorp gave a malicious smile before speaking again.

'I thought you were eager to meet me, Miss Halywell? Or should I call you Ramona? Can I call you Ramona?'

Lord Awlthorp's mannerisms and the way he spoke were so calm and gentle. Ramona shrugged, hiding her unease. Deep inside, she feared the worst may about to happen, knowing what Lord Awlthorp was capable of.

'I have seen you in action, Ramona. How you flushed out Mr Bosham and played him. How you understood my game. Even the precision of your computer code. Marvellous. I know talent when I see it.'

'What do you want? Are you here to kill me?' she asked, keeping her nerves steady.

'How barbaric! What makes you think I would do something like that?' obliged Lord Awlthorp. 'I could have crushed you any time. I could have exposed your forged signature or let Alberyx Enterprises know about you sharing sensitive information with Reginald and even the police. Do you think you did all that by yourself thanks to good old luck?'

'Have you been keeping tabs on me all this time?' Ramona soldiered on.

'Yes, my dear. A little push here and there. Like I did for Mr Bosham.'

'Why?' she asked. 'I could have let the police lead to you, like I did with Reginald.'

'Impossible!' scorned Lord Awlthorp. 'You had no idea of who I was until now.'

'I could now…' insisted Ramona, forcing herself to keep the upper hand.

'You wouldn't.' cut off the man in black.

'Try me!'

'I know what you've been thinking, Ramona. Your ambition and ruthlessness speak for themselves, going to great lengths in your scheming plans. You always wanted to know what lay behind my extensive calculations and the computer programme I asked you to install on that USB flash drive. You, Ramona Halywell, were the only one able to understand it all. I realised then you could easily understand the architecture of my plans and help me accomplish them. You and I, were made for something great!'

Ramona grasped the notion she had achieved what she wanted all along. Meet and work with the genius behind the formulas. She had questions, a myriad of them she wanted to ask.

'Questions will be answered.' said Lord Awlthorp.

Ramona frowned, caught by the man in black almost reading her mind. Lord Awlthorp grinned. An enigmatic smile spread wide across his face.

'What makes you think I am interested?' retorted Ramona.

'A fiery woman, you are, Ramona.' said Lord Awlthorp gazing out of the window. 'Our paths are crossing at the right time, and I need someone special to help me accomplish the greatest plan ever in the history of Wimbledon.'

'You have an interest for the past…if I understood what you were using the Oscillator for.'

'The past. Such a passive concept. People simply accept it for what it is and look at it with nostalgia. Not you and me, Ramona. I simply wanted to peer into the past to shape the future of Wimbledon and learn about the Wynnman.'

'The Wynnman? Here's that name again, and again. Actually, just now…'

Ramona held her tongue and thought quickly, drawing her conclusions.

'Did you put me on the archaeological team for Caesar's Camp?'

'See, I recognise talent when I see one. You were stuck, Ramona. Going nowhere in your petty day-to-day job for a company like Alberyx Enterprises. You were wasted, and your talent better serves a higher purpose. Join me if you wish to fulfil your ambition.'

'Why would I do that?' she replied. 'What's in it for me?'

'There is a story of power and revenge Wimbledon books don't talk about. A story only whispered in the shadows. At the centre of this story, there are hidden treasures to discover, a source of knowledge worth millions, Ramona. Capable to change Wimbledon and the world. Capable to make you and I rich and powerful.'

'What is all this non-sense?' scoffed Ramona, incredulous to what she had just heard. 'I am not interested…'

There was a thud next to her that caught her attention. Something had fallen on the empty leather seat. Ramona looked. A small USB flash drive lay between them. She recognised the dark red casing. She thought it had been destroyed in the fire, when the windmill blew up. At a closer look, she noticed this one was different. A thin purple web of tiny threads ran across the red casing, wrapping the USB flash drive as if they were veins underneath living skin. At the impossible thought, a shiver ran down her spine.

'Where does that come from?' Ramona asked.

'The original USB prototype, Ramona. The one I gave to the late Reginald Bosham.'

Lord Awlthorp closed his eyes and breathed deeply. Ramona did not follow what he was getting at.

'You could not have used this material when you made your copy of the USB flash drive. Clever plan, I must say, but not quite. All you knew was that the dark red casing gave you the creeps, didn't it?'

'What the hell is it?' insisted Ramona.

Lord Awlthorp raised one of his gloved hands, the one showing the dark etchings of scars around the wrist. He then took off his glove and held it closely to Ramona's face. She gasped in horror. The hand was a maroon colour, covered in a dry, burnt skin and exposing a web of veins throbbing unnaturally.

'You don't see the resemblance, Ramona?' he said pointing at his hand and then the USB, 'My skin is what wrapped the USB flash drive. This is the horror I was prepared to face to find the Wynnman. The sacrifice I had to make to bring the formulas to life. Soon you will be able to make that sacrifice too...'

'What? You're insane!'

'Am I?

'Let me out!' ordered Ramona, sitting up. 'I'm not going to be part of this.'

She pushed herself against the door, but it wouldn't budge. Lord Awlthorp's pressed his hand closely to her. Ramona could see the veins and the maroon skin close now and shuddered at the thought that it was the same as the unreal dark red texture covering the USB flash drive. She felt sick.

She tried breaking down the door. It would not open. She banged at the window, and it would not break. She was trapped.

'Ramona, the future is inevitable. He spoke to me and gave me the strength to bring his plan forward…'

'Who?'

'The Wynnman… The three relics will give mind, flesh, muscles and blood back to him… I gave him my flesh and now I gave him my blood…'

Lord Awlthorp muttered those words to himself as if reciting a cursed prayer, speaking convinced of his words. Ramona glanced at him, terrified. Yet, the man in black was not in a trance or crazy-eyed. He was still calm, rational.

'You are crazy!' she shouted. 'Help! Help!'

'You need to see it for yourself…'

Lord Awlthorp took a small knife from his inside pocket and pushed the blade against the scarred skin on his hand. He pressed so hard, blood started trickling. He did not blink. He then cut sideway and quickly removed a piece of his dried, scarred flesh. Ramona turned and shrieked at the horror being committed in front of her.

'Stay away from me!' she cried.

Ramona started rattling the seat in front of her, pounding the roof above her. She tried the rear window. Nothing. Lord Awlthorp sat inert next to her, unmoved by her attempt to escape or call for help. He held the piece of cut flesh in his healthy hand, smearing his fingers with fresh blood. The driver quickly started driving away.

'The ultimate sacrifice, Ramona.' carried on Lord Awlthorp. 'Each time I spoke to the Wynnman I bled. Each time I built one of the USB drives, I knew I would have to give my real flesh and blood to thank the Wynnman for the knowledge he gave me, so that I could help him return. Only he could show such a mastery of life and science. Can't you see?'

'No. I don't want to know.'

The car sped back towards Wimbledon. She hoped passers-by could hear her cries or at least she could catch their attention if they noticed commotion inside the car. Ramona found all the strength she had and attacked Lord Awlthorp, determined to escape at all costs. She cursed her ambition, and where it had led. She lunged forward, ready to hit Lord Awlthorp in the face who kept babbling on, oblivious of her. Or at least, this is what she thought. Before she knew it, Lord Awlthorp raised his scarred hand and a strong pain hit Ramona hard. She looked at her hand and saw the bloodied knife stuck right through her open palm. She screamed with the sudden blinding pain. Then Lord Awlthorp grabbed her by the throat with sheer force, pressing against her with all his body weight. Ramona slapped him hard with her free hand. Lord Awlthorp did not flinch. He pinned her down, almost suffocating her with a force she could not reckon with. Calm and ease had been wiped from Lord Awlthorp's face, leaving a pair of evil eyes ready to swallow her into darkness. Ramona tried to fight back.

'What...are... you doing... to me?' she gasped helplessly.

'You need to see it for yourself...' he whispered to her, merciless. 'It's the only way...'

Lord Awlthorp spoke to Ramona with an eerie, cold-blooded calm, and quickly brought the piece of cut flesh to her lips. The rotting smell reached her nostrils. The smell of blood and decay pervaded. She tried to move her head to the sides. Lord Awlthorp's hand followed it and then pushed hard in her mouth, ensuring she swallowed it. Ramona tasted the awful piece of human flesh she had been just forced to digest. She coughed. Lord Awlthorp watched her and released the grip on her throat gently. Ramona thought it was the chance to counter-attack. Yet, she immediately felt drowsy. Her arms and legs did not respond and quickly became limp, powerless. To her horror, she struggled to get her words out. Her mouth had become dry, pasty. The words of help almost dribbled from her lips like a meaningless jumble of words. An unnatural fear crawled inside her, making her head dizzy. She did not understand what was happening to her. She feared she was dying, considering what she had just swallowed. Lord Awlthorp looked at her, still anxiously waiting. Ramona wanted to ask the mysterious Lord Awlthorp the meaning of all this. She was eager to hear what he had to say. He looked at her and yet she could not recall the face. Her mind had become foggy. Ramona knew she was about to lose her senses.

'What have you done to me?' stammered Ramona. 'Why I can't I...?'

'You will see, Ramona. You will see the power I promise to you. But we have time. Plenty of time to make you see my vision...'

Ramona rolled her head towards the window. She could only see the skies above and the treetops as the car drove on and she slowly drifted into a deep sleep.

She opened her eyes and the car had gone, and so the streets of Wimbledon and her assailant, Lord Awlthorp. She stood in a meadow, in her own clothes. Ramona glanced at her palm. The wound was still there but the pain had subdued. She thought she was dreaming. Her body shivered in the cold. A gentle mist caressed the meadow, lit by a grey morning light. Ramona failed to recognise where she was. A thick tree line all around the edge of the meadow blocked her view. The mist swirled with its silver mantle, guiding her gaze to a small, run-down shack. Grey smoke trails rose from it, mixing with the mist, and the charred walls indicated it had been recently burning. There was a shadow standing outside, turned away from her and facing the wooden shack. Ramona thought she could see right through it. Looking closer, she noted the shadow was not touching the grass; it was clear the shadow was not real but a ghostly apparition blending with the mist. She waited, looked around, usure what to do. The silver spectre stood still, staring at the burning shack as if in mourning.

'Hello?' said Ramona.

She walked forward. Her hand quickly sent a pang of pain and started bleeding as she moved closer to the apparition. The silver spectre then raised a hand, without turning, and showed the bare skin of its wrist. It was burnt, scarred. Ramona recalled the similarity with Lord Awlthorp's hand.

'Lord Awlthorp…?' she called out.

Nothing. Ramona's hand hurt again, but when she looked at her palm again, the wound had healed leaving no scar. She looked up, watching the silver spectre lower its hand.

'Who are you?' she mumbled.

'The Wynnman…' whispered the silver spectre.

Then a whisper echoed across the meadow, loud enough to be heard all around, as if coming from the sky above and the depths of the earth. Two words. Power and revenge.

Snap.

Something snapped at close range. Ramona opened her eyes. The foggy hill before her eyes was no longer there. The shack, the spectre, everything had disappeared as mysteriously as they had appeared. She was now standing in the dark, with a faint neon light in one corner. The place felt cold and humid. She looked around. Some sort of underground cave and a metallic table. Ramona rubbed her eyes to adjust to the lighting and in doing so she saw her hand had completely healed. No scar, no blood, no pain. She wondered if she was still dreaming or if she had woken up from a nightmare. She did not recognise where she was and in the penumbra all she could see were half-opened crates and a bunch of metal panels and wires scattered around the table. There was also someone there with her.

'You've healed.' said Lord Awlthorp, moving into the faint light cast upon the metallic table.

'You? What have you done? Where am I?'

'Does it matter? Can't you see you've healed after I stuck that knife in you?'

Ramona glanced at her hand, turning it at all angles to see if she was being tricked again, to see if this was reality.

'You stabbed me…' recalled Ramona, her voice trailing off.

There was no regret in her voice. Just visible confusion.

'It was necessary for you to understand.' explained Lord Awlthorp. 'For you to see how powerful we could be. Did you see him?'

Ramona could not play dumb. She understood Lord Awlthorp was somehow behind the dream she had just seen. Yet, any rational explanation failed to stand.

'The Wynnman…' she whispered, her voice trailing off.

'Yes, the Wynnman.' confirmed Lord Awlthorp, pleased. 'When I saw him for the first time, I had the same vision as you. He healed my burnt hand and opened my mind. This is only the beginning of what he can offer, what I promise to you.'

'What is that?' asked Ramona.

Her question felt different this time. She did not feel defiant towards Lord Awlthorp. Instead, a sudden hunger to know, to feed her greedy ambition, rose from deep insider. And it felt good, warming up her whole body and making her mind see clearly. She gazed at Lord Awlthorp intensely, feeling good about herself.

'What is that?' she asked again, breathing heavily.

'Immortality, Ramona.' replied the man in black. 'The power to move seas and mountains, and control life and death. Some special knowledge we have been chosen to discover.'

Lord Awlthorp could see her eyes shone differently. He was pleased. She had been touched by the Wynnman, just like him.

'It feels good, Lord Awlthorp.' spoke up Ramona with renewed intensity in her voice. 'I want it. I want all of it. What do you want me to do?'

'The three relics.' reminded the man in black. 'They are now in the hands of Simon Deeley. You are part of his team.'

'Yes…?'

'We need to bring them together and find the fourth relic. The Wynnman will live again!'

'Yes, Lord Awlthorp.' confirmed Ramona, with blinded trust. 'The Wynnman will live again!'

'One more thing…' added Lord Awlthorp.

Ramona cocked her head to one side, suddenly in full admiration of the man in black and keen to please him. She stood by the table, caressing her hair with narcissistic arrogance. Her past self had disappeared, now filled with greed and lust, eager to serve the Wynnman and do what must be done.

'There is another thing you must do.' continued Lord Awlthorp. 'Find out who that pestering friend of ours really is. Mr LoTrova, the baker. He is dangerous, very dangerous, to my plans, our plans.'

Lord Awlthorp's words echoed in Ramona's mind. Enrico LoTrova. The history of Wimbledon. Power and revenge. Her past self, trapped inside, knew more than she was supposed to know. As it sunk deep inside the new persona of Ramona Halywell, she understood she was stuck with the evil path she had chosen. It happened the moment she entered Lord Awlthorp's car. She could not help it, though. Power and revenge felt good, and she had to thank Lord Awlthorp for opening her eyes.

Ramona took one long last look at the man in black before her, just across the table. Now, she finally recognised him. Now, Ramona Halywell knew the real identity of Lord Awlthorp.

The Wimbledon Museum looked emptier than usual when Dr Watkins set foot inside his own temple dedicated to the history of Wimbledon hill. The decision to hand over the black azalea and the urn of crimson liquid to the British Museum, under the pressure of Reverend Green, had left a void both physical and spiritual. In the museum, the space where he had planned to showcase the relics had to be filled in now with something else, something less special. In his heart, relinquishing the idea of finding the Wynnman relics had left a gap he somehow did not know how to fill. The excitement from what he and Simon had discovered about the Wynnman, and how it

479

had led to what they believe to be the third relic, had waned off and left the curator with a bitter aftertaste of incompleteness.

The curator dropped his bag on the desk and dragged his feet around the museum, glancing at the glass cases filled with pieces of Wimbledon's three thousand years history he had collected over the decades. He hoped the brief stroll would comfort him. One thing for sure he had to admit. Ever since parting ways with the black azalea, his sleep had improved greatly. He now slept like a baby, and he felt energised once again. He stopped to look at Hilary Wilsons's diary. The words from the last private owner of Cannizaro House came back to him and felt more real than ever. She too had realised the black azalea influenced her sleep with vivid nightmares. Dr Watkins asked himself how it could be possible, and knew he had to be careful not to let the obsession creep back in. He sighed feeling a shroud of dread cast over him. Ever since the strange encounter with Reverend Green in the Pool of Elixir, Dr Watkins had been questioning himself about what may have happened in between dreams and moments of clarity in the past few months. He felt responsible for something without knowing what it was, something chasing him down, to the point he thought for once he may have been Reginald's accomplice. He laughed to himself. I do not have the guts for it, he thought; it is all in my head.

It was time to move forward and see what had to be done for Wimbledon. He went back to his desk to check his emails and put the small kettle on. There was no water inside, and the curator was in need of a cup of tea to warm him up after the walk from the Fox and Grapes in the cold. He walked over to the backroom where he kept a small sink between the shelves filled with dusty boxes, cleaning products and filing cabinets. He turned on the tap. The pipes let out a lament while he filled the kettle. He then turned to leave but his gaze caught a strange shape in the wall to his right. A metal square with a keypad framed inside it was visible through a gap in the shelf. A few books had been pushed aside to reveal it. Dr Watkins frowned. He had never seen it before. He was meant to know the building by heart as the rightful owner and the sight of this secret keypad deeply unsettled him. He thought about what it may open, and even if he knew, he had no idea of the combination. Before he could make an attempt, a pressure sound came out of the wall and an opening appeared to reveal a secret entrance. Someone had opened it from inside. Dr Watkins swallowed hard, terrified by the inexplicable events unfolding. Now more than ever, he feared something may have indeed happened while he thought he was dreaming about the Wynnman. The question whether he had lived a double life started to haunt him.

The opening led down a short flight of steps into a bare room with a long counter. There were a lot of books and scribbled notes. There were two small, empty stands on top of the counter. No labels showed what may have been standing on each of these. The curator ran his hand over the counter, trying to interpret what he was seeing. The books were all about the history of Wimbledon, Anglo-Saxon folklore, while the notes had a recurring word jumping off each page. The Wynnman. The name Dr Watkins wished he could forget. The whole surface was in disarray, hinting at the fact there had been a lot more books and notes. The place had been emptied, in a rush.

'What is this?' boomed a voice behind him.

Dr Watkins spun around, startled, and grabbed the edge of the counter to hold himself steady. Opposite him, sitting in a corner of the secret room were Reverend Green and Quentin Plainstraw watching him anxiously with their arms crossed. It looked as if they had been waiting impatiently there for quite some time.

'What are you two doing here? You scared me!'

'You scare me too. What is this?'

The reverend stood up and started pacing up and down the room. He waved his hands pointing at the few things scattered in the room. Dr Watkins had the impression the reverend was as shocked as him at finding this place. Furthermore, what made the curator scratch his head was how they had managed to get in. He looked at Quentin, perched on his chair, preferring not to look at the curator in the eye. He looked uncomfortable, as if he did not want to be there but had been dragged without having a choice.

'Ok, Reverend Green, what is the meaning of all this? I am bit confused, and it seems to happen each time I've met you lately.'

The reverend gazed at him with a suspicious look. He appeared to be angry, frustrated.

'What happened?' asked Dr Watkins, demanding an explanation.

Reverend Green nodded at Quentin, and the tall man produced a copy of the Wimbledon Gazette. It was the same copy Dr Watkins had borrowed from Enrico.

'Oh, I have a copy back at my desk…' noted the curator.

'What did you do?' said Reverend Green in an accusatory tone.

Dr Watkins froze and glared at the reverend. He was starting not to like his attitude. Ever since he had made him feel bad about his obsession with the Wynnman, it was as if he was evil.

'You'd better have a good reason to be here before you start accusing me of something…' said Dr Watkins.

'You are the accomplice, aren't you?'

'What?'

'The accomplice working with Reginald Bosham. Quentin heard Enrico LoTrova talking about it. The man who disappeared on the Common but the police never found.'

'Don't be ridiculous!' said the curator rolling his eyes to the nonsense. 'The police dismissed the story. Enrico is not sure what he saw.'

'Then explain this, Dr Watkins.' finally spoke Quentin.

He pointed at the room. The curator was not following their argument. Something did not add up and Dr Watkins failed to comprehend why Reverend Green and Quentin Plainstraw were suddenly here accusing him of being the man in black Enrico had been pursuing.

'What do you want me to say?' he protested. 'I didn't even know this room existed… How did you two know about it? How come you had a code to enter?'

'Don't think we are so gullible, Dr Watkins.' said Reverend Green. 'We've known this room existed for years. We've been here many times with you before, although I never thought we'd come back after so many years. You built it!'

Once again, Reverend Green pulled up events and facts Dr Watkins could not remember. He glanced around the room. None of its blank walls spoke to him. Nothing here reminded him of ever being there. He was sure he had never been here.

'I didn't build this place…'

'You did.' confirmed Quentin. 'It is where we'd gather to hear your latest news on the Wynnman.'

'What? I… I…'

'Come clean, Dr Watkins!' insisted the reverend. 'What have you done with Reginald Bosham?'

'Nothing! This has to stop, Reverend Green. I am not the accomplice. Just because I was obsessed with the Wynnman, it doesn't' mean I am a crook. How could you think I would hurt Wimbledon and everyone who lives here?'

'I don't know. You tell me!' challenged the reverend. 'You have been obsessed with the Wynnman for years. It is the reason you built this room we are standing in. To run your research in the hope of finding something about this sorcerer. Even when I thought you had forgotten all about it, you never actually gave it up, did you? I wonder what you've been up to in this room all this time. I see the place has been emptied recently. Trying to hide something perhaps?'

'Do you really think I would help Reginald Bosham? To do what, find the relics?'

'You said it yourself.' replied the reverend, happy with Dr Watkins's conclusion.

'Quentin, don't tell me you think the same thing?'

The curator turned to the guardian of the windmill. Surely, Dr Watkins thought, he would not be of the same opinion. He was there when Enrico told both of them what he had witnessed. Quentin hesitated, under the concerned look of both his two friends, Reverend Green and Dr Watkins. He did not know what to say and was not keen on taking sides.

'You looked distracted from time to time, Dr Watkins. We thought you were tired after all these events in Wimbledon. When you didn't turn up to help Enrico, and Reverend Green found you acting stranger, he had to follow you to the Old Rectory. We know something is up. We're just worried about you.'

'Hold that thought. You said Reverend Green followed me? How could you say that I was on the Common and at the Old Rectory at the same time?'

Dr Watkins turned to Reverend Green, defiant in proving his innocence to the last. The reverend sneered, incredulous.

'I'm not the one not remembering things well.' he retorted. 'You said it yourself, you don't recall how you went from the museum to the Old Rectory, do you?'

'Still, that doesn't make me who you are accusing me to be. What about Quentin?'

'What about me?' replied the tall man, alarmed.

'Should I just follow Enrico's suspicion about the green soup? How come Reginald and his mysterious accomplice knew about it? Or perhaps you are the accomplice?'

The curator stood tall, determined to fight his way out of this unexpected ambush within this alien room hidden inside his museum.

'I swear... I...' hesitated Quentin raising one hand to him.

'You don't seem to have an explanation either. The same goes for me. Then why am I the one being put on the stand here? Why haven't you called the police, yet, if you two are so sure I am a criminal?'

The curator looked at the reverend in the eye. He thought at first the cover-up plan Reverend Green had suggested in the Pool of Elixir was to protect him as a friend despite the circumstances. Given what was being said in the newspaper, he knew the reverend would not protect a criminal and yet he had taken the time to organise this surprise meeting and face him in person. Even the fact he knew about this room did not make sense.

'Reverend, maybe it's not him...' sighed Quentin, in surrender. 'We're wasting our time!'

'Wasting your time with what?' said Dr Watkins. 'Can you two explain to me what the matter is?'

The reverend gazed at the curator with a deep, intense look. He appeared to be rethinking what he had said until now, pondering what his final judgement would be.

'So?' insisted Dr Watkins.

'Do you believe someone is really looking for the relics, Dr Watkins?'

The curator blinked, unsure what to say about a question he was meant to forget altogether.

'You told me to forget about the Wynnman. You said it was all in my head. Now you ask me this?'

'What if I told you, the peace of our village was at stake, Dr Watkins?'

'What does that even mean? I was looking for the relics to save what we have left of Wimbledon history.'

'Finding the relics is not just archaeology, Dr Watkins. We wouldn't be simply saving Wimbledon history here. We would be saving Wimbledon itself.'

'From what?'

'From darkness... From revenge...'

There was an aura of concern on the reverend's face. A shadow of fear that went beyond being simply worried about Dr Watkins and his health.

'After mocking me about it, you two are now the ones who believe in fairy tales.' reproached Dr Watkins. 'Simon's story about the imprisoned sorcerer coming back to avenge himself is just a legend. Of that, I am sure.'

'Can you be so sure after everything we've seen happening here in Wimbledon?' said Reverend Green. 'I care for this community, and so does Quentin.'

Quentin nodded.

'So do I,' added Dr Watkins. 'but I am not going to start scaremongering people because we think a sorcerer is coming back to life. This is ridiculous!'

'What if someone does truly believe they can bring the Wynnman back?' warned Quentin.

The curator could see fear too in Quentin's eyes as if the recent events had summoned old, painful memories.

'So, it appears you too strongly believe someone is looking for the Wynnman relics?' said Dr Watkins, doubtful.

'Yes, Dr Watkins.' replied the reverend. 'We have to find out who. And quick, before it is too late!'

'Why?'

'Because this is what we were meant to do, my friend. As the team we once were. I wish you remembered!'

Dr Watkins weighed the words carefully. Reverend Green and Quentin believed the theory he had been reluctant to even consider up to year ago. One minute they had been accusing him of being Reginald's accomplice, and all of a sudden, they were desperate to seek the curator's help. The urge in their words and the sudden change of heart left Dr Watkins dumbfounded to understand what they may be up against, what would make his two friends so worried. They hinted at past memories he did not seem to recall; things he had said or done that were just a blur estranged from himself. Upon hearing words about darkness and revenge, the quiet, idyllic image of Wimbledon Village Dr Watkins had forged in his mind all these years appeared to be tarnished by invisible shadows lurking in the dark corners of every street, every building, every meadow, as if evil pulsed beneath their feet. Dr Watkins was a man of history, and as he faced a man of faith like the reverend, he did not know what to make of it. Yet, for the first time he saw terror in Reverend Green's eyes. Terror of what lay ahead.

Enrico will return in
"The Wynnman and the Lemon Smugglers"